$\mathscr{A}$FTER T[...]

A DECADE AGO THE TERRIBLE
DEMIGOD, THE KINSLAYER, RETURNED
FROM HIS LONG EXILE IN DARKNESS,
LEADING AN ARMY OF MONSTERS AND
LAYING WASTE EVERYTHING IN HIS
PATH.

THE NATIONS OF THE WORLD RALLIED,
FORMED HASTY ALLIANCES, FOUGHT
BACK THE TIDE.
A SMALL BAND OF HEROES, GUIDED BY
THE ENIGMATIC WANDERER, BROKE
INTO THE KINSLAYER'S PALACE AND
KILLED HIM.

BUT WHAT HAPPENS WHEN THE
FIGHTING'S DONE?
WHEN THE OLD RIVALRIES ARE
REMEMBERED, WHEN THOSE WHO ARE
HUNGRY AND BROKEN TURN TO THEIR
NEIGHBOURS IN NEED?

*AFTER THE WAR* IS A STORY OF
CONSEQUENCES.

First published 2020 by Solaris
an imprint of Rebellion Publishing Ltd,
Riverside House, Osney Mead,
Oxford, OX2 0ES, UK
www.solarisbooks.com

ISBN: 978 1 78108 803 6

10 9 8 7 6 5 4 3 2 1

A CIP catalogue record for this book is available
from the British Library.

Designed & typeset by Rebellion Publishing

Printed in Denmark

# THE TALES OF
# CATT & FISHER
## THE ART OF THE STEAL

## JUSTINA ROBSON

SOLARIS

This book is for everyone who likes this sort of thing.
I love this sort of thing, so it's for me! Hurrah!
But it might also be for you. I do hope so.

# CONTENTS

INTRODUCTION
*Justina Robson*                                    9

BELT AND BRACERS
*Adrian Tchaikovsky*                               17

SECRETS AND LIGHTS
*Freda Warrington*                                131

TAKING NOTE
*Juliet E. McKenna*                               263

THE UNGUIS OF MAUG
*K.T. Davies*                                     339

Acknowledgements                                  435

About the Authors                                 437

# INTRODUCTION

THIS BOOK CONTAINS some stories about Doctors Catt and Fisher. They first appeared in Adrian Tchaikovsky's novel, *Redemption's Blade*, which is the first book in the multi-author series, *After The War*. As characters they were so delightful that when it came time to write my continuation of that story world, *Salvation's Fire*, I wrote about them too. When that project concluded, the editors at Rebellion, Adrian and I decided they were too good to keep just to ourselves and that they ought to be shared. This book, dear reader, is the result of sharing out the Very Entertaining Characters. It comprises four novellas written by outstanding voices in the field of fantasy and I will not make a pun about them standing out in a field although the lingering traces of Drs Catt and Fisher really, really want me to.

I hope you enjoy the four stories in this volume as much as I did. I think that they are proof that it's a good idea to let people play with your favourite toys. As you will see, each one captures the spirit of the doctors, whilst adding twists, turns and visions that are unmistakably the authors' own, not to mention many additions to the increasing list of Incredibly Interesting Objects which litter the still-unnamed fantasy world of um... well, it's unnamed. I hope the stories inspire you to try further expeditions in the novels set in The Middle Kingdoms, (which is in no way lacking specificity), and further afield.

Meanwhile, it's been a real change of pace and a great pleasure to sit as editor for these stories. The view from the other side of the desk – well, it's a bit hard not to envy it after this outing. I send out requests. I get great stories. It's like magic!

There may have been some small work involved in trying to remember everything that happened or was mentioned in the previous books, of course. As a result of so much material pre-existing it was decided that when these stories were commissioned we would leave as much leeway as possible. We didn't put any restrictions on time, location or the involvement of other characters within the world, so long as nothing contradicted the novels. We also didn't ask for any particular time-stamping and we didn't know what the authors would come up with and if they would write anything that created conflicts.

Although some minor differences have occurred – mostly in terms of how the authors have seen the places and people – there are no changes of note from the original book (*Redemption's Blade*) and I hope you will find these add colour and richness to the experience.

In addition to the technical issues of writing in a pre-existing space the authors have all delivered outstandingly good tales that keep the feeling of the original. This is a tall order (maybe less so for Adrian, but certainly for the new guests!). I was nervous about how it could turn out but as it happens I got to have the Christmas-morning feeling four times in a row. Like tobogganing down a beautiful snowy hill on a huge sofa. Hurrah!

I suppose there must be counterpoint moments to being an editor, where things go wrong, Christmas is forgotten, icy winds blow across Time etc. (No, I've no idea what any of that could possibly mean. Missed deadlines? As if...) I feel I've definitely had a good deal.

Which brings me to the title of this book.

Is it comparing Trump to the doctors? No. Not really. It's purloining a previously used title with great notoriety in order to increase noticeability for this modest volume, and there is the happy accident that it actually does have quite some bearing on the activities and pursuits of the characters herein.

It's not stealing. It's dealing. I'm sure a reader of your perspicacity and good taste can immediately discern the difference.

What? This glove? No. Just for my carpal tunnel. Definitely not a magical glove for channelling other people's words onto the page as if they were your own in order to provide a succinct preface and pave the way for some stories about two very nice old gentlemen.

Argh! Stupid glove. I'm not writing about the doctors, I'm writing an introduction to this book of stories about them!

Stop! Sto-op....!

It is a truth universally acknowledged that when you have accumulated a great many artefacts of power in one place you may expect a visit from the kind of criminal who doesn't think twice about murder as a legitimate by-product of escape.

As a collector of such objects, it is likely that you yourself may be that type of person, or, if not so bold and callous, that you are aware there is only the thinnest of lines between you and the wrong side of the law, between you and the infinitely corrupting power of absolute self-interest.

Ah, the law. Jurisprudence. The practice of arbitration between the truth, the just and the felon, that three-way shuffle executed as a performance art of verbal prestidigitation, rhetoric and scheming.

Better get some practice in at that while you're at it. Establish yourself as a firm figure, a power to be reckoned with, backed-up by a very thorough understanding of exactly what the law intends, what it says and what it carelessly fails to nail down. Precedent shall be your guide, so you should generate plenty of that. Defend the right cases. Draw up the right guidelines. Attend the right committees and donate to the correct causes. But not too much.

Cultivate a raffish competence at that, then in all other matters a raffish incompetence, lest you appear suave. Eschew urbanity. In fashion, determine a firm course toward the eccentric, possibly the risible. This will make you socially deeply undesirable and, therefore, free of obligation and observation.

Do not hire cutthroats or men-at-arms to guard your hoard. All persons are open to corruption, given sufficient incentives, and such a move is excellent advertising for the exact value of whatever you are trying to conceal. You must develop means to defend and keep secret all that you hold; for this reason some traffic with the occult or the panoplies of deceased deities is probably inevitable.

Needless to say you must manage these with the greatest care. Invisibility be thy watchword. Deniability thy handmaid. Diversion thy gardener...

"Gardener?! Really, Doctor Catt?"

"It's rude to read over someone's shoulder, Fishy. Fine. Diversion thy kitchen boy."

"No."

"Housegrave?"

"If Deniability is only a handmaid, how can Diversion be the Housegrave? You might as well say King."

"The Cook, then. Your cook."

"That's better. One does cook up a diversion. Carry on."

"Diversion thy cook."

"Will Deniability be doing the washing-up today then?"

"If you don't let me finish this blasted thing nobody will be doing any washing-up."

"What are you even writing it for? You're writing a guide to – well, you."

"It's my memoirs, Fishy. 'The Art of the Deal', by Doctor Catt, Professor Emeritus, Lawyer, Antiquities Expert, Dealer in Puissant Artefacts of Power and the Arcane. For posterity. I thought I could write them up and then we could use the Court Press to make up a few copies and bind them in something nice and sell them. Pin money for when we have to head off on our travels again."

"But you're telling everyone that our shop is a front for a secret collection of unparalleled world-class objects of immense power and that you have spent your lifetime creating an illusion of mediocrity in order to conceal said shop."

"Well, I… That was merely a first draft, dear boy. One has to get the old cogs moving. Obviously one would only insert this particular first line as an introduction to a posthumous edition in case some oik takes a notion to criticise."

"Are you planning one?"

"I'm planning for all eventualities, of course. I thought I might write down some of our adventures and then later, you know, when adventuring is no longer an option, we could sell them and live on the proceeds."

"You want to live out your retirement on a bard's two pollies, and not a king's ransom for something like Pillifer's Right Glove? That doesn't sound like you."

"One doesn't really write for the money. Vulgar nonsense. One writes for posterity, as I said. For inspiring others to greater things than they might otherwise have imagined. To add to the annals of history. It's not really for me, or even you, you understand, so much as a contribution to humanity, to life in general. Generations to come will need material to inform and educate."

"You want to fill the world with unscrupulous, greedy fortune hunters?"

"I thought you were supposed to be on my side. Instead you're making me sound like a selfish old buffoon."

"Your words, not mine."

"Perhaps it is unwise to leave something so thoroughly erudite and revealing in existence at this time, even as an unfinished doodle. I'll take that grunt as a 'yes', shall I? Pity. I did rather like my opening line. Might not remember it otherwise. It had all the necessaries, didn't it?"

"Because it was written by someone who knew what they were doing."

"Fishy, are you implying that I have somehow *plagiarised* another practitioner of the exquisite art?"

"I'm not implying. I'm saying exactly that."

"Well, my pedantic little friend, you are entirely wrong because I have merely paraphrased her a little, improved, adjusted, added a little piquance, a little zip and sizzle, a hint of things to come being of the gory and salacious variety. *Plagiarism*, as anyone with an ounce of legal knowledge would tell you, is a straight and absolute copy claimed as one's own. Stealing. *Stealing*, Fishy. Like a common criminal. Without a scrap of shame. Whereas I have merely taken something serviceably mundane and uplifted it to stand alongside the greatest of the noble poets and philosophers, nay both. I am hurt, hurt to the core, that you could even suggest, albeit in absolute ignorance and stupidity, that I could have thieved or even misappropriated the hard work of a fellow scribe and claimed it entirely for myself and my own modest reputation."

"I feel suitably humbled."

"Your tone suggests otherwise. What's this?"

"A pottery bowl and a lit candle. Come on, lunch is nearly ready. Do the decent thing and let's eat."

"But I… Fine. We will speak of this no more. Until a later date upon which I shall pen the opus previously mooted in its great length and entirety. Oh dear. It does burn rather well. I think you might have to fetch a bucket of water. I did hear the other day that dust can act almost as well as a black powder in the right air conditions, you know, where there's a lot of it gathered up and about where objects of puissance are kept and cannot be agitated… something about a firestorm… No, really! Quickly! The bucket if you please!"

"Here. Drench the tat."

"I've told you not to use that word in the shop. Befuddling whiskerfication! This is going to take some drying. My shoes are absolutely ruined."

"The price of felony."

"I'm afraid we will have to close up for the day and spend the evening in the tavern until things have aired. There are moulds you know, Fishy, moulds that have spores that last a thousand years and can thrive in common dirt and be carried about for aeons and then sprout and grow at the first signs of moisture to infest the lungs of the innocent…"

"It's duck. Duck with a cherry sauce."

"Oh, I'll change into my other robe first, eh? Here's the mop."

FINALLY. GOT THE glove off. That'll teach me to borrow things from the shop…

And now, without further ado, here are your stories.

*Justina Robson, September 2020*

# BELT AND BRACERS

by Adrian Tchaikovsky

## ONE

"KNOWING YOU AS we do, as authorities on the matter of the enchanted, and given the signal assistance you've provided the cause, we thought that you would appreciate, in addition to your fee, the sight of our most prized relic." The young Constable spoke in tremendously enthusiastic run-on sentences, scattered unevenly with moments of pause for breath. She was a long-faced woman, lanky like most of the Arvennir tended to be, her hair cropped short except for a lock at the front worn long. Her name was Lodovi Setchwort, or at least Doctor Catt thought it was. He and Doctor Fisher had just been introduced to around nineteen separate Arvennir, all of them earnest and most of them young, and his memory for names wasn't what it used to be.

They were in the belly of a barge, a Shelliac vessel heading east for Arven and loaded up with soldiers finally being repatriated after the war, having spent quite a while on other people's doorsteps making them nervous. Travelling to Arven had never been particularly on Catt's list of favourite things to do, what with the locals' prickly customs and general suspicion of foreigners, but there were mitigating circumstances. He was, after all, doing a favour for a fellow collector (in return for a particularly pleasing reward, so perhaps 'favour' was not entirely the word) whilst at the same time and independently delivering a choice piece to a particularly high-status buyer within the Arvennir hierarchy. And, at the same time, he appeared to have fallen in with revolutionaries.

Doctor Fisher had somehow not managed to fall in with the same revolutionaries, despite sharing a boat and all business dealings with them. Instead, they were all reserving their zeal entire for an audience of one somewhat fatigued Doctor Catt, possibly mistaking his veneer of politeness for actual interest. Fisher, for his part, covered his core of surly misanthropy only with a veneer of even surlier misanthropy.

Lodovi had a case out now, and was fiddling with the clasps, all the while keeping up a constant keen patter. Catt was used to the old pre-war image of Arvennir as haughty and nationalistic, with never a kind word to say for anyone born outside their borders. Lodovi and her crop of young veterans, in contrast, had actually travelled and fought in other lands alongside allies from all over the free world. She had seen how things were done elsewhere and, perhaps more pointedly, how Arven was generally regarded. Right now she was in full flow about how much she admired Cherivell, Catt's own home. She singled out the participatory decentralised government, the commercial freedom and the fact that the labourers and workers of that land were not simply accounted as property of a clique of warrior orders. Orders such as the one Lodovi herself belonged to, of course, but she was at least hoping to use that privilege for the good of others.

Catt's own dealings with the woman had been to source a bundle of enchanted war-surplus for the cause: magic blades, arrows, charms against the more common sorts of curses thrown about by Arvennir civic clerics. Nothing, in his opinion, that would actually swing a revolution, which salved his conscience a bit given that he was simultaneously engaged in selling artefacts to the very people Lodovi was trying to unseat.

Lodovi was entirely aware this wasn't ever going to change

a regime on its own, however. She had the case open and was proudly displaying its contents. "As an expert, you'll recognise the power in this and know its proud heritage," she explained. "Gaze upon the Lily Oriflamme, grand standard of Arven, believed lost at the Battle of Struander!"

Catt did indeed gaze upon it, with one of those sinking feelings that seemed to occur to him with distressing regularity, and yet which he really never was able to link with the appropriate causal actions he himself might have set in motion. At his side, Doctor Fisher made a sort of snorting sound that indicated he, too, was aware of a certain looming problem.

The Lily Oriflamme, which had once been merely the flag of the appropriate floral-named warrior order but had gone on to become the rallying point for all the armies of Arven, was a mighty piece of enchantment indeed. It was said that, once it had been planted in the earth, no Arven warrior would desert the field nor know fear; they would flock to its shadow and then stand until they triumphed or until they died. And Catt, no slouch in his magical appraising, was well aware it was a powerful piece of business and quite capable of living up to its reputation.

And at Struander, the first major engagement on Arvennir soil when the Kinslayer turned his mighty armies east, the Arvennir orders had been broken, and the Oriflamme had fallen beneath the iron boots of the Yorughan, never to be recovered.

"We bought it from Grennishmen who'd taken it from the field, seen it fall with their own yellow eyes," Lodovi said reverently. "Parosian here stood in its shadow at Struander. He knew it immediately." She indicated one of her older colleagues, whose grey moustache bristled with pride.

"I'm sure he did," Catt said. "Yes, yes, a magnificent piece of grand standarding. I can quite see how unveiling this in the Chapter Square would lift the hearts of all who stood with you. Such a shame we most likely won't be present to witness the triumphal day, eh, Fishy? Our business likely concluded long before. It is to be hoped."

"Oh, in and out in a blink," Doctor Fisher agreed sonorously.

AFTERWARDS, IN THEIR private cabin, Catt shook his grey head philosophically. "The recklessness of youth," he opined.

Fisher grunted. He had stretched his lean and bony frame out on one of the bunks and was picking at a seam in his old army hat, which Catt happened to know had been destroyed at least three times and yet always turned up again somehow.

"Taking on the Grand Master and the warrior orders, tsk," Catt prompted.

Another noncommittal sound. Fisher's long face suggested he wasn't feeling conversational, especially in matters that might make the pair of them look duplicitous when examined from an overly legalistic perspective.

"It's not as though the rather authoritarian mien of the Arvennir hegemony is not in itself something of a blunt instrument *worthy* of a civic challenge from open-minded quarters," tried Catt.

"Hrmf."

"I myself felt some trepidation when our colleague required that we undertake this journey in person as recompense for his little trinket, even though it has allowed us to tie together a number of disparate articles of business with a modicum of efficiency."

Fisher actually went so far as to nod this time.

"Fishy, I rather feel I'm carrying more than my fair share of this exchange."

Fisher swung his legs round and sat up, re-establishing his hat at its customary slovenly angle. "What do you want me to say?" he asked sourly. "So they're going to go plant a flag and make demands of a pack of jackbooted tyrants? So they're doomed and they're all going to get executed. Probably tortured too."

"Knowing the Arvennir Flower Council, yes," Catt lamented.

"Hm." And Fisher was watching him with that damnable air of his, waiting for the other magical seven-league shoe to drop, and Catt didn't feel he could put it off any longer. "Most especially as they don't have the real Lily Oriflamme."

"Now we get to it," Fisher said sourly. "Catty, your lack of conscience is one of your finer traits as a human being. Don't grow one in your dotage."

"It is not," Catt told him frostily, "a matter of conscience." He fished in their travelling trunk and came up with a blue glass decanter and glasses, pouring out a different colour of liquid into each. "The ruby or the tawny?"

"Tawny," Fisher said. It was a peculiarity of Delshezzor's Miraculous Bibulating Flask that, if you tried two draughts of the same liquid in succession, the second generally had a faint aftertaste of old cod for no particular reason.

"If we actually had hold of the pertinent artefact in our collection," Catt allowed, not without a trace of wistfulness, "then I allow conscience might come into play. However in this case all I can confess to is helping that Chapter Turcopolier, who was it, Matthau Lambsticker?"

"Lemstacker."

"Whatever, helping him conceal the original and replace it with a magnificent piece of false enchantment. Which Lodovi appears to have purchased from some Grennishmen at vast expense. Which only adds to my depression because I failed to see her coming first and had a bridge I could have retailed to her at little more than cost price."

"Plus her little insurrection's going to get stomped flat," Fisher added.

"There is also that. And given Matthau Limpstickler–"

"Lemstacker."

"Are you sure?"

Fisher frowned. "No."

"Well given he died at Struander… Do I tell our friend Lodovi, and thereby assist her in her plans to stand up to the Grand Master? Or do I conceal the truth from her and thereby assist our esteemed client the Grand Master, to whom we are currently taking another trinket of no particularly great power for which he is paying considerably over the odds." He frowned. "Do you think this is going to be the rule, now, with the Arvennir? That they'll pay vast sums for not very much? Only we may be missing out on commercial opportunities."

The late Matthau Lambstickler, or whatever he was actually called, had been about to lead the Order of the Lily into a battle he had known the Arvennir would lose. The Kinslayer's force even then crossing the Arven border had outnumbered them vastly. All they could do was fight to delay the onslaught, to give the forces assembling at the capital of Athaln time to get their act together. And if they had unfurled the real Oriflamme at Struander then they would have won their delay, true enough, but not a man of Arven would have lived to flee the field and fight another day. Desperate, Matthau had paid a certain pair of Cheriveni doctors to engineer a literal false flag operation, while the real Oriflamme, rather than falling into the hands of the Enemy, had been smuggled back to Athaln.

And Matthau had died at Struander, and nobody had ever actually gone on with part two of the plan and unveiled the Oriflamme over the capital when the Kinslayer sieged it, nor had anyone discovered the hidden relic since.

"So, in conclusion," Catt said, and then wavered. He hated being caught in situations where his customers represented opposed interests, but it seemed a lamentably common part of the trade.

"We don't meddle," Fisher finished for him. "And we hope Crabbe's business gets finished quickly."

As if conjured by his name, their associate chose that moment to rap on their cabin door and then push his bulk inside. Doctor

Crabbe was a great decaying hulk of a man, hunchbacked and slope-shouldered so that his bald head seemed to jut out from a rounded hill of flesh and wine-red velvet. He wore round smoked-glass spectacles, even in the gloom belowdecks, and he moved with a ponderous dignity, pale hands out to feel his way. He seemed soft, but when he and Catt had clasped on their own particular deal, there had been a great deal of grinding strength in those white, twitching fingers.

"My fellow doctors," Crabbe's voice was low and unctuous. "We are approaching the very borders of Arven. The Shelliac tell me they will go no further, but we must wait for their kin from within the nation to carry us to Athaln. Is it always so? It seems an inefficient arrangement."

"Some piece of footling demarcation in the matter of Shelliac clans," Catt decided, waving the issue away. "Certainly it is the tradition." Privately he suspected that the boat-people from outside Arven were none too keen to enter in case the locals should make objection to their leaving. The slender, carapaced Shelliac were a race who liked their freedom to go where they would; the Arvennir were a nation with a fondness for hard borders and a tight control of travel and trade. The compromise both had reached was that the Shelliac within Arven would have the run of all the waterways in the land, but no further. Those without would turn back at the borders after dropping their cargo and passengers at a post where officials might weigh and measure them.

Crabbe made a sound of dissatisfaction and adjusted his spectacles, briefly revealing eyes that were small and cold and squeezed almost shut. His teeth clacked together as he sucked on them and he fished in one pocket, bringing out a fowl's leg and picking the lint off before gnawing at it.

"I was going to take the dusk air," he said, between swallows. "Doctors, perhaps you would join me. I have a mind to open the Caskenny brandy."

Catt had not entirely found himself at ease in Crabbe's company, but there wasn't much of the Caskenny around since the war, and it was a strain that magic could never duplicate. So it was that the three of them, learned men and collectors, ended up on deck as the Shelliac trimmed their sails and whistled to one another. He sipped at his glass and listened as Crabbe and Fisher complained to one another about the shortcomings of the boat trade, the Arvennir and just the world in general. Crabbe was one of those people who could always think of a better way of doing something, and Fisher's greatest joy in life was being miserable, and so the two of them seemed to get on remarkably well.

"We were rather hoping," Catt broke in, "that your errands at Athaln might be accomplished with a reasonable measure of haste, Doctor. Local conditions may become inopportune." And he did not, of course, say that belowdecks a whole knot of reformists were planning a great stand against the Arvennir authorities.

"Oh, I don't know about that, Doctors," Crabbe said humbly. "Assuming you are able to secure for me the introduction I have requested, then the pace of matters will be dictated by the obliging nature of the Arvennir authorities."

"Ah, well, yes," Catt said. "Obliging. That is obviously a word many people use in conjunction with the Arvennir. Albeit mostly with some form of negative qualifier."

It was not in any way a matter of conscience. He'd been very clear to Fisher on that point. On the other hand he didn't want to be around to see Lodovi stick her magical fake banner up and then get beaten down, arrested and executed by the Council of Masters and their feared Gryphon Guard. On the other, other hand he *really* didn't want to be still within the borders should some interrogator get Lodovi to explain just who had provided her with all those magic swords.

# TWO

THE WHOLE BUSINESS had started twenty days before when the pair had first met Doctor Crabbe in the flesh. The office Catt and Fisher maintained in Cinquetann Riverport, Cherivell, was not exclusively devoted to their true love, meaning the collection, trading and owning of magical artefacts, Their steady stock in trade was as physicians, and as advocates to a variety of the better-heeled locals, and most especially to visiting foreigners who might fall foul of the intricate web of Cheriveni customs. The magic item trade was, after all, international, and anything that gave them the excuse to be seen meeting with all sorts at all hours was a useful cover. Although, given the corkscrew nature of Catt's mind, he could get just as immersed in tortuous legal argument as he could with the pursuit of errant relics.

Today he returned to the shop after a particularly vigorous course of argument before a magistrate who was not fond of him. The case had not gone overly well, and he had been put to that always regrettable lawyer's ordeal of spinning a narrative for his angry client that somehow both confirmed the overriding virtue of the client, the justice of the Cheriveni legal code that had found against that client, and the legal competence of one Doctor Catt, advocate, notwithstanding the way matters had turned out. It was an exercise well within his gifts, but nonetheless one that always left him feeling fatigued.

When he got into the shop, Doctor Fisher was not behind the counter and there was a large man sitting by the door. Catt regarded this intrusion with surprise. The customers who arrived seeking physic tended to be in sufficient discomfort, the clap being what it was, not to patiently wait, and those seeking jurisprudence had causes either remote enough to book an appointment in advance, or urgent enough that a certain flighty and hunted agitation attended them. This man had none of the above, but simply sat, bulk straining the sinews of his chair as he gnawed away at the crust of a loaf.

Doctor Catt hurried past the counter into the back room, where he found his associate Doctor Fisher standing doing precisely nothing. There was a duster in the tall, glum-faced man's slack hand, but Catt wasn't fooled for a moment.

"Fishy, we appear to have suffered some manner of incursion. An individual of uncertain provenance is taking his lunch within the shop. One might imagine some manner of presence at the counter could dissuade the general public from taking such liberties."

"He's a special customer," Fisher said, and then, with an unaccustomed loquaciousness, "He's a doctor."

Catt felt that two doctors was about the limit the shop could reasonably support, but the word 'special' had caught his notice. "Buying or selling?"

"Both. *Special*special customer. I was waiting for you before I invited him back here. He's got a *proposal*."

"And I thought I would be left on the shelf," Catt remarked drily. He felt a little shiver of excitement nonetheless. It had been a while since the pair of them had actually got their hands dirty in the antiques trade. They were due a holiday.

Doctor Crabbe, as he introduced himself. would not take off his coat, which was vast and leathery without, in Catt's expert opinion, being actually leather. "I am modest, and sensitive about the shape of my limbs," he said. He would not remove his little round-lensed spectacles, for all the low lighting of the back room must have seemed utter dark to him. "My eyes are terribly sensitive, gentlemen." He would not, as it happened, stop eating. "These autumn nights prick my appetite something terrible." The pockets of that coat bore several enchantments of storage, or so Catt's keen senses suggested, and certainly furnished the man with an unending supply of snacks. He sat in their back room, taking up an untoward volume of it, peering mole-like at them and chewing.

"He's the one bought Nystal's Regulating Bracer," Fisher explained.

"A most remarkable toy," Crabbe agreed.

"I..." Lost for words was a rare condition for Catt to find himself in, but he had a bout of it then. The Regulating Bracer was an artefact they'd come into possession of a while back and despaired of finding either a use or a buyer for. Nystal had been an elder magician of broad powers and narrow mind, a misanthrope of the greatest possible bent. He had written a four-thousand page tract on how the world's ills would be solved if everyone within it were *more like Nystal*. And he had not simply meant that they should follow his ideology, but that they should resemble him physically, as like as to twins. He had expended his power in an attempt to create a legion of artefacts that would transfigure people into his image, succeeded in creating precisely one, and then died of, as irony would have it, a congenital condition nobody else in the world had ever suffered from.

All this had been long before Catt was born, but he strongly felt that Nystal probably hadn't looked like Doctor Crabbe, for all he now saw the bracer on the big man's wrist.

"I, ah..." There really was no polite way of saying 'no refunds'.

Crabbe's broad but nearly lipless mouth stretched into a smile. With his eyes hidden, Catt had the odd impression the organ was exercising itself entirely of its own volition, disassociated from any other part of the expression. "I am quite satisfied with the operation of the artefact, Doctor Catt. You may have no worries on that score. I am myself plagued with a variety of ailments which the Regulating Bracer has curbed by making me more the man that Nystal was. In fact, one order of my business here was to thank you for the object, and your couriering it to me." And he brought out a jar of pickles from another pocket and began crunching into them with relish. Catt could only conjecture that his former invalid nature had imposed a limited diet the man was now making up for.

"My esteemed but on occasion uninformative colleague Doctor Fisher was suggesting that you had additional transactions you wished to explore, Doctor?" All this doctor-doctor-doctoring was going to become tiresome, Catt decided.

"I find myself in a position to do you a favour, Doctors," Crabbe explained. "Being in the trade myself, I keep my ear to the ground. Word did come to me that a certain pair of Cheriveni collectors were seeking a certain item that had found its way into my possession. A certain wand, in fact…"

Catt's eyes lit up. "Fishy, does he mean the Gustator?" Because that had been a thorn in their collective sides for a while, a commission they had been tasked with by a very potent individual of Arven, and which had gone unfulfilled for long enough to become a source of serious friction between them and their patron.

"Felix the Gustator's Wand of Varied Diet," Crabbe pronounced. "Precisely, Doctor. It so happened that I had acquired the artefact, at considerable cost, for my own use, but it proved inadequate to assist me." And he finished the last pickle and then necked the vinegar with evident enjoyment. "It is a trifle," he went on, that done. "And yet I understand you have some use for it."

"A matter of idle amusement, indeed," Catt agreed coolly.

"However, if it is surplus to your requirements then we would gladly rid you of the need to store it, perhaps in return for some similarly flimsy trinket."

"Ah, forgive me," Crabbe said. "Only your colleague had mentioned this was required to satisfy a rich and demanding customer of your own, and so I had thought the object considerably dearer to you than you imply."

Catt glowered at Fisher, who chose that moment to resume his desultory dusting. "It might be," he allowed, "that we may have a certain buyer of our acquaintance interested in the wand. However, he is some ways distant, and the cost of securely dispatching the artefact to him will be very high, hence our budget for obtaining—"

Crabbe held up one thick-fingered hand. "Doctor Catt, I have a proposition for you and the esteemed Doctor Fisher."

Catt was generally happier being the proposer than the proposee, but he sat back and lifted an eyebrow, waiting for the man to continue.

"I wish," Crabbe said, "to engage your services. Let us not obfuscate this compact with minutiae. You have been engaged by the Grand Master of the Arven Flower Council to procure the Gustator. I find it needful to travel to Arven, a traditionally hostile nation, and obtain access to certain artefacts held by the Council, which I require to study. If you, rather than expending your resources and your trust on a courier of appropriate qualifications and resume, were to travel in my company to Arven and procure for me the appropriate introductions, many things might be achieved."

"That is a radical proposition deserving of considerable consideration," Catt allowed, privately deciding that under no circumstances would he ever go and place his vulnerable person between the iron jaws of the Arvennir. Their hospitality, so the stories had it, tended to be simultaneously of indefinite duration and short on amenities. "However, our diverse and varied business interests here in Cinquetann are unlikely to permit ourselves—"

"Catty, he's offering to pay," Fisher rumbled in a *sotto voce* that could have been heard out on the street.

"Much as the prospect of remuneration is of value to me, if only to indicate that the world continues to function in an economically appropriate manner," Catt started weakly, but Crabbe shifted in his chair with a creak of wood and held up one hand.

"I appreciate, Doctor Catt, that it is not the acquisition of mere treasure, gold and gems that motivates you. You are a scholar of the finer arts. I am of a similar disposition. Knowledge is my sole motivator. I would therefore not dream of inducing you to take this journey merely for financial gain. I am, of course, offering you the Gustator as part-payment, without which, in any event, you would not be in a position to affect my required introduction. However, in return for your own time and, if I might impose further, perhaps a consultation on anything I should require further insight with, I have an additional inducement. I have located and obtained the only surviving example of The Undiminished Lochago's Sartorian."

"Oh…" Catt said sadly, because he now had the unenviable task of waking within himself a desire to go to Arven, for there was already present a most pressing desire to own the Sartorian.

"Might I… see it?" he asked warily.

From an inner recess of his capacious coat Crabbe brought out…

"Oh." Catt forgot his manners so much as to grimace. "That is… sadly unsightly."

"It is," Fisher agreed, with the sort of admiration usually reserved for blindly adoring parents, "bloody hideous."

"The Undiminished Lochago imbued it with many great enchantments," Doctor Crabbe recounted. "However, perceiving himself as un-aging and immortal, he seldom remembered to imbue his creations with an appropriate resilience to time. Hence the Sartorian has, alas, seen better days. Hence all other examples of the device have fallen into ruin, Gentlemen, this is the last." He placed it on the small table between then.

The Undiminished Lochago's Sartorian was a very badly taxidermied monkey, its glass eyes boggling at uncomfortable angles, its fur mangy, dressed up in a threadbare red coat. It appeared to be grinning like a maniac at Catt's unenthusiastic perusal of it. Its little hands were lifted in front of it as though someone had only just taken away two tiny hammers or some other diminutive instruments of manic violence.

"Does it... still preserve its function?" Catt tried a few of his lenses, seeing that there was certainly plenty of power still within the little beast.

"Impeccably so," Crabbe assured him. "But please, have the fellow demonstrate for you."

"Fishy, your waistcoat," Catt decided. "That purple one I so particularly dislike."

Fisher scowled at him mulishly for a moment and then retrieved the offending article. It was almost as threadbare as the Sartorian, an ancient and vile-hued garment he donned only when he wished to particularly aggravate his partner. Or so Catt always assumed.

He placed it so that a corner of the waistcoat was in the monkey's nasty little hands and then concentrated very hard. Immediately the stuffed creature was in motion, feeding the cloth through its grasp, gnawing on it, whittling away with a large, sharp needle it had produced from thin air.

"Oh, that is profoundly disquieting," Catt decided, watching the thing work. "I do wonder if it looked much better in Lochago's time. I don't know what he was thinking."

"Nonetheless," Crabbe said, and by the time he had pronounced the final sibilant, the work was done. The purple waistcoat, which aside from its hue had always been too short for Fisher's long torso, was now a pleasing burgundy, ornamented with golden floral patterns, and of a perfect fit. As Catt proved to his own satisfaction by insisting Fisher try it on.

A further test of the thing's talents saw it weave a gratifyingly outré pair of pantaloons out of nothing but a pocket handkerchief and some woolly clumps of dust.

"Well that is a remarkable if visually slightly horrifying prize," he was forced to admit. "Perhaps there is some other recompense you might accept for it?" Because, of all the swords of smiting, the crowns of command, the staves of magecraft that all the great makers of the past had enchanted, he knew that *this* was one useful little toy he just had to own.

And Doctor Crabbe had held firm on his price, and so the next day Catt and Fisher had begun preparing for their trip to the nation of Arven, to the city of Athaln, and to the Grand Master of the Council of Orders.

# THREE

THE SHELLIAC HANDOVER at the border went as expected, two crews of the slender, shrimplike people shifting passengers and cargo over, communicating by hand sign and whistles. There was a squat fort half in ruins there, intact enough for a handful of Arvennir soldiers to watch the transaction and check everyone's bona fides. Catt let Fisher go deal with them, and they didn't seem to be in the mood to make things difficult for anyone. He saw Lodovi talking, even joking with them later. Presumably her nascent revolution hadn't got her face up on any wanted posters yet.

The Arvenside Shelliac seemed something of a different culture to his discerning eye. They were more subdued, their boat less gaily painted. They wore more uniform clothes, and he saw them checking quite a lot of paperwork with the guards before poling off from the side. After ensconcing Catt and company in a cramped cabin, they left their passengers to entirely fend for themselves.

"It's no more than one might expect, I suppose. Being a mobile minority in a place as top-down as Arven," he reflected to Fisher.

"Still playing safe after the Red Lines," Fisher said, his nose in a small grimoire he'd brought for light holiday reading.

"The reference is obscure."

Fisher lowered the book the precise minimum distance

required to stare at Catt over the top edge of the binding. "Was, what, two generations back."

"Well, before my time, then."

"Catty, you are a dealer in antiquities."

"After my time, then. Oh, just spill the story, Fishy. Your sense of the dramatic does run away with you."

Fisher sighed. "Not much to tell. Grand Master at the time decided to go kick the Shelliac. Rounded up a load. Burned boats. Was going to run his own trade fleet on the rivers I think, only nobody could make it work like the Shelliac did. The waters ran bloody. All over the country. Red lines, right? Took the Shells a generation to even come back, and then only with a whole load of rules they negotiated with the Arvennir about how it was going to be."

"The Shelliac dictated *to* Arven? My, my."

"Well, by then whole counties were starving because suddenly this amazing network that had been shuffling grain and beer about the country didn't exist any more," Fisher observed, not without some sour satisfaction. "Anyway, everyone treads very carefully these days, and the Arvenside Shelliac are... well, they were carrying weapons *before* the war."

"The deplorable wickedness of the world," Catt tutted. "Now, how many days to Athaln? Because this accommodation is manifestly inadequate."

Doctor Crabbe spent most of the journey up on deck, taking sightings of the stars on clear nights, just watching the water during the day. For want of company that wasn't Doctor Fisher, Catt found himself listening to Lodovi and her band of reformers talk excitedly about all the things they wanted to reform, apparently because he was feeling too pleased with himself and needed to bring himself down with a dose of reality.

It was, he reflected, almost a blessing that she didn't have the real Oriflamme and that she was obviously going to fail horribly, because when you listened to them, there weren't two of the whole pack of them who actually had the same precise idea of what they wanted to reform, or how. He didn't want to imagine how terribly messy and argumentative things would get if they somehow prevailed over the authoritarian Flower Council and centuries of harsh Arvennir tradition. On the other hand, perhaps a bit of mess was preferable to ruthless authoritarian rule, but the many areas Catt prided himself in being an expert on did not include political theory. He himself always liked nice, pleasant, stable places, but generally because that made his own personal brand of self-orbiting chaos easier to practise. One could not, after all, broker shady under-the-table deals if there were people running around kicking over the tables. By the time they were approaching the capital he had begun to perform remarkable feats of social gymnastics to avoid having to spend any protracted period of time with any of his potential interlocutors whilst aboard what remained an inconveniently small barge.

Then the Shelliac reached the checkpoint at the outskirts of Athaln and everyone was promptly arrested.

The first Catt knew of it was Doctor Crabbe descending to the close confines of their shared cabin in something of a considerable hurry and determinedly grabbing his case. This was the first time they'd ever seen Crabbe do anything actually hurried. He was about to pass some mild remark to Fisher on the subject when he noted his partner also shoving various belongings into Mortby's Capacious Valise.

"I may have been dozing," he admitted reluctantly. It was a recent habit that he rather hated in himself, as a sign of age catching up with him. "What has transpired?"

"Catty, *listen*," Fisher advised grimly, and indeed there were boots stomping about on deck where the Shelliac had only padded softly. There were harsh voices with Arven accents speaking harsh Arvenhal, and it sounded as though they were making demands of all and sundry. Catt sighed hugely.

"There has obviously been some manner of local unpleasantness," he suggested. "There is no reason why it should trouble any of us, being as we are foreign travellers with good business to undertake here in Arven. Let me go on deck and make the appropriate noises."

Up top, he was treated to just how the Arven liked to police the comings and goings from their capital city. The river had become a canal walled with stone that went up ten feet before the arching underside of a bridge closed off the sky. They were not only at but within the wall of Athaln. He could see the recent repairs where they'd put right back up all the bits the Kinslayer had torn down. There was even a stolid work crew of Yorughan there now, hoisting great stones into place. He wondered if any of them had been with the army that had inflicted the original damage.

To one side of the barge a distressing number of Arvennir soldiers were engaged in stripping the vessel of its cargo and passengers. They were precisely what Catt thought of when the nation was brought up in conversation: tall, angular men and women, mostly fair, the men with long moustaches, the women with some variant on Lodovi's short hair and one trailing lock. They had lean, long-chinned faces and cold eyes and they wore white tabards over their mail and leather, showing in black the emblem of one or other of the warrior orders. Flowers, mostly, or occasionally butterflies;, the threadbare velvet glove that housed the Arvennir iron fist.

"You there!" Arvenhal was close enough to the middle speech of the small kingdoms that Catt didn't have to stretch himself to understand the worlds. "Present yourself!" The speaker was a big man, broader about the waist than most of his fellows. He wore more armour to less effect, to Catt's discriminating eye, definitely a touch of the ceremonial to him. An official, therefore. Though Catt's senses were being strongly tweaked by the belt the man wore, that looked old and out of place and fairly stank of power.

"Ah, my dear fellow, consider me presented." Catt slid over the deck to him. "Dear me, there appears to be some manner of untoward hostility in your looks. May I present myself as the inestimable Doctor Catt of Cinquetann Riverport, Cherivell, just recently arrived in your magnificent country to conduct business."

On the bank, Lodovi and her people were standing in a close group with a lot of soldiers watching them. They remained armed, though, and Catt wasn't sure quite how arrested they were. What they *were* was definitely within earshot, and so perhaps trumpeting his business dealings with the Grand Master might not be the most politic thing he could possibly do.

"Foreigner," the elaborately armoured Arven observed. Then Fisher and Crabbe appeared abovedeck laden down with bags and scroll cases and sacks, looking as absurdly guilty as any two adult men possibly could. Even though Catt knew that they had not been carrying out some manner of bungling heist of the barge's lower decks, and surely the official must know that they hadn't, the unearned impression of culpability was impossible to dispel.

"You will come with us to accommodations," the official stated flatly. Doctor Crabbe hunched his way over the deck to Catt's shoulder, breathing unpleasantly in his ear.

"Yes," Crabbe murmured. "You see, this is what I require access to. Yes, yes." In that moment he sounded as though his wits had completely flown, the words flopping from his lips like dead fish.

"Not now, Doctor," Catt said. "My dear fellow, there is no need for your accommodations. What it is that you are actually concerned about is, I can assure you, a world away from whatever it is we are in fact about, and you may sleep easily, knowing we are here to enrich your nation with our presence." He was aware that the generalities were not particularly strengthening his case.

"Take them now," the official said, and the nearest handful of soldiers drifted over. In that moment Catt activated his rings of Vital Preservation, that set a filmy golden aura about him, Crabbe took up some amulet adorned with dire images of skulls and lightning bolts, and Fisher just grounded his staff, which was a solid length of wood with which he could get quite a good swing.

"There is absolutely no need," Catt insisted, "for any manner of unpleasantness towards we visiting businessmen—" and then the official did his own trick, which rather trumped any of theirs.

He had taken three long steps back, and Catt fooled himself this was in recognition of the magical puissance of Catt and Fisher. A moment later, though, the man lunged forwards and *changed*.

He grew, big as a bull, and twisting forwards into much the same general shape, save that his body was covered with metallic scales, and silvery batwings spread far enough on either side to brush the walls of the canal. His head became a great beaked horror, lined with hooked teeth, blazing-eyed and fin-eared. An arrowhead tail lashed behind and the paws that were either side of Catt's suddenly prone form had talons that raked runnels into the barge's deck.

He was aware of the inconvenient shapes of Fisher and Crabbe jabbing his back as he lay on them, opening and closing his mouth. The magical protections of Vital Preservation sputtered feebly and then clocked off for the day.

And yet, despite his looking down its very gullet, Catt's professional side was mightily impressed. As Crabbe said, this was indeed what they'd come here to study, though not in such an immediate manner. This was one of the Gryphon Guard of the Council of Orders, the elite fighting force that even the Kinslayer's armies had not broken,

"Enough, Oversy!" someone called. "Please do not eat the

foreigners before we know whether they may be of use!" Quite a light voice, really. Some humour there. The sort of person Catt could imagine sharing a glass of decent wine with should his future go anywhere but into the belly of a Gryphon.

The monstrous creature gave Catt the stink-eye a little more and then leapt back the same three paces, ending on human feet. The Gryphon Guard, Oversy, was smirking at him, one hand fingering that belt. *Ah yes, that.*

An Arvennir woman was bustling up, still armoured and emblazoned as one or other of their orders, but carrying a book and apparently some manner of bureaucrat.

"Accommodation," she said brightly. "I am sure our foreign visitors will not now object to it, while we satisfy ourselves as to who they are and why they choose to visit our lovely city."

"Why indeed," agreed Catt, levering himself to his feet with Fisher's assistance.

IT WAS A sad fact that the life of a freelance collector of artefacts, when conducted with the flair and drive Doctor Catt considered an essential component thereof, did result in him seeing the inside of a remarkable number of cells. With that somewhat jaded position he was forced to admit that the room the Arvennir had found for him and his two fellows was far from the most onerous of dungeons. In fact, it was a relatively spacious high room with decent light, and the only thing separating his case from that of, say, the accommodations of a mid-grade functionary was that he wasn't permitted to leave it. The locals were obviously leery of whatever connections he, a wealthy foreigner, might have, and until proved poor and friendless they were not trying to make his life a misery so much as make sure he stayed put.

Nonetheless he felt that confinement was de facto a wrong committed against him, as a free citizen of Cherivell, and moreover as someone of money, taste and (in his own assessment at least) the wit to normally avoid this sort of nonsense. Stripped of any other way, he was having Lochago's Sartorian run up a pair of eye-watering orange and blue pyjamas as a form of obscure protest.

"I have no doubt," Doctor Crabbe opined, "that your influence will suffice to iron out the wrinkles of this bureaucratic misdemeanour."

"And your own influence?" Catt asked, a trifle sharply.

"Ah, but if I possessed influence that extended to this quarter of the world then I should not have needed to recruit your good selves," Crabbe pointed out.

"Fishy," Catt asided to his comrade, who was sitting like a vulture at the end of the double bed they were apparently to share, "you must exercise yourself more sharply in your choice of friends."

"Nothing to do with me. He's your friend," Fisher intoned.

"I'm sure that's not the case." In fact, Catt was trying to think just how they had first come to correspond with Crabbe. In sunnier moments he might assume he had been the instigator; in times like this he knew it must have been Fisher.

There was a sharp rap on the door, and Catt had wild thoughts of calling out, "Not now, we're escaping!" except that the Arvennir probably didn't have that kind of sense of humour, and would doubtless take untoward steps. Instead he wanly called for whoever it was to enter, watching the little stuffed monkey stitch hems in a ghoulish frenzy of seamstressship.

It was Lodovi Setchwort and a couple of her people, long-faced and gloomy. Catt looked about the room's facilities for accommodating guests, which ran to the aforementioned double bed, and a divan that Doctor Crabbe had staked out.

"Not that I'm not delighted to see you, my dear Constable, but I really don't feel this particular oubliette can cater to any more denizens. Might you not ask your compatriots, our captors, if you could have prison quarters of your own?"

"Prison…?" Lodovi looked blankly at him before his meaning struck. "Oh, we're not arrested. That's just you."

"That seems…" Catt was prudent enough to beckon them in and have the door closed – glimpsing the guard still standing outside to prevent his egress, though not apparently the free passage of criminals conspiring against the Arvennir state. "Constable, if I might make the observation, it seems to be something of a topsy-turvy business when the keen-eyed hounds of the Athaln city guard incarcerate innocent foreign merchants for no good reason whilst permitting dangerous revolutionaries like yourselves to just wander about on your own recognisance."

Lodovi glanced about in such a conspiratorial way that Catt felt he should arrest her himself. "We have friends in many places. There is a clerk here, the woman who took you in fact, who has granted passage for the goods you provided to us, the… articles. And the Oriflamme of course. And us."

"But not us," Catt noted with what he felt was inhuman patience.

"I came to tell you, say nothing of your dealings with us. This is merely a routine detention, undertaken to many foreigners who come to Athaln. It is exactly what we are fighting against." Her voice shook with earnest righteousness.

"I cannot help but note that your fight, whilst generally laudable, lacks a certain specificity in the case of my liberty and that of my fellows," Catt noted.

"The Council of Flowers and the Grand Master have been trying to strengthen their hold since the war ended. Many foreign influences came to Arven during the fight, you must know."

"Kinslayer and his army, not least," Fisher agreed unhelpfully from the bed. "Came right in."

"But our allies, also. They came with their fashions and ideas and ways of life. And many of us have gone out into the world and seen how things are. That Arven need not be run as the private fief of a handful of antiquated orders and the old men who control them. That we can welcome change and become stronger by allowing outside influences in."

"Whilst I do not mean to return tiresomely to my personal circumstances," Catt observed, "speaking *as* an outside influence…"

"Ah, well, yes." Lodovi eyed him sternly. "I would have asked our clerk to expedite your release, save that there has been a mention of the Grand Master of the Flower Council directly tied to you. Which means any interference from me would result in too great a risk. I understand the man is on his way to see you. So: you must not mention us, or any of your dealings with us. Even under duress."

Catt looked into the woman's long, honest face and wondered what on earth Lodovi actually thought was going on. "Well, let us hope it does not come to duress," he said nobly. "I used to say that I could resist all things save for temptation, but I rather suspect that when it comes to the manner of duress involved in the judicial system of Arven I probably wouldn't be very good at resisting that either. But your dealings are safe with us, Constable. The names Catt and Fisher are synonymous with discretion in twenty separate jurisdictions, in my case because I am a fellow of capital character and in his because he mumbles and it is often hard to understand what he has to say. And Doctor Crabbe is not involved in our dealings and therefore has nothing incriminating to tell."

"And I am acquainted with considerable duress and testify as to my fortitude," Crabbe added, from the divan. He was polishing his round-lensed dark glasses, eyes screwed almost shut against the light.

Someone spoke a word from the door, and Lodovi was on her way out, sending Catt a desperately meaningful look as she left. In her absence, he sighed mightily.

"Save me from amateurs who want to make the world better," he bemoaned. "She is going to get a lot of similarly well-meaning people killed, I fear."

Fisher grunted in agreement. "'Specially when that fake flag goes up."

"Oh, do shut up about the flag." Catt was surprised to find his conscience still nettling him. "Should we do something about that, do you think? On the off-chance some manner of rectification falls within our power."

Fisher shrugged. "Maybe. If only to pay them back for having to share a bed with you."

"Me? I will point out that you are the one who snores. I sleep very daintily."

"You fidget."

"That is a vile canard and I will not have it."

There was a particularly nasty chittering sound which indicated the Sartorian had finished its work. The wizened piece of taxidermy held up the garish garment for inspection. It was every bit as offensive as Catt had hoped. The ghoulish little tailor was, at least, one part of this whole business that was entirely satisfactory.

Before he could don the garments, the door was slammed open without any precursory knocking, and a half dozen soldiers trooped in and stood to either side of it. One of them was the big, unkempt-looking Oversy and another a woman who looked far too ascetic and slender to be of any military use, wearing the same elaborate armour and magical belt. Another of the Gryphon Guard.

Catt was about to hail them with as much bonhomie as he could muster when someone stalked in and made a centrepiece to their formation. Someone very definitely In Charge.

He was old enough that his close-cropped hair was white. His head was squarish, as though time had taken the traditional Arvennir features and pushed them down a little each year. He had relatively little neck. As well as the Orchid badge prominently displayed, he wore about his throat a wheel of icons incorporating the sigils of every brand of Arvennir warrior order. It was a nifty piece of enchantment in and of itself, Catt knew, passed down for as long as the orders had come together to found the nation. This was, therefore, none other than the Grand Master of the Flower Council, Master of the Orchid Order, Johannes Keymarque. And, as it happened, a client of Catt and Fisher. How much that would weigh into matters, Catt held his breath to find out.

"Doctors Catt and Fisher of Cinquetann Riverport, Cherivell," Johannes pronounced. "I had not looked for you in person."

"Ah well, you know, creatures of impulse," Catt said vaguely. "Arven being so pleasant this time of year. Plus there were certain matters of research which, selfless as I am, I agreed to assist a colleague with."

"Hrm." Johannes nodded vaguely, as though most of Catt's words had just bounced off the outside of his skull. "And you have it?"

"Oh, certainly," Catt assured him.

Abruptly the tension of the moment was gone. Johannes Keymarque was beaming as though he hadn't just trooped in with a band of soldiers. "Splendid. I offer you accommodation here at my expense, Doctor, but I suspect that your humble tastes may prefer to seek out a licensed boarding house in an appropriate district of the city. I shall give you the appropriate permits and papers you will require, as a foreigner in Athaln. Under my seal, you shall only prosper." He frowned. "Though you should perhaps restrict yourself to those parts of the city used to hosting foreigners. There are untoward elements at work in our city that we are even now rooting out. You would not wish to see anything upsetting. And tomorrow, you shall accept my invitation to dine, and you will bring the item, and we shall discuss any other issues of business you might have in Athaln."

He smiled. It was a remarkable thing, as white and bright as his hair, as straight as the sword he carried at his hip. As utterly devoid of humour as a Yorughan torturer. Although Catt considered the simile and reckoned it was unfair; some of those torturers had probably possessed quite the sense of fun, in their own way.

# FOUR

THE LAND THAT would become Arven had once been just a collection of farming tribes at each others' throats. Because swanning up with a sword come harvest time is easier than actually spending a hard year growing, raiding was endemic, so there arose bands of warriors to protect the fields from brigands and greedy neighbours. After a while, of course, the warriors worked out that they were in a perfect place to take control of the crops and everything else, and that they had more in common with next door's raiders than their own farming kin. So arose the ancestors of today's warrior orders. So were sown the seeds of modern Arvennir government.

Because kings were popular and other countries didn't take you seriously unless you had one, Arven had an on-again off-again royal family, currently off, as in with-its-head, following the Kinslayer's whirlwind tour of the country. It had always been the orders, though, and as they had cemented their hold over the single largest area of land within any set of borders in the known world, so they had both shed and retained their brutal heritage. On the outside, they were sophisticates, fond of fine drink and good things, music and art, and represented by the iconic blooms and moths and similarly delicate icons on their tabards. And yet, Catt was well aware, scratch that veneer just a little and there was bloody iron beneath. The Arvennir orders were not to be trifled with.

"This is, at least, preferable accommodation," he declared. The three of them had found a boarding house licensed to host foreigners, and the paperwork provided by Johannes Keymarque was sufficiently potent to bring their host out into a cold sweat. Arven was, apparently, a jolly place to visit so long as you had the stamp of the Grand Master on your documents. The food and drink and hospitality had been practically non-stop, and Catt had the disquieting impression that their host's own sons and daughters would have been on the menu had he but asked. Thankfully, neither he nor Fisher had ever really had much time for that sort of thing, not for the last few decades in any event. Doctor Crabbe seemed similarly untempted, perhaps because they were nearing the point of his visit to Arven.

"You must, of course, press my suit with the Grand Master," he insisted. "When you have delivered the wand, when he is pleased with his acquisition, you must ask it for me."

"I suppose just dispatching the thing across the city by courier isn't an option then," Catt said sadly.

"Under no circumstances. That would be a grievous breach of faith," Crabbe reprimanded him.

"You don't want to have dinner with the Grand Master, Catty?" Fisher asked with ghastly fake jollity. "Not feeling well?"

"It's just that…" Catt found himself indulging a rare moment of self-reflection, a truly shuddersome experience. "We do these things, Fishy. We go and meet with these powerful and frankly rather distasteful people, and it's all fun and games and passable wine at first. But it seems to me that we do end up in cells or torture chambers regrettably often afterwards, and through no possible fault of our own. Or there was that one fellow with the pit of giant scorpions. You know how it is. They have this thing and they just have to use it, and so paying a congenial visit will so often become an assault upon our continued good health." He waved away Crabbe's objections.

"Oh, we'll do it, certainly. I'd feel rather foolish to come all this way and *not* meet with the man. And perhaps the fact that we've already seen the inside of a prison will serve as our quota for this little adventure. It's just... I'm coming to the conclusion that powerful and unscrupulous people are not entirely *trustworthy*."

Fisher chuckled meanly. "Never too late to learn wisdom, then?"

"Given that you, who pretend to so much, are standing right here beside me, I'm sure I don't know *what* you mean," Catt reproved him, and Fisher had nothing to say to that.

THE DAY AFTER, they went to call upon Johannes Keymarque at the Irongarden which, as an example of Arvennir mingling of fripperies and realities, was perhaps a little too on the nose. It was the central Chapter House where the Flower Council met and decided the fate of the nation and, all to often, its neighbours. The Kinslayer had not damaged it much, though the marks of war were still all about the streets there. The reconstruction effort was in full flow, walls being raised, new roof beams steepling skeletal fingers, masons and carpenters both local and foreign busily trying to restore the heart of Arven.

The Garden itself was a thing of high walls and small windows, designed for defence despite being in the midst of the city. It had been a fortress originally, and succeeding generations had only added to it without taking away its strength. Catt knew just from looking at it that there would be rooms upon rooms underground, the whole edifice extending deep into the earth with stores and cells and hidden sortie tunnels.

Catt felt that, had he been a duller fellow willing to just trudge through the bureaucracy of the place, he would have lost count of the number of sour-faced Arvennir Constables and Turcopoles and similar incomprehensible ranks who looked over his papers on the way to the Grand Master. Instead, he decided to keep himself amused by engaging each one in avid conversation on a different subject of his expertise, thereby colouring their impressions of what, precisely, he was visiting Johannes Keymarque *for*. By the time he and Fisher were actually ushered into the presence, he had left a trail of rumour behind him that the two Cheriveni visitors were simultaneously the Grand Master's commercial factors, lawyers, artistic directors, new chefs, political advisors and doctors for a particularly stubborn case of the pox. Catt's propensity to feel very pleased with himself about all this lasted right up until they were face to face with Keymarque, whereupon it withered on the vine in short order.

It wasn't that Keymarque wasn't pleasant. There was a long table and a lot of servants and far more food than the three of them could eat, even with Catt's gourmandising. Everything was lavishly prepared, and a harpist played from a gallery above, and it should all have been rather charming and luxurious. Except Catt retained an acute sense of the massive stone walls on all sides, not really hidden by the tapestries hung to screen them. And the decoration itself was that curious Arvennir monochrome, not just the order badges but an odd style of representational art. In each depiction, the figures or scenes were shown as though illuminated far too strongly from the right, so much so that the lit portions were just the blank white of the background, and only the shadowed parts could be seen. The impression was uneasy on the eye. *We see only one side of things*, Catt considered, knowing he was being too pat with his criticism. Still, he might not know much about art, but he knew what he didn't like.

Pleasantries continued to hang in the air like flies, but plainly Keymarque was ready to get down to business, and so Catt brought out Felix the Gustator's Wand of Varied Diet. It was a disappointing little thing, to look at, but in the annals of the artefact collectors it had a respectable history. No great thing of power, this, but a quirky little toy that could quite polish the lifestyle of its owner, if that owner was fond of his board.

And that was the odd thing, Catt had to confess, because he'd watched Johannes pick at his food, one dish after another, and take no obvious joy in it. And the man presumably had access to a galley-full of mundane chefs, and so why would he be so keen to acquire this odd little toy? Perhaps he was sick of Arvennir cuisine?

"Perhaps," Johannes said, "you might demonstrate?"

"Gladly." And Catt did like playing with the merchandise when he had the chance, He pulled Fisher's plate over even as the man forked another bite off it.

"Hey!"

"All in the name of demonstration, Fishy," Catt told him gaily. "Now, we have here... what is this? Fishy, have you laden your platter with both the knurl dumplings and the figgy lamb and, simultaneously, and testing the bounds of culinary belief, some of that sweet suet?"

"What of it?" Fisher demanded, aggrieved to find his habits the centre of attention.

"You will excuse my colleague, who is a barbarian," Catt said to Johannes, who was watching them as though they were a pair of performing seals. "However, now I see this grotesque mingling of a repast, perhaps it is not what I wish? No matter, for the magical creation of Felix the Gustator is here coming to my aid. I wish, perhaps, some delicacy of Cherivell to remind me of home: some Lantark pie perhaps, with strained beans and perfectly crisp shulleries as garnish..." And he fixed the dish in his mind and waved the wand over Fisher's half-finished meal with a practised motion.

There was no puff of smoke or glitter, the plate simply now held a portion of the Cheriveni speciality, exactly the same size as Fisher's leftovers. Catt repatriated plate with sour-faced owner.

"I would tell my friend, of course, that he should tuck in to this feast on the basis that it would be entirely better for his liver. However, in that I would be mendacious to the extreme because the wand is no great relic of changing. What Doctor Fisher is there rather dubiously investigating with his spoon is indeed a prime portion of Lantark pie even as my own long-departed grandmother used to bake, and it will appeal as such to his tongue and the sensitive linings of the mouth, even as its aroma does to the nose. However, should he be so boorish as to leave it uneaten then we would see, within an hour, a reversal of the transformation effected by the wand. And, should he, as is surely more proper, proceed to devour the portion, a similar change would occur within him so that whilst his tongue would have savoured Lantark pie, his digestion would be dealing with the unholy mess of different dishes he was misguidedly about to consume. It is a transient thing, even if appealing to the palate."

He paused and eyed Johannes, having forgotten in his enthusiasm for theatre that he was dining with the most powerful tyrant of Arven. Johannes seemed quite enchanted, however.

"And the limits of what it might transform a meal into…?" the man asked mildly.

"To my knowledge, unlimited, so long as both the original and the desired material are indeed meals intended for consumption. It will not, for example, stand to be used to create a short-lived poison that would slay its eater and then vanish from their system undetectably. Felix the Gustator had the device worked with many safeguards, suspecting the motives of others."

"Much good it did him," Fisher grunted and, when he found both Catt and Johannes staring at him, added, "His chef beat him to death with a rolling pin. Professional pride."

"Well," Johannes said heavily. "You have brought it to me. You have found it for me. I had a dozen professional raiders and robbers and academics trying to track it down. I congratulate the pair of you." There was an excitement in him, though he was tempering it carefully, and Catt still couldn't quite understand his angle. The idea of spicing up his breakfast at will did not seem to be the man's motivation.

"Crabbe's question," Fisher prompted.

"I know, I know," Catt said, nettled, even though he had almost forgotten. "My dear Grand Master, as a part of our transaction, we have a request to make that should incommode you not at all but has become part of our own arrangements to acquire this artefact. A little favour we would like to ask, if we may?"

Johannes' cold eyes flicked to him. "And what is that?"

"Our fellow academic, one Doctor Crabbe, has come here with the wish of examining the transformative magics of the Gryphon Guard, those rather infamous belts they wear. We were wondering if one of your elite defenders might spare us a little time at our lodgings, to answer a few questions? We would not, of course, expect such a relic to be simply placed in our hands unwatched."

Johannes stared at him for a moment as though not entirely sure who Catt was or why he wasn't being horribly tortured right about now, but that, it seemed, was just his resting face. A moment later he twitched his head. "These things are possible. However, I must first ensure that this toy is sufficient for my purposes. Come with me, Doctors. Come and see my own academic research."

With minimal escort, Johannes led the pair of them deeper into the Irongarden. There was a new determination in his stride. Another man might have whistled. The appearance of the Wand of Varied Diet had obviously given him a great deal of hope for something that didn't seem to involve the fortress's kitchens.

"We are at a delicate point in the history of Arven, Doctors," Johannes told them over his shoulder as he strode. "Many new ideas coming in, most especially from those of our own who have been too familiar with outsiders. I do not object to outsiders. I am, after all, meeting with you and we have had a very satisfactory commercial arrangement. However, that is because you, Doctors Catt and Fisher, are not here trying to suggest to me that I and the Flower Council should govern in some manner closer to, say, Cherivell."

"Perish the thought," Fisher muttered.

"And yet these ideas keep coming in, so that the orders must be constantly stamping out fires. Or lighting them. Books, papers, ideas, people... And because the rot is within, it can be hard to know who to trust amongst us. Who remains true to our ways. That is what the Gryphon Guard are for, of course. None more loyal. They fought the Kinslayer, yes. Three out of the twenty died on the steps of the Irongarden and their belts destroyed – *lost* to us, the symbols of our power! But they were never the army. They were always for within our borders. Many a naysayer or an agitator has lost his angry words when faced with our magnificent Gryphons."

Catt, remembering the transformation he had witnessed from far too close, nodded fiercely.

"But they are few, and we need more, and there is none now who can make fresh belts for us. And so I have been put to find another guard, powerful and loyal and able to strike terror into the hearts of our enemies within our borders. So that they would not even dare raise their standard." And he eyed Catt and Fisher, back over his shoulder, as though hoping to surprise guilt on their faces. Thankfully, Catt was an older hand at dissembling than that, but he was starting to feel decidedly worried. The suggestion that Johannes knew about his connections with Lodovi's rebellious friends was all about this conversation like a bad smell, and yet Johannes wasn't levelling actual accusations.

"Here we are," the man said at last and, when they entered

the next chamber, after going two flights of stairs deep into the earth, the escort remained outside.

The room beyond was a viewing gallery around a pit sunk even deeper. There were great barred doors down there, and Catt had the definite sense of gladiatorial spectacle held in private, of captive beasts kept hungry. He wondered if this was some obscure part of the Arvennir judicial process. He wouldn't put it past them.

"In days long gone, this was where we kept the Gryphons," Johannes told him. "Supposedly, the earliest Masters of the Orders had the power of command and could get the beasts to do what they said."

"Meaning actual Gryphons, and not merely the products of those remarkable belts?" Catt clarified.

"Indeed, but our power to dominate them waned, so it is said," Johannes went on, "And so did they, hard to keep and fractious in captivity. And in the wild, hunted to death. Or at least, those rumours that claim they remain within the world place them in the most inaccessible peaks, places even the hardiest hunters do not go."

"How remarkable," Catt said. "So, when your guard transform themselves into the beasts, they are recapturing a piece of history?"

"They have kept alive the tradition over the generations," Johannes agreed fondly. "And in all that time their presence, and the terror of the shapes they can assume, have stood between the Flower Council and unrest."

"I will personally vouch for their efficacy," Catt admitted.

"And yet it is not enough," the Grand Master said flatly, leaning out to stare down into the empty pit. Abruptly he put his fingers to his mouth and let out a shrill whistle. "The unrest only grows. We cannot replace the Guard who died at the Kinslayer's hands. Our land is riddled with poisonous ideas that only undermine all we have built."

One of the gates was clanking open, Catt braced himself for what might come out, picturing some sickly runt of a Gryphon brought in by the boldest of hunters, that Johannes intended to rear to strength using some mystical food produced by the wand. Instead, what stepped out was a Yorughan woman, wearing a long dark coat with white edges. A Heart Taker, no less: one of the Kinslayer's magician elite. Not what he'd expect to see here below the Irongarden, walking without chains or guards.

"Shulamak," called out Johannes. "Our new artefact has finally arrived. We are ready to test it."

The Yorughan clapped a fist to her chest. "Yes, Grand Master. I shall bring out a subject."

"Odd company you're keeping," gravelled Fisher.

"Shulamak came to us with some construction slaves. She offered her services, seeking less menial work. And she has proved adept as a handler. She understands her charges as no human could," Johannes said absently, eyes still fixed on the pit. Catt himself was carefully not standing near the edge in case this turned into one of those absurd scenarios where the man of power and no conscience decided to dispose of his underlings in some ironic and entertaining way.

He was also racking his memory, because Shulamak was a particularly notorious moniker amongst the Heart Takers, one of those few individuals whose name had become known to the Kinslayer's enemies. To find her here and free would ordinarily have been profoundly alarming. However he was fairly sure that the original Shulamak had, firstly, been male and, secondly, died beneath the fortress of Bleakmairn. If you were an itinerant Heart Taker seeking an employer without scruples, however, it was probably not a bad identity to take to make yourself seem impressive.

Then, from the open gate down there, he heard an echoing sound. A gibbering and a wailing and a dreadful complaining. Not the roar he might expect from a Gryphon, even one terribly ill-treated. A sound partway between beast and sentient thing, and entirely unhappy, as they were always unhappy. A familiar sound, much as he'd wish otherwise. Beside him, Fisher had gone very still.

"I say," Catt observed mildly. "That sounds awfully like… I mean, if we were anywhere else, and that cacophony met my ears, I might almost think…"

"It's Vathesk," said Fisher.

Catt eyed Johannes, waiting for the denial, but the Grand Master didn't even look at them, though his lip curled ever so slightly.

Shulamak appeared, walking carefully backwards, both hands crackling with the white fire of the Heart Takers' magic. In the shadows of the gate, something huge lurched, barely small enough to fit through. A despairing screaming issued from it, pleading and lost and at the edge of madness. Catt shifted uncomfortably, aware that he had once again put himself in the way of sights he would regret partaking in.

The Vathesk shuffled out into the open space of the pit. Like all its kind it resembled a vast crustacean as much as anything, all carapace and legs and pincers. The Kinslayer had conjured them up, because apparently he hadn't had enough terrifying monsters with which to menace the free world. They were nigh-indestructible, strong enough to uproot castles, proof against most kinds of magic. This one's larger pincers were laden with shackles of immense thickness and Catt wouldn't have bet on them to hold it, if it made a determined bid for freedom.

They had been the slaves of the Kinslayer, like everything else in his armies, but that was not the worst thing about them. For, before being ripped into this world, they had simply been the citizens of their own. Some other place, unvisited by humans, where to be a twelve-foot lobster was de rigueur, and they were philosophers and artisans and scholars with no thoughts of going to war at the behest of a mad demigod.

And now the Kinslayer had met his deserved end, and here the Vathesk still were. Nobody could send them back, and their own magic could not accomplish it, and they were hungry. There was nothing in this world that could sate that famished gnawing within them, though they would make a game try of devouring anything that came their way just in case, including people. They would never starve, Catt knew. The incessant gnawing hunger would never actually finish them. It just drove them mad, eclipsed their intellect, made them into the monsters the Kinslayer had always intended.

And here was one, and from the sounds there were plenty more incarcerated in the cells beyond the grate.

"What do you think, Doctors?" Johannes asked them.

"I think that you have a Vathesk collection," Catt said. He did not personally approve, but he was aware that the profligacies of his own lifestyle were not to others' tastes on occasion, so who was he to judge?

"What is this?" Fisher growled, somewhat less sanguine, only adding, "Grand Master," with grudging afterthought.

"Well, we shall see just what this is, depending on whether the toy you brought me actually performs to my requirements," Johannes Keymarque told them, and tossed the Wand of Varied Diet down to Shulamak.

Another gate down there was clanking open, and what came out was not a monster, but… Catt blinked. What came out was a chef, or at least some servants with a big trolley on which was set out tureens of some kind of stew. He could smell it from here, the sort of stolid, nourishing fare one cooked up en masse to feed a garrison. The Vathesk wailed again, and the servants made a hurried exit.

"Grasp the wand," Johannes instructed. "Picture whatever the slop was that your former master used to feed these beasts."

Shulamak nodded, the little stick almost lost in her huge blue-grey hand. She approached the food and spent a while considering it, stealing the odd glance up at the Grand Master. Even though she was seven feet tall and wearing the most feared uniform in the world, it was plain she wanted to get things right first time for her current employer.

And the food changed to… something. Catt wasn't entirely sure what. Grey-pink blubbery lumps with weird whorls and bobbling cilia. Nothing he had ever regarded before, still less considered remotely edible. And yet the Vathesk lunged forwards a few steps, its smallest arms raking the air.

"Let it eat," Johannes ordered, and Shulamak stepped back and shouted out some commands to the creature in the Yorughan tongue.

Whatever the rubbery stuff was, it was apparently ambrosia to the Vathesk. The monster fell upon the trolley and devoured the lot, shearing open the tureens to get at the contents. Catt watched solid cast iron being shredded like thin paper and swallowed.

"Most remarkable, Grand Master," he noted. "And you have several Vathesk enjoying your hospitality currently?"

"Fifteen at last count," Johannes agreed. "And you cannot imagine how hard it was to safely trap and transport so many. And, when we got them here, what use were they? Unbiddable, murderous, impossible to govern. Even Shulamak, who was a beast-handler in the war, could not make them obey. But she explained their needs to me. How the Kinslayer steered them."

"And so you sought the wand," Catt reflected. "Well, Grand Master, you have certainly done a power of good here. You are the man who learned how to feed the Vathesk! Why, let the word out, they will flock here of their own free will and sign themselves into your service. You have undone a great wrong the Kinslayer wrought. I congratulate you."

Johannes gave him a pitying look, and then Fisher rumbled out, "Except it doesn't work like that."

Catt, who knew full well how it worked, tried to elbow the

man in the ribs, but Fisher was unaccountably a step too far away.

"The Wand's effects are temporary," the man went on, staring down at the Vathesk. "Eat lettuce the wand's turned to lard, you won't get fat. Drink whiskey made from water, the drunkeness wears off. Just as its maker intended. Your Vathesk is fed now, but in an hour it'll be hungry again, as if it never ate."

The look Johannes turned on them was worse than any sound the Vathesk made. "Well, yes," he said. "That they are ravening monsters is their prime virtue. We just need them to be *our* monsters. So, they will learn they can gain some brief relief from their hunger from us, and only from us. Even though it wears off. Even though they will crave another meal so shortly afterwards. We will make them dependant on us for this little nothing that takes the edge off their existence. And for that they will stand beside our Gryphon Guard and our people will recognise the strength of their leaders, and not harbour any foolish ideas. Who, after all, would stand before a pack of Vathesk acting on the behalf of the Flower Council?"

"Precious few people," Catt admitted. "What a remarkable scheme, Grand Master. I am quite in awe of your foresight. Who would have thought the Vathesk could be tamed once more?"

Johannes looked as though he was searching out criticism, but Catt was quite capable of admiring cleverness, even if it transgressed his own personal boundaries. And those boundaries were, he was forced to admit, somewhat mobile.

On their way out, back up in the sunlit portions of the Irongarden, Johannes turned to them with a broad smile. "There remains the matter of recompense, of course. I shall have the appropriate funds authorised for disbursement, and I recall there was your special request?" He seemed all sun and cheer now the wand had lived up to its reputation. And Catt could appreciate that. Even a temporary blunting of Vathesk hunger had been something nobody had achieved since the war. Not that most people had necessarily tried, he supposed, given their view of the things as nothing but marauding monsters. Not that most people had seen the Vathesk as something they wanted to *recruit*.

"Simply that one of your Gryphon Guard might attend at our lodgings so that they and their belt might be examined. A matter of academic study our colleague is most invested in," Catt explained.

Johannes nodded. "I shall send Oversy," he decided. "I believe you and he are already acquainted."

Catt remembered the lunge, the fangs, the talons, that vast bestial bulk slavering over him, all the worse because it was controlled by a human mind.

"Indeed," he agreed weakly. "It will be capital to see such a splendid fellow again."

# FIVE

AND DOCTOR CATT did indeed get to see considerably more of Oversy than he would have preferred, and at a profoundly closer vantage.

How it happened was mostly the fault of Doctor Crabbe for proposing matters, and Doctor Fisher not caring enough to take poor wounded Catt's side (as he saw it) when the suggestion was aired.

"It is a regrettable matter that the people of Arven seem not to be wholly welcome or trusting of strangers," Crabbe observed. "One would almost think that they were suspicious of our intentions."

"Hmm," Catt agreed. This was after he and Fisher had returned from their alarming visit with Johannes Keymarque, but before the great clomping boots of Oversy had carried the Gryphon Guardsman over to their lodgings. "And of course your motives are...?" because that remained one of the many small mysteries encircling Doctor Crabbe.

"Scholarly," the hunchbacked, bald man said, grazing the meat off a shank of lamb in measured, clinical bites. "Possibly academic, in fact, in the worst case. Or in the best case perhaps they may be characterised as positively philanthropic." Which Catt, a circumlocutor of the first water, recognised as a lot of words to say very little.

"Arven don't like us, though, that's a fact," Fisher drawled. He was lying on his bed, fully clothed and with boots on, the military cap he affected drawn so its peak covered his eyes. "Don't much like their own either. Had better welcomes from Yoggs."

"That is not entirely accurate," Catt observed, "although I admit the nature and quality of the hospitality has been reminiscent. As is their leaders' frank willingness to deal with useful outsiders such as ourselves no matter the doctrine passed on to their underlings, which is a sorry reflection on the way the world falls out. Though obviously beneficial. Now, Doctor Crabbe, I am somewhat eager to be gone out of the city before our friend Lodovi does anything foolish, especially anything that might somehow implicate us, so I trust you will conduct your interview with this Oversy in an alacritous manner and thereafter join us on the next barge heading westwards?"

"Ah well, as to that, an interview with the worthy will doubtless be worth its weight in gold, or at least electrum. Possibly brass or some other less valuable but still commercially viable metal," Crabbe had finished the lamb so that not a speck was left on the bone, and he segued seamlessly to a packet of Shelliac boat-tack he had somehow retained. "However, in order to conduct appropriate research on the belt, I must either have it in my hands, or have an assistant taking detailed readings with the lenses and the tuning forks while we talk."

Catt, who was no fool, was already preparing a defensive bristle. "I cannot help but notice that you are not accompanied by any such assistant."

"It is very hard to find appropriately gifted staff," Crabbe agreed, placidly munching. "However, I engaged in a prior discussion with your associate and business partner who happened to offer that you yourself were something of a master of analysis and had a deep and instinctive feel for the workings of magical artefacts, and I naturally presumed that I might rely on our professional fraternity to enlist you. I do not, of course, mean any subordination in my use of the term 'assistant' but simply emphasise the concept of 'assistance' such as is often offered gratis by one man of learning to his peer."

Catt opened his mouth and shut it again, feeling somewhat out-Catted in all honestly.

"This is entirely flattering and I am reassured by my colleague's high opinion of my gifts," he said with a baleful glower at the studiously oblivious Fisher. "We are all agreed, I am sure, that Oversy will not be parting with his belt given the aforementioned Arvennir distrust of foreign influences such as ourselves, but I would table the motion that neither will the fellow be delighted at my professional scrutiny during your interview. And whilst he perhaps lacks the lean hardness of physique that characterises the bulk of the Arvennir warrior orders we have seen, he remains the manner of individual I would be unwilling to antagonise whilst standing within arm's reach."

"A perspicacious summary," agreed Crabbe, "This is why we need a stratagem."

A STRATAGEM, IN Doctor Catt's book, was an elaborate scheme of many interlocking parts designed to effortlessly and (ideally) invisibly abstract from some other the precise treasure one might be seeking whilst exposing oneself to a minimum of personal danger, discomfort and indignity, and ideally not having to pay for anything in currency or in kind. That was the manner of stratagem he himself aspired to, when such sleights of hand and mind were called for.

They did not, in his strongly-stated preference, involve hiding underneath a table.

Oversy had arrived at last, pounding on the door as though about to arrest the lot of them, then stomping in, all six feet and three hundred pounds of him. A second viewing did not recommend him much. A big man whom nature had intended for great strength, but who had let it go to seed through too much large living, Catt decided. The Gryphon Guard were plainly not held to the same strictures as the average Arvennir order soldier.

He would have wine, yes. He would have food, too. He had whatever Crabbe offered, in fact, planting himself at the table the scholars had shrouded and dressed for him. Catt, from his secluded vantage, could only picture his narrow glare at all of it. His answers were curt and grunted, hostile from the start. He was here on sufferance and didn't trust them a jot.

Doctor Crabbe took a seat too, his absurdly hard knees jabbing Catt's shoulder blades. Catt had been trying to put as much space between himself and the lower regions of Oversy as possible but that 'possible' was being eroded moment to moment.

*I should have found a polite but firm way to absolutely refuse to have anything to do with this*, he decided, and yet somehow the conversation had never given him the handle to that door. It was, he knew, all Fisher's fault. Somehow Fisher and Crabbe had cooked this lunacy up between them in his absence, even though he couldn't even have said when they'd had the opportunity.

The underside of the tabletop brushed his wispy hair. His back hurt already. Crabbe was taking his sweet time with the interview.

And there, before him, was the belt, blazing with magical power, the belt of the Gryphon Guard. One of a limited edition of twenty, of which only seventeen remained in Arven hands. An artefact as old as the nation, passed down through generations of guardians until it cinched tight about the belly of a man who smelled as though he had not taken it off in a month.

There was precious little to recommend Oversy's nether

regions, in fact, a topic upon which Catt rather felt he was becoming an unwilling expert. His viewpoint gave him the Guard's enormous legs, his filthy boots, the tassets and greaves of his fancy armour, the belt and the belly that swagged over it. The whole smelled of sour sweat, spilled wine, old blood and more recent vomit. And, from the heavy sounds of jug and beaker from overhead, Oversy was more fond of the wine than the board at his hosts' table.

Crabbe was just getting started, asking about the institution of the Guard, the transmission of the belts, what attunement or training might be required. What had recommended little Oversy to the Guard, he asked?

"Born to it," the man grunted, and then, after a few more enquiries. "The right families. The right orders. Can't trust this with just anyone, ho hey?" And the sound of more pouring.

It was, he confirmed by monosyllable, the way with all the Guard. The Masters of a handful of orders controlled the belts, and the belts went to their favourites. Given they were the bulwark between the accepted order and any civil objection, that seemed entirely rational to Catt. Not as though you could hold a raffle, after all.

"I won't ask you to demonstrate the artefact's use within doors, obviously," Crabbe went on. "However, as a man of learning, the operation fascinates me."

"Turn into a Gryphon," Oversy said flatly. "What more is there?"

"The operation itself, though," – and Crabbe's voice did not in any way betray that he had given Catt a kick beneath the table – "is unorthodox. Transformation magic requires a defined matrix in order to encompass the desired new form. It is a challenging matter. One man's Gryphon is another's wyvern, so to speak. And yet I understand the Guard are meritoriously uniform when transformed. Is the Gryphon-ness within the belt, one wonders? Or within the wearer's mind, with the belt merely as a servant of his desires? This armguard of mine, for example," and doubtless Crabbe was pulling his sleeve down to expose Nystal's Regulating Bracer, "was designed by a very vain magus, intent that it would make the wearer a man more approximating the maker's own attributes, and thus the matrix within is very limited in scope, capable only of that transformation."

"Why wear it then?" Oversy wanted to know, a question Catt had himself poised.

"Oh, I am an admirer, obviously," Crabbe claimed. "Also, Nystal was of a sound constitution and there are certain embarrassing physical ailments that I am a martyr to, and which he himself was proof against. Hence to become more his manner of man brings me a surprising range of comforts I would otherwise be denied. And is your belt the same," another kick, "or might it have within it a certain flexibility of purpose?"

Oversy grunted again and poured another beaker, two bottles down and not sounding blurry in the slightest. Apparently the magical technicalities of the belts were not part of the curriculum of their wearers. Catt hunched forwards, shuffling silently on his haunches and holding his nose, shifting from one coloured lens to the next to study the intricacies of the belt's construction. It was, despite the overall suboptimal situation, an education. *They knew how to craft in those days*, he allowed, and doubtless there had been hands more than mortal in their manufacture. And yet, the more he peered within, the less Gryphon he saw. Doctor Crabbe was, he conceded, on to something with this line of questioning.

At last the wine soaked deep enough in that Oversy started talking, though in slurred and mumbled Arvenhal that Catt had to strain to make out. He was talking about when he first received the belt, his initiation ceremony. He had gone below the Irongarden, to that very pit Catt and Fisher had so recently visited. They'd given him one of the belts, from the hands of the elderly, sickening retiree who had held it before him – some uncle or similar, Catt understood. One of the other guard had been there, and transformed, knocked him down, bellowed into his terrified young face with its stale beast breath and its grey stony fangs. He laughed about it now, but Catt reckoned there was still a germ of that fear in him, from that moment. It had bloodied him a bit, he boasted. And he had called upon his own belt and become the Gryphon, and known he was one of the great, a bulwark of Arven, defender of the Flower Council. He laughed, and then told Crabbe frankly, "To keep out freaky little men like *you* who would dilute our great nation."

"Quite and indeed," said Crabbe mildly.

Abruptly, the man had kicked back his chair and was standing, though his odour remained as an unwelcome guest clogging the air beneath the table.

"Right, enough's enough," he decided. "You got the Grand Master to agree to this, but there's no more wine and the food's not all that. Enough questions from you." Catt saw the man's boots take a broad set stance and pictured him jabbing Crabbe in the chest. "Enough prying into our heritage. The Gryphon Belts have protected our country from every threat for a thousand years. Just hope we don't get called to protect it against you."

And then the boots were clomping off to the door, which rattled the frame when Oversy slammed it on the way out.

With some difficulty, Catt extricated himself from beneath the table. Crabbe was staring after the vanished Oversy speculatively, while Fisher sat in the corner, perusing a book with every appearance of disinterest.

"May we take it as read," Catt announced to the world at large, "that I consider myself most vilely abused by being employed in this manner and, were it a matter purely of personal dignity, would now follow that uncouth fellow through the door and have no more to do with this project."

"Oh, do smooth your hair, Catty," Fisher told him.

"And one might look for a little more support from an individual who has always held himself out as one's business partner," Catt added. "The disloyalty is hurtful."

Crabbe glanced between them. "Placing the personal to one side, might I enquire as to your conclusions as a man of learning, Doctor?"

"Ah, well." Catt seated himself at the table and found that, indeed, the wine was gone. His own flask of brandy would have to suffice. "As to that, and should I indeed relinquish my grievances, I congratulate your scholastic instincts, because you have come to the very heart of the matter vis the functioning of these remarkable belts. They are not, indeed, Belts of the Gryphon or any such business, for all that is what they have been used for and touted as for many generations. In fact, their functioning is not unlike the shamanic amulets we saw over in Undremark that one time, Fishy. They have a matrix within then that attunes itself when given over to a new user. In Undremark they were used to grant sight through the organs of an individual's familiar animal, and once bestowed, would work only with that singular beast. With these belts, the functionality is similar. When a new recruit is inducted into the Gryphon Guard, they are given the belt, but the belt must be taught what it is to transform them into. That story Oversy told, about being menaced by an existing Guardsman in Gryphon form imprinted the image on his mind and taught his belt what was expected of it." Catt rubbed at his chin, the opportunity to descant on the subject, not to mention the brandy, wearing away at his earlier indignation. "I note he said the business was performed down in that beast pit they have the Vathesk in now. Johannes did say that, in times long past, that was mews for actual Gryphons. Save that, of course, no set of eyes has been laid on a living Gryphon for an age. I wonder how many generations of their Guard have taken their shape-changed forms only from the existing holders of the belts? A remarkable thought, that a vanished monster has been kept alive and extant, in some way, by the transmission of these relics from wearer to wearer over the centuries!"

Crabbe was nodding keenly. "Indeed, quite remarkable," he said, and there was an odd, husky tone to his voice. It was the sort of tone Catt associated, from frequent personal experience, with someone who has a scheme, and which scheme has just been advanced by way of knowledge or trinkets brought to them by Messrs Catt and Fisher esquire. In a disappointing number of those past instances, Catt had discovered the scheme he had unwittingly advanced turned out to be a Bad Idea, at least from his perspective, and he surveyed Doctor Crabbe with a worried eye. However, the man didn't immediately fall to cackling and rubbing his hands, nor spontaneously grow a moustache to twirl, and so if villainy was afoot, it was at least of the longitudinal kind that might give Catt the chance to vacate the country first.

"I trust, therefore, that academic curiosity is satisfied?" he advanced. "In which case, there is nothing holding us in this lovely demesne save for the innocent desires of a sightseer?"

Doctor Crabbe opened his mouth in a manner that indicated that there might be some other demands upon his time here in Arven, and at that point Oversy kicked the door back in and re-entered. He had another of the Gryphon Guard with him, a white-moustached old man with a stoop, plus a half dozen soldiers from the Dogstooth Order.

"That's the one. The bald one with the eyeglasses," Oversy identified. He leered at Catt and Fisher. "Gentlemen, as you are men of letters, here's a piece of paper for you."

A document was thrust into Catt's hands, on the basis that Fisher was still placidly sitting across the room and hadn't even got up when the soldiers entered. He unrolled it, noting the various weighty seals appended to its foot.

"This would appear to be a warrant of arrest signed by my good friend Johannes Keymarque," he noted.

"Amazing what an education'll do for you," Oversy slurred, still riding the tide of all their wine. "My lord the Grand Master doesn't feel that foreign magicians prying into the sacred relics of Arven is so good a thing. Not with the way things sit right now." He bullied further in the room and gave Catt the benefit of his breath. "Freaky little bald men asking questions about the Guard. Why, he could be in league with all sorts of dissidents. You're just lucky you weren't here when he was about it, little Cheriveni, and that your friend over there didn't say a word. And that you did a favour for the Grand Master, maybe."

Catt bristled. "A favour, I might point out, that was in part recompensed by your coming here to answer my learned colleague's questions. For which recompense, by this paper, he is now being taken up."

Oversy chuckled. "Oh, he *thought* he was quizzing me, but it was me who was quizzing *him*, and when I got back to the Irongarden I told the Grand Master straight up. Don't trust the hunchbacked freak, I told him. He's up to something sneaky. Best bring him in and give him to the Yogg so she can pry his purposes out of him. She's good at that."

Catt, who had satisfied himself that neither his own name nor Fisher's were on the warrant, redoubled his bristling. "This is entirely unacceptable. We are Cheriveni academics, men of note and import. That you can so cavalierly lay hands upon one of us sets a dire precedent you cannot possibly—" and then he ended the sentence with a premature squeak because Oversy had become the Gryphon, slavering and snarling there before him, crushing the table with his increased bulk, wings scraping the walls and ceiling, floorboards groaning under his weight.

"You were saying?" the other Guard, the old man, asked, cold-eyed. "Perhaps you would like us to suggest to the Grand

Master that you will pine for the company of your fellow, and should be permitted to join him?"

Catt cast a helpless look at Crabbe, who seemed unusually placid in the face of this oppression.

"No, no," he muttered. "This is obviously an internal matter for the Flower Council. We would not dream of interfering." He backed off as Oversy reverted to his human form and the pack of them took Doctor Crabbe away.

# SIX

DOCTOR CATT WAS not at his best when waiting upon someone else's pleasure. This might not be intuitive to any who knew his home nation of Cherivell, a place of infinite gradations of laws, protocol and procedure. However, the Cheriveni constructed their paper castles of jurisprudence and etiquette specifically so that others might wait upon them. Catt took the reversal with poor grace.

He was, for the form of things, attempting to achieve his desires in a civilised fashion. Specifically, he was attending at the Irongarden to petition for the release of Doctor Crabbe. He had been waiting for almost two hours and the trickle of servants and officials assured him that the Grand Master had been informed of his presence but was, of course, a very busy man. And if there was a little extra needle in their tones, at fobbing off a Cheriveni with such niceties, he was doing his best to rise above it.

In the end, and after the second hour had passed, he did indeed gain his desired audience, for all of two minutes. Johannes Keymarque greeted him from behind a laden desk, with a friendliness no more than skin deep.

"Ah, Doctor Catt. Perhaps you have some new and useful artefact you wish to proffer for sale?"

"No indeed, although should you have any requirements I

will of course bend my professional powers to the utmost in their fulfilment," Catt replied politely. "However, I am here to bring to your attention a curious misunderstanding that has occurred. Specifically, my learned colleague Doctor Crabbe appears to have been taken into custody for no more than an honest scholarly curiosity, and I wished to alert you to this untoward turn of events so that you might reverse it."

Johannes regarded him mildly. "How regrettable," he remarked. "And did you see whose seal it was upon the relevant document?"

"I believe that it may have been your own, Grand Master."

Johannes, to his credit, kept an admirably straight face. "Well this is a most unusual quandary, and I will of course investigate it. Should some manner of error have crept into our proceedings here then I will of course rectify it in the fullness of time, Doctor."

"There was some mention of aggravated questioning at the hands of—"

"In the fullness of time, Doctor." One of Johannes' bony hands indicated the papers on his desk, doubtless all of surpassing urgency, and Catt knew when to cede the field.

HE RETURNED TO find the lodgings full of Arvennir in full order regalia, which gave him a nasty turn. He wouldn't have put it past Keymarque to go through all that charade while there was another warrant already out for the arrest of Catt and Fisher. A moment's blinking confirmed that this particular band of locals was comprised of Lodovi Setchwort's adherents, however. They had a map of the city spread out on the smaller replacement table Fisher had purloined from somewhere and the woman herself was in full flow about their glorious revolution.

Catt sidled in, braved their suspicious stares, and shuffled over to Fisher where he slouched in the corner.

"I'm away for such a brief moment and yet it appears things have already become considerably worse," he observed mildly. "What, might I ask, is going on?"

"They needed somewhere to plan their uprising," Fisher replied, as though that explained everything.

"I'd venture to note that this would be *their* problem, but now it appears to have become *our* problem," Catt said.

"Doctor Catt!" Lodovi was abruptly at their collective elbow. "I heard what happened to your colleague. This is exactly the sort of tyranny we are striving against."

"Yes, yes, a dreadful development," Catt agreed weakly. "Constable, what is actually going *on* here?"

"We are going to make our stand before the Irongarden," she told him fiercely. "In two days we hold the Feast of Agassi, a reminder of all it means to be Arvennir. We will gather and make our demands, and exhort the populace to rise up, for justice and progress."

Catt nodded placatingly. "Well I'm sure that will go well for you."

"We will release the prisoners held beneath the Garden, your friend included."

"That is very kind of you."

"The Flower Council will be forced to recognise our demands."

"That would be very accommodating of them, if out of character. How many do you actually have, to stand there and force the might of the Arvennir government to make any concessions?"

"Oh, there are not so many of us." Lodovi indicated the score or so cramming their lodgings. "But the people are with us."

Catt felt a certain presentiment of disaster. "One might observe that, whilst the sympathies of the people may well be broadly in alignment with your aims, tired as they are of being constantly oppressed by the armed might of the Warrior

Orders, the actual presence of the people may yet be dissuaded because of that armed might, backed as it is by monstrous Gryphons." *And now Vathesk*, he added silently to himself, although he wasn't going to expound on that particular delightful development because he wasn't keen to expose his own part in it. *All entirely innocent, and yet how these things stack up…*

"But we have the Lily Oriflamme, of course," Lodovi told him. "When we raise that flag, it shall give courage to all who flock to it."

"Ah, yes," Catt said weakly. "That. Jolly good. Of course."

He retreated to Fisher's corner and hauled over a chair. His legs were feeling shaky.

"This is not going to go well," he murmured. "Not any of it."

"No," Fisher agreed morosely. The voice of Lodovi sailed to them, telling her comrades of great tomorrows when Arven would show a different face to the world, when her people would not be under the heel of the orders' boot. And Catt found he could respect that. After all, everyone there was wearing order colours and yet conniving to lessen their own share of the common good for the benefit of those beneath them. Except…

"Between you and me, Fishy, I really don't see this uprising business going terribly well."

"No," grunted Fisher, taking an uncommon interest in the state of his nails.

"There honestly aren't that many of these fellows here, and sheer enthusiasm was never a great substitute for a headcount, no matter what the Forinthi ballads always claim. And I don't think Arvennir ballads even do make those claims."

"Not after they executed all those balladeers," Fisher agreed.

"And there's the matter of those damnable Gryphons."

Fisher shrugged. "They weren't all that against the Kinslayer."

"Granted, but primarily because the Kinslayer had plenty

of his own monsters, and the Yorughan to boot. But I rather think they are quite effective in civic put-downs. I don't really want to imagine a half dozen of those beasts ploughing into a protesting crowd, tooth and claw. Which is a shame because it is a sight all too easily imaginable." Catt shuddered.

"Indeed."

"Even assuming anyone turns up except our friends in this room."

"Well, they'll put the flag out," Fisher noted. "And people will come just seeing it. Not as many as would come if…"

Catt lowered his voice. "If it was the real flag, yes."

"And as it's not…"

"Not the real flag, yes." The barest whisper, and a guilty glance over his shoulder.

"Then," Fisher finished heavily, "as soon as the claws come out, there's no great supernatural upsurge of courage and steadfastness. And so it's all that panic-panic, running around like headless chickens with a fox in the pen, all that." He sighed. "Don't imagine there's much we can do about it though."

Catt nodded sadly. "I really don't want to witness any of that, frankly," he decided primly. "Barring one or two small dissatisfactions, one might think this was a good time to vacate Arven before the Grand Master finds some blank arrest warrants and doodles in a few more names."

"I'll pack our bags, shall I?" said Fisher, making no move to do so.

"Well that would seem the wisest course of action," Catt agreed, similarly unmoving. "Save for some small matters of scholarly principle."

Fisher looked at him sidelong. "That's a thing with you now, is it?"

"You wound me, Fishy. You positively wrong my noble character. I am a man of learning, part of an elite siblinghood spread across the world, borders, species and creed no object, so long as a love of knowledge is given its head. And thus, one cannot but take it amiss when one's colleague in erudition is hauled off by thugs at the behest of a tyrant. One feels that some manner of token action is required above and beyond kicking one's heels in the Grand Master's antechamber. One feels this particularly when the Grand Master has a pet Yorughan inquisitor to hand."

Fisher regarded him levelly. "You want to go spring Doctor Crabbe."

Catt sighed. "Well no, not really. I *want* to go home and forget any of this nonsense ever happened, because very little of it has left me feeling happy or fulfilled. But I feel that leaving our fellow to his fate, however vexing his manner, personal habits and the demands he has made on me, would be a terrible precedent. Speaking as someone who has, through no fault of his own, found himself in similar predicaments from time to time."

Fisher's eyes swivelled left and right as though trying to work out where all this uncharacteristic self-knowledge had come from, but at last he just rolled them in exasperation. "This is just because Keymarque made you wait around, isn't it?"

"It was a profoundly impolite approach to someone with whom the Grand Master had recently concluded a satisfactory business transaction," Catt agreed. "It's only natural justice that we express our indignation by way of, for example, an impromptu jailbreak. And, while we're there..." Catt's eyes took on a faraway look Fisher knew only too well. "It is always possible that we might chance upon some other prize. I rather suspect the Irongarden has been accumulating little treasures for rather a long time."

"You want to rob them now, as well?" Fisher noted. "So much for the moral high ground."

"Not in any way. That is a base accusation," Catt retorted, though with little real fire. "However, should we come across items whose provenance suggests that the Flower Council has no good or beneficial title to them, we might abstract them with an eye to repatriating them to their true owners, if such should come forwards. And there is also another matter of relatively pressing import." He looked over his shoulder. Lodovi had drawn out some lines on their map and everyone was nodding very earnestly at her. They were so very young, Catt thought, and so determined to change the world. Winning the war against the Kinslayer had given them a sense of immortality and power over destiny that were both entirely illusory. As Johannes Keymarque would doubtless teach them in two days' time.

"We never saw much of the Irongarden on our official visit," he noted, half to himself. "It might be that I shall take the opportunity to see a few sights."

# SEVEN

THE FIRST STEP was, after they had shooed all the revolutionaries out of their lodgings, to actually enter the Irongarden in a capacity other than carefully monitored official visitors. In this, it turned out that Doctor Crabbe was, in absentia, their best ally. Or, at least, the payment he had already made for their services. That the Undiminished Lochago's Sartorian he had provided them would be a key element of their attempt to retrieve the man from durance seemed to Doctor Catt entirely appropriate. Plus, he had discovered that playing with the wizened little creature was a pleasure in itself.

"We shall require new outfits, Fishy," he declared. "How ambitious do you feel? How native is your Arvenhal?"

"It'll do," Fisher said. In fact, being taller and leaner of face, he would pass fairly convincingly for the sort of local who'd gone off to war and come back, and lived a life of endured privation in between. Catt himself, being shorter and plumper and considerably more avuncular, was more a match for the officials they had seen within the Irongarden itself, many of whom were, if not of his age, then at least resembled the age he allowed himself to appear as, and tended to show more signs of soft living than the actual troops.

And of course Catt had been to the Irongarden twice now, and had a keen eye for costumery at the best of times.

For himself, he had the little taxidermied tailor run up the kind of get-up that the Grand Master's secretary had worn, complete with the badge of the Order of the Foxglove, mostly because that particular organisation was not well represented right now in Athaln and he'd be less likely to meet with people who'dwant to know why his face was unfamiliar. The monkey got to work in its horribly spry way and made the required garments out of cobweb and sunlight to his order and as fit his imagination.

Fisher proved more difficult, not for any intrinsic awkwardness in his nature, although it was a character trait he certainly held dear, but because Catt wanted him in the mail armour of an order soldier, without himself being of a martial nature. The first three attempts came out like a mummer's costume of knitted wool painted silver, which would raise some questions on any close inspection. In the end, Fisher himself had to take over, and the resulting garment sat particularly ill on him, baggy at the crotch and knees, too short at the wrists. He also ended up with a white tabard showing a black thistlehead, an order neither of them was remotely familiar with, though privately Catt felt the choice was appropriate for the wearer.

They donned their new outfits with, in Catt's case at least, a certain childlike enthusiasm, then examined themselves critically in the Extendable Mirror of Pergon, a device Catt tended to keep in his inside pocket for moments of vanity.

"The effect is…" he was forced to admit, "imperfect. We look rather as though we were a pair of foreigners who had decided to attend some manner of costume ball as comedy Arvennir."

"Hrm," Fisher agreed, trying to tug his mail into a more comfortable position about the groin.

"Stop fiddling with yourself. That also looks inauthentic," Catt told him. He frowned at his reflection critically. "The overall ensemble is lacking something. Some piece of Arvennery that we have not achieved." He stroked his immaculately barbered chin and then caught a sudden inspiration.

"I have it! But... I wonder if we might be asking too much of the little thing." He knelt before the Sartorian, which was crouched on the bed like a nightmare awaiting its next client. Its glass eyes, slightly skewed, stared both at and past him.

"Is this within your capabilities, my little fellow?" Catt asked it, concentrating on the effect he was after. The little monkey hands hesitated, then started their work, plucking woolly strands from the coarse bedsheets and weaving them into...

Mere minutes later, Catt admired himself anew, stroking the luxurious grey moustache adhered to his upper lip, which dangled down to some inches past his chin.

"I rather think this is exactly the thing. *Terribly* Arvennir, don't you think?"

"You look absurd," Fisher told him.

"On the contrary, I find this lends a certain gravitas to my physiognomy previously absent. Why, I would venture that a really serious moustache would aid any manner of sombre negotiations such that we might clear an additional four per cent of our fees, our opposite number being given such additional evidence of our sagacity. I think I may keep it, or even attempt to grow one naturally hereafter. I really am rather pleased. You, of course, look like the most dreadful thug, but that is, alas, also key to fitting in here."

Fisher's moustaches were darker and even longer, and further lengthened his already stretched face. The Sartorian had, of its own notion, given him a brass bead woven into each, so that if he turned his head sharply they jangled together or occasionally hit Doctor Catt in the eye.

"Much as I would like to continue adding to our ensemble," Catt decided, taking a prudent step back, "it is time we called upon the Irongarden and put these disguises to the test."

\*     \*     \*

IN TIMES PAST there had been a Cheriveni magician who was also a clerk in that nation's well-developed bureaucracy, and who was, as a third string to his lute, a profound lecher and pursuer of other men's wives. His name had been Maturio and he had bent his arcane talents to enhancing the more mundane aspects of his life by creating the All-Satisfying Writ. This enchanted document, when presented in an appropriately officious manner, always appeared to be the exact credentials allowing the bearer to be where he was and pass where he chose, thus allowing Maturio access to his wide range of paramours. Catt understood the man had been remarkably popular behind closed doors.

Given his current errand, therefore, it was a particular shame that Catt had been in possession of the Writ only a few weeks beforehand but had traded it on before coming to Arven. Not that he particularly wanted to romance the Grand Master's wife or any such tomfoolery, but the artefact would have let him waltz blithely into the Irongarden without having to exercise his less creditable talents.

As it was, he was going to have to lower himself.

Doctor Catt came by his collection of artefacts by a variety of means. Mostly he traded for them with other collectors or hired agents to track them down and purchase them. While the purchase prices were ideally considerably under value, bought from the clueless who didn't know what they had, the transactions were still of an entirely legal nature. On other occasions it might be that his research would lead him to some item unclaimed or abandoned, or at least in the possession only of beasts, monsters or the dead, thus requiring a more dynamic abstraction. However, there had been moments when he had been required to take more direct and less legitimate action over some trifle that he simply *had* to possess, and that was not for sale in any coin he could muster. This was mostly a holdover from his youth, when he had not been the prosperous and happy fellow he now was. He was not proud of those times, but the skills had stayed with him.

So it was that he bustled about the front of the Irongarden until he spotted a clerk inbound who looked to be of about the same status in the Arven hierarchy as the outfit that he had crafted for himself. He then crossed paths with the luckless man and, after a jostle and an unctuous Arvenhal apology, came away with the sealed documents the man had been carrying inside his tunic.

"In we go then, Fishy," he murmured, and he and the armoured Doctor Fisher strode up to the gates of the Irongarden as though they owned them, waved the pilfered documents at the officials, and then were inside.

The Irongarden was, of course, a large and labyrinthine place, and the Arvennir had unaccountably failed to pin up maps for the first-time visitor. However, the pair did at least know their way downwards, and Catt reckoned he'd had a sniff of cells and prisoners on their way to see the Vathesk. They had a number of false starts trying to get to the lower levels without dog-legging past the Grand Master's own chambers, and at one point they nearly walked straight into Oversy as the man shambled along with a couple of his belt-wearing peers, a shabby and undisciplined knot within the clockwork of the Arvennir governance. The man didn't even glance at them, shoving past with the natural arrogance of the elite. Catt saw every other orderman, servant and clerk scurry out of the Gryphon Guards' way too. Plainly, if you wore the belt, you answered to nobody save the Grand Master and the Flower Council.

They had hoped to track Doctor Crabbe by sympathetic magic, having brought a half-eaten sandwich the man had left behind when hauled away, but such means tended towards a straight-line approach which didn't take into account inconvenient obstacles like walls and floors. In the end, what their noses did lead them to was the kitchens, and a little skulking observation was able to identify food for prisoners on the basis of its poorer quality and shorter portions.

"Poor Doctor Crabbe," Catt murmured. "He was always fond of his dining. I do hope this isn't too hard on him." And by that time they had followed the servants down to where the cells were, and where the sandwich might act as a reliable guide.

"And now," Catt added, "I think I shall leave you to conduct the final part of our plan, Fishy. After all, we are about to enter a place short on clerks but long on guards, and you will be more inconspicuous than I."

Fisher eyed him narrowly. "And what might you be about, while I do all the work?"

"I think I might drop in on an old friend. Or at least visit the quarters he was formerly resident in, before his wartime demise. You remember old Matthau Limbtickler?"

"Lemstacker," Fisher corrected for the umpteenth time. For a long while, he stared at Catt, then shrugged. "I better go get Crabbe out then."

"If you would be so kind. Meet you back here presently."

Matthau Lemstacker had been a curious man. Catt remembered him well: so lean as to be hollowed out, bent beneath the weight of his responsibilities, not a warrior's warrior at all. He had been Grand Turcopolier of the Order of the Lily, a senior quartermaster's rank that wouldn't normally result in a battlefield command. His company had already been mauled once, and the Kinslayer had gone for the head, leaving him the ranking officer. He'd been given a diverse army made of offcuts from all the broken and mauled bits and pieces left over from the Kinslayer's advance on the Arven border. He'd been ordered to hold as long as he could to allow the defence of Athaln to ready itself.

And he'd had the Lily Oriflamme.

Catt himself had been scouting about ahead of the Kinslayer's advance, keen to snap up a few choice pieces, simultaneously helping himself and denying them to the enemy. Somehow Lemstacker had known of his reputation and come to him with a problem. He knew he couldn't win, basically. Very shortly there would be a battle, and his people would die buying time, which was their job and he was resigned to that. The Oriflamme, sacred relic of his order, would fall into the hands of the Kinslayer, however, and he didn't want that. And so he and Catt had cooked up a piece of trumpery.

A false flag. A simulacrum of the Oriflamme so exact nobody would ever know. Catt had possessed the means, and in return for some goods in trade and a little cash had performed the service. And Matthau Lemstacker had ridden hotfoot to Athaln and the Irongarden with the real flag. And, apparently, told absolutely nobody what he had done, because history recorded the Oriflamme lost at Struander when the Kinslayer crossed the border. And while history didn't particularly care to record that one Matthau Lemstacker fell on that field too, it was nonetheless true.

Of course, his room wouldn't be just sitting vacant, but the Arven warrior orders had a rigid hierarchy, and there would be a new Grand Turcopolier of the Order of the Lily, and they would have the same chambers in the Irongarden as Lemstacker had once occupied.

And, of course, they remained occupied, and the grey-haired woman stared at Catt with narrow suspicion when he appeared at her door. It was immediately apparent that some feud existed between Lily and Foxglove he hadn't been aware of, but Doctor Catt was nothing if not adaptable. He put on a haughty air, as of clerks the world over, and explained that the Grand Turcopolier of *his* order had a list of requisitions, items currently held by the Lily, which it was absolutely essential be provided to the Foxglove yesterday. He waved his sealed document, which said no such thing, but of course the outraged woman wasn't remotely interested in seeing any such list. Instead she stormed off to give her opposite number a piece of her mind, and Catt was left in possession of the late Lemstacker's chambers.

He brought out his lenses, thinking of hidden catches, secret compartments, all the usual. After all, the Arven warrior orders presumably employed cleaners to turn out these rooms on a regular basis, so the flag couldn't just have remained undiscovered under the bed or something similar. Hurried analysis showed no such places for secretion. The walls were stone and solid, the furniture wooden and likewise. There were no hidden chambers behind the drapes, nor extradimensional spaces enchanted into the ceiling.

Uncomfortably aware that, unless inter-order relations really degenerated, he wouldn't have long until the room's current owner returned, he tried to hone his magical senses. Maddeningly, he felt that he had come close to the damned thing in his search already. He could virtually smell the power of the Oriflamme on the air, and yet somehow Lemstacker had stashed it somewhere utterly beyond his reach.

Had the man been a magician? Catt thought he'd had some tricks. Nothing that would win any battles. He remembered sitting with the cadaverous Arvennir before the battle. What was it the man had been doing with his hands...?

Conjuring tricks, he recalled. Making his cutlery disappear, producing objects from his sleeves. A nervous habit, really, without any showmanship to it. Just a little exercise in illusion to keep his fingers from shaking.

Catt blinked. He'd been on the very point of starting to disassemble major pieces of furniture, and that would likely be hard to explain when the Grand Turcopolier came back. *But what if I'm being too clever for my own good...?*

Because he had been rooting behind the drapes just a moment

ago, and now his residual memory was telling him that one hadn't been as thick as the others. Thinner cloth, older, more worn.

Catt took a step back, looking at what seemed very much to be a faded tapestry, just another of those odd Arvennir black and white art pieces. Nothing to call it out from its fellows, to the eye, but to the fingers...

*In plain sight, you sly fellow.* One last enduring illusion from Lemstacker, who would never come back to reclaim it.

When the Grand Turcopolier did return to her office, after a blazing row with her baffled counterpart from the Foxglove, she was baffled to find one of her curtains missing.

DOCTOR FISHER, LEFT to his own devices, was not of the false-documents-and-blather school of infiltration. Nor did he feel that the general mood of the cells beneath the Irongarden was likely to be conducive to such an approach. Oh, doubtless Doctor Catt would have gone in with his usual boundless confidence and, in Fisher's experience, that did tend to bear fruit rather more often than was strictly reasonable. And the rest of the time it went horribly wrong and the man then required rescue, all too often from Doctor Fisher. And the one grand disadvantage of being caught breaking into a prison was that the locals, by definition, had facilities on hand with which to welcome you.

Fisher skulked. He was a good skulker. In an earlier, prouder life, before he'd gone rogue and cast his lot in with Doctor Catt, he'd never have dreamed of anything so insalubrious as skulking. He'd been proud and mighty and angry, and gone about things in a very direct way indeed. And in the end, after all of that nonsense, he'd looked back on his violent and energetic career and decided that very little of it had really achieved anything, and that he hadn't really enjoyed it as much as might have been thought, and maybe it was time to change his name and step into the background and just take things a bit easier. He had learned, among other things, to skulk, and discovered an unexpected joy in the habit. He had also learned to be surly, sarcastic and self-centred, but right now it was the skulking he was deploying.

He had become a world-class skulker. The baggy chainmail did not inhibit him. In fact, given that it was sufficiently ill-fitting to disguise his human outline, it actually assisted. He shifted from shadow to shadow through the subterranean halls of the Irongarden, sneaking into guard rooms to rifle the registers, holing up in alcoves as patrols went past, helping himself to a turnkey's packed lunch and then padding away even as the argument broke out. A good throw-down over a missing pastry was exactly what he needed to draw all the bored and malingering guards over, while he made tracks deeper into the cells.

They were mostly empty, and he wasn't sure if that was a good or bad thing. Perhaps the Arvennir were practising a light touch with their prisoners. More likely, he suspected, they knew full well that someone was going to take a stand come the Feast of Agassi and had considerably thought ahead and cleared some room. Doubtless Lodovi and her people would be down here soon enough.

*Very much not our problem*, Fisher considered, for all it rankled.

Doctor Crabbe was not named on the ledgers, but one new prisoner was already picked out in the records as having made multiple requests for food, and that sounded sufficiently familiar to put Fisher on the trail. Typically, they hadn't just thrown Crabbe somewhere convenient and near the stairs, but had stowed him in a cell down on another level again, even danker and darker than the first. They were close enough to the Vathesk pit that Fisher could hear the gibbering and wailing of the creatures as they, too, demanded to be fed. And would be fed, he supposed, with that damnable wand. And would still be hungry afterwards, and desperate for more. Would that turn them into tame monsters for the Flower Council? Fisher was rather afraid that it would.

He had not seen any guards for a while now, and assumed the lower levels were not popular with them for health reasons. That did give him a clear run down the stairs to the lower bays, and a solid oak door with rusting hinges and a clunky great lock.

Skulking was not the only bad habit Fisher had fallen into, of course, and the lock was the matter of a few moments under his deft ministrations. Opening the door was another matter, though. This was the point where skulking would cease to serve, if there were guards on the far side. And doubtless there were.

He gave it a tiny push. The hinges screamed a little, just warming themselves up.

He opened it a further crack, to further protest. And yet there was still no outcry from beyond. What were the guards about, he wondered? He was minded to write a letter of complaint. Were they deaf? Asleep?

He continued opening the door in little fits and starts, constantly trying to minimise the squealing of the hinges, achieving nothing and yet reluctant to just throw the thing open. Each time he listened. Each time there was silence. Each time he tried ever harder to move the door with infinite stealth, and each time the hinges wailed and complained ever more until by the time he had the door ajar enough to slip in he was sure the entire garrison would be waiting for him on the far side with swords drawn.

There were indeed a solid half-dozen guards there. There were only three cells, and so the number seemed disproportionate. Fisher guessed that some of them were not natively to be found at this low level but had come down out of solicitous feelings for their colleagues. Despite the shameful state of the door hinges, they did not leap up and stare at him, challenge him or even throw him in one of the cells. All three doors were standing open, and it would have been very little effort to make a prisoner of an elderly Cheriveni scholar. Or possibly it would have been rather more effort than that, but they weren't to know. Nonetheless, not a one of them took a step to do their manifest duty in the face of an intruder.

This was likely, in Doctor Fisher's expert opinion – for he and Catt were medical men alongside their other areas of expertise – because they were every one of them dead.

Really quite a lot dead, in fact. It wasn't as though they had simply lain down to sleep and passed peacefully to their final reward, whatever that really amounted to in these latter secular days. They hadn't eaten the same bad prison food or caught some virulent plague passed to them by their charges, which Fisher reckoned was an occupational hazard of hanging around unhygienic places like jails. They had not, en masse, tripped over each other's spear shafts and died of comedy pratfalls.

They were all over the place. All six of them. They had been, and he made the assessment as a man with considerable experience of the topic, torn bodily apart. Limbs had been severed, as had a couple of heads. There were great crushing wounds on the bodies. Steel mail had been sheared away like fancy crimped paper on some noble's birthday surprise.

Doctor Crabbe stood in one of the open doorways, adjusting his cuffs. There was blood on his boots – there was blood on Fisher's boots now, already – but nowhere else. His look, from behind those little spectacles, was of mild inquiry only.

"Right, so," Fisher noted. "It's like that then. Can't say I didn't have my suspicions."

Crabbe blinked myopically at him, an act which, right then, was not fooling its sole living audience of one. "Is it a rescue?"

he asked. "That is more kindness than I had necessarily looked for under the circumstances. I'm afraid I had already made a start on my own."

Fisher made a vaguely affirmative noise. His eyes strayed just once more to the carnage that was painting the walls and layering the floor in loose organs, and then he mastered them and made a butlerian 'after you' gesture to the other man.

True to his nature, Crabbe was chewing, as he stepped out through the door. Fisher had no intention of enquiring what it was those big, omnivorous teeth were working over.

# EIGHT

DOCTOR CATT HAD been anxiously waiting around, smiling cheerily at passing Arvennir with the Lily Oriflamme stuffed down his tunic. By the time Fisher and Crabbe made their appearance he felt he was definitely wearing out his welcome.

"What, may I enquire, kept you?" he demanded in a whisper.

"Had to clean our boots," Fisher told him, which he took for a particularly opaque figure of speech.

"While I was kicking my own heels awaiting you, it did occur to me that we had not approached the logistical difficulty that is our colleague here," Catt noted, glancing anxiously about, because Doctor Crabbe was very much not moustachioed or attired as a local, and his physical appearance was unlikely to pass for the sort of Arvennir one didn't glance twice at. "I was pondering the old saw where we pretend to be his captors moving him from one place to another, and thereby remove him from the Irongarden entirely."

"Hrm," Fisher considered. "Can't see them just letting us walk all the way out with him. I reckon in this place the prisoners come in, but they don't come out again. Anyway, we have a plan."

Catt blinked at him. "You made a plan. With Crabbe? Without me?" He felt wounded.

"We have a barrel."

They did indeed have a barrel, some large tun that smelled of aging olive oil, but was entirely empty now. Catt eyed it leerily. "He'll fit in that, will he?"

Fisher shrugged. "Only one way to find out."

Doctor Crabbe, despite his bulk and awkward shape, was somehow able to pour himself into the barrel, seeming to fill it entirely as though he had something of the glutinous liquid to his makeup. Catt wondered if it was the influence of Nystal's Regulating Bracer, although he hadn't particularly heard that Nystal liked to spend any significant time cooped up in barrels.

"Whilst this stage of the plan is accomplished," Catt noted, "we now have a barrel of Crabbe which, I suspect, is rather heavy."

They lugged it as far as they could, trying their level best to seem like professional Arvennir about a routine task, and then reached the foot of the stairs that led up to ground level and the eventual exit.

"There is no way," Catt puffed, "that we, two middle-aged Cheriveni, are going to be able to accomplish this."

Fisher looked mulish, or at least more mulish than usual, but Catt was struck by a sudden inspiration.

"Doctor Crabbe, would you exit the barrel, if you may?" They had got it into a shaded alcove, and Crabbe decanted himself with an unpleasant fluidity of movement.

"I give you," Catt explained, "the Satchel of Prodigious Contents."

It was his standard travelling pack, enchanted to hold far more within than its rather scuffed outsides would suggest. He and Fisher had long understood that, of all the trinkets and toys a gentleman might wish to take into the world, something that allowed you to carry quantities of food, drink and comfort without requiring a bevy of servants and a coach was by far the most essential.

"Doctor Crabbe, might you climb into the satchel. Take care you keep your head outside, at the least, or I wouldn't answer to what the preservative field might make of you."

The satchel's opening shouldn't really have been large enough but, as with the barrel, the man proved strangely jointless at need, and soon Catt was holding a small bag, from which a large bald and bespectacled head protruded, his flabby-fingered hands hooked over the lip. He was still chewing. The effect was disquieting.

"I confess," Catt, no stranger to strange sights, found himself entirely thrown off by the sight, "that this may not have been the solution I thought it was. I don't know how we'd get something like this past the guards."

"Stick it in the barrel," Fisher said prosaically, and they did, and in such a manner they left the Irongarden with Doctor Crabbe, just as some sort of outcry could be heard emerging from the cells below them.

As per prior arrangements, Lodovi met them close to the Garden. She had been outraged at Crabbe's arrest, which represented everything she felt she was fighting against, to wit the offhand tyranny of the Arvennir state. While they had been enacting their rescue, she had found them alternative lodgings over an ironmonger's in a decidedly drabber part of town. The place was one of her meeting houses, and it was already elbow-jostling with keen young Arvennir when Catt, Fisher and Crabbe got in. There was precious little room for them, and they made a little cluster next to the pile of their belongings Lodovi had arranged to bring over.

"My fellow academics," Doctor Crabbe said. He was out of both barrel and satchel now, and appeared entirely unchanged by the whole affair, although again, perhaps the bracer he wore was partly responsible for that. "I confess myself humbled by your assistance, which has gone beyond any contractual relationship standing between us."

Catt peeled off his fake moustache. "It is, as they say, a trifle. Or perhaps it may be regarded as a service performed on credit, to be borne in mind when we should enter into our next commercial arrangement." For want of anything else to do with it, he stuck the moustache on the withered lip of the Sartorian, which was squatting atop the pile of their possessions.

"I suppose," he said, "it is time for us to plan our exit, the three of us."

He cast an unhappy eye at Lodovi and her people. More of them were coming in, some looking quite senior in this order or that, some not so young. She was getting herself up on a box, ready to speak to them all.

"Exit, right," Fisher agreed. "I think we're *done* Athaln. Doctor Crabbe, you concur?"

Crabbe wasn't looking at the gathering revolutionaries. "There are some finishing touches to my researches that remain undone," he murmured. "In the manner of a practical test of my theories."

"I would advise undertaking such niceties outside the border," Catt suggested. "I do not believe the Arvennir government shows an appropriate respect to either theoretical or applied learning."

"Doubtless you are right," Crabbe agreed. "And yet one's researches are all too often tied to the locale of one's topics of interest."

"Well," Catt said firmly, "*We*, at any rate, will obviously vacate the city before this Feast of Agassi business. Which signifies I know not what. I say, Constable Setchwort, what even *is* this festivity of which you speak?"

"It marks the day that Grand Master Agassi walked the entire border of the nation, using his miraculous Fleeting Boots, thus forever separating the chosen people of Arven from the rest of the world. A philosophy that our leaders have espoused ever since, to our detriment," she explained.

"What a remarkably insular legend," Catt noted. "And these boots, might they be preserved...? No? Alas, so goes time and the world. Well, all very creditable that you should choose such a day to make your doo... grand stand, Constable. I wish you joy of it. We will eagerly await news of how matters fall out with you, from the far side of the same border that Agassi trod."

When she had returned to her people and her box, he shook his head.

"Youth, enthusiasm and hope, and the worst of these things is hope." But then Lodovi was making her speech. It seemed very similar to the previous one but there were more listeners, and Catt suspected most of the audience had followers of their own they would regurgitate the words to. Out of respect, but mostly because it was hard to carry on a conversation over Lodovi's strident voice, he sat and listened with all appearance of interest. She spoke about how the common people of Arven had been crushed under the fist of the orders, unable to own even the land they tilled, virtual slaves kept in the darkness of ignorance. Then she spoke about the people she'd seen in lands to the west – Cherivell and Forinth and all the little lands the Kinslayer had trampled. The people there had hope and pride, she said. They were given to, and so they gave back. Those nations were smaller than Arven, and perhaps their armies were not as mighty, but they were places of light and life and promise. Arven must change, she said. Arven must grow towards the sun, for if it continued to simply serve the wants of the old men on the Flower Council, it would forever fall behind, become the joke of the world. And she spoke with passion and fire, and Catt could see everyone nodding. It was all terribly depressing.

He stood, just as she finished. Fisher plucked at his sleeve, but he gave the man a meaningful look, as of *You know what to do*, and then approached Lodovi, hoping Fisher did indeed know what to do.

"Constable, ladies and gentlemen, stalwarts of the Warrior Orders," he addressed them, taking possession of the box and finding it didn't actually make him taller than most of them. "My name is Doctor Catt, a scholar, physician, lawyer and general polymath of Cherivell, one of the nations Constable Setchwort has just referred to in such flattering tones." And they were smiling a little, anticipating a big hurrah from the friendly foreigner, and in that he was going to disappoint them.

"I have heard the Constable's words," several times in fact, "and I am broadly in sympathy with them, you understand. Greater openness, greater freedoms, the iron hand of et cetera and so forth. All fine sentiments. Who, after all, would not want such change to transpire? Save for that cabal who currently benefit from it, of course, and you may be assured I bear them no love. I have only just returned from retrieving my esteemed colleague Doctor Crabbe from the dungeons of the Irongarden, so you may imagine I am not best pleased with the whole organ of governance ensconced therein."

More nods, more smiles, and here came the turning point of his patter, right on time.

"But," he told them, a finger in the air. "The problem with overthrowing the established order is that the established order doesn't like it. And while you here are obviously valiant order soldiers who are willing to throw off that yoke and work towards the betterment of those less fortunate than you, I rather feel the majority of the armed might of Arven won't see it that way. And won't take kindly to you hoisting a flag and making demands, do you see?"

"Our cause is just," Lodovi told him. "That is why we will prevail."

"Ah, well, that is what we call a logical fallacy, where the first syllogistic statement does not in any way imply the sequel," Catt said. "Stories are full of just causes triumphing. History texts notably less so."

"Doctor Catt," Lodovi told him. "We cannot just do nothing. If not us, then who? If not now, then when? Every generation there have been people like us who dared not act. Even if we fail, we must show the Flower Council that it does not rule unchallenged."

"And then there are the Gryphon Guard," Catt went on, as if she hadn't spoken. "I have seen them up close, and I'm sure many of you have. Terrifying creatures. Just the sort of hounds you'd set on a mob of protestors if you were an authoritarian regime. They have seventeen of them, and that seems enough to quell quite a sizeable demonstration."

"They won't dare unleash them," someone there said, and Catt decided he had done as much as he could. There was a limit to how far words would carry you.

"Well," he said quietly, "I wish you all the best of it."

When he'd sat back down it was a moment before he could make himself look to Doctor Fisher, and when he did, the man's long face was no clue. He felt sick to his stomach.

"Did you?" he was forced to ask.

"I did." Fisher looked as unhappy as he felt.

"I never thought it would come to this, Fishy."

"I know."

"Revolutionaries going off to get themselves mauled by beasts. Us on the run from a pack of brutes. Blood on the streets tomorrow. And now... this. I am quite beside myself with misery."

"Hrm."

"I feel as though I am betraying a deep-rooted principle of my existence, Fishy."

Fisher let out a long and mournful sigh, shaking his head at the dire turn the world had taken.

And Catt's eyes finally strayed to the rolled up bundle of argent cloth on the table next to Lodovi's box, which was absolutely not the rolled up bundle of argent cloth that *had* been there before he began making his vain counterarguments. None of the dissidents had seen Fisher make the switch, and the fake flag they had originally possessed had been swiftly whisked out of sight.

"Letting an artefact of rare power go," Catt whimpered. "For *free*. I honestly don't like this man that I'm becoming, Fishy."

# NINE

WHEN THEIR CHAMBERS were finally rid of the revolutionaries that seemed to have infested the place like rats – revolutionaries now unwittingly provided with the potent exemplar of the fake relic they had been carting around – Catt took a deep breath and surveyed their possessions, working out what could fit into the Satchel of Prodigious Contents. They had arrived in leisure upon a barge, luggaged as befit prosperous visitors to another land. They would leave as sneaking fugitives, no doubt. Though the thought was depressing, it would not be the first time. Catt felt aggrieved that this particular seemed to loom so large and so frequent in his life. Was he not congenial by nature? Did he not seek to live and let live with his fellow human beings, and any and all other sentient creatures too? Wherefore this constant persecution from the universe, that so often saw his innocence hounded across the nations of the world by angry tyrants, monsters, aggrieved former business associates and egregious sufferers of buyers' or sellers' remorse?

"I am at a low ebb, Fishy," he admitted to Fisher, sitting on a box of clothes he would likely have to leave behind – at least there was the Sartorian to make up for that loss.

"Just remember we were paid for the flag by Lemstacker. So it's not like we did the whole switch for nothing," Fisher said philosophically.

"That is not the thrust of my gist," Catt told him. "It is just... Do you not feel that we are *unappreciated* in our time? We, erudite men of pandisciplinary learning, who seek only to make the world a better place. Mostly by ensuring that potentially hazardous items of magical power are abstracted from the hands of those who might misuse them and into our own eminently safe grasp."

"And now you've actually given something risky to someone and you're sour," Fisher finished.

"That is not it at all. And don't make out that I'm regretting my admittedly regrettable charity. That only casts me in an even worse light."

"I had assumed," broke in Doctor Crabbe from the door, "that it was because your theoretically creditable substitution of the genuine flag was likely to lead to considerably more bloodshed than had you simply left them with the fraudulent object."

Catt glowered at him. "I beg your pardon?"

"Had they unfurled the fake," Crabbe continued with ponderous logic, "then doubtless Constable Lodovi and her immediate circle would have been either captured for later torture and execution or turn apart by the savagery of the Gryphons." And Catt appreciated that he made it sound all very theoretical, an ethics question for abstract speculation. "Should the courage imparted by the genuine Oriflamme inspire another few hundred citizens to stand alongside them, I feel the introduction of seventeen Gryphons into any struggle with the regular civic forces will still decisively turn the tide. Only in that case considerably more people will be rent limb from limb. Especially as, as you are well aware, the Flower Council has more to deploy now than mere Gryphons. Do you not think?"

The thought of a pack of Vathesk tearing into even a formation of trained soldiers was painful, let alone a mob of panicking civilians. Catt mustered a variety of counterarguments, none of them convincing even to himself, before admitting, "Well yes, I do think, hence my attempt to dissuade them. But... I felt somehow that they should at least be given the chance to run their doomed ship as fully into the storm wave as possible."

"That's not how ships work," Fisher noted.

"As though you know anything about ships. I felt that... I felt... Oh dear, I do believe that my earlier sleight of hand with the flag, to the orders of the late Matthau Lambsticker, made me in some way culpable for their misplaced enthusiasm. And now I have interfered and things have got worse, which is precisely why one does not get involved in these lamentable affairs. I shall be wiser hereafter. And now we must pack."

"Do," Crabbe said, opening the door. "I shall rejoin you presently."

"I strongly advise you not to wander," Catt cautioned him. "If you intend to complete your researches, we will likely be gone, and you will likely be reimprisoned."

Crabbe's smile was bland. "I require provisioning before we travel anywhere. My stocks are low." He patted his empty pockets.

Once he had gone, Catt stuffed as much of value as possible into the satchel and then scratched his head. "We will of course require some manner of disguise."

Fisher held up something like a hairy dead serpent. "Still got my moustache."

"I wonder if we should attire ourselves as ordermen again, or whether that might not be pushing our luck. Perhaps meagre peasants would attract less notice. A pair of charcoal burners or travelling vermin catchers or something similarly invisible to the great and good. What might that look like, I wonder?"

"Just keep it simple," Fisher suggested.

Catt was racking his brains to think of any actual poor people he had seen, but he hadn't frequented those parts of the city, and the rural peasantry's inability to travel freely or meet foreigners was part and parcel of Lodovi's grievance with the state.

"Well let's do what we did last time then, but change the orders and the insignia. A travelling tax collector and his bodyguard perhaps. Some such mid-level annoyance that should see us passed rapidly from hand to hand." He crouched before the Sartorian and gave it the pertinent instructions.

The monkey stared at him glassily and did nothing.

"Perhaps I have overtaxed the poor creature's mummified brain," Catt considered, and tried to picture his desires more carefully. Again the Sartorian just sat there.

Catt took out a couple of his lenses and squinted at it, in case some of its puissance had leaked out with the sawdust that sporadically drifted from its seams. After a reflective pause he said, "Fishy, would you put your head out of the door and tell me whether Doctor Crabbe is within eyeshot."

"He is not," Fisher confirmed a moment later. "Problems?"

"This is not the Undiminished Lochago's Sartorian," Catt stated. "This is a monkey. Long dead, and dressed very much in the same garments. Which garments have been run up by the *actual* Sartorian, which is not here. Which, I rather feel, may have been in the possession of Doctor Crabbe when he left these rooms a moment ago. Whose intent, I rather also feel, may not have been to purchase some snacks for our trip but instead to abandon us for his researches and, in doing so, to steal from us the very object he had provided to us in payment for our considerable services, including coming to this misbegotten country. Fishy, we've been *robbed*!"

"Most likely," Fisher agreed glumly.

"Betrayed, Fishy, betrayed! And by one whom we have so recently saved gratis from persecution and torment at the hands of the authorities! There is no gratitude in the world!"

"None at all."

"And now we are torn between pursuing the rogue to recover

our rightful property and the far more sensible course of just abandoning this city and this nation before further adverse events transpire!"

"It is," Fisher agreed, "a puzzler."

Then they heard heavy steps on the stairs outside the door, and for a fragile moment Catt felt that he had maligned Doctor Crabbe, and that everything was about to resolve itself in some way that would restore his rosy view of the world and its regard for him.

It was not Doctor Crabbe come to return the Sartorian, though. When he flung the door open, it gave him an entirely unsought view of Oversy and a squad of soldiers.

He flung the door closed again. "Not today, please!"

There was a moment of baffled silence, because this was not usually how one treated the agents of the Flower Council on their home turf. Catt turned to Fisher to discover that worthy already throwing open the window for a deft exit, when Oversy refused to take no for an answer and entered. Specifically he entered through the closed door, and also through its frame and part of the wall, in full Gryphon form.

Catt fell over at that point, landing on the false Sartorian and revealing it to be a plush mockery, not even real taxidermy. Who could have known the clever little monster could run up a duplicate of itself so readily? Fisher got halfway out of the window before two soldiers fetched him back. Oversy – a Gryphon still – placed a taloned paw on Catt's chest.

"Doctor Crabbe is not here," Catt informed him stiffly. "He is at large, a larcenous fugitive. You should probably go track him down."

The monstrous beast growled, but then shrank down into Oversy's still not inconsiderable bulk.

"Oh, we'll take you, Doctor Mouth. We'll find him soon enough but I have a warrant for you two as well. Suspected of spying, theft and murder."

"I am," Catt protested, "a man of peace! Fishy, tell him we don't know anything about any murders!"

Doctor Fisher said no such thing and, looking at his face, Catt had a rather familiar sinking feeling.

"My esteemed colleague Doctor Fisher," he murmured, as the pair of them were stood together to have manacles thrust on them, "is it possible you may have neglected to tell me about any trifling details such as, for example, some mortal bloodshed."

"Things happen," Fisher grunted.

"And did *you*—?"

"Nope." Fisher shrugged. "Don't think that'll make much odds though."

CATT HAD MOSTLY expected to be cast into an oubliette and left to his own devices. In fact he would have preferred it, given that his devices were likely more varied and useful than the Arvennir anticipated, and several had survived undetected during an unnecessarily rough search of his person. However, it appeared that Grand Master Johannes Keymarque was going to spare some of his valuable time to reacquaint himself with a former business associate, for old time's sake.

He had himself behind a grander desk now, considerably fancier than any sane man would require. There were golden icons there, of various of the orders, and a variety of trophies and banners hung about the walls. This was the pomp and circumstance room reserved for formal judgments and impressing ambassadors, Catt gathered. He supposed he should feel honoured.

"Well," Johannes said smoothly, "here we are."

There were four of the Gryphon Guard in arm's reach of the prisoners, and the room was capacious enough that they could all have transformed and just about stayed the right side of the desk. Catt therefore felt that his ability to make current repartee was inhibited.

"There has obviously," he tried, "been some manner of dreadful mistake."

"I agree," Johannes told him. "When two agents of a foreign power come to our land and conduct espionage, associate with known dissidents and even effect entry into the Irongarden to commit mayhem, I feel that they have indeed made a mistake. The sort of mistake that it is impossible to recover from."

Catt bristled, despite Oversy's sour breath at his shoulder. "I greatly resent the suggestion that I am in the employ of anyone. I am a champion of free enterprise and endeavour, and entirely my own man. Ow!" This last because Oversy had cuffed him across the back of the head.

"You are a Cheriveni. Who would believe that Cherivell's gold does not line your pockets?"

"If it does, then I have earned it fairly, or at least under lawfully valid contracts entered freely into by the other party, regardless of any second thoughts they may later inculcate. Ow!"

"You are wondering why Guardsman Oversy chastises you," Johannes noted.

"It seems an untoward use of his authority." And, at the third swat, "My dear fellow, we are trying to have a conversation!"

"We are not," Johannes told him. "I am speaking, and you, with all your complicated words, should not feel that your opinion is being sought. You are foreign spies. If, in fact, you are not foreign spies then this serves my purpose even better, for I might execute you as foreign spies without offering direct insult to Cherivell."

"...Execute...?" Catt echoed, and then flinched as Oversy raised his hand again.

Johannes leant forwards over the desk, his expression very

much displaying the satisfaction of the outwitter as against the outwitted that Catt far preferred to bestow on others rather than receive himself.

"As you are well aware, there is a wretched pack of disloyal fools who intend to make *demands* of my Flower Council tomorrow. To stand before the Irongarden with some absurd flag and suggest that we should *change* the way we do things around here. You have been aiding them, foreigners who wish to weaken our great nation. I am very happy for them to gather their strength in one convenient place, Doctor Catt. That is far easier than chasing them all over the city to round them up! And when they are gathered I shall set Oversy on them, and all his fellows, as you might imagine. And I shall unleash my Vathesk, too. Their training is coming along very well, now we are able to bribe them with a little breakfast before sending them out. They're so hungry, Doctor. Even temporary respite will buy their service forever. Even if their hunger never abates. It is really the perfect arrangement. Like buying them with fool's gold that costs us nothing."

"In which case," Catt got out quickly, "some manner of gratitude might be in order. Ow!"

"I would rather ensure that the details of our arrangement were conveniently forgotten by all, first and foremost by ensuring that neither you nor your wisely silent friend ever mention the business again. But I may as well make one final use of you. When our dissidents are dead or in chains I shall show our citizens what we do with foreigners who seek to practise on our good nature. I shall feed you to the Vathesk, Doctor. Or would you prefer one of our native Gryphons?"

"I confess to no real preference between these options," Catt returned dourly, and then, "Ow! My dear Oversy, he was asking me a question!"

"Have them placed in the cells, and double the usual guard," Johannes decreed. "I don't want a repeat of last time."

\* \* \*

THEIR CELL WAS cramped and damp and on the same low level as Crabbe's had been. Catt felt that it ranked low amongst the various incarcerations he had endured. The large number of guards without, though obscurely flattering as a mark of the threat Keymarque apparently felt he posed, kept up a constant noise that disturbed his thinking, and the only entertainment he had been left was the company of Doctor Fisher. As Fisher's main topic of speculation was an in-depth exploration of whether it would be preferable to be devoured by a Gryphon or a Vathesk, this was not as diverting as might have been wished.

"The Vathesk," Fisher ground on, "have lots of mandibles, and I reckon that they'd probably eat you alive, starting at your feet maybe. That would hurt. But then I bet the Gryphons play with their food, so you'd be clawed and mauled for a while before they ripped your guts out. It's a quandary, really."

"Oh, do be quiet, Fishy," Catt told him miserably. "I see now that, when I have been held and you have been free, the chief advantage was not, as I had thought, that you might be in a position to liberate me, but that I was spared this moribund kind of talk."

"Just making conversation."

"Please restrict yourself to topics of solely theoretical application."

There was a rattle at the door and a burly soldier came in with two metal cups and a plate of something Catt could only characterise as 'slop'.

"I cannot help but observe," he said wanly, "that one plate is being provided between us."

"I regret that a peckish spell overcame me on the way from the kitchens," the soldier confirmed, and from beneath his helm he turned upon them the moonish face of Doctor Crabbe, complete with meticulously tailored false moustache.

Catt leapt to his feet. "My dear fellow, whilst I feel I have a variety of very genuine grievances to lay at your feet, I will happily place them in abeyance while you reciprocate the rescue that we previously performed for you!" he said in a fierce whisper.

But Doctor Crabbe only gave him a sickly smile. "Alas, while I would be delighted to perform such quid pro quo, I am currently deeply engaged in the final stage of my researches, which stand in a perilously precarious state. I really cannot concentrate on any subsidiary projects until they are complete. Given the negative attention it would draw I am unable to effect a rescue at this time. I am, of course, deeply sorry, and will try to get round to your needs as soon as my own are satisfied."

"They are going," Catt said with remarkable restraint, "to have us devoured tomorrow. Devoured. It will be both undignified and inconvenient to have to await the culmination of your researches before this can be rectified."

"I am sure, as fellow men of letters," Crabbe said, "you understand that even the most dire events can be instructive and an opportunity to broaden the vistas of our learning. Goodbye Doctor Catt, Doctor Fisher. I hope we shall meet again."

And then he was gone.

# TEN

THEY SPENT A cold and sullen night in the cell, neither of them much speaking to the other. Catt himself was sure that Doctor Fisher was in some way to blame for their predicament because, as memory served, their initial contact with the treacherous Doctor Crabbe had come via Fisher, and it was Crabbe to blame for everything. Although, admittedly, as Johannes was plainly on to Lodovi and her dissidents, there was no need to cast Doctor Crabbe as an active informer of Catt and Fisher's whereabouts. The moment they entered Lodovi's precious safe house the news would have been hotfooting it to the Irongarden with venomous glee.

Simultaneously, he was very sure that Doctor Fisher's surly silence came out of misplacedly blaming him, the innocent Doctor Catt, for their current mess on the entirely irrelevant basis that Catt had been responsible for all the actual details of their multiple double dealings with the Arvennir. And, Catt thought to himself haughtily, if a man's going to be blamed for sound business sense, what is the world coming to?

Around an hour after midnight, having found no rest in the sparse dampness of their accommodation, he got up to shout at the guards, the absent gods and the general concept of injustice in the abstract. This led to Fisher – who had a more robust constitution where sleep was concerned – shouting at him to pipe down, and to him making no friends whatsoever amongst the guards and other prisoners. When a guard turned up with a club threatening to put him to sleep the hard way, Catt presented him with a nineteen point petition elegantly written in a formal Cheriveni lawyer's hand, and demanded the man go hotfoot to the Grand Master to present it. The guard used his own less than formal hand, and the threat of the club it held, to insist that Catt eat his own petition there and then, and may the ink poison him. Still, Catt told himself as he chewed over the last few clauses, he had at least taken a stand for civilized conduct.

Fisher, of course, was already asleep by then, and snoring fit to wake the dead.

Likely not much after the unseen dawn, heavy fists came to bang at their door. Catt started out of a fitful sleep he felt he'd only just fallen into, and beheld the less than welcome face of Oversy the Gryphon Guard there with a handful of turnkeys and soldiers.

"Good morning to our most esteemed foreign guests," the Guard boomed with murderously fake cheer. "Were our beds soft enough for your padded behinds? Is the fare from our tables fit for your delicate digestions? Rejoice, for it is the Feast of Agassi, when we remember how our land was separated from the world of weakness and chaos to be the greatest of all the nations. And you, lucky foreigners, are called to the chambers of the Grand Master on this auspicious day! How fortunate you are!" He seemed drunk already, and not in a pleasant way. His florid face ran with sweat. Catt had known enough people whose penchant for inflicting violence came deep-rooted in their nature to recognise that Oversy was spoiling, not for a fight but just for blood.

*Hopefully not mine.* But no guarantee of that, and plainly the man wouldn't turn down the chance if it were offered.

"Pray take us to our good friend the Grand Master," Catt

said, with dignity. He did his best to glide elegantly from the cell but Oversy tripped him on the way through the door, a mean schoolboy trick. Catt ended up on his face, and had to rely on the silent Doctor Fisher's arm to right himself.

"I'm not enjoying myself very much, Fishy," he confessed in a whisper.

Fisher was looking at Oversy as though he might do something unwise, but perhaps thankfully he restricted himself to just looking.

JOHANNES KEYMARQUE WAS looking in the very best of cheer, however, so at least today was going well for *somebody*. He was being dressed in elaborate formal robes as the prisoners were brought in, an outfit as fancy and impractical as Oversy's flashy armour, but vastly more expensive, all white fur and black velvet and platinum thread. Catt looked at it mournfully, feeling that if there was anyone in the room who could have truly done such vestments justice, it was he himself, and how might one go about becoming the Grand Master of the Flower Council so as to inherit them?

"My esteemed guests and former business associates," Johannes addressed them with the sort of broad smile that goes nowhere but the lips. "I am delighted that you have remained with us for this, our festival day. The Feast of Agassi is always a cornerstone of our calendar, and today in particular will be recorded in the histories. Today Arven re-establishes itself as the lion of the world. Today we remind the lesser nations beyond Agassi's sacred borders that we are *strong*. They think, because the Kinslayer breached our lands and the walls of sacred Athaln, that we were laid in the dust as they were? They shall be taught otherwise. They think that they can encourage those fools among our citizenry, among the very *orders* themselves, to upset the natural balance of our nation? They shall be shown, in no uncertain terms, that Arven does not bend! Arven does not yield! We do not *change!*"

Catt did his best at a beneficent smile. "I always admire a man who knows where he wishes to go and how to get there, Grand Master. May I be the first to offer my congratulations for your clarity of vision. I shall, of course, spread the word of Arven's resurgence from here all the way back to Cinquetann Riverport."

He won a very small nod for his sheer chutzpah, but it was plain Johannes was not to be swayed.

"Later today, I feast with the Masters of our warrior orders, Doctor, but before then, I shall appear above Chapter Square before the Irongarden and address our populace, giving them the Council's promises and dictates for this year to come. You will be sadly unsurprised to hear that a band of would-be revolutionaries intend to present themselves there to defy me, and to sway the mob against me. I will deal with them, and the people shall see where true strength lies. And then, I shall require one further favour from you and your sullen compatriot, alas unrecompensed. We have had no executions on the Feast of Agassi since long before the war, but I will bring back the old tradition. I will show our people how foreign spies are dealt with in our great nation."

Catt licked his lips. "You do not think that such extreme treatment might hamper your nation's ability to find men of enterprise willing to trade with you in future? So that perhaps a light whipping or some time in the pillory might amply make your point."

"Arven will not need to trade," Johannes told him, "when it can take."

Catt felt that form required him to raise some other rational arguments, but he really wasn't feeling up to it, plus Oversy's carious breath was at his shoulder and he didn't want to be struck again.

Shortly after that, they were out on the balcony, overlooking the square before the Irongarden. Catt looked gloomily over the ancient buildings that lined it, the tall, narrow townhouses, all decorated with order symbols, and most still scarred from the war. A fair crowd had gathered, and if they didn't look particularly festive, they didn't look openly rebellious either.

Johannes leant on the balcony, backed by half a dozen Order Masters and three soldiers apiece to ensure neither Catt nor Fisher somehow had it away on their toes at this late hour. Oversy had gone, and Catt was grimly certain he knew just what part of the festivities the man was preparing to partake in.

For a moment he actually thought Lodovi wouldn't show, having finally understood how fatally doomed her whole venture was, but no. There she was, pushing through the crowd, and a score, two score of ordermen at her back, tabards showing a variety of innocent-looking blooms, together with a scattering of butterflies and some sort of hummingbird. She had the furled standard in her hand, and Catt still didn't know if he'd been right to do what he'd done. He supposed he was about to find out, though he took precious little joy in the prospect.

"Grand Master!" She had a fine battlefield voice. "Forgive us for this intrusion but, on this sacred feast day, we are come to present our petition for the future of Arven!"

Catt, whose own petition had left a sour taste in his mouth, literally, could only wish her joy of her own.

Johannes lent on the stone balustrade of the balcony, plainly enjoying himself, regarding Lodovi with amused indulgence. His own voice echoed from the surrounding buildings when he called back, "I see there Constable Setchwort of the Lily. What is this untoward intrusion? You need not push forwards to hear my words to the nation! They are for all!"

"Grand Master!" Lodovi, still painfully, formally polite. "We represent the many in this city, in this nation, who have known our nation in its isolation before the war, and who have known our nation when it stood shoulder to shoulder with our allies against the Kinslayer, and who recognise that the latter is the stronger! We beg that Arven takes its place amidst the world as friend and partner to Forinth and Cherivell and Tzarkand and the rest. We are strong, and so it behoves us to use our strength to build bridges, not walls! We are strong, and so we should use that strength to help our own people to their feet, and not keep them on their knees. Grand Master, you have it in your hands to make us not only strong, but a shining example to the world!"

Johannes let the echoes of that die, and for the slightest moment – so impassioned had been her voice – Catt thought Lodovi had somehow reached him. Then he shook his head as though about to correct a forward child. "Constable!" he called. "We are strong, it is true. And we are great. No nation greater. But you have been too long amongst foreigners. You have forgotten that they are leeches who would drain the blood of our strength. You have forgotten that they are thieves who would steal the coin of our greatness. You have lowered yourself to work and sleep and live amongst them, and now you have come back here altered. You show yourself as no longer one of *us*. You profane Agassi's day. You come here armed with foreign weapons, enriched with foreign coin. You speak out as though your words are any more than wind before the authority of the Flower Council. And I have your two confederates here with me, and before I go to feast, I shall have them hung from this balcony as a warning to other foreigners not to meddle in the affairs of our nation."

And there were cheers, but they were scattered and obviously thinner on the ground than he would have preferred, and Lodovi was speaking again.

"I see them there," she shouted. "Two old men who came

here for trade, a pair of dotards who sought nothing more than fair dealings. And you will release them unharmed."

"That," Catt said to Fisher, "was not as politic as it might have been," but Fisher shushed him, eyes narrow.

"It is time that Arven was governed for the people!" Lodovi went on. "Not for a handful of old men!" And there was a murmur from around her, a shuffling, a wavering back and forth over a delicate fulcrum.

"I do not see 'the people' with you, Constable Setchwort," Johannes told her. "I see forty traitors."

With a move as deft and elegant as Catt could have wished, she unfurled the standard.

He felt the touch of it – no more than that, because he was neither a soldier nor Arvennir. The crowd eddied back from her, for a moment leaving Lodovi quite alone in the centre of the square. People stared up at the argent Oriflamme and its black lily emblem. Johannes hissed through his teeth, and Catt was abruptly certain the man had known about the false flag, but not about the substitution of the real one. It gave Catt a little private pleasure to know he'd at least soured the man's day a little.

"People of Arven!" Lodovi called. "You who have felt the rod! You who have fought, and been overlooked, cast off, kept down! Now is your chance! Rally to me, and we can change the world!"

And more of the same, but Johannes was giving hurried orders already. In the square, some people were leaving, others were pushing in, a great swirl of chaotic citizenry all weighing their courage and examining their priorities. And above them all, the brilliance of the Oriflamme, giving heart, giving hope.

*Oh dear.* Soldiers were pouring out of the Irongarden, two score, three, but more than that, there were the Gryphon Guard. He saw Oversy down there, and the old man and the skinny woman, and a pack of them unfamiliar to him. Seventeen, was his quick count. Every one of them that remained, forming a loose line before the Council's regular defenders, standing with easy confidence. And they were not imposing, Catt saw. They were not powerful fighting men honed by battle. Their armour was ceremonial. They carried nothing worse than a knife between them. And yet it didn't matter. Their duties had never required them to be strong or swift or even fit. They had other bodies they would fight in, that were always at the cutting edge of savage ferocity. Perhaps the transformation would even flush the alcohol out of Oversy's bloodstream.

And the people rallying to the flag knew them, and the whole crowd was trying to push back, to put a distance between them and the Gryphon Guard that the square's confines would not allow. Even the Oriflamme could not overcome that knowledge. Seventeen gryphons would carve through that close mass of people like wolves in a sheep pen.

Johannes permitted himself a chuckle, just a small one, as befitted the dignity of a Grand Master.

"Clear the square!" he called. "Deal with the ringleaders."

Oversy was first to move, thrusting himself forwards, lunging onto all fours, snarling, saliva spilling from his mouth as he bared his teeth.

"Raaaar," he said. "Grrrr. Blaah."

The square went very silent.

"Roar," added Oversy awkwardly. He remained very much a big man pushed into overly fancy armour, only now he was on his hands and knees as though impersonating a dog.

One of the other Gryphons took a leap forwards, hands crooked like claws, and stood there, making little raking motions in the air. A woman amongst them leapt and ended up on her face on the ground, coming up with her nose streaming blood.

Johannes' face was quite, quite blank. Even Lodovi just stared, too bewildered to take advantage of the situation.

Oversy was craning past his paunch to see his belt. Then the crowd gathered beneath the Oriflamme surged forwards a few steps and he took some lively paces back, pale face turned towards the balcony.

Johannes recovered first. "Send for the Yogg!" he hissed. "Set the damned Vathesk on them."

More messengers ran off. By then the Gryphon Guard had retreated prudently behind the regular soldiery, who were forming a thin-looking cordon about the front of the Irongarden. Lodovi's clear voice rang out, rallying her people, hailing more of them from the side-streets. The mass of dissidents was looking less and less like a forlorn band of the doomed and more and more like the will of the people.

The doors of the Irongarden were flung open. Johannes leant forwards over the balcony to see. "Now," he hissed, and shouted, "Clear the way, there!"

The soldiers parted, left and right, not sure what was coming but sure they wanted no part of it. For a moment, nothing emerged from the inner gloom. Catt pictured the pincers, the scuttling legs, the ever-hungry mouthparts of the alien Vathesk.

Someone emerged from the Irongarden.

It was a Yorughan woman in the robes of the Heart Takers. She was running, running as the Yorughan never ran. Running as though all the monsters in the world were at her heels. The slapping of her boots on the flagstones was the loudest sound in the square as she pelted between the two wings of soldiers, veered sharply when she saw Lodovi and the Oriflamme, fled the square and was never seen again in the city of Athaln.

Johannes' mouth and throat worked. Catt half-hoped the man might drop dead of an apoplexy right there and then, but instead he shouted, "Close the gates!" and then, "Hold the rabble back!" and then he was retreating back inside, away from a balcony that seemed suddenly vulnerable to thrown stones and bottles in a way it hadn't a moment before. Retreating with his followers and his prisoners, even as Lodovi's people surged forwards and the soldiers fell back against the Irongarden's walls.

Catt and Fisher were hurried downstairs by the rough hands of their captors, with no clue as to whether they were now hostages to be bartered with, or whether they would get an accelerated execution out of pure spite. They came down a sweeping flight of steps, skidding and slipping in their collective hurry, and below was a grand hall all set out for the feast of Saint Agassi. Catt saw a great long table groaning with every possible dish that the culinary artists of Arven could ever have conceived of, lined with liveried chairs set for the Masters of the Orders. Even under guard and threat of death the sumptuous spread had him wondering if the Arvennir had a tradition of a last meal. If only because a man could gorge on what was laid out there for several days before being dragged off to the executioner. There were racks of ribs braised with red and purple berries, coils of bitter white sausages arranged in geometrically pleasing pyramids and a great aurochs joint as large as a man set before the head of the table and garnished with oranges and pomegranates and some manner of small candied fowl he could not identify. There were bowls of that heavy suet Fisher had decided was fit as a savoury garnish, tureens of turtle soup and a magnificent cake iced with spun sugar in the shape of the Irongarden itself. There was more wine in more varied receptacles than Catt had ever witnessed in one place. There was a flatfish cooked with cloves and lemon that must have been nineteen feet long while alive, and retained both its head and its final expression of goggling exasperation. And Johannes would probably not now be enjoying this truly lavish banquet, given recent events outside the gates of his stronghold, yet *someone* was taking advantage of the free meal, even if the Flower Council had likely lost its appetite.

There was a confusion of odd old men down there, sitting about the table and tucking into the food with great gusto.

Johannes plainly didn't know them but, though Catt couldn't claim a personal acquaintance, they had a worryingly familiar look. As though, he thought, this was a family reunion, every one of them a cousin or similar relative. They were bald, myopic-eyed, moon-faced. They had high shoulders and crooked backs. They tore into their food with great robust teeth, seeming too large and too many to fit behind their rubbery lips. And there, at the head of the table, was their exemplar, wearing his long and shabby coat and his little spectacles, sitting in the Grand Master's big chair and chewing his way through an entire suckling pig. Doctor Crabbe, no more, no less, who looked up and waved a gnawed bone in greeting to all and sundry.

"What is this?" Johannes Keymarque fairly howled.

The Gryphon Guard had piled in by then, fleeing whatever was going on outside. They, too, stare at the gaggle of old men devouring their master's dinner.

"Fishy," Catt said, "I feel I may have missed some key developments."

Fisher was actually smiling. Not a big smile, certainly not a very merry one. Mean satisfaction was about all he could manage. "Look at what they're wearing, Catty," he said.

The strange old men, Crabbe's cousins, were in fact wearing a bizarre and mismatched assortment of garments: robes, surcoats, tunics, stockings, gowns, nothing of a pleasing combination of cuts and colours, really quite the offence to the eye. As though, Catt considered, someone had got hold of a certain tailoring monkey, and yet had absolutely no feel for the finer points of fashion. He bristled a bit at the thought, and when Johannes ordered Oversy to take hold of Doctor Crabbe he almost applauded the move.

Oversy, seeing here, at least, someone he could throw around and bully, grabbed Crabbe by the wrist. Mildly, Crabbe transferred the large piece of pudding he'd been holding to his other hand.

"Unhand me," he suggested. "I am at my repast."

Some of the other Crabbe-ish men had stood up, still mauling the feast for choice titbits, and were drifting over, and Fisher's hoarse voice repeated, "Look at what they're *wearing*."

Catt did, and finally saw what it was Crabbe's cousins were all sporting, along with that mismatched motley. "Oh dear me," he said. "Oh very dear me very much indeed." He felt right then he'd rather be out in the square with the mob.

Oversy hauled Crabbe to his feel and yanked at him, hoiking him towards Johannes. Crabbe, reaching for another handful of pudding, went in the opposite direction. The leather cuff that sheathed his arm from wrist to elbow, and that Oversy had hold of, came off.

Nystal's Regulating Bracer. And Catt had seen an engraving of Nystal, who had so wanted the world to resemble himself. He had wondered that, even with the bracer, Crabbe had not particularly approximated the man.

He saw now that the bracer had been performing a heroic service; that it really had made Crabbe far closer to the bracer's creator than anyone might have expected. Nystal, after all, had far fewer limbs than Doctor Crabbe's native form. Nystal had not owned to an invulnerable craggy carapace or such huge and shearing pincers. He had not possessed so many faceted eyes or complex ever-busy mouthparts.

Doctor Crabbe's various sense organs regarded the frozen Oversy, who stood in his huge Vathesk shadow. With a tiny squeaking noise the Gryphon Guard did his best to offer the bracer back.

One pincer sliced the man in half almost absently, even as various smaller limbs were fitting the artefact back on. A moment later it was merely Doctor Crabbe who stood there, unpleasantly naked save for the bracer as his clothes were now all in rags on the floor. One hand was to the elbow in Oversy's blood, but that didn't stop him reaching for a leg of chicken with it.

"Doctor Catt, Doctor Fisher," he called cheerily. "We are having a feast. Will you join us?"

"Alas I am unaccountably without appetite," Catt said, stepping prudently away from the nerveless Arvennir and drawing Fisher with him. He eyed the other men in their mismatched outfits, each one of them wearing an identical belt. An old belt, an Arvennir belt from generations gone. He glanced at the half of Oversy that still wore his own belt, marvelling that the Sartorian had been able to produce a fake so perfect as to fool a man who'd worn the garment for decades.

And Crabbe had swapped those fakes for the true belts of the Gryphon Guard, somehow. Only, their current wearers had never seen a Gryphon. They had been forced to find another model to infuse the matrix of the artefacts with. The first one that came to hand, in fact. When Crabbe had gone down to the Vathesk pens and distributed his gifts to his kin, they'd only had his mostly-human image for a model.

But, as mostly-humans, they could eat. They could fill their human bellies for the first time since the Kinslayer had hauled them into this world, and unlike the dainties conjured by the wand, it was real food, and they would stay fed so long as they remained human long enough for digestion to take its course. And what Crabbe's plan was after that, Catt had no idea. Nor did he have any intention of getting in its way.

Crabbe, still butt naked, sat back down in Johannes's chair, smearing Oversy's blood across the arm. The Grand Master was staring, shaking, trying to find some words that would undo all this and restore him to his accustomed place as master of all he surveyed.

They all heard the solid crash as Lodovi's people broke the door down and entered the Irongarden, doubtless with that damnable banner waving over them and getting caught up in the doorway. The usual. The transformed Vathesk barely looked up, but Johannes Keymarque and his cronies suddenly had their existential dread replaced by something rather more immediate.

"Let's get going," Fisher grumbled, but despite himself, Catt held on at least until Lodovi entered the feast hall to stare perplexed at all these squinting bald men in their mismatched clown clothes, devouring a feast laid out for five times as many people until they were sucking the last shreds of meat from between the tines of the forks, and drinking soup dregs from the tureens.

"They'll be moving on soon," he said softly to her. "They won't be any trouble. I'd pack them a nice big lunch, honestly, whatever you've got in the castle larders. Load it onto a handcart for them, I would. You don't want them getting peckish anywhere near the city limits, honestly. And whatever you do, don't get in their way. They've a mission." And he thought about how many other Vathesk there were, flotsam cast up on the shores of the war after their conjurer the Kinslayer met his end. Crabbe knew, Catt was willing to bet. Crabbe likely knew where they all were, too. And probably he had some ideas about other transforming items, or maybe they'd just pass the belts around whenever it was lunchtime.

*Not*, Catt decided definitively, *my business. Just one more regrettable incident in a life fraught with them.*

"And I don't know what you're smirking at," he told Fisher.

"I don't smirk."

"Then you were doing a very good impression." Catt's eyes narrowed. "You always did have a soft spot for the Vathesk, if I recall."

"Don't know what you're talking about."

"When we were at Dorhambri, that disagreeable business, you freed a few of them there. To general panic and chaos on all sides thereafter."

"Can't rightly recall," Fisher said.

"Was one of *those* Doctor Crabbe?" Catt demanded. "Have you *known*, all this time?"

"Now you're just sounding paranoid," Fisher said, not looking at him. "Mess like this, no way anyone could see it coming."

Catt sighed. "I don't suppose our possessions are anywhere convenient to lay hands on? I would rather be shot of this place at our earliest convenience."

They discovered at least some of their goods, confiscated from Lodovi's safe house at their time of arrest, after Fisher browbeat an Arvennir clerk into being their local guide. And, on the top of their little stack of boxes and bags, there sat a hideously wizened monkey, long dead, badly stuffed, but at least not a cunningly knitted imitation this time. A note was appended, in Doctor Crabbe's precise handwriting. *For services rendered. I will contact you shortly for the next leg of our dealings.*

But Doctor Catt had seen at least eight of Doctor Crabbe's legs already, and he decided that he wanted nothing to do with any more.

# SECRETS AND LIGHTS

by Freda Warrington

## ONE

"NOT MUCH OF an apprenticeship so far," Crombie said, mock-resentful. "All they've had me do is sweep floors and run errands."

"We all have to start at the bottom of the ladder," said Crombie's father. "Ladder, get it?" He rocked with delight at his own joke.

"Get on with you," said his ma, swiping him across the backside and placing a well-wrapped parcel of lunch into his hands. "It's only your fourth day."

"You're lucky to have got this apprenticeship at all," Pa added. "Better than sweeping floors here at the inn, I should think."

That was the truth, Crombie thought, as he started the hour-long walk along the main track from Fort Town to the site on the ocean-facing eastern tip of the island. At least they paid him a few coins, unlike his parents. He looked carefully around him, forward and back; there were a few others walking, but no sign of *her*, Mistress Galt. As she and her father were lodging at his family's hostelry, the Fort Isle Inn, he always kept an eye out in order to avoid the embarrassment of meeting them en route.

The inn stood proud above the harbour town below; a plain, handsome brown stone building with a good bar and decent-sized guest rooms. It was the grandest accommodation

Fort Isle had to offer, which wasn't saying much. Usually the senior supervisors from Arven travelled from town to site by horseback or wagon. But Galt was unpredictable. Sometimes she walked.

This morning he was early, so he cut through a field and took the long way round along the cliff path. The day was bright and fresh. On his right lay pastures of rough grass, gorse and heather; on his left the sea, with waves exploding madly onto the rocky shore far below. Crombie felt rather delighted to be alive.

Fort Isle was a stump of rock some three miles off the coast of Arven; mercifully not too far north to be hit by the truly bitter weather. Only seven miles long and six across, it was a jagged diamond shape with its points rounded off by rough weather. The island was formed of granite, lava and serpentine, or so he'd picked up at school when he wasn't truanting to help his sheep-farming uncles. In their view, school was a waste of time when all you needed to learn here was farming or fishing.

The highest point of the path gave a fine view. Stretches of grass and heather with the occasional farm. Few trees. Wide open ocean to the north and east. Behind him, a handful of larger buildings: the inn, the Governor's house, the school and small mansions from which matters of fishing, farming and sea trading were managed. Then a jumble of houses and cottages spilled down to the harbour. Scores of fishing boats, the ferry, even the Arvennir vessels looked tiny from up here. Mevroan, the mainland harbour that faced them across the Straits of Fort, was no more than a grey line.

Over twelve years back, they'd avoided the worst of the Kinslayer. His forces hadn't made it beyond the capital, Athaln – let alone to the Straits of Fort – before Celestaine of Forinth, alongside other heroes, had killed him. A large number of refugees had, however, sought safety on the cliffs and thin grassland of Fort Isle. There weren't many actual Arvennir, as they were too proud to flee from conflict, but other races had crowded in; intelligent beings with strange features, pointed ears, scales and tails and whatever else the gods could imagine. Crombie, once over the initial shock factor, got on well with most of them. He would sit and listen to their tales, even when accents or cultural confusion made the narrative hard to follow.

The original islanders were believed to descend from the same lines as the Arvennir; there were physical similarities, although the Forters had evolved tougher and without the airs and graces, or the aggression, of their wealthier cousins. Since the newcomers had muscled in, the modest harbour town was growing bigger, busier and more full of trade than in the past.

Crombie liked this. He was seventeen, just old enough to remember a time when the island had more seabirds and sheep than people. The stories his parents told of storms and complete isolation filled him with horror. Why hadn't they died of boredom? At least these days there were places to go, interesting folk to meet, a ferry that ran five times a day to the mainland.

At present, the ferry and other vessels ran constantly, conveying limestone blocks and other building materials from mainland Mevroan to the island. Arvennir cargo ships kept coming and going too, a rather more disturbing sight. He could see them as he walked, ploughing their way along the coast to the construction site. Sails full of wind, waves churning to foam in their wake. Crombie saw the thrilling sight of the new lighthouse ahead; a tower of pure white stone that dazzled even with scaffolding, ropes and chains all over it.

The construction crew was close to reaching full height. Then there would be the lantern house to construct, topped by a dome. They'd built up to this point in only two years; although Crombie hadn't taken much notice before, now that he was employed there he'd become amazed by the speed and efficiency of Arvennir construction. It would be twice the height of the existing lighthouse, which looked, in comparison, like a decrepit little farm silo a couple of miles to the right.

Most of the itinerant workers – folk from other nations employed by Arven – were housed in makeshift barracks and tents, a hundred yards inland from the construction. Their bosses, though, had better accommodation in Fort Town itself, even though it meant a bumpy five-mile ride to the far coast each day. General Orendion himself was, of course, the guest of Governor Gredlen.

His parents were making a decent fortune accommodating so many guests. Crombie was pleased for them, although he felt like an outsider in his own home; Arvennir folk all over the place, stomping up and down stairs, shouldering him out of the way or demanding food in their rooms. He'd got to know many folk of different races, but only the Arvennir made him nervous. No one more so than Mistress Galt and Commander Embran, who occupied the two best rooms on the floor down from his attic bedroom.

He strode up past the new lighthouse and looked over the cliff edge. Some nearby Arvennir guards, tall and elegant, eyed him suspiciously. Pitiful on the rocks below, the wreck of the *Arven Pride* rocked uneasily on the tide. Arvennir ships were majestic, with graceful sweeping hulls and excessive black sails; terrifying to their enemies, but a heart-stopping sight to behold.

To see such majesty smashed on the rocks made Crombie sad.

His heart jumped about. The height was dizzying; he always felt an odd prickle of fear when he looked down, a tingling in his hands. Almost nausea. What cargo had the ship been carrying? The Arvennir didn't seem to know, or care; he'd never heard anyone mention it. This all felt so odd; yes, exciting, but also wrong to have all these strangers striding about. Disturbing.

Even though he was early, the working day had already begun. Arvennir, Fort Isle and other workers were gathered around the site foreman, an islander called Jorgan, for the morning briefing.

"Oi, Carrot-head!" Jorgan had a startlingly loud voice. "Nice of you to join us! Go bring us some hot drinks. I've got a special job for you later."

"Right you are, sir," Crombie called back. He felt a thrill of anticipation: something other than floor sweeping today?

"A very important errand," grinned Jorgan, waving a piece of paper at him.

MUTUAL DISTRUST BETWEEN the Forters and the Arvennir wasn't serious enough to have made the islanders rejoice at the shipwreck. On the contrary, they'd done everything they could to rescue the marooned sailors. There had been some fatalities, including both the captain and the merchant who might have given answers about the cargo, but the majority of the Arvennir crew had made it safely onto the island. At first they'd been wretchedly grateful for the inhabitants' help. Later, as they recovered, their pride reasserted itself – tinged with resentment by the humiliation they perceived themselves to have suffered – and their gratitude had waned towards condescension.

If only they would leave! But they couldn't. Rather, some had gone home, but more came. There was a valuable wreck to salvage and a lighthouse to build.

Crombie always tried to be friendly, but they weren't the easiest lot to get on with. The island governor, Gredlen, a wealthy farmer, declared that the King of Arven seemed to think he ruled Fort Isle now.

"If you help someone," Crombie's father grumbled, "they never forgive you."

Naturally the islanders had looked down at the wreck of the *Pride* and planned a looting expedition. Why not? The Arvennir were rich and the Forters, for the most part, were not. An attempt to get aboard the ship had proved too difficult, what with slippery rocks, shifting wreckage and the peril of angry waves. Next thing they knew, a flotilla of Arvennir navy vessels rolled up to take charge of the crew and to guard the wreck day and night. Ominously, they even had cannons on board.

Arvennir flags were planted, to the fury of islanders. White flower on a black ground, signifying one of their military clans: the Order of the White Lotus.

Days of delicate negotiation had begun, mainly between Governor Gredlen and General Orendion, head of the Lotus Order and the senior official appointed to lead the Arvennir deputation. Discussions had started in a civilised fashion, but soon gathered pace downhill.

On the fourth day of talks, at a public meeting in the town square, the two men's conversation had deteriorated into a raging argument. They were on a makeshift stage, each with his own podium. A scattering of their senior assistants stood behind. Gredlen was not a small man; he was stocky and muscular, with swept-back hair of brown-going-grey, and a fierce jutting beard. He looked diminutive, thought Crombie, next to the lofty Orendion.

The Arvennir's list of demands grew ever-longer and more ridiculous, complained Gredlen. But Fort Isle was being pig-headed, refusing to compromise, countered Orendion. Such were the accusations flying back and forth as Crombie and his parents stood near the front of a large crowd, listening with a mixture of boredom and dread.

"Is this an invasion?" Gredlen shouted suddenly.

"Of course not." Orendion's steel tone didn't change. Gredlen, everyone noted, was doing most of the raging.

"Because it looks very like an invasion to us. You were not given permission for flags."

"We've a responsibility to rescue the crew of the *Pride* and to secure Arvennir Crown Property—"

*Oh, Crown Property?* Crombie had thought, suddenly alert. *That could be anything, though. Doesn't mean value, just that it belongs to their King.*

"Hence the heavy artillery on your ships?"

"They are navy vessels. Of course they carry weapons. A mere precaution, you understand."

"Against *us*? We're not thieves, not looters! Your crew have received the full hospitality that Fort Isle could offer. In return, our island is now swarming with armed Arvennir troops! This is just a small rock with nothing to offer, but it's *our* rock. It can't be worth a scit to you, yet your men and women are swanning about the place and raising flags as if you own it! This looks *very* like an occupation to us. So tell us, what are your intentions? When do you plan to leave?"

Grumbles and applause rose from the onlookers.

"I hear your concerns, Governor," said Orendion, his voice dropping a few degrees colder. "Let me set your mind at rest. I assure you, we have no designs on the sovereignty of your splendid island, and once the operation is concluded, we will leave you in peace. You have my word."

Crombie frowned. *Orendion's acting like he's going to be in big trouble with the King if he doesn't do what he's here to do. Or is he just like this all the time?*

His unshakeable tone seemed to throw Gredlen off balance. "I would like to believe you. But we need deeds, not words."

"Mm. I'll assume that's not a suggestion that the Arvennir are ever less than truthful. There *will* be deeds."

A pause, filled with hostility between the Arvennir and Fort Isle officials so intense that Crombie wanted to flee, and would have done had he not been firmly hemmed in.

"What deeds?" said Gredlen. "What do you mean by *operation*?"

Orendion huffed through his patrician nose. "You've rather despoiled the early hospitality you showed us with this openly aggressive attitude. Must I spell out that the grounding of the *Pride of Arven* was *your fault?*"

"*What?*"

The Governor's disbelief was echoed by the audience in ripples of outrage.

"Silence," said Orendion, raising his palms. Crombie wondered, *Who's he to start giving us orders? This isn't right.* "The maritime disaster of an Arvennir vessel crashing onto Fort Isle's brutal rocks was entirely the fault of this island's inhabitants. And you will pay us recompense."

Over the uproar that followed, Gredlen raised his voice. "We, pay *you?* What the devil are you implying? I'm dreadfully sorry that the gods placed this rock in your way! We've been here for countless thousands of years. *You* are the ones who grounded yourselves – did you expect the island to move aside, to save you the trouble of steering around?"

Laughter. But Orendion stood like an iron statue, unamused. "I'm referring to your defective lighthouse."

"Ain't nothing wrong wi' my lighthouse!" This anguished cry came from a nondescript islander, fifty-ish, his weather-beaten face dark against pale tunic and trousers that looked as ragged as his salt-bleached tangle of hair and beard. "I'm the lighthouse-keeper, Viktor Dremin, in case you were slow on the uptake. I've manned that old lighthouse since I were a kid and my old ma and pa were still alive. Kept it in good nick. Never let the light go out or the beam fail, no matter the weather. That wreck weren't our fault!" He pointed a shaky finger at Orendion. "No wrecks for a century, until you lot came along!"

"Viktor," said Gredlen, trying to calm him. "We know that."

"Tell *them!* What am I s'posed to do now? Am I out of a job, or what? I've done nothing wrong."

"You are free to keep your job, Master Dremin," Orendion said thinly, "as long as the islanders are willing to keep paying your wages, as well as those for the new lighthouse keepers.

I imagine your pay will be more a gesture of good will than anything. The old tower won't be needed in future."

*I think I'd like to kill that Orendion,* thought Crombie. *Who's he think he is?*

"Damn that," Viktor snarled. "I won't be treated as a beggar when all I've ever done is work."

"And that won't happen, Viktor," Gredlen added firmly, apparently trying to support the keeper and silence him at the same time. His wild appearance and ranting were not helping the Fort Isle cause. "He's correct. Our lighthouse is not defective."

"The Athaln government disagrees. Our investigations show that its light is faint and inadequate. It's wrongly positioned. On the night of the wreck, the captain and crew swear that there was no light visible at all."

"Ram's balls!" yelled Viktor.

"That is a complete falsehood!" Gredlen said over him. "We've had no wrecks since it was built! You seek to blame this upon Fort Isle, rather than on your own incompetent steering abilities? Your crew was probably drunk! This is *not our fault!*"

Orendion cleared his throat. "Furthermore, Governor Gredlen, there is no lighthouse at all where there *should* be one. We had hoped to make this request in a rather more formal, measured fashion. However, as you seem to prefer a direct approach – and don't misunderstand me, I respect a straight talker – *the price Fort Isle will pay is the construction of a high specification lighthouse built to modern Arvennir standards!*" The last words were yelled, making the whole crowd jump and put their hands over their ears. He concluded calmly but just as loudly, "A. Brand. New. Lighthouse."

Afterwards, Crombie understood that losing control of one's temper and yelling at a man superior in strength, wealth, numbers, arms and everything else was a swift way to lose an argument and all control of the situation. The recompense to be claimed by Arven was destined to be challenging and impossibly expensive. Perhaps if Governor Gredlen had been more diplomatic, the penalty would have been less onerous.

Over the clamour of dismay and astonishment, Orendion looked at Viktor Dremin and said, "Perhaps we could find a few light duties for you at the new tower?"

Only Crombie and those nearby had heard his answer as he turned his back and shuffled away. "Stuff yer job. Condescending git."

There had been protests and petitions and negotiations, but the Arvennir won, as they always won.

Two years on, and here was Crombie working for the 'enemy' – positively excited by the silver white tower daily increasing in height. Hundreds of shining limestone blocks were hauled up on straining, rattling chains. Workers ran up and down the ladders all day. There were ladders inside, too, and a staircase taking shape to connect the four floors. Air full of white dust and the delicious smell of a new building.

His first couple of hours passed like the preceding three days. He was running around with drinks and food, sweeping up, carrying ladders and tools to where they were needed, shouted at, teased – but one day he might graduate to a bit of carpentry. A young man needed ambition, so his father said.

Then Jorgan the foreman appeared, waving a folded piece of paper as if this meant something crucial. "Crombie. Special job for you, remember? You still up for it?"

"Yes, of course sir."

"Need you to take this list of supplies across to Volt's. That's the stone masonry suppliers over in Mevroan, since you're looking blank at me. The heavy stuff, he'll ship over to us. The light stuff, you'll carry back in a rucksack. Shouldn't take more than three hours. All right?"

Crombie had never been to the mainland, despite the ferry; never had time. He had no idea where the supplier was. "Yes, sir."

"Don't lose that list. It's important. You do know where the mason's is, don't you? Right near Mevroan harbour?"

"I'll find it," he said, faking confidence. He took off at a run before the foreman could give this excitingly important assignment to someone else. The main way back to the town and harbour was only six miles, but that was far enough when you were in a hurry. Fortunately one of his uncles came past and gave him a lift part-way in his horse and cart.

As he stood on the dock, waiting for the next ferry, a young woman stepped out in front of him. She made him startle; his heart thumped in his ears. Mistress Galt.

Even though she was lodging with his parents, he'd tried to avoid her. A brief nod in passing was all the communication they'd had in two years. Still, he'd seen a lot more of her in the past few days, as she was the Project Supervisor of the lighthouse. Her father, Commander Embran, was Chief Project Officer and a man who frankly terrified everyone. Galt had his height, poise and intimidating demeanour; *resting rage face*, some said behind her back. Reddish fair hair parted in the centre and drawn back tightly; a neat work uniform of tunic, loose trousers and boots in autumn browns.

Crombie found her completely menacing. He was also aware that he was developing an infatuation with her of embarrassing dimensions. She was strong and mean and unapproachable and... perfect.

"Crombie?" she said. When she smiled, her rage-face transformed and she became quirkily pretty, eyes as blue as the sea. "Where might you be going?"

"Mistress Galt." He made an awkward half-bow. "I'm, er..." He pointed at the ferry boat that was now angling itself in to dock. "Across to the stone mason's for supplies."

She stood looking at him with a slight smirk. He had no idea what this meant, or what to say in response. "You're the new boy, aren't you? How do you like the work so far?"

"I-I-I – it's good, thank you. Very interesting. Don't mind what it is, I like working."

"Well, that's an excellent attitude. We Arvennir aren't such monsters, are we?"

"Of course not, ma'am."

"I hope we'll be friends, eventually. A joint project for the benefit of all." She was still smiling. He wondered what she wanted, felt himself sweating beneath his collar.

"Yes. Are you, um, travelling…?"

"Not today," she answered, to his relief. Moving closer, she said softly, "Would you do me a favour? Post this letter for me? I'll pay you for your trouble."

He took from her a roll of paper, sealed and stamped with the island's crest. "Um, yes, of course… What trouble?"

"Don't look so alarmed! I don't mean it's going to get you *into* trouble. Just trouble as in errand." Her grin disarmed him.

"Where?"

"I've written the address on it."

"No, I mean where do I take it to post it?"

"Have you never sent a letter before?" She spoke teasingly, which he didn't much like. "Just ask the mason, Volt. He'll put it with his post. A courier comes round to fetch it all."

"All right, that's no trouble at all. It's a pleasure, Mistress Galt."

"You're so good." Her face and tone of voice went serious. "It's really important. Thank you so much, Crombie."


THE STONE MASON's yard was huge, with a warehouse so big he saw it as soon as he stepped off the ferry. The cool sea-breeze was filled with the scent of brick-dust and stone cutting; Crombie fairly danced along with the thrill of new places, new duties.

Walking in through the wide-open gates, he saw two Arvennir males arguing over who had actually purchased a particular stack of limestone. One was off Fort Isle, dressed in Embran's work team uniform; the other seemed to be from a city with an urgent building project. Crombie scuttled past, hoping to avoid the fracas before swords were drawn. Winding his way through stacks of rock, brick and timber, he found an office that opened out into the vast warehouse. He breathed in the smells of seasoned wood, cut stone and mortar, plaster; he loved building smells, so enlivening and full of promise.

'You're new, aren't you?' The merchant was scowling at him from behind a counter, as if wondering why he was gazing into space like an idiot.

"Um, yes, sorry. Good morning, Master Volt. I've got a list of supplies needed for the new lighthouse..."

Volt was already taking the list from his fingers. "I guessed that, lad. What do they call you?"

"Carrot-head, mostly," said Crombie. "But I'm Crombie. It's only my fourth day."

The merchant gave a kind of smirk while retaining his scowl. "They can only get worse, then. The names, I mean. Right, let's see... Double-ended screwdriver."

Volt walked off and disappeared round a corner. Crombie waited. And waited.

And waited.

Eventually Volt reappeared with an armful of bags. "There we are; left-handed nails, same as right-handed nails. We're out of soap staples, so I've given you regular staples. Screwdriver with *one* business end – bit difficult to use without a handle, see – and shingle froe, tick. Frog fettler, no idea. A high-grit sanding block should do."

"I thought you'd forgotten I was here," said Crombie.

"It's on the list, lad," said Volt. "A long stand."

His face cracked into a grin, while Crombie groaned.

"Might've known they'd take me for an idiot! Those bastards!"

The mason chuckled. "Oh, don't take it to heart. I needed a few minutes to sort out that pair in the yard, anyway. Every new apprentice gets the same treatment. Like an initiation. Some of 'em figure it out when they read the list, but most don't."

"You're worse than my father!"

"I'll take that as a compliment. They know I'll always send them stuff that they have to pay for, so the joke's on them, in the end. This last one... *A scale from the upper right wing tip of the moth of* – what's it say? Under-thon? Can't help you with that, son."

"Another made-up thing, I s'pose."

Volt went on squinting at the list. "It sounds so ridiculous, it may be real. Only place I've heard of for weird stuff like that is a place in Cinquetann. Catt & Fisher, apothecaries and whatever."

"Where's Sink-tan?"

The merchant's eyebrows twitched ever so slightly. "You don't know... Well, it's a river port in Cherivell."

"Never heard of it. How would I get there?"

'Well, if I were you I wouldn't start from here. Let me think... river boat is the quickest. Takes a few days, mind. Not cheap – you need a knack for bargaining. A Shelliac vessel might take you, but you'd have to get *to* the river first."

Crombie felt a flutter of anxiety. Surely they didn't expect him to... and he couldn't be away from work for days. He'd get the sack, or worse. Whoever had written this list couldn't be serious... but what if was a double bluff? What if they genuinely did need this scale thing, whatever it was? Maybe it was something the island magus Paulian needed. *What shall I do?*

He opened his rucksack to load it, and saw the scroll at the bottom. He took it out and stood there, pondering his options.

"Anything else?" said Volt, a bit impatient now. "Want me to put that letter with our post? No trouble. Give it here."

"Thank you," said Crombie, loading his pack with tools and nails until he could barely do up the buckles. *Damn, I nearly forgot her letter! How could I?* "Er… what *is* Catt & Fisher?"

The merchant was now staring at him with a blank yet twisted expression of confusion. Crombie glanced over his own shoulder to check if something monstrous had come in. "It's a shop. Special kind of shop. Lad, you…"

"What, sir?"

He waved the rolled-up parchment. "This here letter you've given me is *addressed* to Catt & Fisher."

"Oh. Is it? I, I didn't write it."

"You don't say. Take a few deep breaths. Just head back to the site. The heavy stuff will be over by boat this afternoon. Tell the gaffer I'll invoice on the new moon, as usual."

Crombie left quickly with the rucksack over his shoulders and leaned against the outside wall for breath. He was sweating with embarrassment. How stupid must everyone think he was? Of course they'd play a prank on him, and of course the merchant would play along – albeit in a kindly fashion. Served Embran right if they were charged for tools even sillier than the ones they'd written on the list. Commander Embran, though, would not be paying. It was the islanders who were picking up the bill.

One decision was easily made: he was heading straight back to Fort Isle. Trying to find Catt & Fisher with no clear instructions, no plan, no nothing, would prove a terminal misadventure for him. Let Galt worry about it.

The two arguing men had gone; there was now a large sticker on the limestone stack, presumably denoting who had actually ordered it. In bold black, it looked like two words. Apparently Fort Isle had won that one.

But Galt's letter. It was important somehow. He knew only

by an evanescent gut feeling, because he could never admit the humiliating truth of how much school he'd missed. He couldn't read.

# TWO

At Catt & Fisher's shop, a small amorphous entity, like a white cloud, was working its way around the crowded shelves, feasting on dust. It polished as it went. Its movements were jerky, its mood not good; there was so little dust to clear. Catt guessed it must still be hungry.

He would try to find it a dust bunny from the back office as a treat. "Is that cannibalism?" he wondered out loud. "After all, we *call* you the dust bunny. You need a more fitting title. Hare of Perfect Cleanliness?"

The shop bell clanged, and Fisher came in with his usual business-like strides – albeit aided by a walking staff – that often made Catt think something was amiss when it wasn't.

"Letter!" said Fisher. "I intercepted the courier. By the gods, dead or otherwise, I hope it's something interesting. Life's verged on boring just lately."

"I wouldn't say that." Catt padded out from behind the counter in a long, shabby blue robe, his white hair standing on end from all the magnifying goggles he'd layered on his head. Although the packed shelves gleamed with all manner of peculiar items of bronze and bone and gems, it was rather a dark gleam. He lit a lamp to make the reading of the letter easier.

"Mm. How could I possibly be bored, Catty, sewing all those silver stars onto your new hat?" The hat, presently sitting on the counter, was a big floppy cap of indigo velvet that Fishy had made him. Catt loved it. All he needed now was the matching indigo robe.

"Quite so! Who d'you think it's from?"

"Someone in Fort Isle. Do we know anyone in Fort Isle?"

"I don't even know where it is." Doctor Catt chuckled. "Who would you like it to be from?"

"Celest would be nice. You?"

"Um... Tricky?"

Fishy groaned. "How delightful *that* wouldn't be."

"Nonsense, Tricky and Ralas would be fun. Shall we bet a silver polly on it?"

The bet made, Fisher broke the seal and unrolled the thick paper. "Mistress Galt!" they said in unison.

> Dear Catty and Fishy,
>
>   I hope this letter finds you well and up to your usual mischief. I need, of course, a little advice – help – something of that sort. Have you heard of the grounding of the *Pride of Arven* on Fort Isle, and the new lighthouse they're building? My father (I bless him through gritted teeth) is the chief officer, chief engineer, chief everything, and I am his project supervisor, which means a sound, beautiful and costly project that the islanders (blameless souls) will have to stump up for. No one seems to realise that they can't pay; they'll be in debt for decades. Anyway, that is not your concern!
>
>   My father continues as exasperating as ever.
>
>   Earlier today I saw an item on a list that the work crew had written for a new apprentice, Crombie – but, you know, it was a prank list, with *a long stand* and the like. Also some genuine items, so that his trip wouldn't be wasted – and the mason would understand, even though poor Crombie didn't.

But there was one item on the list so odd that... how do I explain? A feeling hit me, like a rock to the stomach, that it meant something and therefore I should check. You know. Hence I'm scrawling this urgent letter to you.

Would you not agree that such a project – a new lighthouse of exceptional height and *extreme brightness*, all for the benefit of sea captains who are less skilled than they might be – can only reach its full potential with the aid of a little, dare I say, magic? Physical protection may not be enough. The methods of lighting we have available will need a boost of particular energy, or they simply won't achieve the desired luminosity. And so on.

I have some ideas. I have a few knick-knacks that may be combined to produce certain effects. But as you know, my dear friends, I'm not a professional magus. I work very much by instinct, research, and all that I learned from you, which is probably nought-point-nought-one of what you actually know, let alone what you can *do*, especially *you*, Fishy.

So I write to you with two requests. First, any advice upon securing the protection and power of this lighthouse is greatly desired and would be hugely appreciated. Second, a specific item: I'm sure I read of it in a very old book of building methods, years ago, but the book is nowhere to be found in my collection. Its title, as best as I can recall, was *Recondite Arts of the Sagacious Architect*. I suspect my father burned it along with some other volumes. So I can't verify the origin of *A scale from the upper right wing tip of the Moth of Underthon*.

Those are the words I saw scribbled on Crombie's list. Enigmatic, no? Have you even heard of such a creature or such a charm? I don't know if it even exists, nor even what good a dead bit of insect may do. My memory of that old book may be faulty, but the idea is pulling at me. You know, I hope, that my heart is sound and my instincts are good. What I am certain of is this: all buildings are better with magical help. And the lighthouse needs this particular magic protection or it may fail and then the islanders will be blamed and – well, I do not want their fate on my conscience. But all this must be done with the utmost secrecy.

Please write back to me; I'm staying at the Fort Isle Inn, but need you to address it care of the mage Paulian. I await your response with anticipation! With dearest regards,

Galt of Athaln

PS. In case you wonder at the subterfuge – you doubtless remember my father as the most stubborn opponent of all things magical in the known world. That is why we must keep all our investigations and plans a complete secret. If he finds out, he *will* kill me, but not before I kill both of you! Much love, G.

"Well, this is a turn-up," said Catt, spreading the letter on the counter. "*Fascinating*. Mistress Galt! You cannot complain that this is boring!"

Fisher's surly face softened and his eyes went misty. "Oh, she was a bright girl. I knew she'd go far. Very likeable, no nonsense about her."

"Indeed, she was. One of the few we both agreed was likeable! Remember that Tzarkomen lad who was obsessed with killing and reanimating creatures, and... cooking them for supper if they stayed dead?"

Fisher pulled a face. "Waste not, want not. Rather you hadn't reminded me. What about Sheft, the Oerni girl, who remotely set fire to the bathroom for reasons I'll never fathom? They weren't even the worst."

"And isn't that the very reason we withdrew the bounteous gift of our knowledge and swore never to take another student? Galt was different, though."

"Mm, and I remember her father," said Fisher. "They were here rebuilding part of the council chambers... she'd vanished and he sent someone to shadow her. Thus Embran found her here."

Catt put a hand to his chest. "I thought he was going to destroy the very shop!"

"Indeed, and so difficult to remove that I thought..."

He stopped, but Catt filled in, "Oh, I was sure your temper was going to make an appearance!" He made the face of a shocked aunt about to faint.

"Focused rage," said Fisher. "There's a difference."

"Oh, quite. No idea where my image of you as a holy terror comes from, dear Fishy! I think she's onto something, don't you?"

"Galt? Really?" Fisher gave a small sigh. "And, dare I guess, you want to go chasing after it, whatever it is?"

"But of course! Let's sit down with a hot brew and talk. The book title rings a bell."

"Catty, where's that silver polly? Neither of us won the bet, remember?"

"Oh, goodness." Catt drew the coin from a pocket. "How did that get there? So absent-minded!"

"Put it back in the money box where it came from."

"Putting it back and locking the box."

"And I'll make the tea," said Fisher mordantly, "on the grounds that I always make the tea."

"But you do make the best tea, Fishy." Catt picked up the letter, turned and stopped. "Hold on," he said. "What in heaven's name does she mean by, 'let alone what you can *do*, especially *you*, Fishy'?"

"I have no idea," Fisher answered, deadpan.

# THREE

GALT STOOD ATOP the almost-finished tower and looked down at the sad sight below: the wrecked *Pride of Arven*. Sea-currents washing in from the north did more damage each day. The sodden sails flapped like drowning crows. The emblem of the White Lotus was unrecognisable. A constant groaning issued from the straining, breaking timbers as they were manhandled by the waves. As a salvage job, it was near-impossible; if the wreckage slid off the rocks to be swallowed, well, that would be the end of the cargo. If it wasn't ruined already.

She wasn't even sure what had been in the hold; wine, silks, gold? Traded or pillaged? As long as the cargo hadn't been alive, she didn't much care. The story was that a merchant had been importing rare goods for the King; she wondered how much trouble Orendion might be in, if he failed to retrieve anything. The aggressive yet effete culture of Arven had always rubbed her up the wrong way. She'd fallen out with her father Embran years ago, although they still managed to work together. She had to admit to herself, she embraced the advantages of her privileged position. Everyone knew she was Embran's daughter and his second-in-command, so they afforded her the utmost respect, as she deserved.

It wasn't only that they were terrified of Embran's wrath. They knew she was damned good at her job, stood no nonsense, and yet was rather more approachable than her father. They weren't to know that Embran's father had died early in the Kinslayer war, nor that his wife Angalah, her dear mother, had been lost in a later battle... still, everyone had suffered loss, and did that really still excuse his temperament?

Building was going efficiently, as most Arvennir projects did. Scaffolding, ramps, block and tackle, ropes and chains, workers and materials all in their right place at the right time. She looked down the swooping white wall of the tower with some satisfaction. Her friend, Captain Jennvi, who also happened to be her aunt, looked up from the ground and waved.

Galt was tempted to shout down, "Beer later?" – but they were meant to maintain a professional distance. Jennvi was her late mother's sister. Practical and unemotional, she wasn't the type to be a substitute mother to Galt. Nevertheless, there had always been a firm trust between them that didn't need words.

She wondered if sending the letter to Catt and Fisher had been a mistake; likely nothing would come of it anyway. Yesterday, there had been a sheet of paper doing the rounds with everyone adding plausible-sounding comic items that didn't actually exist. There had been a lot of giggling, which had stopped abruptly as she interrupted a knot of men and asked to see it.

There were some red faces among the workers. Nothing dangerous or offensive on the list, just silliness mixed in with real materials. At the bottom, someone had written, *A scale from the upper-right wing tip of the Moth of Underthon.*

"What's this?" she had asked. A ghost-memory stirred, but wouldn't connect with her conscious mind. When no one answered, "Who wrote, 'the Moth of...'?"

"Don't know," several voices mumbled, and one said, "The mason will know."

She handed back the paper to them, letting her stern expression become a smile. "All right. Carry on. Don't take too long over it."

By which she meant, 'As long as you don't overdo the mischief or waste any more time.' They understood. The relaxation of group tension followed her like a warm wave as she strode away.

The words bothered her, though. A wing scale from a mythical moth? Her father wouldn't approve, even though it was a joke, albeit an obscure one. Probably invention, but still it gnawed at her. She wished she still had her copy of a very old book called… she dug in her memory until she saw the faded gilt letters. *Recondite Arts of the Sagacious Architect.*

After lunch, she sought out the island's mage, Paulian. His small stone temple stood near the eastern cliff-edge, a desolate place of tough grass and a couple of wind-thrashed trees. He must catch the full force of every storm up here, she thought.

A weedy specimen in a ragged brown robe over thick woollen trousers, Paulian lived in a sort of wooden lean-to behind the temple. Some protection from the weather, then. Galt, having seen him creeping around the site some days in his capacity as a healer, had brought a basket of food and drink with her. He thanked her in soft, nervous tones. "Would you like to talk in the temple, Mistress Galt?" he asked. "My dwelling is not fit for visitors."

"Fresh air's fine for me."

He pushed back a twirl of uncombed, thinning brown hair. "Is it, is it, is it about Commander Embran?"

The poor man was petrified of her father. He wasn't alone in that. Hence the creeping around. She dipped her head in a gentle, *everything's all right* gesture, trying to seem less menacing. "No, Brother Paulian. Forgive me if I alarmed you; it's nothing to do with Embran. I only need to ask you a question. May I?"

"Oh. Yes, of course, ma'am."

"Do you know what's meant by *A scale from the upper-right wing tip of the Moth of Under – Umberthon – something?* I can't remember the word exactly. Misspelled, I suspect."

His thin face lengthened, turning even paler. She could nearly read his mind: was this a trick question? Was she testing him on suspicion of magical interference in the building project?

His voice shook. "Forgive me, no. No idea."

"Paulian," she said, patient and firm, "I'm not spying for Embran and I'm not trying to catch you out. I just thought you might know if it means something, or if it's from a story or legend, or some kind of forgotten artefact. If it means anything, please tell me. I promise on my life that you won't get into trouble for it."

"Oh. Um, ah, ah… I'm not sure. It's really nothing. I think it was a builder's superstition, from the olden days, so long ago it's forgotten now. It was er, errr… a little joke, like touching wood, or making the symbol of Gordeos? For good luck."

"I see. A superstition. A saying or a symbol to ward off evil? Likely they didn't take it seriously, but it had to be done anyway."

"Yes, that's it," he said with a hearty exhalation. "A little ch— a little ritual of the building trade. From hundreds of years ago."

He'd stopped himself saying the word *charm*. Ever since Embran had arrived, and decreed a ban on magic or belief in magic or even any mention of it, Mage Paulian had shrunk in on himself in terror of some awful punishment. Galt felt sympathy for him, but also annoyance. He demonstrated no defiance, no backbone, no courage. A mage needed some degree of bravery, at least. He was a poor example of a mage, by any standards.

"You've been really helpful," she said kindly. "Thank you. I know we Arvennir are a great nuisance to you, and I apologise, but it's not forever."

For the rest of that day, as she went about her work, the words ran round in her thoughts. Just a tradesman's ancient ritual, but not forgotten; meaningful enough to be written down. Was it important? Was it anything?

As soon as her shift ended, she rushed back to the Fort Isle Inn without waiting for Embran. She shut herself in her room and started to search through her oldest books of architecture for any mention of charmed amulets and suchlike, any rituals or spells from centuries past. Her lost book hadn't made a miraculous reappearance, but she couldn't help looking, just in case.

An unwelcome memory rose of Embran making a bonfire in their small garden in Athaln, grimacing fiercely as he threw ten or so books onto the flames. She hadn't asked him why, as he'd been in such a foul mood. But she recalled it was not long after her mother, Angalah, had died in the eighth year of the war. Galt had been thirteen.

With hindsight, it was obvious that *Recondite Arts of the Sagacious Architect* was one of the books Embran had destroyed. More occult content than he could tolerate.

The magic angle bothered her. Embran was a complete sceptic. Arven, as a nation, might still speak of gods and guardians; it seemed to make them feel special, enlightened and chosen, as if they needed any excuse. Some form of divine affirmation.

Since the Kinslayer's death, though, there was a small but growing movement of dissent. Embran was a strong supporter. The gods were long-dead, he insisted. If ever there *had* been magic in the world, it had ceased to exist with them. Only foolish folk chased artefacts, imagining they had powers of healing, or strength, or invisibility, or breathing below water, or making or unmaking or a thousand other improbable attributes. He disapproved of charms, curses, blessings, haunted bones, god-faces carved into new buildings for good luck. Any builder caught binding enchanted gems into the foundations would be dismissed on the spot. Concealed spells of warding scratched into the rafters would result in severe punishment – of everyone, until someone confessed. Then the guilty party would have to sand the wood until the inscription was gone; or, at worst, replace the entire beam.

"Keeping back a tide of superstitious sewage." This, Embran claimed, was his second most important job, albeit unrewarded. "This is the new age of development," he would tell his daughter. "The gods are gone, and with them all the demigods, guardians, demons, ghosts, spirits of good and bad luck, mindless energies with the power to change the wind or cause a storm at a mage's bidding. This is *our* world now, made new: clean and strong and magic-free."

Galt didn't entirely agree. Like her mother, she sensed things, *knew* things. But there was no question of talking to her father. Their last exchange on the subject had been an utter catastrophe that still made her wince in anguish when she thought of it.

That night, after a light supper of stew and a glass of wine, she sat down and wrote her letter to those who might know.

# FOUR

DOCTORS CATT AND Fisher strolled along the river bank, taking their time as the weather was delightful. Catt had a cane in one hand, while Fisher sported a large net on a pole. This, the more salubrious end of the shopping district, had either escaped the Kinslayer's bane, or had been restored. The old houses, painted in shades of blue, red, and orange, dropped long reflections into the water. The shop they sought was a sombre dark blue, with wide windows and large glass doors. An establishment of style and wealth that only the elite dared to enter.

*Tiny and Dedley*, read the lettering curved over the doors. *Purveyors of Fine Arts and Collectibles*.

Catt and Fisher entered side by side. The counter was actually an enormous fancy desk with a glass top, positioned to their right. A short, bald figure standing behind the desk looked up as the bell rang and issued a barely audible sigh. Catt heard it clearly, because Mr Tiny always sighed when he saw them.

"Gentlemen," he said, leaning on the desk top with neatly-folded hands. "What a pleasure to see you both. It's been a long time. Pre-Kinslayer, I believe."

Catt politely doffed his new hat. "Good afternoon, Mr Tidy."

"It's *Tiny*."

"I'm dreadfully sorry to hear that," Fisher put in with a sideways smirk. Tiny turned boiling red.

"Hilarious as ever, *Mr Fish*."

"And yet you always fall for it!"

"Excuse my friend," said Catt. "And please forgive me. It's an easy mistake to make because this establishment of fine repute" – he swept his hand around – "is always so utterly immaculate. Your diligence put us to shame."

"It's a matter of pride. Brings our customers back. And how is business with you?"

"Ah, our dusty, web-laden shambles of a premises," said Fisher. "As well as can be expected. We're so envious. Everything here is so shiny. Isn't it *shiny*, Catt?"

"Like a mirror."

A voice from a back room said, "Do I hear sarcasm? I know those supercilious tones." Mr Dedley came bustling into view; he was as short as his partner, though considerably broader and hairier. His greyish hair and moustache were the least tidy things in the shop. The points of his ears stuck out at right angles, like beaks from a bird's nest. "Mr Catt and Mr Fisher."

"*Doctor* and *Doctor*," Catt said amiably. Their rivals always got it wrong on purpose. The ridiculous thing was that they had no need to be rivals. Tiny and Dedley sold art and antiques; there was almost nothing of magical provenance on the premises. Yet they maintained their feud, partly because each pair of merchants found the other so obnoxious, but mainly because it was fun.

"And how may we help you, good Doctors?"

Catt gave a bright smile. "Actually, we've come to help you. It's time your lighting had a check and service."

Both men looked up at the ceiling, where several white globes floated with no means of support except the esoteric energy with which Catt and Fisher had imbued them. They were the shop's source of dazzling diamond light. Tiny and Dedley had paid a fortune for them, a few years back. Coming to an agreement on price had, in fact, taken the best part of a night that had ended with the art dealers frazzled, Catt and Fishy all smiles.

160

"What? But they run on... magic, or whatever you call it. Since when do magical items need *servicing*?"

"You'd be surprised," said Catt. "Delicate balances can go off-kilter. A collision might give rise to a heart-stopping shock, and you certainly wouldn't any of them to go rogue and burst through your pristine front windows."

"Potentially hitting an innocent passer-by," added Fisher. "Could prove expensive."

Both dealers looked comically alarmed. "And how much is this *service* going to cost us?"

"Oh, nothing," said Catt. "Not a scit. Servicing was all included in the original price."

Fisher flourished his net. "May we get on?"

Time stood still for three seconds as Tiny stared at them with round eyes. "Very well. Splendid. This is so absurd, it must be genuine." He turned side on and swept his hand graciously, offering the freedom of the shop. "Do continue. Try to be quiet, we have customers on their way."

Smiling benignly, to show that it was all gentle teasing and everyone was friends, Catt and his companion glided past the desk as if on cat's paws and into the main body of the shop. Fisher deployed the net to catch each globe in turn and bring it down to shoulder level. Then Catt made a perfunctory check of the vibrations, feeling a gentle tingle of energy between his palms. They were all fine; simple spelled things that would run for decades. Meanwhile he went about his central purpose; carefully eyeing every single item on the beautifully arranged shelves.

"Feel anything?" Fishy whispered as he carefully eased a globe out of the netting and let it float back up to its natural height.

"Not sure. Possibly, but it may well be wishful thinking. I'm becoming positively myopic, searching for something that's potentially the size of a thimble with a grain of dust inside. And yet... I'm certain there's something here. Last time we were here, I sensed *something*."

"Not much help."

"But I'll know it when I see it."

While they were shielded from the counter area by a couple of glass cases, Catt opened the drawers of various polished wooden escritoires, dressers and jewellery boxes. Empty. He searched about for hidden latches to secret compartments without success. They moved into a further display room, the very back one where they were fully out of sight. There was nothing to see but fragile old plates painted with elaborate designs, all protected in locked display cases.

Catt noticed a dusty scent that made his throat tingle. He swallowed hard to stop himself coughing.

"Bring that light down a bit lower, Fishy," he croaked. "Here. *Ahem. Cack.*"

Middle shelf, near the back corner where all was in shadow, there was a large square frame. Fisher's light illuminated a delicate-looking fan sandwiched between two sheets of glass, standing vertically in a frame of dark walnut.

"What's that?" said Fisher. "You always find something to distract you that's nothing to do with what we're actually looking for!"

Catt didn't answer, because he couldn't speak. He indicated Fishy to be quiet as he leaned in for a closer look. Certainly no speck of moth-dust. The fan was a tall oval about four handspans across, brownish, with a ragged top edge like silk so old it was close to disintegrating. As the light moved, faint shades of blue and green rippled over it, peacock-like. What an odd thing... He popped his jeweller's loupe from a pocket and looked more closely. There were no marks on the frame to identify the item, but he could still feel that tingle at the back of his tongue.

"*Hrmm.*" Fishy cleared his throat. "Could be... bit of energy. Faded."

"Can I help you gentlemen with anything?"

Dedley's voice behind them was so loud that they both jumped nearly out of their skins. Catt dropped the loupe. The globe escaped Fisher's net, shot up and bounced off the ceiling before settling at its normal height.

"Good grief, Mr Dedley, don't do that!" Catt put a hand to his heart and struggled with a fit of coughing and spluttering. Dedley grinned.

"You're here looking for something in particular. I knew it."

"Really, casting such aspersions upon us ill-befits you and your prestigious establishment—"

"All right, well caught," Fisher interrupted brusquely. "What is this object here? We'd like to see it more closely, if it's no trouble."

"That ugly old thing?" Dedley shook a bunch of small keys, selected one and opened the cabinet. He eased the framed material from its shelf and set it on a polished round table, where it sat looking unrepentantly ugly. "Been there for years. I don't even know where it came from. You could have simply asked, before you messed around with all our light spheres. You two are ridiculous!"

"Hm, well, that aside," said Fishy, "it's a long story. Catty, are you all right? Could you bring him a glass of water, Mr Dedley? We promise not to steal anything."

"Such an unworthy thought never crossed my mind."

While Dedley left them alone, they leaned down to examine the unknown framed object. It looked fragile and sad, pressed within the glass panes. "You've seen this before, haven't you?" said Fisher, eyes narrowing.

"I suspect so. Years ago. It hopped into my mind when I read Galt's letter."

"Can't argue, Catty. As soon as you brought my attention to it, I *knew* I'd seen it before. The old instinct stirring."

"Oh, me too, me too. This is why we make such a good team!

An odd thing seen years ago that just *might* be a moth wing? You felt that wisp of power, that catches the throat like pepper?"

"I think there's very little power left in it," Fishy sighed. "A few centuries old, I'd say."

"I don't think it's an item truly worthy of our collection... Still, we might, *might* be able to scrape a few scales from it for Galt?"

Dedley took a while, but when he returned, in addition to water he had a huge ledger under his arm. "I've brought the catalogue. If you'll bear with me, Doctors, I may be able to find the details, date, provenance and suchlike..."

"I must say, you're being enormously helpful," Catt said with a smile. "Not unwell, are you?"

"Haha. Truth is, I hate the damned thing. It's neither aesthetically delightful nor of any value."

"How much d'you want for it?" Fisher put in. He helped Dedley to hold the book across their forearms, the table being too small to take both frame and open ledger. Dedley began flicking through the pages, swift and experienced.

"Nothing. Just take it. But *do not* tell Mr Tiny. Swear? He'd hang me up by my intestines if he knew I'd given it away, especially to you two. I'll distract him while you make your escape, all right?"

"Most generous," Fishy said with a rare grin. "We owe you a favour, at least a small one."

"Ah, here we are. Oval membrane pressed in glass to prevent further damage. Believed to date from... good gods, nearly a thousand years old? Provenance uncertain, probably shed in the wild near Forest of Feltek and discovered there. Reputed to be *One wing scale of the Moth of Umberanaetheon*."

"It's what?" Fisher was trying to read the handwriting at an angle.

Dedley repeated the words, but Fishy interrupted, "Don't you mean one *wing*, or fragment thereof?"

The short Cheriveni shrugged. "What it says is one scale. If you're going to quibble..."

"No, no, we'll quibble back at the shop," Fisher said quickly. "We'll take it. And not a word to your partner, we swear."

"Excellent. I'll mark it sold in the ledger, so we don't get mixed up during stock-taking. Under your cloak, Doctor Catt? I'll go and distract Tiny while you two tiptoe out."

As he was whispering, the table trembled. All three men were at least two steps away. They watched in disbelief as the frame slid sideways and tumbled towards the floor, as if pushed by the paw of an invisible cat. Fisher lunged to catch it, too late. It hit the hardwood floor with a tremendous *crash*.

Wood splintered, broken glass flew everywhere, and Mr Tiny came rushing in from the front of the shop.

"What the blue blazes was that? Dedley?"

No one could answer, because the wing-scale turned to a whirl of dust on contact with the air, and the other three were incapacitated by a mutual coughing fit. Catt knelt down, almost in tears, trying to capture some fibres on his finger. Dedley crouched beside him and promptly caught a glass shard in his palm.

He stood up with a yelp of pain and cradled his injured hand, dripping blood everywhere.

"*What the hell do you think you're doing?*" roared Tiny. "Dedley, not on the floor, it'll stain! Great gods, have you gone collectively mad?"

"I can explain," said Fisher.

"You two, always trouble!"

"Tiny, the thing just *fell*," said Dedley. "It was no one's fault. Everyone out, before we all get cut to pieces."

"Just fell, did it? Threw itself from a height to end its misery? *Don't bleed on the carpet, either!*"

A woman, resplendent in satin and jewels, had opened the shop door. Her jaw dropped and she backed rapidly out again.

"That's it, frighten off our best customers to add insult to injury!" Tiny gasped.

"You're the ones doing all the shouting and bleeding," Fisher put in.

"We're most terribly sorry," said Catt, looking back at the mess of wood, glass and – nothingness. "Dedley, let me see that hand."

"We'll sweep up," said Fisher.

Tiny threw his hands in the air. "No, just get out, before you do any more damage! You're banned! *Go!*"

"MIGHT HAVE BEEN a small earth tremor," said Fisher as they dawdled home. "Or vibrations transmitted within the floorboards. Perhaps that table wasn't standing square, and it was *very* highly polished…"

"Or some unseen power didn't want us to have it," Catt said mournfully. "Or the scale itself didn't want to be had."

There had been a short pause before they left the shop while Catt treated Dedley's hand with a healing unguent and a bandage. Fisher had left a stack of silver coins on the desk, which Tiny regarded with contempt. Then they had, as requested, got out.

"Certainly an interesting excursion."

Catt looked at his fingertips. "I tried to gather up a bit of the dust but there was just nothing. Oh, Fishy, what a wasted trip we've had."

"Nothing's ever wasted," Fisher replied with smug lilt to his voice. "Look." He pulled back his left sleeve to show Catt the end of a rolled-up document.

"A map? Did you steal that, you rogue?"

"Of course not. Didn't you notice the coins I left? Cost me a fortune! The things I do for you."

"A map of where?"

"Patience. Wait until we're home."

"Good. I love surprises. As long as they're not bad ones, like Embran coming in without opening the door." Catt paused, thinking. "It's a map of the Forest of Feltek, isn't it? Clever chap!"

"Hold your chariot," said Fisher. "I'm hoping it will prove to you that travelling to Feltek would be *impossible*. Because I know you, Catty."

"Ha. You do indeed know me too well." His eyes narrowed. "One single wing scale."

"But was it *literally* one scale from one wing from the Moth of Umberanaetheon? A forgery, an enlarged drawing? Painting on silk? Unfortunately, we'll never know."

"Oh, my dear fellow, I *have* to know," Catt said. "From what I could see in my brief examination, it appeared to be *literally* one scale of a moth wing, singular. One single scale."

"But it was the size of a dinner plate! A serving dish, even. How many scales are there on the average-sized moth?"

"Several… hundred… million," Catt said very slowly.

"Yes," said Fisher. "Let's just think about that for a minute, shall we?"

# FIVE

THE WEATHER TOOK a turn for the unhelpful, with strong winds and sea fogs hampering completion of the lighthouse. Crombie kept his head down and worked through it, ever-obliging, with the result that everyone would come to him for help with everything, from the smallest task to hanging from a wildly-swinging chain in order to steady the ascent of limestone blocks.

"Measure ten times, cut once!" Galt's voice echoed off the raw stone. An Arvennir worker had made a beam too small. Fumbling to put it down, he dropped it on his foot and yelled with pain. "Oh, wonderful," groaned Galt. "Is Paulian around? Medic!"

"I'll find him," said Crombie. He looked around to make sure Embran wasn't nearby, then found the mage crouched behind a stack of timber. "Paulian, can you come? Hurt foot. Maybe broken; it looked nasty." Paulian hesitated. "It's all right, Commander Embran's not here. You're safe."

"I don't know what's wrong with you lot," the mage whispered. "Past few days, nothing but broken feet, broken hands, scrapes and bruises – these Arvennir and their workers are the clumsiest lot I've ever seen. They're meant to be so superior to us?"

"I know," said Crombie. "I think it's just a run of bad luck."

"Captain!" Galt summoned a nearby officer, a bright-faced

woman of middle age with a stocky physique and confident demeanour.

"Ma'am?"

"Jennvi, get this man to the infirmary. Quickly."

"On it."

The captain snapped a command. Two soldiers arrived to stretcher the workman to the makeshift infirmary they'd set up in one of the outside sheds. Crombie went with Paulian to help him, then ran back to the site of the accident – an interior scaffold platform on the second floor – where Galt was still voicing her exasperation. "Another entry in the accident book. If you check, you will note there have been nine serious injuries in the last five days, plus numerous cuts, bruises and knocks. What is wrong with you all?"

All the workers looked pale, and said nothing. "Seriously, I want to hear about every single problem, no matter how insignificant. We need to address this rash of accidents before we run out of craftspeople entirely! You realise that not only am I in charge of the smooth running of this project, but also the safety of every single one of you. You are my responsibility. Has every single safety instruction escaped your memory? Right, you can all down tools for the rest of the day. Tomorrow, I'll be conducting a refresher course on how to build a lighthouse without killing yourself or anyone else! Jorgan, you'll assist me. First thing tomorrow. Outside. Safety lecture."

Crombie became aware of Embran's large figure in a doorway. "Galt." His voice had an impressive resonance, like someone striking a huge war drum. "What's happening?"

As the workers streamed out of the main door to avoid his dragon gaze, Galt walked to her father and confronted him. "I'm trying to halt the run of avoidable injuries that has afflicted us. Because that's my job."

Less tall than his superior, Orendion, Embran was a wider and more menacing figure. His hair was dark and cropped, but he sported the beard of a berserker. Crombie knew he'd been formidable during the Kinslayer war, both at sea and on the field. He always looked as if he was about to slice your head off, even while sipping coffee at the inn's breakfast table.

"I'm glad to hear it," he said. "I'm beginning to wonder what the devil is going on."

"Fresh start in the morning. Safety checks on all equipment. Stricter guidelines. This is my responsibility, Father."

"But also mine," he said. "And the word 'sabotage' has crossed my mind."

He looked past Galt and caught Crombie's eye. Crombie realised he'd been standing there, gawping like an idiot. He turned and fled out of the main door, following the others.

HE AVOIDED THE crowd of grumbling men and women outside, went to a secluded buttress and sat on the foundation stone where he liked to eat his lunch. There was shelter from the wind here. He'd barely unwrapped his feast of cheese pastries, pickled fish and chopped raw vegetables when Galt appeared in front of him. She looked stern and disgruntled.

"Mind if I join you?" she said. "This is the least draughty spot on the whole site."

"Yes, no, I mean, it's fine." Crombie was less tongue-tied with her than he used to be, but her presence still turned him to mortar; the way it wobbled before it set. "Isn't it warmer inside, though?"

"At the senior site personnel reserved dining area?" She sneered and sniffed. "As long as I can escape from my father, I don't care where I sit. Your ma and pa seem nice; ever feel glad to get away from them?"

"Yes, they're all right." He handed her a baked cheese pasty, as she had nothing to eat. She accepted gladly. "Even so, yes, I love getting away from them. They're always teasing me, like I'm a cross between a puppy and a donkey, but they're not cruel or anything."

"They adore you," she said, looking out at the fog on the waves. "I love my father, too, even though he's a complete nightmare. But sometimes I think that no matter how much you love someone, you will still want to kill them at times."

Crombie swallowed an overlarge mouthful of pasty.

She smiled. "So, eating out here is a better choice than running a blade through Embran, bless his monstrous heart. This business with the accidents has put him into one of his cantankerous moods. If you can spot the difference."

"He didn't upset you, did he?" Crombie was glad she raised the subject of the accidents first. He didn't like to ask delicate questions of his superiors. He passed her a bottle of small beer.

"Me, upset? Of course not. But it's an odd thing to start happening when we're so close to the end."

"*You* don't think it's sabotage, do you?"

"I doubt it. I think people are just being clumsy because they're tired, or complacent. If you saw someone creeping around sawing through ropes and the like, you would tell us, wouldn't you?"

"Of course I would. But I haven't seen anything, and I'm running all over the build more than anyone."

"Wasn't you, was it?"

He gasped, but she smiled. "I'm teasing, Crombie. I know you wouldn't. Everyone says you seem to be in ten places at once, you're so busy. You don't have to work *too* hard, you know. People will only take advantage."

"I don't mind. I like being busy."

"And you're a really good worker. Jorgan says so. Even Embran says so. You posted my letter, and made sense of that joke list for Volt. You behave with common sense; I respect that."

"Thank you, Mistress Galt."

"Just Galt. Your ma's pastries are delicious. Would she give me some, instead of that fancy Arvennir food Embran demands? Says it reminds us of home, but it's such a fuss for her to make and I don't even like it."

"Course she would!"

"And, I hate to ask this, but would you do some observational work for me?"

"You mean spying?"

"I wouldn't put it like that. Crombie, I trust you. Just keep an eye on people. Look at plans to see if the measurements have been altered. The same with written instructions. That sort of thing."

He cringed inwardly. What to tell her, except the plain truth? "Miss Galt, I can't read or write," he blurted. "I'd be useless to you."

"Oh? That's unfortunate. Just watch and report back, then. At least there'd be no danger of you writing down what I say and passing notes to my father about my secret… secrets."

"I'd never do that, in any case."

"I know. You are the only person I trust, Crombie, if you didn't know. Well, there's one other, but she's Arvennir. Can't risk it. So you're my right-hand man."

"I am?" He felt himself blush. Why must he be a tall, gangly youth with the sort of gormless face that only his ma could love, while Galt was at least ten years older, grown-up and glorious? Fate was never fair.

"I can teach you your letters anyway." She spoke as if it was the easiest thing ever. "Why didn't you learn at school?"

"Sheep," he said. "I mean I was helping with the sheep more than I was at school."

"So when you went to the mason's, you had no idea what was written on that list?"

"None." They both laughed; the episode seemed funny now. "Master Volt was all right; he didn't make me feel stupid, or only a bit. He even told me where to ask about the moth wing thing! Only it's hundreds of miles away, so…"

"Mm. Not as mad as it sounds. I'll explain when I can."

"Oh, did you get an answer to your letter? I did post it, I promise."

"I know you did, Crombie." She patted his shoulder. "And no, no reply yet. But it's rather soon for an answer to have come back."

"The mason said go to Catt & Fisher, and he said the letter was *addressed* to Catt & Fisher, so I was a bit puzzled, but after all, it's none of my business. My grandfather, he was a carpenter; I remember he said, in the old days, stuff about putting charms and things in when you build, to protect the building and make it really strong. The Arvennir don't do that, though, do they?"

"Hush," she said. "Don't speak of such things, especially not to Embran, unless you want to be whipped."

"I don't." He gulped. "Very much not. I'll do absolutely anything to help you stop these accidents, though."

As he finished his sentence, a shape came hurtling from above, right past their eyes, and landed with a grim *thump* on the grass in front of them. Hardly two feet away. Galt clasped his arm and they stared, speechless, at what was clearly a workman's body.

They both looked up at the top of the tower, and down again at the prone, twisted figure. Galt went forward onto her knees and felt under his chin. "I can't find a pulse," she said. "Crombie, it's Jorgan!"

THE ARVENNIR AUTHORITIES arrested Paulian. Soldiers held him in the town square, while General Orendion, Embran and Governor Gredlen looked on. Gredlen was ashen, watching Jorgan's family who stood at the side of the crowd, hugging each other and sobbing. Wife, parents, sister, assorted children.

"An unexplained series of accidents is one thing," said Embran. The assembled crowd was silent with shock. "But now there has been a death – a murder – this has become an entirely different matter."

"We've questioned every worker who's ever been on site," said Galt, standing beside her father. "We can't find a single witness to Jorgan's fall – he seems to have been alone at the top – nor to any of the lesser accidents. That is, I saw him hit the ground, but did he overbalance, did someone push him? No one has seen *any* incident caused deliberately by another person. And I pride myself on the highest standards of safety on my sites. This is unprecedented."

"That being the case," Orendion continued, "there is clear suspicion of magical attack. A search of the island's mage Paulian, the *only* mage to our knowledge, of his temple and his dwelling, revealed a stash of suspicious items. Herbs, ointment, tinctures, instruments, amulets, spells and many more sinister items that might be used with malice."

"No," said Paulian, his voice very faint.

Crombie couldn't listen to much more of this. He stepped forward to confront the Arvennir. "Paulian's a healer! Those are the tools of his trade. He's the one who's been in the infirmary *healing* all the broken bones – why would he make work for himself?"

"I don't know," Embran growled, glaring down at him. "To *make* work for himself, so as to appear less... redundant?"

"You don't even believe in magic!" Crombie retorted, adding, "Sir."

"Who told you that? Yes, I loathe magic and wish to see it expunged from the world. That's not to say it isn't a real and malevolent force! You do *remember* the Kinslayer, boy?"

"Paulian's hardly... He's our healer. Also, he's terrified of you, Commander Embran. I'm sure he would never do anything against you. What reason has he?"

"Why are you defending him?" Embran's gaze could have melted iron. Crombie knew he was one step from an abyss of trouble.

Orendion's voice drowned them, ear-shattering. "What reason?

Rebellion against Arvennir directives. Sabotage. Defiance against Embran's ban on magical workings. I'm sure he has countless motives. Paulian was the only non-construction worker frequently seen on site. And all the victims were Arvennir."

"Jorgan wasn't!" This was Governor Gredlen. He went over to Jorgan's family and stood with him.

"Perhaps, then, Paulian had a specific grudge against him. Collaborating with people he perceived as the enemy?"

"We're not enemies," Gredlen said. "You said as much when this started."

"But you, the islanders collectively, have never wanted this lighthouse. Someone has taken action to sabotage it. If not Paulian, who?" Orendion waved his arms around the crowd, as if making an open-hearted plea. "*Someone* has caused these accidents with ill-intent. If you give yourself up now, the mage will be released and your punishment will be less severe. If you know who's responsible and give them up to us, there will be a reward. If you know but *don't* tell us – expect the direst of consequences."

Embran pointed at Crombie and said, "What about *you*? Might be as simple as someone drugging all the tea and making us clumsy."

Crombie felt the blood draining out of his head. Embran gave a sneer and looked away. Apparently it was a joke, the worst and cruellest joke ever, he thought, but how could he be sure?

The only sound was a collective indrawn breath.

"Release our mage," said Gredlen. "Otherwise we'll have no healer. And you've no proof against him; this is not a fair trial."

The Arvennir officials muttered among themselves. All the time, Galt stared straight into Crombie's eyes. He had no idea what the look meant, but it sent chills over him.

"Very well. In the interests of fairness," said Orendion, "we'll release him – if I have a volunteer to keep him under house arrest?"

"I'll take him." The voice came from Viktor, keeper of the old lighthouse, who hadn't been seen around since his protest at the public meeting two years ago. He looked more unkempt than ever, like the hermit he'd become. Then Crombie felt bad for not going to see him... but why should he, if no one else had? Victor Dremin was notorious for alienating anyone who tried to befriend him. "There's a lock-up room, a cellar, like, under my place. I'll stick 'im in there. What? Who said that? Of course I'll feed 'im! I'm not a barbarian!"

"Good. Keep in mind you'll pay a large fine if he goes missing, Mr Dremin. Understood?" said Orendion.

"Whatever." Viktor hobbled over to Paulian, grabbed the ropes that tied his hands, and marched him away.

"You know, they'd never have bailed him if the dead man had been Arvennir, not an islander," murmured Crombie's father.

Crombie saw Galt's face relax, and she gave him the slightest of nods.

And at that moment he knew who the real culprit was. Or might be. Certainty was like quicksand; concrete one moment then sinking liquid the next. It struck him that *uncertainty* must be killing the Arvennir, especially Embran. No wonder it must have been tempting to grab the most obvious suspect and behead them on the spot. Case closed.

THE NEXT MORNING, after Galt's long and thorough safety workshop, a handful of surveyors was allowed back on site, while the remaining workers were sent back to their accommodation. Crombie didn't know what to do with himself. He was unsettled, couldn't stop thinking about Jorgan and Paulian. So he just walked, with the sea wind blustering at his back.

He was wandering aimlessly on the cliff path when Galt caught him up and walked beside him. Her presence felt reassuring. The trauma of seeing a man crash to his death in front of them was, apparently, a bonding experience.

"How are you bearing up, Crombie?" She spoke softly and put her arm through his.

"I don't know. I'll be fine. But all this is awful. Are *you* all right, Galt?"

"No, not really. I hope Viktor takes care of Paulian; he's saved his life, at least for now. Embran's beyond rage."

"You don't think Paulian's guilty, do you?"

"I don't think so, but I don't *know*. Crombie?"

"Yes?"

"You *don't* know who or what caused these accidents, do you?"

"As if I'd tell you, and get handed over to Orendion's officers!"

"That's not fair. You can't think I'd tell them?"

"But if you didn't, that would put *you* in the wrong, too. No, Galt, I promise I don't know what's happening."

"And you weren't drugging the tea?"

"Why would a thing like that even cross my mind? I almost wish I had, now! At least I could have put Embran and Orendion to sleep for a few days!"

She laughed. "Teasing. I believe you. Where are you going, by the way?"

"Nowhere in particular," he said. "Just clearing my head. You?"

"Well, I'm heading down to meet the ferry to see if there's an answer to my letter yet. Come with me?"

GALT HAD BEEN visiting the ferry landing every day, sometimes both morning and evening, to see if any post had come for her. It was too soon, she knew, but she was impatient. Besides, her apothecary friends had special charms to make things happen more swiftly… Surely they had an enchanted dove or a trained crow, at least? Wasn't her letter worth a little magical acceleration? On the other hand, their reply might be just that they couldn't help. She wouldn't blame them.

And if her father happened to find a letter from Catt & Fisher, no matter how carefully she tried to hide it, there would be hell to pay. In fact, he would literally send her down to the underworld as payment. She might be a grown woman, but he still claimed the right to barge in and search her room as if she were still thirteen.

There were about thirty people disembarking from the ferry, others waiting to board.

"I don't see the courier," said Crombie. Taller than most, he was craning over their heads.

Then, after everyone else had gone, she noticed two grey shadowy outlines on the ferry landing. They must be a trick of the fog on her vision. She simply couldn't believe what she was seeing.

"Crombie, can you see two people… just over there?"

"Where? No. Just mist moving around."

To her, though, they became absolutely distinct. Still grey shadows, but unmistakable. "Catty?" she called softly. "Fishy?"

They unshrouded and there they stood, in the very flesh; as dear as grandfathers to her, the taller Fishy with his quiet, watchful demeanour, and her Catt, with his wild white hair escaping a floppy velvet hat, and his broad smile. "You're here, you're here!" she cried, and burst into tears. She flung herself on them and they shared an awkward but joyous three-way hug. They smelled of the shop; herbs and incense and exotic resins.

Crombie hung somewhere behind her; she forgot he was there for a few minutes.

"I can't believe it. All I hoped for was a letter and here you are!"

179

"We simply had to," said Doctor Catt. "You can't send us a letter saying, 'Help me with this magical dilemma', and expect nothing but a note in return, 'Do this, do that, and you'll be right as rain'. We needed to see for ourselves."

"It sounds a serious business," said Fisher.

"It is. Actually, it's even worse since I wrote. A man died. It's about the safety of the building, because if it fails, the islanders will be the ones to suffer…"

"Yes, we gathered that. We've done considerable research."

"Besides, Fishy here was so bored he made me a new hat and embroidered fifty silver stars on it!"

"It's beautiful." Galt was laughing and crying.

"I certainly don't do it for the gratitude," said Fisher. "Where shall we stay? Feet up, tea and cake, then we can talk."

"Come with me. The Fort Isle Inn – oh, damn and dragon's fire."

"Galt? Don't tell us…"

"Yes, my father's staying there too. And if he sees you, he will kill you."

"Shroud," said Fisher, and the two men faded to near-invisibility. Crombie would have given a month's wages to know how they did that.

Half an hour later, they were cosy with him and Galt in his attic room; they daren't use Galt's larger guest room, for fear of Embran suddenly bursting in. He was prone to that, Galt complained, and if she locked it he just forced the lock and barged in anyway.

"Doesn't want to find his paragon of a little girl with a gentleman friend?" said Catt, settling into a shabby old armchair as if it were the pinnacle of luxury. At least Crombie had a decent wood fire going; it masked the squalor with a classy glow. Fisher sat facing Catt, in a similar but non-matching chair, while Crombie and Galt perched on stools. The two doctors seemed to have filled his space messily with staves and cloaks and themselves, though only one bag Crombie could see.

"More that he thinks I'm an extension of him," Galt sighed. "Walking reference book, bringer of refreshments, person who knows where the laundry room is. Also, he seems to fear I might be *up to something.*"

"Sorcerous somethings?" said Fisher.

"Like my mother, rest her soul, often was."

"And are you?"

"I'd like to be. Some chance, alas."

"Well, we'll have to see about that." Catt sounded excited. Crombie felt oddly excited too; he could sense an aura around these two old apothecaries, layers and layers of strange magic and stranger experiences receding to infinity. The things they must have seen and done! And to have two such legendary beings in his humble room seemed more thrilling by the second.

Fisher poised the tips of his long fingers beneath his chin and spoke portentously. "Let's start, shall we, with the business of the *Eight Wing Scales from the Eye of the Upper Right Wingtip of the Great Moth of Umberanaetheon?*"

"The what?" said Crombie. "That's not what it said on that list!"

Galt glanced at him, *shush.* "Crombie's correct. That's the proper name, is it?"

"Indeed it is. Whoever scribbled it down for you only half-remembered it. But they remembered enough."

"And we've been up to our knees in ancient tomes and scrolls trying to find some reference to it," Catt added, as if this task had been his idea of the best time ever. From the oblong leather bag, he produced a textbook and placed it in Galt's hands. "Also, we brought you a gift…"

The book was of modest size, the spine only the depth of a

finger joint. Brown and badly worn with age, the cover looked close to disintegration, and its title was almost gone; not that Crombie could have read it anyway. He caught its fusty scent. Galt, though, reacted as if Catt had given her a golden crown.

"Oh!" Speech deserted her for a moment. "*Recondite Arts of the Sagacious Architect*! I knew I hadn't imagined it! I could kiss you both! This was in your collection?"

"Devil of a job to find it, but yes," said Fisher.

"One of the oldest tomes on architecture known, replete with the benefits of magical relics in the noble trade of building," Catt said proudly. If you turn to page—"

"No, don't tell me! Page 183?" Galt carefully turned the flimsy leaves. Crombie saw that each page was dense with indecipherable runes, while the smell of age almost made him choke. "Yes. Here it is. A reference to the Great Moth!"

"Not the easiest passage to decipher," said Fisher.

"Let's see. '*On the protection of... the edifice modern? Various relics may be employed, though the most powerful of these are lost to... previous ages...*' So the best charms were gone, even by the time this book was written? I'm skipping over a list now... Here we are: '*And the most powerful of these were reputed to be Eight Scales from the Eye of the Upper Right Wingtip of the Great Moth of Umberanaetheon. The ancients employed the scales as follows; one scale sealed within each plane or slope of the roof. The optimum number being Eight. This was said to bestow protection of unimagined strength against storm, fire, battle, ill-intent and other magics. No detail was left as to the harvesting or placement of such scales, yet this myth is with us still'*."

"Says it's just a myth, though?" Crombie put in, deflated by the lack of evidence.

Catt joined in eagerly, "But we found a number of other sources, connected with the magical warding of structures, that mention the moth. There are extra morsels of information, albeit contradictory. And we *found an actual moth scale!*"

Galt sat forward, alive with curiosity. "Where is it?"

The two men related a rather long but amusing tale about a fracas in a china shop.

GALT CARESSED THE book like a cat while they spoke. Eventually, Doctor Fisher drew out a rolled-up document that looked far too long for the satchel that had contained it.

"This map…" Crombie cleared crockery from the low table, so that Fisher could spread it out and weigh down the corners with tea cups.

Catt knew that the faded lines probably meant nothing to Crombie, nor even to Galt, but since the first thrilling time Fishy had unfolded it, he'd examined every pen stroke. The paper was thick, yellowish and crumbling round the edges; it was a treasure of genuine provenance, not a tea-aged piece of fakery. Catt could sense and smell its musty yet enthralling potential.

Places had names, but these were barely legible, and as for the language – anyone's guess. A root tongue for old Arvennir, perhaps.

"Ah … isn't that the coast of Feltek?" said Galt after a while. So we're looking at… the great Forest. And a lot of mountains. Middle of nowhere. Is this where they found…"

"The Moth of Umberanaetheon." Fishy nodded. "The heart of the forest is marked with a symbol."

"Damp and nearly impassable terrain, as I recall," said Catt. "Very rocky, with chasms carved out by long-extinct rivers. Warm climate, humid, so plenty of wildlife and insects and the like."

"Have you been there?" Crombie asked.

"No. I read a lot and I have a good memory, as you may have noticed."

Fisher said, "Well, I have been there, and you're pretty much spot on. It's a labyrinthine country. The forest is all giant roots and vines and carnivorous flora. We'll certainly collect some interesting plant specimens there. But that aside … very sparsely habited. Some non-human tribes up in the thickest parts of the forests, but more likely to hide than attack."

"That's reassuring, but why would we want to go there?" said Galt. "Surely the mythical moth is long dead."

"But we don't know," said Catt, overcome by the familiar thrill of treasure-hunting. "We must find out. Some things are longer-lived than you could imagine."

"Going into the wilderness to find a bit of an insect doesn't sound the best idea," Crombie said slowly. "What am I missing?"

Catt leaned back in his armchair. He loved explaining, as much as Fisher loved keeping secrets. "The scribble on your list wasn't a joke, lad. This is serious. Our belief, or rather our best guess from the research, is that these wing-scales have a definite arcane warding power to protect a building from danger. The old writings tell us that a roof is powerfully protected by scales from this moth. Insufficient detail, as we said, but eight scales would seem to form a kind of radiating shield. An umbrella! And, believe us, your lighthouse needs that protection; from weather, from magical attack, and so on. As Galt says, if the lighthouse fails or collapses, regardless of what caused it, the Fort Islanders will get the blame."

Crombie swallowed hard, as if trying to keep his stomach in place. "Yes, we will, Doctor Catt. You're dead right there."

Fisher's face looked gaunt and serious in the firelight. "Our investigations went deeper still. Without going into our full workings with the Phial of Prediction, Malach's Shattered Ruby or the Cards of Telling, we learned that your tower *must* be created, and it must be protected in order to protect Fort Isle itself. Constructed and warded correctly, it will be empowered to repel the Arvennir – no offence, Galt – so that they can neither crash their ships on your rocks, nor ever invade and conquer you."

Crombie was speechless, while Galt sat up even straighter. "No offence taken, Fishy. I want full protection for Fort Isle as much as they do. I've no desire to see my own people grab this small island, just because they can. What must we do?"

Fisher patted the satchel at the side of his chair. "We've brought some essentials with us. Five light-sacs from the Eternal Glow-worms of western Spiria – a million times more effective than lighting one hundred candles every evening, or whatever your old keeper does. The specially-crafted glass sphere to hold them, a selection of crystal points to control their position and timing. All sorts."

"None of which Embran would allow," said Galt.

Catt grinned. Even Fisher broke a smile. "Hence we'll be working in secret."

"Oh, and I have some warding amulets," Galt said in a sharp whisper. "One is Imrath's Rose Quartz of Silence – casts a shield round us, so no one outside can hear anything. And a mirror of power. It's believed to be from the stash of Torquil the Majestic – folds down almost to nothing, but opened out, it's something to behold." She described its size with outspread arms.

"How the devil did you get your hands on those?" said Catt, sitting up straight.

"Don't be envious, Catty," she replied. "You can't possess every single artefact in the world, you know."

"Hmph. Doesn't stop a man trying, though."

"They're spoils of war that Angalah, my mother, passed to me. After she died in battle, the navy sent them directly to me, which Father didn't know. Unfortunately, he found out and went mad. He confiscated some of my relics, damn him, but not everything; I'd hidden things in different places, so at least I saved the rose quartz and the mirror and some crystals." She paused; Catt suspected a brief struggle with tears. "She left a letter, too, warning me that some were extremely dangerous and not to mess with them until I'd learned about them. So I've never quite known how to use them, until now."

"This is wonderful," said Fisher. "A spelled mirror is *precisely* what we need to boost the glow-worm sacs. Parabolic?"

"Exactly, albeit with little hinges so fine you can barely see them when it's fully open."

"Perfect. Your lighthouse will be legendary."

"Why are you doing this for us?" said Crombie.

"We're not," Fisher said aridly. "It's to help Galt. And to take almighty vengeance on her father, Commander Embran."

Crombie looked at Galt. Her expression didn't change, but she mouthed, *Tell you later.*

"What's that little red blob on the map?" Crombie asked.

"A symbol," Fisher tapped the map with a hard fingernail. "Catty, lend him your glasses."

Catt fished in the satchel, brought out umpteen pairs of goggles as ugly as fish eyes, and handed him a pair. "These should do. You won't decipher it. Even I couldn't tell what it was, first time I looked. How dare someone concoct a symbol I don't recognise? The nerve!"

Crombie squinted, his nose nearly touching the map. "All I see is a tiny red smudge, with some vague lines curving through it."

Fisher's mouth went flat in a meaningful smile. "It's a secret symbol of the Guardians. It indicates a portal."

"To… Umberanaetheon?" Galt looked pale but interested.

"See, Fishy, another lucky guess!"

"Not at all. A considered answer," said Fisher.

"Oh really?" Catt raised his palms at Galt and Crombie. "When I came out with the answer, Fishy said it was a lucky guess and called me an old fraud! See what I have to put up with?"

"That's nothing to what I have to put up with," Fisher retorted. "I showed Catt this map to prove that locating the Moth of Umberanaetheon would be impossible and a completely fruitless, possibly fatal quest. And yet, somehow the sly old devil talked me into it."

"You are a pushover, Fishy," Galt said with a smile.

"He always gets his own way," said Fisher.

"Ha. Only because he *wants* to be talked into it!"

"How are we going to get there, if it's impossible?" Crombie sounded too panicked to join in the teasing. "Going through a portal? That doesn't sound safe. That sounds absolutely terrifying and insane."

"That's why it's fun," Catt said, bubbling with glee. "Lad, we eat terrifying and insane for breakfast!"

# SIX

NIGHTFALL FOUND THE four of them walking up from the town to the new lighthouse. Fisher wanted to take a look, he said. There were Arvennir guards, of course, and light and noise from the workers' accommodation, but the two doctors had contrived to shroud all four of them. Crombie found the shrouding an odd experience. He couldn't believe he was actually invisible, yet he couldn't quite see properly, either. They walked in a gauzy mist.

Catt, Fisher and Galt climbed stairs and ladders to the very top, while Crombie waited at the base, keeping a lookout. There were unseen pressures moving around in the darkness, brushing past him, pushing at him as if to see what he was, moving on then returning. They were soft and blunt and mindless as sheep, yet not benign. He stood trembling violently in the darkness, wondering if he'd ever see his companions again. Wondering if he'd live to see daylight.

Then footsteps, a gentle bustle of people descending. "I know the smell of power," said Fisher's voice. "There's an unnatural force around, but I don't recognise it. Catty?"

"It feels like... a muddle. A number of energies without a purpose. Not Kinslayer-level evil, but nothing beneficent, either. I don't like it, Fishy."

"Directional," said Crombie. His teeth were chattering so much he could hardly speak. "It's coming from the south. I

189

think. I've felt it before, thought it was just the wind."

"Strong enough to push Jorgan off the tower?" said Galt.

"Oh, certainly," Catt answered.

Fisher shrouded them again as Galt hurried them outside. The wind was cold and threw blasts of rain in their faces, but Crombie was sweating.

"And what's to the south?"

"Um." He paused, struggling to breathe. He felt like the world's greatest traitor. He couldn't answer, but he had to. "The old lighthouse. Where Viktor went with Paulian."

"Ohh," said Galt. "I should have guessed. Right before our eyes – my father was so intent on accusing the only magus, Paulian, we didn't even consider that Viktor might be responsible."

"For what?" Catt sounded out of breath as the ground grew rougher. A lamp lit up on Fisher's staff, so they could find their way across the rugged path.

"No, this is unthinkable," said Crombie. "I – I suspected Viktor as soon as he took Paulian away. But then I thought no, Viktor wouldn't do this. He's no sorcerer."

"That we know of," said Galt.

"He's worked on Fort Isle all his life. He wouldn't do anything to hurt us. But…"

"But you said he was furious when Orendion first announced the new lighthouse," said Galt. "And why wouldn't he be? Offered a job, he took it as an insult."

"Someone, enlighten me?" said Catt.

Fisher had caught on. "Viktor has lost his life's purpose, Catty. His lighthouse has been tossed on the rubbish heap. And so has he."

"But I still don't think he'd attack the new tower." Crombie was almost in physical pain with guilt. "He's not like that. And like you said, he's no sorcerer. I've never seen him anywhere near the site. Have you, Galt?"

"No. You don't want him to be the culprit, Crombie, and I

understand that – yet your suspicions went straight to him."

"Well, let's go and have a word." Fisher's tone was incongruously light.

Half an hour later, drenched and bedraggled from rain, wind and sea-spray, they reached the shorter tower. The lantern house glowed, so Viktor was, apparently, still performing his duties. Fisher used Catty's cane to knock on the door.

Rain whirled around them as they waited. Crombie was still shaking. Catt said, "I hear footsteps."

The door, a small arch of wood, grey with age, opened a hand's width and Viktor stared out, as if looking straight through them.

"Uncloak, quickly!" Fisher whispered – he and Catt having forgotten – and the shroud dropped. Viktor, holding up a lamp with one hand, started backwards. His face was a picture of terror, glaring eyes and all. He looked dreadful.

"Someone's coming," he said.

"I know, it's us," said Fisher. "We're so sorry to have startled you, Master Dremin."

"It's me, Crombie. These are my friends; Doctor Catt and Doctor Fisher, and Mistress Galt. You know me. It's all right, there's no need to be frightened."

"May we come in?" Catt asked politely.

"What d'you want?"

"Only to talk," said Galt. "Please. We're concerned about you."

"Well, that's a turn-up. All right. I got nothing to lose. *Nothing* to lose."

A shambling figure in pale, dirty-yellow rags, he opened the door fully and let them into a simple room: stone walls, wooden floor. Circular, but for an oblong extension where there was a fire in the grate and a battered trestle table.

Paulian was sitting at the far end of the table, staring at them. Crombie noticed him, and at the same time he felt a dozen different forces assailing him; blunt, stinging, hot, cold, and a mixture of scents, foul and sweet and all peculiar. He heard Catt gasp, "Fishy! It's *flooded* in here!"

"What's he mean?" said Viktor, backing away towards the skinny mage.

"Salvage," Paulian said, so quiet Crombie barely heard him.

"That this building, your home we assume, is full of supernatural energies so strong that even Crombie here smelled them from two miles away," Fisher said. He looked around, sniffing at the air.

"Don't know what you mean." Belying his stubborn words, Viktor still looked terrified.

"We can all feel it, smell it and sense it." Galt sounded angry now. "Magical attacks upon the new lighthouse? They're emanating from here, apparently."

"It's not us!" Paulian exclaimed, standing up.

"Who, then? Tell us what's happening." Catt's voice was gentle, in a way that commanded trust. Crombie caught a sense of the two doctors' power, which they carried easily around with them like eyesight or hearing. The four went deeper into the room. Strange winds whirled and pushed around them. *So this is how magic feels,* Crombie thought. *Still no idea what it is, though.*

"Help us," Viktor said suddenly, eyes like saucers. "Help us!"

"How can we help?" asked Fisher, as if trying to calm a cornered wildcat.

"Told you, there's someone coming." He pointed, hand shaking, at a small window. "Arvennir troops."

Doctor Catt whipped a little bronze horn from the satchel and put it to his ear. "Great demons, he's right. About ten minutes' march away."

Crombie and Galt stared at each other.

"They often come, to make sure Paulian ain't run off," Viktor went on. "But never this time o' night, and never so many."

"Commander Embran's with them," said Catt. "I'd know his roar anywhere."

"*What*?" Galt's yelp of horror made everyone jump. "Viktor, we all need to get out of here. And tell us what the *hell* you've been doing!"

"Here," said Viktor. He limped-ran to the far corner where Paulian stood and pulled up a trap door. "Down there. Weren't us, I swear. I swear."

Fisher caught his arm. Crombie saw white fire, very faint, crackling from his hand. "Not if you have some plan to trick us into the cellar and lock us in there. Won't work."

"I yelled until he let me out," Paulian said. Whatever this non sequitur meant, Crombie went as cold as he'd been hot a moment ago. He felt as if the energies were fighting each other, crawling up his body beneath his clothes.

"No, no. I need yer to *see*. Before they come."

"I'll go down first, then," said Fisher. "Bear in mind I can blast this trapdoor open if you try anything. Is there a way out at the bottom?"

"Of the cellar? Yep. Out onto the rocks. It's locked, though."

"Doesn't matter," said Fisher.

Two minutes later, all six of them were down the ladder and in the small, dank cellar room. The trapdoor was shut, and Fisher had put some kind of locking charm on it. Crombie suspected Embran would simply smash his way through.

The air shook with waves, fires, dancing lights, floating waters like tiny storms. Like watching a war down the wrong end of a telescope. The pressure was overwhelming, the lights so disorientating they made Crombie's eyes throb. "I need to get out," he said, panicking.

"In a minute," Galt said, taking a firm hold on his arm.

"Fishy, look!" Catt, by contrast, sounded thrilled. "All these artefacts! Look, the Shadow Compass of Onhar! All these beautiful relics! Help me get them into the satchel, quickly!"

The centre of the damp floor was heaped with countless strange items: knives, censers, jewellery, carvings, glass bottles, skulls covered with jewels, ceremonial things Crombie couldn't even identify. Together they appeared, and felt, like a never-dying bonfire of poison.

"No," said Fisher. "Catty, restrain yourself. Don't touch anything."

"But—"

Fisher physically held him back while asking Viktor, "Where did you acquire this hoard?"

Viktor slumped. "Off the shipwreck."

"That's impossible," said Galt. "No one could get near it."

"No, it, it's true," said Paulian, looking as hangdog as Victor, his warder. "Victor swims like a fish. Literally. Can hold his breath for an age. He taught me too, when I was a child. We swam down together, many times, and brought things out. Magical salvage."

"How did you know what you'd found?" Catt sounded almost offended.

"I'm a mage!"

"Then you should know, as a mage, that relics of power need to be treated with care and respect. You can't just pile them in a jumble! It makes them… cantankerous."

"We thought… we thought they was things as could help us," said Victor. "But they drove us off. They hurt, they burn, they send you mad. That's why I threw them all down here. I put Paulian down here, like I promised, but had to fetch him out again. He's me friend. Couldn't listen to 'im screaming like that."

"Some mage," Catt muttered. "Irritate magic, it will irritate you back."

"Why would the Arvennir have a cargo of relics?" Fisher demanded of Galt.

"I don't know. The merchant who was importing them –

he must have been a sorcerer, but they say he drowned in the wreck, so no answers from him. We're notorious for coveting objects of beauty, value and power. Not unlike you and Catt, dare I say it? It's said they were destined for the King, although I dread to think what he was intending to do with them. More powers, new weapons, I expect. It's only Embran and a few others who are anti-magic."

"Maybe your father has a point," Crombie said miserably.

She added cautiously, "There were no drowned remains of... living beings, were there?"

"Like what?" asked Viktor.

"Like Yorughan. Or other races."

"No, nowt like that. Only bales of cloth, and maybe stuff that had melted, like salt."

She dropped her chin in relief and mouthed, *Thank goodness*. Crombie asked, "Why would they have Yoggs, of all things?"

"You call them 'things'," she said. "Some Arvennir orders have made an unfortunate venture into enforced labour. Don't mention it again; I'm so ashamed I could burn the King's palace down, yet I continue doing his will. I'd like to be a hero, but I'm not."

Catt had the trumpet to his ear again. "They're here," he said.

Fisher sent a silent pale beam of fire from his hand and a tiny door flew open, revealing sea and rocks outside. "You two, out," he said. "Keep into the cliffs and run. There must be caverns you can hide in."

Viktor and Paulian exchanged looks and obeyed – or made the fastest progress they could, Paulian helping the older man. They'd just made it outside when the ceiling – the floor above – thundered with the boots of a dozen Arvennir warriors.

Embran was shouting incoherently, his voice shaking the very walls. Catt cringed at the noise. "How did he know?"

"He was sending guards up here to make sure Paulian stayed

put," Galt answered quickly. "He was always suspicious. Perhaps a guard sensed the energy – it's so strong, a dumb rock would sense it. My father loathes magic, but that doesn't mean he can't sniff it out."

"What are we going to do?" said Crombie.

"This," said Fisher. He took Galt's right and Crombie's left hand, and forced their little fingers together through a gold ring. "Keep hold of that." He held a staff while Catt had his malachite cane. Then all four of them joined hands, forming a circle as best they could. "Do not let go. On my command, all take one step forward towards each other."

There was shuddering crash as Embran axed his way through the trapdoor. "Give yourselves up! We know you're down there, with your foul magics—"

A ball of burning rag was thrown down through the hatch, missing Crombie's group but starting flames at the edge of the relic heap. He heard Embran scream, "*Galt*!"

"One step forward, hold on, eyes closed," said Fisher. "*Now*!"

"We've never tried this before," Catt remarked, just as it was too late.

# SEVEN

ONE STEP TO Feltek felt like a *whoosh*, halfway between falling and fainting. Not Fisher's first experience by any means, but every transition was different and always unnerving. Catt would be fine, he knew, but Galt and Crombie? He felt they were still falling. His hearing had gone for a moment, only to be pierced by yells of panic. He opened his eyes.

No firm ground, certainly no forest. They'd dropped straight into a portal: a long chute of amber, red, and fiery-orange rock. And they were all sliding down out of control, at an approximate angle of forty-five degrees. Catt was in front, feet first, his robes up about his ears, while his bare and somewhat hairy calves were red-blotched where he'd hit the rocks a dozen times. Fisher was on his side, enduring the raw pain of stone tearing against his ribs. Heaven knew what would be left of his clothing, let alone his skin.

Above was a ribbon of sky – he hoped – that was charcoal-grey yet glowing. Both doctors still held onto their staffs, and the satchel, for dear life.

Galt was coming down head-first, her skull on Fisher's shoulder, while Crombie was part-tangled up with her and emitting an impressive roar of physical shock.

"Have they still got the Ring of Faultless Striding?" Catt shouted.

"How should I know?" Fisher was trying to remember what items were in the satchel, and what might save them from a grisly landing.

"Yes," Galt gasped.

*The Palm Stone of Balance*, Fisher thought, and reached out to it with all his senses, of which he had at least eight. Its peculiar property was to be always hot underneath and cold on top, which created constant air convection. A draught, that could be magnified to create a cushion of air.

As cushions go, it was thin and weak, but just enough to ease their fall from a violent descent to a more gentle glide. And then the flat ground rushed up and stopped them. Catt landed first with an impressive somersault and the others came tumbling down on top of him.

"Everyone off, please," Catt gasped with remarkable composure. "One at a time. Steady. That's it, carefully. Good. Good."

"Any broken bones?" Fisher drew Catty's robe back into its proper arrangement, preserving his modesty. The other two were on their feet. He saw a selection of torn fabric, scraped skin, blood, wild hair and wilder eyes. "I'm most dreadfully sorry about that."

"Started how you mean to go on?" said Galt, raising an eyebrow.

"That," said Crombie, bending over to recover his breath, "was *amazing*."

They went through the process of dusting down their clothes, sharing the water from a flask stowed in the satchel, using it to cool their bruises, and checking that everyone was intact. Behind them lay the steep scarp of fire-coloured rock, and ahead was a plain, also orange in colour but dull. And above, the ominous charcoal sky from which came a peculiar light. Enough to see by, at least.

Galt said, "I hate to ask the obvious, but where are we?"

"The realm of Umberanaetheon," Catt answered. "At least, that's the destination we calibrated for."

"There's nothing here," said Crombie. He sounded on edge. Probably the shock of entering a new realm where everything felt odd, not to mention the question of how they were going to get back.

Catt was tinkering with a round object like a small clock or a hand-sized watch; Fisher barely glimpsed it before Catt slipped it out of sight with a conjurer's dexterity. "This way," he said, pointing straight ahead with confidence. Then, "Oh, Fishy, may I lean on your arm? I feel a bit dizzy. The universe should *know* by now that I hate being thrown around, but does it care? Pah!"

"CATTY, ARE YOU seeing what I think I'm seeing?"

They'd walked for perhaps half-an-hour when they glimpsed an outcrop on the horizon. Soon it resolved into a hill with some kind of house in front of it. And further on, they saw that the house was in fact a fortress; a gigantic brown mass with a great tower on the right that sloped down to lower battlements on the left.

Fisher was confounded. As a structure, it looked all wrong for its purpose. The overall shape was hazy. Its form was curved and sloped, not straight and square and crenelated as you'd expect a fortress to be.

After another twenty steps, all doubt vanished.

There was no fortress. To be precise, the moth *was* the fortress. A vast shape, seemingly collapsed towards the left and sloping upwards to the right where a rounded, furred shape resolved into a moth head the size of a small palace. Two great curving banners unfurled from it: moth antlers.

Side-on and in silhouette, the whole titanic creature appeared brownish, but as they drew closer touches of colour appeared.

Peacock colours, and flashes of red and orange. The body was bigger than an Arvennir war vessel. The wings swept down from the thorax high above to sweep the ground, like vast drooping sails, or tent flaps.

"Halt," said Fisher. "Need a careful look before proceeding. Times like these, what I'd give to have Celest, Heno and Nedlam with us…"

"Only if you're anticipating an attack," said Galt. "It's not a dragon. Just… bigger. But furrier."

"I've never liked moths," said Crombie. "Don't know why. It's the way they go round your head, making that whirring noise… rather see a dragon any day. But we're not planning to hurt it, are we?"

"You've such a kind heart," said Galt. "We need to get in close, get the scales, and run. Focus on that."

"There's no way that thing could take off… is there?"

"And whirr round your head?" Catt said with a grin. "Great dragon's teeth, I can't believe it's real. The mythical Moth of Umberanaetheon!" Catt lifted a short double tube to his eyes. "Binocular telescopes," he explained. "Well, I never. Fishy, could you extract my notebook from my inside pocket? Please write down, 'Note to self: Contact author re updates to revised edition, *Encyclopaedia of the Natural and Unnatural Worlds*'. Oh, and take a sketch."

Note-taking done, Fisher reached into the satchel and brought out a crystal orb held in a silver casing. "Instant sketch," he said aside to Galt. "Orb of Trapped Light."

"How does it work?"

"Aim at the desired object and push this tiny switch across – apart from that, I have no idea. That's the trouble with magical items – we know they work but we don't know *how* they work. Energies sneaking through from another dimension – that's one theory. Magic is just a word for *what we don't know yet*."

"Fishy, stop talking so much!" said Catt.

"And *that's* a debate for another day," Fisher retorted.

"Are you sure it's real?" said Crombie. He looked rigid with nerves, but Fisher admired him for not fleeing. Someone who could be terrified yet not run away – that was a person of courage.

"Why?" said Galt.

"Well, it's not moving. It might be asleep. Or dead."

"Or made of sailcloth over a huge pile of rocks," said Fisher.

"Why would anyone do that?"

"Why does anyone do anything? Moth sculpture festival? Or to scare intruders like us away. Or they wanted to live in a moth-shaped tent. I don't know."

"Moths do this," said Catt. "Stay in one place, waiting for a mate to find them."

Galt pulled a face. "I surely hope this one's mate doesn't show up."

"It's a little-known fact that the Kinslayer was terrified of moths," said Fisher.

"Was he?" choked Crombie.

"No, of course he wasn't! That we know of. You're so gullible, dear fellow."

"I hate to be the bearer of bad news," Catt said gently, "but it's real, indeed. The anthers are moving. I could pick out the individual scales. You can see it breathing, or whatever it is that moths do. Spiracles."

"What's going on at the tail end?"

"I have no idea. It's resting on some peculiar flora, I think. Galt, look."

She took the binoculars and gasped. Shortly after, Fisher discovered why: the 'fortress' was transformed to a creature of heart-stopping beauty. Such intricate patterns; green and black swirling along the edges of its wings. Peacock stripes spreading between the shoulder and wing tip, curving tighter and tighter until they framed circles within circles – bronze, red, purple, orange, and at the very centre, the pupil of the eye, red again. The patterns moved constantly with the light, mesmerising. Every detail was sharp; the fur on the body and the scales were made up of fine strands of a hard substance, hard, yet soft and furry – feathery in an unexpected way.

Catt had said that moths had no defences, except the thick fur and scales that made them so unpleasant for predators to swallow. Beautiful, unearthly creature from head to wings, and along the fire red thorax, but then where the abdomen should have ended, a horror. Four great, thick, snake-like tentacles splayed out. The moth wasn't resting on them; they were part of its body.

They writhed like huge serpents, each covered in a forest of long spikes.

Fisher cleared his throat and she quickly handed him the binoculars. "Its back end. Look," she muttered.

"Good heavens, Catty. Have another glance. Those serpent things are attached."

Catty did as he said, looked for two seconds, and threw the binoculars back to him. He actually screamed. "*Gaaah*! I can't stand snakes! You know that, Fishy! You're not getting me anywhere near that damned thing!"

The taller man hugged his friend. "Sorry, dear fellow. Didn't mean to scare you. But they're not actually snakes. Just some kind of... tentacles. All right?"

"I'm no fan of tentacles, either."

Galt said, "I thought tentacles were all in a day's work for you two. Come on."

Thus she somehow took charge of the mission. The Great Moth loomed over them as they went closer, Galt in the lead with Crombie at her shoulder, the doctors following. "Crombie and I will get the scales while you two work out how we're going to get home. All right? Fishy, hand me the storage case out of your satchel."

He handed her the entire satchel, which weighed surprisingly little.

"How are we going to get up to its wing?" Crombie asked.

"You can climb, can't you? You'll go up onto the right-hand wing – I think we'll have to duck underneath its body to avoid the tentacles – and I'll be on the leg so I can take the scales from you without damaging the moth. *Do not hurt the moth*, under any circumstances."

"What if it tries to kill us?" said Crombie, almost treading on her heels.

"It won't," she said, hoping she was right.

"Those things might, however," said Fisher behind her.

A swarm of pale beige creatures was coming to meet them – insect-like with long bodies and lots of long, spindly, jointed legs. Their upper halves were raised up, pincers held like forearms. Their abdomens curved up also, like scorpion tails. They made a rustling, pattering noise as they rushed over the hard ground.

Next to the moth, they were tiny: each, however, was still the size of a small house. Against the charcoal sky they had an unearthly yellowish luminosity.

"Wait wait wait." Galt stopped and stuck her arms out to halt her companions, only to realise they'd already halted several steps behind her. She could hear curses and indrawn breaths. "Doctor Fisher, advice please!"

"Run like hell," said Catt.

"No, we have weapons. Protective staves. Shrouds up," said Fisher.

The swarm kept coming. The doctors formed up alongside Galt and Crombie, staves at the ready. All Crombie had was a butchering knife from the inn's kitchen; Galt had nothing except the satchel and no time to rummage inside it. But he held up his knife, the blade shaking, ready to protect her.

"I don't think the shroud's working," he said. "They're still looking at us."

One of the swarm, twice the height of the others, emerged and pattered to within three steps of Galt. The body was something between insect and dried frog. A skeletal frame, poised on four legs while the powerful front pair was held up, edged with saw-teeth and thorns, like weaponised arms. The whole creature was held together with folds and webs of dried parchment; translucent, yet impenetrable. The head was triangular in shape but the face was humanoid, like that of a very old woman, lined and tanned brown with immense age. Five eyes, red and glaring; the outside two enormous faceted domes, the centre three small, like holes full of fire. Her terrible jaws were half-open, lined with rows and rows of sharp edges and snapping mandibles on either side. Not quite the size of a dragon, but certainly of a height with Viktor's lighthouse.

She looked less than pleased to see them.

Her triangular head rotated as if to give the gigantic eye-domes the best angle of view. Galt thought she saw ten thousand reflections of herself. The great forelimbs twitched. Now Galt was trembling as much as Crombie. A moment from being lifted by those saw-edged forelimbs and her head bitten off between the mandibles.

"It's the Queen," said Catt.

"Queen Mantid." Fisher was icily calm. "Whatever she does, the others will follow. So, the Great Moth has a bodyguard."

"A very angry bodyguard," said Galt. "Is it worth trying diplomacy, before she eats us?"

"If only we'd thought to bring an offering," said Fisher. "An enormous, juicy fly."

Catt stepped forward slightly and bowed. "Your Majesty, Queen of this realm, we intend no harm. We came to admire the Great Moth of legend. We humbly request a few scales from its illustrious wing. Would you allow us?"

In response, the Queen Mantid reared back and lunged at Catt. She made a terrible sound as she came, chittering and creaking – a language they couldn't understand. The others massed behind her, rustling horribly as only dry dead things could.

Two sounds came out of her that resembled human speech. "*Protect. Skitterae.*"

Fisher shoved Catt out of the way and took his place, swinging his staff. A ball of fire flew at her and she swerved out of its path, as – Galt thought – he had intended. She'd never seen such rage in the eyes of such an alien, malevolent being before. Even Embran could not have competed – and she even half-wished he was here now. That depthless malevolence burned all hope out of her.

"You two," Fisher whispered. "Back away. Circle around and run straight to the moth. Catt and I will distract these… pests."

"Seriously?" Crombie whispered, but if Catt was still afraid, he didn't show it. He and Fisher closed up together, hurling light and fire from their staves. The Queen and her swarm turned towards them, as if drawn by the light and heat. The two warrior-apothecary-mages backed away: Queen Mantid followed, raging.

Galt and Crombie ran.

CROMBIE TOOK HIS direction from Galt, who was heading to the right, circumventing the mass of mantids. They ran, keeping low. The odd light made it hard to see, but he couldn't feel the shroud any more. Couldn't the doctors have given them *any* magical protection?

"Anything in the satchel?" he said between gasps.

"No idea. Can't run and look for power relics at the same time."

Then they reached the moth. It towered over them; anthers

waving gently at the head end, wings cloaking it from thorax to ground, lethal tails writhing at the back. Curving behind it was a low, crescent-shaped hill, covered in rough vegetation. A long proboscis curled and uncurled from its mouth parts.

"We can't risk going under the head," he said. "We'll get strangled and eaten. You sure *this* isn't the right side?"

"I assume the books meant *its* right, not us looking at it head on." Galt went straight to the edge of its wing and lifted it up like a stage curtain. "Get under there, go between its legs!"

They crept through together between the first and second pair of legs, though there was plenty of head height. The smell down there was terrible, as if a million animals had excreted and died. The moth did not move. On the far side was the small curved hill that contained it. Actual grass and ferns grew here among the rocks. And now the wings hid them – as long as Catt and Fisher kept the mantids busy.

Crombie gasped for fresh air. The wings on this side were an almost perfect mirror of the left. He looked upwards at the huge furry head, and along the wing edge for the curving spiral that enclosed the wing-eye.

"Let's get on with it," Galt said, overtaking him. "Quick, before the bugs come looking for us. They might not be as dumb as they look."

She knelt down, delving into the satchel and bringing out the carry-case Fisher had made; stiffened leather, divided into narrow compartments by strong yet silk-soft fabric. "Get on with it!" she repeated.

On this side, it carried its wings several feet off the ground. Unable to reach, Crombie began to climb its sturdy rearmost leg. He had to cling on each time it twitched, trying to throw him off, but there was plenty of rough fur to help him. He kept eyeing those horrific, undulating tentacles. They were a good distance away, but would easily reach him if the moth decided to start lashing them around. He reached the wing-edge and hauled himself up onto it. The slope and the rough-soft scales under his hands and knees were the strangest thing he'd ever experienced. Green-black patterns and swirls of red and bronze, so close up, made his eyes whirl.

"The eye," hissed Galt. "The red peacock marking. There. Pluck the scales from the very centre."

"This isn't the upper wing," he said, trying to catch his breath. "It's the lower."

"No it isn't! It's the way they're folded! Upper on top of lower, both pointing down to the... the tail. Tails."

He crawled down backwards, ever closer to the eye – closer to the tentacles, tails, whatever the hell they were. Venomous? He might not know until it was too late. Every time the tentacles writhed, they released that vile scent – a cross between musk and the urine of a thousand elephants. He kept going, trying not to choke or throw up.

"Go for the centre of the eye. The smallest circle, where it's red."

*Yes, I've got the message,* he thought, teeth clenched. He was nearly there. Dangerously close to the thick tails, which whipped around blindly as if trying to knock him off. He clung to handfuls of scales – they felt like tough silk – and a few came loose. *Why can't I just take these and jump off?* he wondered. But Galt kept urging him on.

Then he found his hand stretching and reaching the red centre. "Keep steady. Pull them out gently."

Hands cramping with effort, he reached in and pulled out the first wing scale. It stuck a bit, as if it needed to be unhooked. Then it came loose; and it was, as Catt had said, as big as a serving dish. "Sorry, moth," he whispered. "Hope this doesn't hurt."

"To me!" Galt, on the ground below him, stretched up but couldn't quite reach. She climbed a short way up the rear leg. Then he dropped the scale, but the air took it like a leaf and it caught on the wing edge. A spiky tendril whipped around to dislodge it – and he saw it float down, undamaged, into Galt's outstretched hands.

"They're just scent glands," she called.

"You think?"

"Just keep going. Next," she said, and their second attempt was better; straight from his hands to hers without wind or scent-spikes intervening. "Are you counting? One. Two. Three…"

Each scale he passed down, Galt packed with extreme delicacy between thick folded paper, then slid each folder into its own individual section of the protective case.

Crombie was growing strangely fond of the moth, despite its wicked pheromone stench. It was so placid, so furry. He kept talking softly to it as they worked. He felt its slow thoughts touch his. *Pain. Can't move. Help?*

*"Sorry,"* he thought back. *"Nearly finished. Sorry I made your wing sore, but we thank you for this…"*

*Not wing. Leg.*

And as he dropped the final scale, he noticed what was causing the pain.

"Eight," said Galt. "All undamaged. Less fragile than they look. Great work." She was slipping the last one into the case and fastening the buckles, but he was looking at something else.

The moth was tethered, from a cuff around the top of its middle leg to a metal ring in a rock, by a thick green rope. The tether horrified him.

"Come on, we're done, get down!"

Crombie ignored her. He was clambering up the wing edge towards that middle leg, his butcher knife clenched between his teeth.

THE QUEEN MANTID was not a quitter. Fisher drove her back and back with all the fire he had – and he truly didn't want to harm her, just keep her at bay while Galt and Crombie worked – but she didn't seem to care. She hissed and reared, swinging her forelimbs like clubs. Endlessly trying to stab him with that tail sting. She spat, and her venom hit his cheek, burning. Even worse, itching. He tried to rub the itch with the back of his hand, but that made him vulnerable to her vicious strikes.

Catt, meanwhile, was swinging his own staff of fire at her minions. They were easier to drive back, it seemed, but they just wouldn't give up. Each time he cleared a half-circle, they'd crowd forward again, and away from his violet flame, and back in, on and on like a pendulum. Every time Fishy glanced over at Catt – who at least had separated the swarm from their Queen, and away from the moth itself – he looked more exhausted. His posture was growing worse, his swings slower.

The truth was, Catt was not a young man. Nor was Fisher. Even with magical aid, how long could they keep up this sort of thing? How he longed for the battle power of Celest and Heno and Nedlam – she and her merciless war hammer! – to do the dirty work while he and Catt scuttled around picking up the spoils in their wake. This, *this* was all wrong.

If Catt died, he would never forgive himself.

*One day our hubris will kill us*, he thought. He tried again to calm that painful itch with the back of his hand, and the Queen Mantid seized the chance to wrench the staff off him. Next he knew, her grasping forelimbs were carrying him up towards her jaws. The saw-teeth and thorns held him firm, sticking right through his clothes into his flesh. Pain paralysed him.

From an alarming height he could see Catty below, fighting on.

And Fisher had one advantage that his dear friend lacked. He reached into himself and turned inside out – that was how it felt – a wrenching shape-change into a wolf-monster that was a complete horror of vast jaws, fangs and claws and a deafening battle roar.

He bit the Queen Mantid in the face. She dropped him. As he went down, his claws raked down the hard casing of her neck and thorax.

Fisher was two personalities in one body, or one person with two shapes – he never quite knew. He liked being the grouchy old apothecary who kept his beloved Catt safe, even though Catt was convinced it worked the other way round. Much as he resented all the chores that his friend could easily have done himself – even down to darning Catt's socks – he still did them. Making him a beautiful new hat for no reason was pleasing, in a perverse way. Fisher quietly saved their skins and let Catt take the credit, all the time, because he preferred to divert attention away from himself. This was who he really was: a Cheriveni scholar (lawyer – doctor – butler?) called Fisher who ran a little shop. But who he *really* was couldn't be denied. A Guardian named Fury, a warrior. All the Guardians, alive or gone, had their unique features, and Fury's was the ability to rip monsters in half without trying too hard.

He'd defeated mad Guardians and pit-bred horrors a thousand times more savage than a mantid.

"Stop!" he panted, crouching on the ground in front of her. "I don't want to kill you, but I will if you don't stop fighting us. Call off your swarm – hive – troops."

The mantid backed away, chittering at him. A few seconds later, he heard the rustling of mantodean feet approaching their Queen, and Catty calling for him from another direction.

"Fishy? Where are you?"

By the time the two found each other, Fury had pulled himself back into his humanoid form and drawn his torn clothes around himself as best he could. Catt hadn't seen him transform this time. For all his faults, Catt was a sensitive soul. He couldn't cope with the existence of Fury. So Fisher had spent many years protecting him from the savage reality as best he could, and would for many years more.

\* \* \*

CROMBIE FINISHED SAWING through the rope, then managed to sever the thick leather cuff and let it drop to the ground. As he did so, the moth stirred. It took a few steps forward that shook him like a bumpy cart, then opened its wings. He made a grab for the furry pelt of its thorax and clung on with both hands, but his body was still lying mostly on its upper wing. Sudden colossal wingbeats threw him up and down so violently that he thought his spine would break.

The Great Moth took off, fluttering upwards. For a few seconds Crombie was airborne, dizzy, disorientated: glimpsing the ground dropping away and feeling a micro-second of flight exhilaration. The orange plain, the charcoal sky with its odd black light, and scores of giant luminous insects below – the sight burned itself into his memory, ready to star in his nightmares forever more.

Then panic set in. That was a hell of a distance to fall and growing greater by the moment. And he couldn't hang on. His arms hurt, every sinew stretching like wire. He couldn't feel his hands. The moth banked steeply, and the dip of its great wings flung him towards the ground. He landed with a hellish impact on a bush that eased his fall, only to bounce him off onto hard earth. The second landing thrust out all his breath and made his bones shudder with pain.

"Crom! Anything broken?" cried Galt, kneeling over him.

"Everything, I think."

Stones, soil and grass rose in the downdraft made by the moth. It lifted their hair and nearly carried off the satchel. Galt ducked on top of Crombie. Looking skywards over her shoulder, he saw the mighty wings filling the sky, the enormous furry body rising, big as a dragon if not more so, the legs dangling. The whirr of the moth's flight was deafening. The world was a tornado of chaos. He heard people shouting, but it was just another noise.

The whirlwind eased as the creature gained height and curved away across the sky. Its wingspan flashed with iridescence against the darkness, green and red and bronze, majestic. Dwindling in size.

Gone.

Crombie managed to get back onto his feet as Catt and Fisher came bustling towards him and Galt. They both looked done for, but the creepy pale insects kept their distance, running around on top of the crescent hill.

The Queen Mantid was slithering downhill towards the humans, her forelimbs raised but flapping as if fractured in multiple places. She was limping. An ooze of green blood ran down her keratin face and down her front. She looked so desiccated, Crombie was amazed to see she had any blood in her. She stopped to point at something in the hillside and began screeching, her voice like a rusty hinge.

Then all Crombie could see was Doctor Fisher bending over him as Galt rocked back to squat on her heels. "Is he all right?"

"I think so," she said. "Crombie? Can you move all your limbs?"

"Um, yeah. Think so."

Fisher tested his pulse and felt along his limbs. "See if you can roll onto your side. Take it slowly – that's it. Just rest for a few minutes. Lad, you are going to be all shades of black, blue and purple tomorrow."

"Better than dead," said Galt. She stroked his hair. A pleasant, warm sadness went through him. "The doctors have medicine to help you." A small green bottle approached his lips. Obediently he sipped from it, then Fisher stoppered it and slipped it back into the Endless Satchel where, no doubt, it had its own place away from the precious wing scales.

"That was a prodigious fall," said Catt. "What's Her Majesty pointing at?"

The doctors and Galt rose to look. "Catty!" said Fisher. "What the actual...? Is that what it looks like?"

Crombie's curiosity won over pain. He got up onto his hands and knees then found his feet, dizzy. Galt held his elbow. He saw an opening part-way down the right-hand crescent arm of the hillside. Not so much a cave as a hole in the world; a round tunnel that distorted light. It contained holes within holes within holes, and each one seemed to be a bubble or a lens revealing a great bustling space, full of wings and antennae, insectoid legs and segmented bodies. Huge bugs shining like jet, others fat, spindly, web-covered, nursing fuzzy nests of eggs ... an alien realm. The green medicine made him feel odd. To his perception, the bugs were of normal size, while on this side, he and his companions had shrunk to the size of dust grains.

"It looks like a portal," said Catt. "Smells like one, too."

The Queen Mantid came down towards them, less menacing with a bad limp. She scraped out some humanish words, hard to understand. Catt listened keenly and translated. "She says it's a portal to Skettera. And that we're fools. Also, '*What have you done, what have you done?*' quite a lot."

"What's Skettera?" asked Crombie.

"That place." Catt waved vaguely at the hole. "She says that whoever let the moth free is ... an idiot of the highest order. Did we not realise that the moth was protecting the entrance?"

"Clearly not," said Fisher. "Protecting or blocking it?"

The Queen was practically dancing with rage in front of them, dipping and waving like an insect-phobic's nightmare of a mantis performing its courtship routine.

"She says both," said Catt. "Oh dear. To protect the Sketterae from other races, and to protect us from them."

"You couldn't find a better way than using a live creature?" said Crombie. "I know it's only an insect but... they're still living things. Tying it down was just cruel."

"*Not business of yours*," said the Queen, clearly enough for all to understand. "*Change a thing you not understand. Foolish. Was only way.*"

"She says the moth was the only way to safeguard…"

"We all got that, Catty," said Fisher. "Apparently we've done something dreadful."

"I had to," Crombie protested. "It was cruel to keep it tethered up like that!"

"You – ridiculous," the Mantid hissed at him. "It not care. No brain, not care."

"It asked me to free it!"

"You regret this, you boy. Have *no idea*."

"I'm not apologising!"

"We were all responsible," Fisher said in an exasperated tone.

Crombie watched the portal. It looked infinite in there, like an enormous cave without walls. Each cell overlapping every other cell. A universe-sized hive of bustling, crawling creatures with too many legs, too many eyes, too many joints, more than any living creature should possess. Crombie wondered if the Sketterae even had an interest in leaving their own realm. Why would they?

"We're terribly sorry," said Catt. "Look, we'll help you block it up with rocks. We have some small enchantments with us that will help. Then we'll be gone."

The Queen Mantid scowled at them as if she were still capable of biting all their heads off. She angled her triangular face to glare at Fisher. "Demigod set us, ward Moth that wards Sketterae. We fail. Wardens no longer, we. You, Guardian, understand?"

She went still and silent then. Crombie wondered if she'd died.

"Let's get out of here," said Fisher, shouldering the satchel and lifting one of his several staves.

"Best idea you've had all day," said Catt.

They went back the way they'd come; not quickly as they would have liked, as Crombie could barely walk.

"How are we going to get back up that chasm?" said Galt. "Will the first method work again? We might end up anywhere."

"This." With a flourish, Catt produced the odd-looking small clock again. "The Shadow Compass of Onhar from Viktor's lighthouse."

"Oh, Catty, *really*," Fisher groaned.

"I'll adjust it to find the direction of Fort Isle and then – just trust me, for once."

# EIGHT

"I *TOLD YOU* not to take anything from that stash," said Fisher as they trudged over a field full of Fort Isle sheep.

"It worked, didn't it?"

"You all right, Crom?" Galt asked anxiously.

"I fell off a moth," he said, and started giggling.

"We need to get him home, but where are you two going to stay?"

The doctors looked at each other and shrugged. "Did we pack the Bounteous Domicile?" said Catt. "Oh Fishy!"

"Why is it always my job to remember these things? Perhaps we could shroud up inside the inn, if there's a spare room. The last thing we need is Embran seeing us, at least before the project is finished."

As they neared the town, a scrawny figure in the robes of a mage came to meet them. Reaching them, Paulian stood there with tears running down his cheeks and no words coming out. All, even medicated Crombie, took turns trying to comfort him. Finally he managed to speak.

"The old lighthouse burned to the ground. Me and Viktor, we stood on the rocks below and watched. Then Viktor just... walked away. Said nothing. Walked off the rocks and into the sea. I tried to go after him but..."

"He didn't want you to," said Crombie.

"They pulled his body out the next day."

"Paulian, I'm so sorry," said Galt, hugging the skinny mage. "This was Embran's doing. He set fire to the cellar, just after you escaped."

"Barbarian," Catt said under his breath. Fisher turned and glared at him. Crombie had no idea what the look meant, but later he found out: as much as he loved his old friend, sometimes Fisher silenced Catt as a precaution, in case he was mourning the delicious trove of lost relics rather more than he was mourning Viktor.

"Come to the Inn with us," said Crombie. "You shouldn't be on your own."

"Where have you been?" Paulian asked. "I couldn't find you for two, three days."

"Weirdest place," Crombie began. "I did something terrible—"

"NO he didn't." Fisher spoke over him. "Just searching for something useful, which we found. All is well."

"I wish that were true," said Galt. "There is still the big question of how we're going to complete the lighthouse to *our* requirements, while Embran's around. Ideas, anyone?"

CATT AND FISHER always had an idea, of course. It was their stock in trade.

Lennion's Skiver was a potion to give anyone a harmless yet completely debilitating fever for a few days. Side-effects (reported by one client in ten) included a throbbing headache and stomach cramps, dry mouth, rash or hallucinations. The perfect solution for those who wished to take a few days off work while not actually sick – not seriously, at least. Thus, during the crucial phase in which the lantern house was built and roofed, Embran was forced to take to his bed while Galt stepped in as Chief Project Officer.

She deployed as few workers as possible to complete the

build. Just those who worked well and asked no questions about changes to the plan. Also Catt and Fisher, both shrouded; and Crombie, who proved remarkably dextrous and resourceful. She put up the Rose Quartz of Silence to thwart potential spies. And she set Captain Jennvi to keep a lookout.

"I heard Embran is quite poorly," Captain Jennvi said into Galt's ear while they were taking a brief break. "How is my beloved brother-in-law?"

"Not well at all," said Galt, trying not to smile. "But he will be perfectly fine in a few days."

"What are you up to?"

"Nothing, Auntie Jenn. Just finishing the build in the optimum way, rather than letting Embran make an unholy mess of it. Not a word to him, all right?"

"Goes without saying. You're just like your mother, Galt," said Jennvi. "Recklessly brave. A rogue. But a good rogue."

"Would you tell me something about her? Yes, I know you've already told me a lot," she added, as Jennvi frowned. "Something in particular. About my father too. Later. I need to know why he…"

At that moment, Crombie came past hefting an armful of timber. "D'you want this on the top floor, Miss Galt?"

"Yes, but get someone who hasn't nearly broken all his bones to carry it!"

"I can manage!" he insisted, striding manfully up the stairs.

As he went, Jennvi smiled. "That boy has *such* a crush on you."

"What? Don't be ridiculous!"

"You're telling me you haven't noticed?"

"That's absurd. He's like my little brother! The brother I never had – so that makes me his big sister." She felt her face heating. "You really are the worst aunt in the world."

Jennvi only went on smiling, shaking her head.

\* \* \*

"WE HAVE VARIOUS ways of producing light without heat," Catt had explained. "The globes in the antiques emporium belonging to our dear friends – they were made with simple charms of an evanescent luminosity, a soft magic. But the living Sacs of Spiria are extremely powerful. Old magic from the demigods' time. They're not to be treated casually."

Fisher added, "Catt and I will place them *just so* to provide the best illumination."

"Optimal, unending illumination," Catt added gleefully.

Now the lantern housing itself was finished after days of work, the moment of truth was here. Glaziers, metal-workers and other craftspeople had been dismissed. All was sorcery (and some clockwork) from here on. Fisher and Catt raised a charmed glass sphere – created by a relic of Making – to float in the centre of the space. "Keep back now," said Fisher. "Don't touch anything."

"By all means, we're leaving this part to you." Galt, Crombie and Paulian stood back, watching as the two mages carefully positioned the fist-sized sacs to float inside the glass sphere. Galt couldn't see how they went in, but they seemed to slip easily through the sphere as if it were a soap bubble. Then various crystals of power were positioned in a circle to calibrate everything.

The landward side of the lantern house was blanked out with metal panels; the light would pour through the storm glass on the seaward side. Finally, when the doctors gave the word, Galt unfolded and positioned her mother's mirror against the blank wall: a remarkable parabola of lenses that sat behind the sphere, multiplying and reflecting the glow outwards like a beam from a white sun.

The most delicate and secret part of the project, prior to this, had been placing the eight sections of the domed roof under cover of dusk. Catt and Fisher had spelled each moth wing scale to strengthen it, then each one was carefully sandwiched between the outer and inner layers of the roof sections; shingles and underfelt, trusses, sheep's wool for insulation, curved inner panels made to the perfect fit by a master carpenter. But the last step – inserting the moth scales behind the panelling – had to be done by Catt and Fisher, with only Galt and Crombie to secure each panel to the ceiling ribs when they gave the word.

Galt had held her breath so hard, willing the scales not to tear, that when the last one went in safely she nearly fell over from dizziness.

One last mechanism had gone in just before the sphere and mirror: a half-cylinder of black metal that moved on small wheels around the lantern room, fitting just inside the walls on a track. This occulting shade was designed by Galt to rotate at variable speeds, operated by a clockwork mechanism on the floor below. Closed, it blacked out the light; open, it would allow the light to shine and flash messages clear across the ocean.

"It's DONE," SHE told her father the next day. He lay propped up on pillows, looking ungroomed and extremely grouchy. She saw a glimpse of a copper chain around his neck before he pulled his nightshirt collar up to his beard.

"Hmph," he responded. "I'll be glad to get out of this damned bed so I can take a look for myself. I'd hate to have to demolish and rebuild what's been done in my absence."

"You'll be impressed, I promise. You trust me, don't you?"

"Indeed. Trust myself more, that's all. I shall be inspecting your work as soon as possible."

"No, you won't. You'll wait on the ground with everyone else for the grand unveiling."

"The devil I will."

She put her hand to his forehead. "I think your fever's going down, Papa. Drink this."

There was no Lennion's Skiver in the mug of hot herbal tea she gave him; she could afford to let him get better now. He pulled a face but drank it anyway. When he'd swallowed about half, she asked calmly, "What were you doing in the old lighthouse that time?"

"What? What the devil were *you* doing there?"

"Trying to stop the magical attacks on our work crew."

"As was I," Embran growled.

"Did you know that Viktor is dead?"

"Who?"

"Viktor Dremin, the lighthouse keeper. He threw himself into the sea because you burned his life and home to the ground."

"Serves the devil right. He'd hoarded items of evil power to attack *us*!"

"Not on purpose. Those relics were salvaged from the *Pride of Arven*. Intended for our King, so I understand. Viktor couldn't control them and neither, I suspect, could the Arvennir sorcerer who had charge of them. They were probably what drove the ship onto the rocks in the first place."

"All this does is seal my belief that all things of magic are evil! What is your point, Galt? Are you trying to twist me to some other point of view? Ever your mother's daughter. You suggest that this entire unfortunate episode is the fault of Arven? You're verging on treason!"

"The whole island knows what happened. We told Governor Gredlen, and he told everyone. I'd never seen General Orendion shame-faced before. He will want to question you; let's hope that both you and I don't lose our jobs."

"*What*? Why? What have I done wrong?"

"How do you think the King will react when he finds that his precious cargo was deliberately destroyed by *you*, a trusted commander?"

"I'd say he should be grateful that I saved him from unimaginable harm!"

"But he won't be. My point, Father, is that you set fire to Royal Arven property, relics you didn't even understand, burned down the old lighthouse and caused a man's death – and you don't even care. You have *no idea* what I've been through to ensure that the new lighthouse doesn't fail." She stood up. His gaze on her was unfocused.

"Galt – my dear – come, you still love your old father despite my harsh actions and words? I forgive you."

"Finish your tea," she said. "I trust you'll be fit to attend the grand opening?"

No Skiver today; instead she'd given him a strong herbal brew of sleeping and forgetting.

# NINE

THAT GLIMPSE OF copper chain plagued her. It looked suspiciously like an item her mother had left her, which Embran, to her outrage, had confiscated. But why was he wearing it? He was hardly a man for personal adornments. Maybe she was mistaken, but she couldn't delve into her father's shirt to settle the matter. But until she knew for sure, she could not let the suspicion go.

Closing her eyes, she inspected her memories. After her mother's death, more than fourteen years ago, the navy had sent back her belongings, including the pendant, to Galt. She'd been outraged when Embran found and confiscated it; she'd noted her mother's warnings of danger – *"Name: Acicular But Once. Keep this safe, don't try to use it until you know what you're doing. Or ever."* – yet he refused to trust his daughter's common sense. Embran had kept it in a small, plain wooden box. He thought she didn't know where he hid the box or its key: he was wrong. Five years ago, she and Embran had been engaged in some construction work in Cinquetann Riverport. Before they set out, Galt had slipped the little box and key into her pocket.

She was the daughter who must pretend not to know anything. Actually, she knew quite a lot, other than engineering. She knew how to find a certain shop, and having given her father the slip, found herself pressing a hand to the door and letting herself through into the gloomy, glowing interior.

The shop of Doctor Catt and Doctor Fisher was quite the most disturbing place she'd ever entered. A cave packed floor to ceiling with strange objects; some enchantingly beautiful, others hideous enough to scare the skin off a demon, all alien. Candlelight and other light sources she couldn't identify gleamed on everything. A cave of treasure. The wall of energy coming at her stopped her in her tracks; the whole space was taut and swollen with invisible powers as if it might explode. A glass counter held her gaze, but she couldn't seem to take one step towards it.

"Good afternoon to you, ma'am." She hadn't seen the tall man behind the counter, beckoning. "Come, come. We don't bite, despite rumours to the contrary. Doctor Fisher at your service."

The current that had held her back slackened. She walked towards him, putting on her most intimidating demeanour.

"Good day, Doctor Fisher."

There was an awkward pause, broken by Fisher shouting, "Catty!"

She jumped, but managed to hide it. "I understand," she went on, "that you are the experts to come to for... evaluations."

"Indeed, we are. How can we help?" As he spoke, a slightly shorter, friendlier-looking gentleman appeared from a dark space – hallway or room – behind the counter.

"Doctor Catt?" she said, letting a smile reach her face. "I'm Mistress Galt, daughter of Commander Embran." They both went a bit pale at that. "I'm here incognito; no one, least of all my father, must know I was ever here. Understand?"

"You have our word." The two dealers looked at each other, eyebrows lifting, as if to tell each other, *This may be something interesting.*

"I have this pendant. It was my mother's." She took a small

box from a pocket. Catt quickly spread out a square of black velvet to receive it. With reverence she opened the lid and placed the heart-shaped cage on the fabric, curling the chain behind it. It was an ugly thing, really, she thought. Heavy and base-looking, the metalwork too coarse to be called filigree

"Did you wish to sell it?" Catt asked, leaning over it with an optical instrument of some kind. He already sounded disappointed. After examining it for a good five minutes, he passed the magnifier to Fisher, who paid special attention to the cage, and ran the chain through his fingers.

"No," she said. "I just want to know what it is."

"Hm," said Fisher. "Little to no financial value."

"I've heard that you say that to everyone."

Catt grinned. "Scurrilous rumours!"

Galt leaned on her elbows on the counter. "All I ask, gentlemen, is that you are honest with me. It's not about monetary value. Just give me your honest, expert opinion."

"As I was saying." Fisher cleared his throat. "It's copper, or an alloy thereof. I can balance it in the scales against copper scits, and the number of scits will be its precise value. There is a stone inside it... I can't see that it hinges open to remove or replace the gem."

"No, it's soldered. I could do it, but have no reason to."

"And it's not even a gem. Looks like a piece of common white quartz, although it appears someone had a go at carving it into a shape."

"A polished cylinder, pointy at one end." Catt put a finger on the cage, as if trying to glean something from the stone. "Any idea how old it is?"

"I hoped you'd tell me. I've no idea where Mother got it. Spoils of battle, possibly."

"It looks old," said Fisher. "I've seen things similar that were thousands of years old, but this may be a copy, no more than a century or two."

"Good." Galt took a steadying breath, sensing this was going to be a slow process. "And do you have any idea what it is? I mean, it's hardly decorative. Mother never said, and if she ever wore it, it was hidden under her clothing. Father hates it. He confiscated it from me, and I've no idea why."

"So you stole it back?" Catt gave her that lovely look of mischief again. She rarely liked anyone, but she found herself warming to him.

"Exactly so."

"This may seem an odd question, but does it have a name?"

"Yes, she wrote it down for me. 'Acicular but Once'. Strange name for a pendant, isn't it?"

"Interesting. 'Used to be a needle'? What sense are we to make of that?" said Catt.

"No idea. 'The Imperial Moonstone of Queen somebody' would have been much preferred, of course..." Galt tried to smile. "She wrote that I shouldn't try to use it, that's all."

"Here's the thing," he said, lowering his voice. "It may be an amulet of interest. It may contain a power of some kind, or its power may have waned over the centuries, or it may be a lump of dumb stone."

"We don't know," added Fisher. "Can you leave it with us?"

"Can I stay?" She must have sounded so sweet and plaintive that the doctors, with an unconvincing show of reluctance, both agreed. "I must confess, I'm *so* exasperated with my father that I need to hide away for a few hours. I've earned a respite."

"Of course, of course," said Catt, beckoning her through to the back. There was a small cosy room with a fire in the grate and shelves full of bizarre items. They brought her tea and cake, and she curled up in an armchair watching her two new friends leaning over the pendant in a pool of unnaturally bright light.

She suspected they had other back rooms, darker and more dangerous, some for business and others where no customers ever set foot. The secrecy was rather thrilling. This was, in fact, the most agreeable afternoon she'd spent in months.

The three talked and laughed for a couple of hours, bonding nicely. Fisher, although more reserved than Catt, had an acerbic wit that delighted her. She dozed a little, but woke feeling refreshed, and confident that they wouldn't dare put anything suspicious in her tea. They'd taken a liking to her. Besides, there would always be some customers who could be hoodwinked and others, like her, who most definitely could not.

For three days in a row, she sneaked away from her father and his building project and spent an hour gossiping over tea with the two apothecaries. She had an excuse ready for her absence, but Embran didn't seem to notice. Catt and Fisher were becoming her firm friends; they had a store of outrageous stories that she mostly believed, and more than that – she was learning things, storing them away for future use.

"Any ideas yet?" she asked on the fourth afternoon, as Catt continued poring over her pendant.

Catt sighed and sat back, pushing his magnifying glasses up into his white hair. "Nothing clear, I'm sorry."

"There's definitely *something* in it," Fisher added. "You can feel a slight energy."

"Yes, I've noticed that," said Galt. "Didn't know if I was imagining it. Just a *feeling*, but…"

"Learn to trust your instincts, young lady." Fisher wagged a finger at her. "If you sense something, there's a ninety-nine-per-cent chance it's real, and—"

"A ninety-nine-per-cent chance that you have certain sensitivities to certain powers," Catt finished.

"That's interesting." She sat up straight and put down the empty cup she'd been cradling. "Could I develop those instincts? Understand them?"

"Absolutely," said Catt, "if you're prepared to work on them. Read. Experiment."

"And alas, the only way we can discover the purpose of this artefact is by experimenting," said Fisher. "Try things with it until something works."

"I have an inkling it may have been some kind of way-finding device." Catt held up the pendant and angled it to demonstrate. "A bit like a compass, but not. I think the gem inside is charmed to point in the direction you're looking for."

"How would I tell it to do that?"

"That's the puzzle. You'd have to bond with it in some way... Such spells can be dangerous, though. Damage the mind if not done correctly." He mimicked his head exploding with both hands. "My apologies for being so vague. We can't be sure yet."

"We'll be in Cherivell for another few weeks," she said. "How much longer do you need it? I'll pay for all your extra time, of course. I'm so glad I found you."

As Fisher started to mumble about settling money another day, and Catt protested that her company was payment enough, there was a terrible noise from the front of the shop.

First a demolition-level banging that brought them all to their feet. A man shouting in a deep, loud voice. Then – since Catt had locked the shop door and put up the 'Closed' sign – a gut-wrenching crash of glass and screaming hinges.

"What in all the demons of—" Fisher began, his voice drowned by roaring.

"Galt! *Galt!* Where the devil are you? I know you're here, you wretched child!"

"Shit," said Galt. Meanwhile, Catt and Fisher were rushing down the hall into the shop, just in time to see the raging form of Commander Embran bringing down an axe straight through their glass counter. Artefacts tumbled and rolled everywhere.

"You pair of devils!" yelled Embran. "I know my daughter is here! Give her up!"

"Wait, stop!" Fisher threw up both his hands, just as Embran was preparing to take a swing at a display case.

"Sir, please, be calm, your daughter's safe and there's no need..."

Doctor Catt spoke contritely while Fisher, Galt couldn't help noticing, had an odd glow about him, something dangerous and spiky that might leave either him, or her father, in a bad way. And if Embran either destroyed the shop or ended up dead, she'd never be able to live with herself.

"Father, it's all right, I'm here!" She ran out from behind the counter, straight into range of his axe. He dropped the weapon instantly as she grabbed his arms. "I'm fine. Look what you've done to the door, and the poor counter! Please stop. Let's talk outside. Don't be angry with these two good men, they've done nothing wrong."

"They're sorcerers, or think they are," Embran growled, dripping sweat on her upturned face. "What in blazes do you think you're doing here, you idiot girl?"

She tried to press him backwards toward the doorway. He wouldn't budge. "Bring me the pendant," he said.

Catt looked despairingly at Galt, who nodded. He turned, and was back in ten seconds with the copper amulet. By then, Embran was holding out the little wooden box to receive it. He snapped the box shut, locked it, manhandled Galt across a carpet of broken glass.

"If I ever see or hear of you two charlatans again, if you come within ten miles of my daughter, you will both die. Comprehend?"

Her last sight of Catt and Fisher was of them both standing behind the smashed counter, faces frozen, hands raised as if someone were aiming a bow and arrow at them. "I'm so sorry," she called over her shoulder. "I'll pay for the damage. So sorry."

# TEN

CROWDS GATHERED ALL day around the new shining tower, Arvennir and islanders mingling in an unprecedented show of friendliness. Stalls of food and drink bustled with trade; the infirmary was now a makeshift beerhall. Bands of musicians played all day – sometimes two at a time, producing intervals of horrible cacophony. This was a celebration, a holiday. A huge whirl of heavy-footed dancing broke out.

Crombie was less happy than he might have been. Did no one realise how voices were amplified and bounced around by the interior of the lighthouse, even whispers? He'd heard Captain Jennvi's words to Galt, *"That boy has such a crush on you,"* and Galt's horrified response, *"That's absurd! He's like my little brother!"* It was only what he might have expected, but still, hearing such words spoken out loud was excruciating. He burned with embarrassment every time he remembered. For the remainder of the build, he became cool and reserved, both with Galt and her aunt. Learned to smile without emotion, so they wouldn't notice anything had changed. *Hated* Jennvi, at least for a few days. It had been an icy slap in the face – but it had, perhaps, made him grow up quite significantly.

He was quite pleased with his own dignity – not that either of them seemed to notice.

\*     \*     \*

As DUSK FELL, the gathered masses grew quiet, the atmosphere electric with anticipation. The only people inside the lighthouse, one floor below the lantern room, were Galt, Crombie, Paulian, Doctor Catt and Doctor Fisher. Crombie was uncharacteristically quiet, Galt thought. Nerves. She'd managed to keep her father out of the way by maintaining his slight sedation; he was down below, with Orendion and Gredlen, still under the weather but apparently well enough to join the official Arven deputation. Galt had set Jennvi on guard at the main entrance.

All the officials were down by the main door on the seaward side, ready to raise the ceremonial banner. White Lotus and Fighting Ram: symbols of both nations on the same flag. Perhaps they could remain friends after all, bonded by a mutually beneficial venture.

Fisher held the winding handle that would rotate the occulting shade within the lantern room above, thus unleashing the light beam for the first time. Later it would be set up to rotate on a timed mechanism, but for now it would be held open manually in order to impress the crowd.

Then he stepped back and indicated for Galt to operate the handle.

"You should do the honours," he said. "This is your achievement."

"Not without help," she said, "but thank you. Crombie, join me?"

A thin bugle call sounded from below, signalling that it was dark enough, and time for the grand reveal. Together, Galt and Crombie turned the long handle, using their weight for leverage.

"Four turns, then brake on," Fisher reminded them.

Above them, the half-shade turned, the open side aligning

with the storm windows. A beam of pure light rushed out across the ocean.

Brake on.

A roar went up from the crowd below.

Every sailor and every flying creature all the way to the horizon turned to stare.

NOT WAITING FOR the others, Galt ran down the flights of steps to the ground floor, slipping past Jennvi and ducking under the banner. She ran straight into her father's embrace. He was unsteady on his feet, gaze unfocused; she should have realised that beer on top of sedating tea would be too much, but at least it stopped him trying to get inside the lighthouse to examine what she'd done. There wasn't much going round his mind at all, except alcohol. He hugged her, lifted her in the air and set her down.

"See?" she said. "It's done. It works!"

"My genius girl," he slurred.

A few days ago, she'd cornered Jennvi and asked her the question. *"What turned my father so against magic?"*

"He's told you. The Kinslayer's creatures killed his father, your grandpapa, with fire magic. Just a few years later, Angalah died too, in battle. You know this."

"Yes," Galt said firmly. "That's true. But I need to know the *real* reason." And Jennvi had given in at last, and told her.

NOW THE CELEBRATIONS began in earnest. Speeches were made. Fireworks exploded. Arvennir and Forters danced, with each other and with all the strange and scaly races that shared their island. Eventually Galt bumped into Crombie and danced with him, too, spinning round and round.

"D'you think we should be celebrating this much?" he

whispered in her ear. "Because of Jorgan, and Viktor, and the sailors who drowned... Seems a bit disrespectful."

"You try stopping them," she replied. "For now – be glad it works! And think how much you helped! We'll mourn the dead tomorrow and then, thank the *heavens*, all the Arvennir can go home."

"You're going... with your father?"

"Let's not speak of that."

She spun away from him and ran towards the front of the lighthouse, to marvel again at the starbright beam they'd created.

A SHINING LIGHT in the darkness had the power to draw night creatures towards it. The brighter the beam, the more things came. Out at sea, a black cloud was rising up steadily from the horizon, approaching slowly, like a black sheet being drawn across the entire sky.

By the time the merrymakers noticed, it was almost upon them. A sound came with it. A furry buzzing noise growing louder and louder. As Crombie looked up, he saw it was not a cloud, not a single dark sheet of magic, but layer upon layer of bugs in flight, separating into individual creatures as they came. Wings like sails, legs dangling like giant scaffolding, hair on their bodies thick as forests. They swarmed and rushed and rustled until the sky and the air itself were thick with them.

People cried out, waving their arms around like windmills and throwing themselves flat to the ground. Crombie heard the angry roar of the Arvennir – what fresh evil was this, what malevolent magic this time? *To arms*, they yelled, voices muffled by a million wings and segmented bodies. *Man the cannons*.

Where the dazzling white lamp had beamed out, bright enough to delight the gods themselves, darkness began to blanket the dome. A thousand giant moths threw themselves at the crystal panels of the lantern house. Not only moths but fat, shiny flying beetles, long thin wasps, flying mantises, hideous forms he'd never even seen before with faces ugly enough to terrify the Kinslayer.

They were practically queueing up to reach the light, swarming over the glass in thick layers – occasionally letting a lacework of light through their mass of whirring wings. Those who couldn't get near enough simply filled the air. They sucked in the air through their spiracles until the humans cowering beneath were struggling for breath.

"Sketterae," said Doctor Fisher, suddenly at Crombie's shoulder. "Knew the damned things were lethal in some way. Didn't realise it was by dry drowning."

Catt was with him too, but no sign of Galt. A voice was shouting yet whispering at the same time; where was it coming from?

"You cursed, hellbound idiots. We warned you – Moth was guarding portal to Skettera. Without her to stop them, Sketterae came pouring out—"

"And naturally, were attracted to the brightest light for miles around," said Doctor Catt.

An old woman, a bundle of long thin bones held together by yellow parchment skin, stood on four legs in front of them. She seemed to be wearing almost nothing except rags. Crombie saw that she had six limbs; four legs bent under her, two arms dangling in front. Glaring red eyes.

It was the Queen Mantid, transformed to human size. "Where is moth?"

"We haven't seen the moth," Fisher said, bending down so he didn't tower over her. "Flown to new lands far away."

"But she came this way." The nearly-human Mantid scraped her face with a forearm. She still had a streak of green blood there. "Sketterae follow her. They know her scent. They smell power in the dust of her tails. So they follow."

Leaning on his cane, Catt asked her, "Are there usually this many? They must have had an awfully fecund breeding season."

"We work to protect *your* world. Our task, given us by your demigods. Keep Sketterae in their own realm."

"I'm sorry, Queen Mantid," said Crombie. "We didn't know you were trying to protect us. This is all my fault."

"Nothing's ever *all* your fault, lad," said Catt. "Even the Kinslayer couldn't have claimed that."

"What the hell are we going to do?" said Fisher.

"Don't know. They never escaped before," hissed the Queen. "Not in such numbers."

"Come on, Catty, rack your giant brain. There must be something."

"Dare I venture to suggest that you rack *yours*, Fishy? Perhaps we have a walnut shell about our persons that we can crack to fling out a vast spider web of infinite diameter, strength and stickiness?"

"We did have something like that once – wasn't it to do with an enchanted bridal gown, though? Not very sticky, as I recall."

"Shut the occulting shade!" said Catt. "Blackout. No light, nothing to attract them. They'll go after their moth again."

"I'll go," Crombie began, but then the ground and sky rocked with explosions coming from the Arvennir navy ships. Yellow fires flashed above their heads. A column of air opened up, moths spiralling upwards like a tornado. A second later, they began raining to earth. A hailstorm of boulders with spindle legs.

"They're going to kill us and knock the tower down if they carry on with the artillery," Catt gasped, hanging onto Fishy's arm. "Gods grant their aim's as accurate as they boast it is!"

"Stuff's exploding in the air, not down here," said Fisher. "The Arvennir are very good at blowing things up, you have to give them that."

"I'll tell you what's going to happen." Crombie stood up. A moth hit him on the side of the head with an audible thud. He staggered. The cannonade repeated, deafening. As it died away a new sound began. Through the ringing of his ears, he recognised it as the twang and *phshewww* of Arvennir arrows.

"That," said Crombie. "The Arven troops are going to massacre them all."

"That's going to leave a mess," Fisher said gloomily.

"I don't think they possess sufficient arrows," said Catt.

The Queen Mantid hissed. "So they kill a few hundred, and as creatures die they release a scent of distress that finds way back to Skettera, and hundred-thousand more pour out in answer. Not only moths but hive creatures. Wasps, scuriti, urgota – stings like swords. Beetles spit venom. Things I can't even name. Fling poisonous barbs from their legs, things that eat human flesh or lay eggs inside you, leave larvae inside human bodies until they consume whole host. Body and mind. Dragonflies the size of this island with wings sharp enough to sever heads as they pass."

"Fine, we get the picture," said Fisher. Catty had gone greenish-white.

"What price then your precious lighthouse?"

"It's not right," said Crombie. "They're living creatures. Yes, they should stay in their own realm, but it's not their fault they were drawn here – and all the Arvennir can do is slaughter them?"

"They're only bugs," said Paulian, supporting an injured woman as he passed them.

"They're not, though, are they?"

"They hold magical energies. They have their own plane of existence. They might even have some level of intelligence, who knows?" said Catt.

"I'll go up," said Crombie.

"My boy, you can still barely walk!" said Fisher, which was the truth.

"Right, then, I'm off to find Galt. She'll help." Crombie had lost patience with the debate. He'd never wanted anything to die – but nothing mattered more than Galt's life.

AFTER CROMBIE LEFT, the Queen Mantid also ran into the dark. Apparently no one was interested in two elderly doctors who no longer had any help to offer.

"Why did we come out unarmed?" Catt groaned. "The one night we assumed we'd need no weapons, no shrouding, no magical protection of any kind – how did such complacency possess us? We *never* do this. Until tonight!"

"We should get inside the lighthouse, Catty," said Fisher. "Safer there. Maybe get up to the winding handle—"

"You pair of devils," said a voice behind them. The voice was deep and rough with aggression; unmistakably, inevitably Embran. "I knew the moment I spotted you that you'd fouled the lighthouse with your vile powers!" A dagger came up at Catt's throat, and a sword at Fisher's. They were both yanked back against his armoured chest and held there by arms as powerful as a Yogg's. Beer breath washed over them. "If *one* of you moves, or tries any demonic tricks, the *other* dies first. You understand?"

"You've made yourself admirably clear," squeaked Catt.

"This is your doing, isn't it?"

"Not entirely—" Fisher attempted.

"You brought an attack of monsters as personal revenge against *me*!"

"No, nothing personal—"

"And I warned you that if I ever saw you again, you'd die. This is all your doing. I saw you, casting your curses down in the old lighthouse. Should've known then – only way the project was finished so fast was by sorcery. You've corrupted my daughter and brought devastation upon this blameless island!"

"Wait, were you not *blaming* the island for the shipwreck not long—"

"Shut up, you piece of shit." Embran silenced Catt with the edge of his dagger. Catt hardly felt the cut until he felt it stinging and itching, blood trickling down.

"Ouch," he said.

"Start walking," growled Embran. He spoke with ominous precision, as if trying to disguise how drunk he was. "Behind the huts over there. I've a few lessons to teach you; you belong with the insects, and you are going to die among them, like the insects you are."

# ELEVEN

GALT HAD RUN to find Embran as soon as the cannons set off. She didn't even know why, after all he'd done; it was a familial instinct that overrode all the details. Through the dark and the veils of membranous wings, she saw him halfway between the lighthouse and the accommodation huts. He was walking, rather slowly because he was forcing two figures along in front of him.

Catt and Fisher.

She nearly screamed with anger. How utterly predictable of him! And she should have known – they'd been wandering around fully visible, and she hadn't thought to warn them. *Too busy*, she thought as she ran full-pelt towards the three, *showing off my work to my father to realise he was bound to do this.*

"Father!" she yelled. "Embran! *Father!*"

He stopped, turned to face her, awkwardly turning the two doctors around with him. She saw their frightened faces and the blades at their throats. She was so furious now that she was sure she'd spew fire if she tried to speak. Fisher had power, she knew – but so did her father, and she feared that if he died, he'd take Catt with him.

"Father, please," she managed, halting ten steps from him and holding out her palms. "Please, let them go. They've never

243

done anything but help us. We couldn't have completed the lighthouse at all without their help."

That was absolutely the wrong thing to say. Embran bared his teeth.

"They cursed the lighthouse – *both* lighthouses, old and new. They've corrupted you with their lies, Galt. Walk away. I'm going to extract a full list of their crimes before I execute them – and that is something I won't allow you to witness, even though you are no longer my daughter."

"Over my dead body!" she shouted back. "You've finally lost your mind! You harm them, I'll throw myself over that cliff-edge!"

That made Embran pause. He stared at her but his eyes were black and empty.

Then he began to turn away. Embran's turn was perfectly timed to allow a moth the size of a sheep to come swerving in sideways and collide with his chest, knocking him clean off his feet.

Galt ran to him, stumbling over gods-knew-what detritus on the ground. Explosions shook the world around her, fire and smoke half-blinded her. First she extracted the sword and the dagger from the melee of tangled limbs. Fisher managed to disentangle himself, then they both helped the shocked Catt to his feet. She saw his neck was bleeding; the cut looked superficial but painful.

"Galt, bless you. Thank goodness," said Fisher. "Catty? It's all right, we've got you."

"There's an infirmary set up in the lighthouse, ground floor." She pushed strands of hair off her sweaty forehead. "Take these weapons, will you? Hand them in to the guards and tell them that under no circumstances are they to let Embran anywhere near you."

"I doubt he's going anywhere for a while, dear Galt." Catt gripped her hands and gave her a pained smile.

When they'd gone, with an effort she hauled the great moth body off Embran. Then she crouched over him, sweat and tears forming an unpleasant slick on her cheeks.

"Father?" She shook him urgently. "Father! Wake up. Come on, you can't be dead. Get a grip."

Despite all that had happened, she still loved him. Love was buried so deep in her heart and mind, like a tangle of thorns, nothing would ever dislodge it. His pain when her mother died – unimaginable. That, however, excused none of his behaviour. Such focused aggression had its place in battle; in times of peace, though, it began to look like severe derangement.

He was out cold but breathing. A handful of soldiers gathered, but held back while she attended to him. "He's alive," she told them. "Help me get him into the lighthouse, out of harm's way. Don't put him *anywhere* near Catt and Fisher. He's just tried to kill them."

"Who?"

"The two doctors. Oldish, long robes – you can't mistake them."

As she held Embran's shoulders, her fingers found a familiar thick chain around his neck. She froze. *Oh yes, Father. This!* She started fumbling to take it off him, but her reaction was too slow. His men were already there with a stretcher and she had no choice but to let them load him and carry him away. Through the swirling onslaught of huge, plated, angry insects, she ran after them.

The ground floor of the lighthouse was weirdly quiet and peaceful. It was a large space, with a handful of injured folk already there. In the light of many lamps, she saw Crombie's parents doing their best with water and bandages, Paulian and other townsfolk assisting.

Her wayward doctor friends were nowhere to be seen.

"I'll stay with him," she told Embran's stretcher-bearers. Once they'd gone, there was a moment in which she and her father were alone. She felt beneath his tunic, found the chain again and carefully drew it out. Thick copper-coloured metal, and suspended from it – a pendant like a heavy, heart-shaped cage.

Acicular but Once. Her mother's pendant. She had been right when she'd guessed that was what he was concealing from her. She held back a growl behind her teeth, fumbling to undo the clasp. She slipped the chain free with the most delicate touch she could manage. Now was not the time for him to be woken by copper links scraping over his neck.

"You sneaky bastard," she said, folding the pendant inside her palm. She felt the rattle of the carved stone it held. She opened her fingers and saw that the stone was purplish and dark, like a bruise. Dead. Was that her father's game? Not just to hide it from her, but that he'd discovered he could smother and kill its magical power? He hated magic – and magic, it seemed, also hated him.

Her heart sank. Killed her mother's power? *Did this to protect me, Father? All right, maybe your intentions were good, but… I don't need protecting any more.*

At first the gemstone felt inanimate – then there was a jolt of heat that made her startle, and a peculiar steady rhythm started thumping against her palm. Through her fingers came a pinkish glow. "So," she whispered. "That's it. You didn't take my power relic to use it. You took it to disable it. You always knew it would work for me, didn't you? But… I understand now. The pain of that day… I can't imagine how you bore it. I understand, but it's time to let go now. All right, I know it's *never* time to let go. But I have to do this. My dear father."

Embran grunted.

Quickly she stepped away, fastened the chain around her own neck and settled it under her clothing, out of sight. She wiped moisture from her eyes. When she turned back, Paulian was sidling towards her. "Mistress Galt?"

"My father's hurt. He was thrown off his feet. Needs help, obviously. I know he's not the most popular… In fact, can you bind him with some rope so he can't get up? He's just tried to murder Catt and Fishy."

The mage, looking more serious but less nervous than the previous times she'd met him, lifted a pacifying palm. "Of course, no matter who he is… *Murder?* Anyway, no matter, all the injured are treated the same. Crombie's parents are here too, and other healers from town. They're very good."

"Thanks." Her shoulders dropped with a touch of relief. "Sorry for snapping, Paulian. Why are you staring at me?"

"I, I, I sensed…" He flicked his fingers towards her right hand, which she was resting over the lump the pendant made on her breastbone. "Sort of energy. Just a wisp. I don't know. Forgive me, I should mind my own business."

"Just look after him," she said.

Outside, back in the gloom and the eerie, humming storm of the battle, she sat down on a stone block and leaned against the lighthouse wall. Her mother's pendant; it still throbbed like a heartbeat. And her father had had it on his person all this time – he who despised all magical things – as the best way of preventing Galt from getting her hands on it. But she now knew why, and that wasn't easy.

Clearly it hadn't pulsed with power for him. It had awoken only for her; woken up at her touch. "Mother," she whispered.

Her relationship with her father, already distant, had never been the same after the incident in Catt & Fisher's shop. She couldn't forgive him for his behaviour that day; he couldn't forgive her for taking the pendant to people he saw as dabblers in evil powers. "*What got into you?*" he had demanded. She tried to explain with calm logic, but he wouldn't listen. "*How did you find me?*" she asked in return. Her absence hadn't gone unnoticed after all; he'd sent someone to follow her on the third day, he answered, and they had seen her enter the forbidden shop. How dare she steal her mother's pendant? *It's my pendant*, she retorted. *How dare you humiliate me like that? I'm an adult now. Am I to be allowed no right to my own life, my own decisions?*

The answer, in perpetuity, was No.

After that, she and Embran barely spoke. Rage burned out into cold silence. She continued working for him – why should she be driven from her job, after all? – but now they exchanged words connected only with work.

A couple of days ago, when she'd finally got Jennvi into a secluded corner of the Fort Isle Inn and plied her with ale, she'd told her aunt all this. Jenn hadn't known of Catt and Fisher's involvement, so it was a fair exchange for the information Galt needed.

"How much do you know?" Jennvi had asked.

"That my granddad, Embran's father, was killed in the early days of the Kinslayer war. And that my mother died in a river battle, only two years from the war's end. That's the reason he gives for hating magic: the Kinslayer's sorcery."

"It's a pretty strong reason."

"Yes, but I know there's something else. The navy sent her personal effects straight to me, so Embran didn't intercept them. Not right away. I kept some of the charms and crystals, but there was something about that particular pendant … Come on, Jenn. There's a mystery about my mother that no one will explain. But I'm a big girl now. I need to know."

"Embran swore me to secrecy." Jennvi looked unhappily into her tankard.

"Embran is up there," she pointed at the ceiling, "recovering from his fever, with *my pendant* round his neck! Why?"

"I never knew what Angalah saw in him. Of course, she was the beauty; full of energy, flowing dark hair, up for anything. I got the brawn and the common sense, so can't complain."

Galt had to gulp down a sudden wave of grief. Memories of

how she'd wept in secret for weeks. Then sat staring at nothing for weeks. "You weren't much alike, but equals in fierceness and strength. Embran adored her. He used be nicer, in the old days... like a big friendly bear..."

"Yes, he definitely changed for the worse after she died." Jenn took a long drink of beer, then a deep breath. "All right. It wasn't a river battle; rather, a skirmish some thirty miles from Nydarrow. As part of the naval brigade, we'd often fight on land. Forty of us were sent to patrol the nearby villages after reports of Kinslayer attacks, but everywhere seemed deserted that day. I was there, with Embran and Anga – you know she liked to search corpses for power relics, when Embran wasn't looking?"

"So I gathered."

"Anyway, we were patrolling a row of barns and cottages, with a small castle ahead of us – the Yoggs came out of nowhere, other creatures too. One minute silent, the next hell broke loose and we fought like demons, sword and axe and arrows – could we have taken them? Forty of us, at least a hundred of them. I know Embran thought we were more than a match, and so did I: wishful thinking. We were screwed, Galt. I didn't notice what Anga was doing at first, but she had that copper pendant, amulet, pointed at the enemy like a tiny dagger. I heard her chanting under her breath. Then her hand lit up with this weird, shimmering pinkish light – don't know how to describe it, I was half-blinded and it was over so fast. And all the Yoggs *vanished*. Gone, like they'd been sucked into another dimension."

"That... doesn't sound like a bad thing..."

"The disaster was that over half our own troops went with them. Never seen again. Not intentional, obviously, but there it was; Angalah had killed half her own comrades, using a magic relic."

"Great gods," said Galt. "I had no idea."

"No, it was covered up. We were in shock. Embran was mortified. I can't begin to imagine how your mother felt."

"What did she do?"

"Arvennir don't flee, do we? One of our men was still ahead of her. He turned round, staring – I'll never forget his face – and she ran forward. Straight onto his sword."

"What?" Galt was trembling. So was Jennvi. A pall of shock settled over her: her mother's end, and what Embran had seen… the imagined scene began to play repeatedly in her head, more vivid each time.

"Well, wouldn't you? I couldn't have lived with that on my conscience. I think she'd been experimenting with the amulet, but had no idea of its power … Embran beheaded the swordsman, even though it wasn't his fault. Then he fell to his knees and roared like a hundred demons over her body; I've never heard anything like it. Anyway, naval officers soon came and took him away. Others came for my sister; the pendant was still in her grasp, so it just went with her other belongings. I found Embran much later, chained because he was mad with shock. He raged against Angalah for using sorcery, and the despicable magicians who'd made such a thing, on and on. And *that* is why your father loathes magic to his bones."

*That's why.* Thoughts went careening round her head. *That's why. Father, I didn't know. Mother, Mother, please, I'd give my life for it not to have happened. When the sword went through you, it went through him too. And through me.*

Galt managed to speak, after a long silence. "But if she hadn't, you might *all* have been killed."

"By the enemy's hand, though. It's different."

Galt nodded. "They always told… told me my mother died nobly."

"Sweetheart, she was as brave as they come." Jennvi held her hands across the table. "But that day, she made a terrible mistake."

\*　　\*　　\*

AFTER EMBRAN HAD reclaimed the pendant in Cherivell, she had never seen it properly again – until this moment, as she sat against the lighthouse wall buffeted by dark wings and cold winds. Knowing why he hated the Acicular but Once. Still despising him for how he'd treated Fishy and Catt, still feel that burning pain of watching Angalah end her own life.

No wonder they hadn't told her. It was never going to go away

"Hey, Galt!" She looked up to see Crombie standing next to her. He leaned against the wall, gasping for breath. "You all right? I couldn't find you anywhere."

"I'm fine. Not injured, or only a bit. You?"

"I'm just frightened, is all. They're killing these monster insects, but more keep coming, and I can't stand to see them killed, but what else are we going to do? I was trying to go back up and shut the shade, but I can't even see straight. My ma and pa. I need to do *something*…"

"My father," she said, pointing her thumb at the door to the lighthouse. "He's in there with the healers. He was knocked unconscious while taking Catty and Fishy to be tortured and killed."

"*What*?"

"I know. I found this on him…"

She pulled the copper amulet from her neckline. Crombie blinked at it.

"Yes, I know you wonder why I'm fussing over a piece of ugly jewellery. I'll explain, if we live. But I need to fetch Catt and Fisher."

"It's lit up."

"What?"

"There's a white light coming out of the pendant, look."

A glow and a blue-white wisp were escaping from the point of the gemstone and through a filigree hole at the bottom point. The whole cage twisted in her palm and set the wisp angling upwards.

And suddenly she knew what the pendant was for, and the stone within it, and what her mother had done wrong. She dropped it back beneath her clothing.

Nothing happened. Just a glow passing through her shirt and her fingers, a weak little wisp of magic.

"Mother?" she whispered. "Angalah? Did you leave anything of yourself in here? If you did, please help me now."

"What's going on?" said Crombie, worried. "There's power coming through your hand. I can smell it. Pungent."

"Stay right here," she commanded. "I'm going to find Fishy and Catt!"

She raced towards the Arvennir position with the world exploding around her – heavy moth bodies, artillery, archers, people panicking and running, no air to breathe, no light to see by – all the time yelling for Catt and Fisher, yelling at the troops to cease fire. Where was General Orendion? Sheltering well out of the way, no doubt. An arrow whisked past her shoulder.

"This is Galt of Athaln, Chief Project Officer! I command you to *stop firing*!"

Her voice was, for those seconds, supernaturally loud. To her amazement the archers heard her, and the troops down on the ships heard her, and the firing stopped. "And I need a volunteer to go up to the top and turn the occulting shade. The blackout shield thing."

"I'll go," said Jennvi, stepping up to her. "Tell me what to do."

"Floor below lantern house, pull brake lever off, give the winding wheel four turns clockwise. Brake on again, leave the light shielded for ten minutes to see what happens, then reopen – it only goes one way, so four more turns clockwise—"

"Got it," said Jennvi, already on her way. Galt followed her into the lighthouse.

"Catt! Fisher!" she yelled across the pale stone space. And there they were, appearing right beside her like ghosts, before her voice had stopped echoing.

Within a minute, Galt and the doctors were outside with Crombie again. "What my mother did wrong was this," she said, gasping for breath. She took out the pendant and again felt it twist up towards the sky. "Angalah pointed it horizontally, straight at the enemy – sorry, long story, bear with me – and that's why the wrong people got caught. It needs to be—"

"Straight up at the sky!" said Catt. "Of course. *Now* I see."

"We work together. Clasp your hands over mine. Put all your instincts behind it."

"What?" said Crombie. She ignored him as Catt, then Fisher, placed their palms in prayer position over hers. They raised the quartz point within its cage as high over their heads as they could. With shared instinct they all knew what to do: three pairs of hands layered round the cage, a tiny gap for the light to escape, all their energies gathering, ready to be unleashed—

*Mother*, she pleaded in her head. *If you're there, lend us your strength*. Wishful thinking, but so what? It came to her that this very last surge of magic left in the stone was her mother's spirit, and that if they did this, Angalah's spirit would be gone forever, but there was no other choice.

*This is what I want. This is why I'm still here*, her mother's voice whispered in response. *Stayed with you for a moment of utmost need. Sweetest love of mine, you need… your friend…*

"Crombie!" Galt snapped. "You too! Hands round Fisher's!"

"Er – right. I'm here." It wasn't hard for him to join the huddle as he was so tall. She saw him tense up and close his eyes.

The lighthouse beam was already dimmed by the layer of Skettera bodies crawling on the lantern house windows. As the shade turned all the way, thick darkness fell. From the stone within the pendant, the thin white light strengthened, blazed upwards and sent ripples flowing out across the dark pond of the sky. Hesitantly, then in an increasing rush, all the moths and beetles and all the flying things of Skettera rose up in a single body, swirling in wild patterns like starlings at twilight.

The effect was weirdly beautiful – creatures rising and rising on an uprush of air and light until the silver ripples simply... swallowed them.

The last creature she saw vanishing into the sky was a pallid, skeletal streak; the Queen Mantid, still shepherding her grisly flock. Then the whole atmosphere sucked inwards and slammed shut. The island shook; all the remaining humans still on their feet hit the ground. The vacuum left Galt deaf for a few minutes. Ripples went on flashing across the sky like some impossible circular storm.

The lights pulsed, filling the whole sky with pale, icy rainbows until they rushed outwards and were gone. A bright speck snapped down to a pinpoint and vanished. Darkness, silence. Peace.

Galt sat up and put her hand straight onto a large beetle body. Its carapace gave way with a crunch, plunging her hand into semi-liquid entrails up to her elbow.

As she was trying to extricate herself from this moderate horror, she heard a voice louder than the others. "Galt!"

"What?"

"You made a portal." It was Doctor Catt yelling at her. "You and the boy. And us, but mainly you two. You made a *portal*!"

"Bloody well done," added Fisher, panting for breath. "Even better – you closed it, too."

"Quite," said Catt. "Last thing we needed was some fresh monstrosity coming through."

Crombie was bent double with his hands over his ears. Galt carefully wiped her arm on the grass – damn, these entrails took some removing – and looked at the scene around her. Ground covered in boulders, most of which were moth corpses; or actual boulders, or... she didn't want to know. Not yet.

Arvennir army and navy personnel milled about, some shouting orders while others stood around in shock. Islanders, likewise: sitting, standing, but all with eyes, or mouths, or both wide open.

"Crombie, you all right?" said Fisher. "You're a natural."

"Easy for you to say." He straightened up, red-faced in the plain lamplight. "Felt like a bolt of lightning went through me." Then he keeled over and lay panting on the ground. "We did it!"

"Yes, we did," said Galt.

"Splendid work," said Catt. Galt took her pendant from him, just as he was about to slip it into a pocket.

"Safe-keeping! I was going to give it back!"

"Of course you were, Catty."

Fisher leaned on his knees. "Yes, great work. And you two have *both* got the mage instinct – just needs honing with instruction and practice."

"A very great deal of instruction and practice," Catt said tersely.

The stone was dull again. Empty. "It won't work any more, in any case," said Galt, suddenly weak with shock. "Did you work out what Acicular but Once means?"

Catt begrudgingly shook his head. He and Fisher both looked at her, waiting.

"A needle that could pierce open a portal. The needle was the light piercing the sky. It was only meant to work once."

"Many relics are like that," said Catt. "Massive energy, then they run out of steam, as it were."

"But this one worked twice. I can't explain yet, but I think my mother put her spirit into it to replace the magic she'd used. And now… her mission accomplished… she's gone." Her voice faded. She felt Fisher's hands and Crombie's on her back, holding her steady.

High above, Captain Jennvi was cautiously rotating the shield around to its open position. The lighthouse beam reappeared and continued to shine without effort, as if nothing had happened. With every Sketterae corpse that tumbled from the dome, it shone a little brighter. Imperial, aloof, impervious.

"Oh dear." The voice was Governor Gredlen's, a few strides away. In the partial light, Galt saw General Orendion lying dead, pierced by the deadly sword-sting of an angry passing scuriti wasp. The rest of the Arvennir officers – except Embran – stood looking down at him, stunned.

"Well, there it is," Governor Gredlen addressed the Arvennir contingent. "There's your damnable lighthouse. Happy now?"

"ANYTHING ELSE YOU need, my dear?" Catt asked.

"Do you have a remedy for my father being a stubborn idiot?"

Catt smirked. "Alas, no... However, if this unfortunate unfolding of events hasn't shaken him up, nothing will."

"I almost wish that Skettera wasp had stabbed *him* through the heart, instead of Orendion. I know that's not fair, after what he saw in the war... but... none of that excuses him trying to kill my friends!"

"At least the General won't have to face the King's wrath for losing the cargo," said Fishy, with an ill-suppressed smirk. "I strongly advise pleading ignorance."

"I'm sure we will," said Galt, "but how can I ever atone for the fact that Embran tried to *torture and murder you*?"

"Not the first time," said Catt. "If we added up all the times we've been tortured and murdered... well, *nearly* murdered..."

"On top of that, he's never going to forgive me for using sorcery in the lighthouse!"

"Oh, just buy him a few beers," Fisher said. "That should do the trick."

"Have you *met* my father? I did what was necessary, but he doesn't see it that way. I'm half-hoping the King will throw him in prison. There *must* be enough charges we can raise against him. He's not sane. He's not *safe*."

"Failing that, we have plenty more *interesting teas* back at the shop, next time you're passing," said Catt.

"I'll be sure to drop in." Her spirits seemed to lift, and she punched Crombie on the arm. "You should meet me there sometime, little brother. Broaden your horizons!"

A happy thrill went through him. He lowered his head so she didn't see him grinning like an idiot. Also trying not to let any tears break loose.

Commander Embran's ship was boarding. He was already on deck with Captain Jennvi; Crombie saw him gesticulating at Galt, summoning her to join him. *Why didn't that bastard die with Orendion?* he thought grimly. *There's no justice.* At least Embran looked a bit grey, subdued, less of the raging bear.

"Why are you even going back with him?" Crombie asked.

"To make sure he behaves," she said darkly. "I will get him locked up, if that's what it takes. And I certainly won't be staying in Athaln. Time for a new start. My own architecture venture? Yes. That's my dream."

Doctor Catt and Doctor Fisher were travelling on the regular ferry. It was already by the dockside, ready to leave before the Arven ship. "This is us," Fisher said to Catt, lifting the Endless Satchel onto his shoulder. "This has been another one for the memoirs, eh?"

"Another day, another understatement." Catt patted Crombie on the shoulder. "Take care, dear boy. Any more magical troubles, send us a note."

*Time for a new resolution,* he thought. *Galt started me reading, now it's up to me to go on learning.* "Thank you, good sirs. As long as it's nothing urgent... although..."

"Yes, notes can travel fast by carrier dove," said Fisher.

"And *we* can travel fast by certain uncomfortable yet effective means." Catt winked. "As you well know, my boy."

With a couple of brisk nods, they turned and left, joining the line on the ferry gangplank. "One thing you did right," Galt called after them. "Catt didn't get his new hat dirty! It looks beautiful!"

"Fishy's making me a matching cloak!"

"In your dreams," said Fisher.

Crombie felt as if someone were pulling at his heart, kneading and stretching it like a lump of dough.

Galt, having waved goodbye to her apothecary friends, hung back. She took Crombie's hand and pressed something metallic and heavy into his left palm. "You'll need to keep this. If something *really* urgent happens, you know how to use it."

It was Embran's pendant: her mother's pendant, to be exact. "No, I couldn't, it's yours, I mean it's... no."

"Don't argue with me. This is purely practical. Look, it's got a different stone inside. Fishy broke it open so I can keep the quartz. Catt's replaced it with a turquoise, for communication. Put it on! I expect you to keep it safe. And rename it!"

"I promise." He obeyed, fastening the thick chain round his neck and tucking it into his shirt. *Galt's Turquoise*. That was it. Nothing fancy.

"Make a wish. Your dearest wish."

He put his hand up to the pendant and held it firmly, feeling the tingle and throb of energy within it. *My wish would be to marry you, Galt, if I were ten years older and not an island bumpkin who can't even read, and we'd be so happy and have three beautiful red-haired children and you'd build a perfect house and I'd run a perfect little farm...*

"Honestly, it would just be nice if everyone stopped calling me 'boy' and 'lad' and 'son' and 'oi, you' all the time," he said drily.

"No, don't *tell* me the wish!" Galt kissed his cheek. "But respect is a good thing to work for. And it will come, Crombie, and you'll suddenly wonder where the years went. I'm sorry we didn't have more time on your reading – but you will keep up your studies, won't you?"

"Promise. And, um, thank you for being the big sister I've never had. Couldn't have wished for a better one," he said, and meant it. More words than that, he couldn't find.

With a sweet warm smile and a wink, she went. Hardly fifteen minutes later, he was watching the ship cast off and move out into the ocean waters. All the islanders were crowded around him, cheering and waving goodbye, not so much with sadness as with happy relief to see the back of the Arvennir.

*Right,* he thought. *This is my proper wish; that the Great Moth is alive and enjoying her freedom somewhere. And the same for Galt. Safety and happiness.*

People drifted back to their homes, but Crombie stayed there until dusk began to fall and the ship was well out of view. The beam of the new lighthouse shone as bright and proud as a moon, transforming the waves and the fog into an enchanted plane where demi-ods might float about.

"If I can learn to read and write, I could learn to be a mage," he said to himself. "I don't have to stay on Fort Isle. I could go and have adventures and help people."

"You could," said Paulian the mage behind him, making him startle. His voice was downbeat and he stood with his arms inside his sleeves, looking deflated. "Indeed, you should."

"You wrote the moth wing on the list, didn't you?"

Paulian gave no answer. Instead, "They've offered me a post as new lighthouse keeper. Because I... know how everything works."

"They have? That's wonderful, but... your healing duties?"

"That will continue. I'm only one of five or six keepers."

"I think you will love it up there."

"You could join us. Becoming a mage, though; if that's your calling, it's an interesting path, if a lonely and twisty one. Good luck, friend."

"Kind of you, Paulian."

"Just bear in mind that no one will thank you for it."

# CODA

"AND WHAT NAME should we bestow on that particular collection? Artefact, singular or plural?" said Catty.

"Let's just live in hope that those *sods* of organic magical items actually function as they should," said Fisher, slicing cake. They were home, cosy in a back room of the shop.

"Artefacts of *organic* origin are strikingly rare. Especially those that no one will ever find again. What about 'The Eight Wing Scales of the Great Moth of Umberanaetheon'? Too obvious?"

"Sounds perfect to me," said Fisher.

"Oh, do you have your Orb of Trapped Light to hand? Let's see what it captured."

Fisher drew the crystal orb from a pocket and projected it at a wall, or the only clear square of wall there was. The instant sketch lit up. The image was hazy, but showed what they remembered in full colour: fire-dry earth, the small hill behind the colossal queen moth, the Moth of Moths. The Queen Mantid in the corner, ready to attack.

"Look at that. It was all real! I hope the Sketterae survive, and find realms more pleasant and fitting for beings of their stature."

"Where people like us don't scream and squash them."

"Me too, Fishy," said Catt. "I'd better start making notes and drawings before any of this slips my memory. The Sketterae!"

"Any relation to the Kelicerati, I wonder?"

"Mm. My instinct says not. There may be many different orders of gigantic bugs who dwell in their own gigantic bug dimensions... as much as I hope never to encounter one ever again. This is going to be quite the essay."

He bent down and opened the satchel. As he hunted for his notebook and pencil, the bag fell on its side and a heap of charred relics tumbled out. Jewelled skulls and carved bones and phials and the rest.

"Catty!" Fisher shouted, nearly jumping out of his chair. "I told you to leave that stuff alone! How the devil did you sneak it out without me noticing?"

"Long years of practice," said Doctor Catt. "Sadly, I didn't get everything."

"Small mercies."

"Dear old friend, you *know* I couldn't leave them in an unseemly heap. The energies get too agitated, and then... bad things happen."

"Mm. That said, I dread to think what fragments of malevolence are still inside those items. *What* have you brought into our previously mostly safe abode?"

"Who knows?" Catt smiled happily, rubbing his hands together. "We're going to have months of marvellous fun finding out."

# TAKING NOTE
### by Juliet E. McKenna

## ONE

IT WAS A tediously quiet morning in the byways of Cinquetann Riverport. Doctor Catt had taken stock of every last herb in the shop, fresh and dried, both in jars and bunches. He had sorted them into alphabetical order, and made a list of those which he or Fisher needed to replenish. At least that was a conversation which promised some passing entertainment. Either that or a heated argument, depending on whether or not Fisher had decided it was Catt's responsibility to see to such things. Perhaps they could agree that one of the ever-hopeful waifs and strays who visited the shop to sell their trinkets could be persuaded to do the hard and dirty work of harvesting.

Yes, that was a better idea. Catt smiled contentedly as he tidied up the papers on his little desk, though he resisted the temptation to call Fisher out of the back room. The old fidget had insisted it was Catt's turn to tend their customers while he was doing whatever it was that he considered so important with that battered Forinthi ear trumpet. Catt hadn't been listening when Fisher had explained the details, but he knew his partner would resent being interrupted. They could discuss herbs after lunch. At the very least that would break up what promised to be an equally boring afternoon.

A figure outside the shop window momentarily shadowed the glass. Catt sat up straighter on his stool. He shrugged his shoulders to settle his blue and silver robe more neatly, as befitted a scholar and antiquarian. He practised his most welcoming smile: the one that would convince anyone desperate to trade some treasure saved from the recent years of upheaval that they would get the fairest price right here.

The figure walked on by. It was hard to make out who they might be through the small, grimy panes that made up the shop front. Just a few days ago, one of the dispossessed who washed up so often hereabouts had offered to scour the glass clean of years of wind-blown, rain-plastered dust. Catt had almost been sorry to turn her away. He respected the incomers who would offer to do whatever menial service they could see a need for, rather than simply sit on a street corner and beg. But he wasn't about to explain that enabling passers-by to see into this particular shop was as unwelcome as it was unnecessary for him to be able to see out through these windows.

He lifted the hinged lid of his sloping desk, and tucked his lists under a polished mirror in an ornately carved ashwood frame. He waved a hand across the glass. The mirror showed him the street outside as clearly as if he were standing in the shop's open doorway. Catt studied the retreating figure now sauntering past the cobbler's shopfront. The stranger's hair was hidden by a neat hat, so he couldn't see how long or short it might be. Nevertheless that was a woman, he decided, leather jerkin, buff breeches and black boots notwithstanding. There was something unmistakeably feminine in the stride and the sway of those hips, as she passed the cheesemonger.

Not a traveller though, or at least not a recent arrival. She carried no pack and wore no cloak in the mild spring weather. She must have such resources though, or other means as her garb was clean and tidy. More than that, there was none of the hesitation in her step that he was used to seeing in those who had arrived in Cinquetann with only the clothes they stood up in.

He watched her go on her way, wondering what those resources might be, how they might be reflected in the weight of her purse, and how she might be enticed over their threshold, when she returned to the heart of the city from whatever errand brought her to these back streets. Then the bell on its coiled spring over the door jangled. Catt hastily closed the desk lid on his Mezish Farsight glass and looked up to see who had just entered. His smile faded.

"Atrat," he said without enthusiasm. "What do you want?"

"No, wait, listen." The scrawny Arvennir spoke quickly, as if he was countering objections or dismissal before Catt had uttered any such thing. "I have news of an opportunity for you."

"Really?" Experience made Catt sceptical.

"Really," Atrat assured him. He reached into the unbuttoned breast of his tattered Cheriveni gown and pulled out a folded piece of paper.

"Really?" Catt heaved an exasperated sigh, as he swiftly and discreetly assessed the paper. It was new, clean and uncreased, apart from being folded into four.

Flattened out, it would be exactly the size favoured by the bill posters who papered the riverport with exciting news from out of town, invitations to forthcoming entertainments, or offers of well-paid work. So what had Atrat filched from one of the paste-brush and bucket brigade? The Arvennir was far too idle and spindly to have joined one of those energetic gangs. Bill posters had to work faster than the Housegrave's street reeves could order such affronts scraped off the walls. Those who had paid for the service in good faith were politely informed of the correct procedures for making use of the designated noticeboards, and handed the appropriate scale of fees, along with directions to the clerk who would take their payment and write out their receipt. Repeat offenders could try explaining themselves to a grim-faced judge.

"So what is it?" Catt asked with a finely honed lack of interest. He got down from his stool and walked over to stand behind the shop's glass counter.

Encouraged, Atrat advanced. He unfolded the paper and smoothed it out with his nail-bitten, grimy hands. "There's to be a sale in the Oerni enclave at noon tomorrow."

"So what else is new?" Catt demanded. "Oerni buy and sell as readily as they eat and breathe."

"No, wait, listen," the scrawny Arvennir protested. "See? It's a special sale. Lady Escarene of Varra Hecklen is hiring the Exchange Hall to hold a special sale of family heirlooms, to raise coin to ease her people's distress. Apparently the Hemlock Commune where they've been living has been badly flooded."

"I heard about that." Catt was already reading the details. The paper was upside down from where he stood, but that was no hindrance to him. He shook his head, pitying. "There were no lords or ladies left alive after the Varra Hill kingdoms were destroyed, and precious few of the peasantry. This is simply some scam."

Though he wondered what the con might be. The paper was good quality, as these things went, and the printing was clean and sharp-edged. Work like that didn't come cheap, so if the woman was a cheat, she had coin to stake. That must mean she expected a worthwhile return on her investment. As a loyal citizen – well, as a mostly law-abiding resident – of Cinquetann, surely Catt had a duty to expose those who came here to deceive the honestly gullible? Leaving such a villain stripped of the purse that financed her deceits – as well as acquiring anything else of interest – would be doing all Cheriveni a public service.

"Doctor Ulpian doesn't think she's a charlatan." Atrat's expression wavered between triumph and apprehension that he had overstepped some unanticipated mark.

"Really?" Now Catt's interest was genuine.

Atrat nodded eagerly. "His Marincol was asking the bill

posters about it. Who had paid them and when? What inn is the lady staying at, or does she reside elsewhere? She wanted to know if the lady would be holding any advance viewings of her treasures. She said her honoured master would be willing to pay a small sum for that favour, in return for a consideration on the price of any pieces he might wish to purchase in advance of the sale itself."

"Her honoured master? My honoured arse," Catt muttered.

Atrat looked at him anxiously.

Catt pursed his lips. "I expect you think this news is worth something?"

"As your honour sees fit." Atrat clasped his hands together under his chin. He stood there round-shouldered, as if he expected a beating was as likely as some payment.

Catt reached into the pocket in his robe where a cut-purse would lose at least the top joint of any questing finger. Then he changed his mind and used his other hand to reach into the pocket that a cut-purse would never find. He took out two pollys.

Atrat's red-veined eyes brightened. Catt proffered the silver, only to withdraw his hand as Atrat stretched out his open palm.

"I am paying you to keep watch on Ulpian and Marincol from now until noon tomorrow. Come and tell me if there's any sign of the lady granting either of them an audience. At once," he stressed as he dropped the coins.

"At once," Atrat promised fervently as his fingers closed tight on such largesse.

He stood there, beaming.

"Go on then," Catt prompted.

Atrat nodded eagerly. "Of course."

Catt watched him leave the shop. As the bell jangled, he turned to see Fisher emerge from the back room, scowling.

"Who was that?"

"Atrat the Arvennir."

"You gave him money, didn't you? When did you become such a soft touch?" Fisher said without much heat.

"He's useful. Who's going to pay any attention to a runt of an Arvennir who couldn't fight his way free of a wet bath towel? Besides, he brought us that." Catt gestured at the bill advertising the supposed sale.

Fisher picked up the printed bill and read. The corners of his lugubrious mouth turned down even further. "Are we interested in this?" He sounded doubtful.

"Ulpian certainly is." Catt told him what Atrat had reported.

Interest kindled in Fisher's deep-set eyes. "What could a noble lady once of the Varra Hill Kingdoms have for sale that would interest him – and us?"

"Something that would have enabled such a noble lady to get out of the Varra Hill Kingdoms ahead of the Kinslayer and his ravening hordes?" Catt suggested. "It's not as if the poor fools had any warning that screaming death and destruction was about to emerge from the depths to slaughter and scatter them all."

Fisher nodded. His expression suggested he was already thinking the same. Though he was still inclined to caution. "If she is really Varran-born. She could well be some wayward opportunist from one of the communes. We've seen more than one with a knack for selling a convincing story and passing off a few trinkets of brass and glass as gold and diamonds."

"A possibility," Catt allowed. "So would you know a genuine Varra Hills accent from before the war if you heard one?"

Fisher's look of scorn said that foolish question didn't even deserve an answer. He turned to survey the shelves behind the counter. His gaze passed over the brass farm and saddle animals and the models of handcarts and carriages, dull with lack of polishing. He ignored the lead flasks, once crisply stamped with the insignia of the towns that had made them, and whatever symbol designated their contents. Most were so battered and deformed by years of passing from hand to careless hand that it was anyone's guess what they held. Rasping broke the silence as Fisher rubbed his stubbled jowls with a leathery hand, as he contemplated the tattered and discoloured ends of the scrolls stacked in the triangular cubby-holes down by the floor.

Catt waited patiently. He picked up the bill advertising the sale when Fisher stooped to retrieve the scroll he was seeking. Folding and tucking it away in another pocket left his hands free as the taller man unrolled the map he had selected on the glass counter. Catt took a smiling brass pig and a high-stepping colt from the shelf to weigh down the end closest to him.

"Careful with the Prince of Porkers," Fisher said absently as he studied the faded lines on the parchment. "Remember what happened last time."

"Oh, yes." Catt hastily swapped the pig for a bristling hedgehog. The brass figurine looked disgruntled as he put it back on the shelf.

"Here we are." Fisher was leaning on one hand to stop the scroll rerolling itself. He used the other to jab a long, swollen-knuckled finger at the map. "Varra Hecklen was to the north of Varra Buyil, and south of Varra Dermi. Varra Tinat was to the west and Varra Pagad lay to the east."

"I don't imagine we'd catch her making any mistakes about that. We're hardly the only ones who have maps from before the war," Catt pointed out.

Fisher looked up at him, mildly irritated. "If you take a look, and take a moment to recall the path and progress of the Kinslayer's reaving, you'll see it's not beyond the bounds of possibility that a woman with some magical means at her disposal, as well as the wit to use it, could have stayed ahead of the tide of destruction."

"Oh." Catt leaned over and drew the band of lenses that he wore pushed up on his forehead down to cover his eyes. He waited a moment as the lenses rearranged themselves and then nodded slowly. "I see, indeed."

He pushed the silver band back up and the sallow glow in the lenses faded. "So what do we do now?"

Fisher sucked his teeth. "Ulpian is bound to realise this will interest us. If one of his minions didn't follow Atrat here, I'd be very surprised. That fool is as stealthy as a black rat crossing a snowfield."

"Quite so." Catt smiled, content. "So while watching him and watching us takes up all Marincol's attention, we can decide who to use as our proxy."

"That's easier said than done." Fisher scowled. "If Ulpian sees anyone known to work with us at the sale, he'll drive up the price of anything they bid on, just out of spite."

"So we make sure he will have no idea who is bidding against him on our behalf, to empty his purse all the faster." Catt's smile broadened.

"So who do we trust?" Fisher's gaze returned to the map. "Who has the wits to tell if this so-called Lady Escarene is all that she claims? Come to that, who can tell us what she has for sale?"

"I was thinking about the Lantir captain who called here last market day?" For the first time, Catt sounded tentative.

Fisher looked at him sharply. "He'll want a substantial favour from us in return. There would have to be something for sale that we really want to acquire."

"True," Catt conceded, "but a Lantir will know if she's truly a Varran as soon as she opens her mouth. Who knows, depending on whereabouts in Lannet he and his ragged band lived before the war, they may even have some direct knowledge of this woman."

"Perhaps." Fisher traced the now obliterated border between the unlucky kingdoms with a thoughtful finger. He smiled without much humour. "Ulpian certainly won't expect us to be dealing with Lantir mercenaries."

"Exactly." Catt was smiling again.

Fisher nodded, decisive. "Let's see what this captain can find out. How well he does making a few enquiries should tell us if we can trust him to bid on our behalf."

"Once you buy a Lantir, they stay bought," Catt protested.

Fisher snorted. "That's no guarantee you're buying one with brains. I'm not handing over a purse for someone to spend our gold on Trispin's Ever-full Flagon."

Catt waved that away. They both knew full well where the flagon was. "So do you want to come with me, or shall I go and see them on my own?"

"I really need to finish work on that ear trumpet before the moon rises," Fisher said reluctantly.

"And we know that'll be a worthwhile investment of your time." Catt rubbed brisk hands together. "Let me see what I can find out while you carry on undisturbed."

He waved a hand and the bolts on the front door slid across to secure the shop. Following Fisher into the back room, he shrugged off his blue and silver robe and hung it on a hook by the rear exit to the alley behind the shop. He took something from a jar on the window ledge beside it. Then he donned an unremarkable cloak of blue-grey broadcloth and raised the hood before he opened the door.

Outside, the alley ran past the backyards that lay behind these shops. Similar yards served the buildings facing the next street over. An open drain scored a wavering line down the centre of the beaten earth that separated them. Pausing at the shop's rear gateway, Catt looked up and down the gentle slope. Marincol knew better than to hire underlings who would keep watch standing out in plain sight, but he would bet Fisher's Forinthi ear trumpet that someone was lurking behind that slightly open gate over yonder.

He was unconcerned. Their yard had no actual gate to open and close to alert Ulpian's spies. If anyone paused to look past the fragments of wood still clinging to the rusted hinges askew on the gatepost, all they would see would be a few chipped pots and splintered half-barrels filled with rainwater or possibly worse, if the smell was anything to go by. Of course, if anyone ignored the "no entry' sign nailed to the fence, that would be a very different story, but such trespassers would only have themselves to blame. Catt tossed the meaty titbit he'd taken from the jar to the closest land squid. The water in the barrel briefly seethed with tentacles. He made a mental note to remind Fisher that these juveniles would soon reach the size when they really should be released and replaced.

At this distance, he would go unnoticed by the watcher across the alley. Catt strolled towards the centre of the town. He stepped aside politely as the streets grew busier, and he couldn't avoid getting within arm's length of people. Men and women alike stepped aside for him as and when necessary. Not that any of them would have been able to say who they had just passed, even if they dealt with Catt and Fisher regularly. The twilight cloak had been a truly worthwhile acquisition. So much more useful than anything conferring invisibility. That only ever caused problems sooner or later, though selling such trinkets to those who didn't realise the drawbacks was always profitable.

He headed for the Dogged Drummer. The mercenary captain had insisted on telling him where his small company was quartered, in case he or Fisher changed their minds. That was another recommendation as far as Catt was concerned, at least for this particular task. Lantir were nothing if not persistent. Whether or not that ever enabled the far-flung remnants of Lannet's population to regroup, and then to reclaim and restore their ravaged homeland was another question, but that wasn't Catt's concern. Other than the leverage that desire gave him of course, to persuade them to do what he wanted.

# TWO

CAPTAIN ZETTIS RECOGNISED Sergeant Fasro's distinctive knock. He finished making the day's updates to the list that he was compiling. They were making good progress recording the names and residences of the Lantir to be found in Cinquetann. Then he looked up. "Enter."

His lean and grizzled subordinate held the door open and ushered Doctor Catt inside. Fasro didn't say anything, but that didn't signify. The troops joked that the sergeant hoarded his words like a miser. At least, they said that until they made some misstep. Then they learned how searing his unstinting eloquence could be.

"Doctor." Zettis stayed seated at the table. Meagre as these rooms they had hired might be, this unexpected visitor was on their territory now.

"Captain." Catt beamed as if this meeting was a treat he had been looking forward to all day.

Zettis looked past him. "Wine for our guest, sergeant."

Fasro nodded and withdrew, still without a word.

Zettis looked at Catt, unsmiling though not unfriendly. "What brings you here?"

The apothecary or alchemist or whatever he truly was chuckled. "Ah, the Lantir way. Straight to business as always."

Now Zettis smiled briefly. He inclined his head, as if he

273

acknowledged the compliment, whether or not the Cheriveni had meant it as one. If the tubby old man even was Cheriveni. Fasro might not be much of a talker, but he had a sharp ear for accents. After their visit to the shop, the sergeant had told his captain he had his doubts about Doctor Catt's origins.

"Please, make yourself comfortable." Zettis gestured at the chair on the other side of the battered and stained table.

Doctor Catt draped the cloak he carried slung over one arm across the back of the chair and sat down. "I have been thinking about our conversation the other day. Doctor Fisher and I were so sorry that we couldn't find any way to help you."

Zettis didn't recall seeing any sign of that, but he allowed himself to look politely hopeful.

"As it turns out, you may be able to do us some service." Catt beamed, apparently delighted. "Just as we find ourselves in possession of a rare and precious artefact that will bring untold benefits to your people, when you return home."

"Is that so?" Zettis leaned forward, resting his elbows on the table.

Doctor Catt leaned forward as well. "We have received Coulan's Plough of Plenty in trade for a particular service. Forgive me, I cannot say more about the precise circumstances, for our client's sake. You may rest assured that this plough is the genuine article though."

"What does it do?"

"Whatever soil, however impoverished, that it is used to cultivate will produce a bounteous harvest, however inclement the growing season might be, whether the weather is too hot or cold, whether the rain is excessive or even wholly absent."

Zettis curbed an urge to say that he knew what inclement meant. He recalled the verdict Fasro had brought him, after the sergeant had made his enquiries about the traders to be found here in Cinquetann. Everyone agreed that while it would be a good idea to have "buyer beware' tattooed on the backs of your hands before crossing Catt and Fisher's threshold, the devious old men never told outright lies about the curious, and not infrequently dangerous, items that they acquired and traded onwards, when doing so would benefit them.

"That would indeed be a useful tool to have when we return home. While we are still gathering our people and the necessary resources, it would be an unwieldy encumbrance, alas."

"Ah, never fear, that is not the case. Unless and until the plough is buckled to a beast's harness, it is small enough to carry in a trooper's backpack, still leaving plenty of room for everything else." Catt cupped his hands about an average boot length apart.

Zettis reckoned if his jolly, white-haired visitor smiled any more broadly, the corners of his mouth would reach his ears. "Then that would be a valuable asset to own. The service that you're asking must be of commensurate worth." The old man could learn that both of them at this table knew long and scholarly words.

Catt looked more serious. "It is, and you are uniquely qualified to do it."

"Please, do explain," Zettis invited, as Fasro returned with the wine.

He listened attentively as the doctor explained. Shorn of the old man's incessant circumlocutions, the first phase of the task had two facets. Decide if this woman was truly from the Varra Hills Kingdom that she claimed as her homeland. Establish what she had for sale.

"We can certainly make every effort to do this for you," he assured Doctor Catt, "and you may rely on our discretion."

"Excellent." The old man beamed. "I will call on you at midnight, to see what you have learned. Then I will return first thing tomorrow morning, to let you know what pieces we would like to acquire, and the prices we are willing to pay."

Zettis smiled. "As to our price, I take it that we're agreed the plough will be ours even if we learn this woman is a fraud, or if she is genuine but with nothing of any worth to sell."

That was a statement, not a question. He looked for Catt's reaction.

"Naturally," the white-haired scholar assured him.

"Then we have no time to lose." Zettis rapped his knuckles on the table and rose to his feet.

Doctor Catt took the hint and stood up as well. Fasro opened the door with another rattle of the latch to conceal the fact that he hadn't shut it completely after bringing the wine.

"My sergeant will see you to the door." Zettis waited as Fasro escorted Catt out.

Then he sat down again and poured another few fingers of wine into his own goblet. A few moments later, a Grennishwoman in a shapeless dun smock and leather leggings slipped into the room. At least, she referred to herself as such rather than accept her kind's usual neutral designation, and that was all Zettis cared to know. She set the cup she carried down on the table. Small like all her people, she had to use both of her six-fingered, two-thumbed hands to lift the wine jug. Zettis knew better than to offer to help her. Just as he knew better than to ask if she had heard what their visitor had to say. Fasro would have gone to find Deshiri before he went for the wine. She would have started making enquiries as soon as she heard the key details of Doctor Catt's proposal through the not-quite-closed door.

"This Lady Escarene is staying at the *Light of Truth*."

She pulled the vacated chair closer to the table and climbed onto it. Deshiri was short even by Grennish standards. She leaned forward to reach for her cup and drank with the delicacy that always surprised those who saw her ungainly Grennish limbs and her gangling walk, and expected her to be clumsy.

"Interesting." Zettis considered what the lady's choice might mean. There were more expensive inns in Cinquetann, as well as a great many more that were cheaper. So the lady was not being profligate, but she was prepared to pay – and had the means to pay – for a certain level of comfort and cleanliness, as well as the assurance of security.

Deshiri gave a murmur of pleasure as she swallowed the wine. Then she fixed Zettis with a stern glare. "You can drink less expensive vintages, you know."

"There are some things where Lantir never economise." He grinned at her. "Besides, if we're paying for the best wine, we can't afford enough of it for the company to get drunk enough to start trouble. That surely saves us coin in the long run."

"Any of the company drunk enough to risk falling foul of Fasro would be too drunk to stand. But enough of this merry jousting. How do you propose to satisfy Doctor Catt's curiosity?"

Zettis raised a hand. "First things first. Have you heard of this Plough of Plenty?"

Deshiri nodded. "It was in the catalogue of artefacts that the Reckoner circulated to every scavenger team. Though there was no indication in the copy that I carried to say if he sought to destroy it, or to lend it out to those he favoured among his minions."

It still gave Zettis chills to hear the Grennishwoman speak so casually of her service among the Kinslayer's hordes. Not that she and her kind had had any choice, he reminded himself yet again. More than that, unlike so many of her kind, Deshiri now sought to make amends. Most importantly, she had convinced him and Fasro that she wasn't only doing so to escape having her throat cut alongside so many others. There was no denying that Grennish made easy victims for those out to wreak vengeance on the Kinslayer's one-time minions.

She finished her wine and jumped down from the chair. "Time's a-wasting. Let's go."

"As you command." Zettis put his pens and inkwell away

in their box and closed the leather portfolio on his list. He had other records in there: the company accounts as well as the muster roll and testimonials from those satisfied with services rendered. He wasn't bothered about leaving it on the table. No one would get in here without Fasro knowing.

He grabbed his cloak and sword from their peg as he followed Deshiri out of the tavern. She walked a few paces ahead of him, taking two strides for every one of his. It didn't look as if they were walking together, but he was close enough to intervene if anyone tried to attack her. Today though, she merely suffered the usual sneers and contemptuous glances.

Deshiri had explained that she was used to it. Other races and humans in particular simply didn't like her kind. When you were used to your own folk always having the same arrangement of eyes, ears and limbs, it was unnerving to see that the Grennish could have any number and combination of such things.

Zettis was forced to admit it was far easier for the company's troops to accept a Grennish who had two arms and legs like them, and a face they recognised, even if her slit-pupiled eyes were over-large and wide-set over an oddly snub nose and an under-slung jaw. People here stepped aside for Deshiri though. Fear of the Kinslayer's hordes lingered, whether the populace realised it or not.

It wasn't far to the *Light of Truth*. The inn was a substantial three-storey building on the main highway entering the town from the west. There was a spacious yard to the rear reached through an arch to the left of the main entrance. Deshiri slipped through on the heels of a man leading a pack mule towards the stables. Zettis walked up the steps to the main door facing the street. He found a broad entrance hall. As well as the tap room to the left that served the passing trade, there was a salon to the right where those with rooms here could sit and eat or relax and chat as they chose. Doubtless, the muscular lackey at the salon door would keep any riff-raff out. Zettis also had no doubt that the amiable matron who sat behind the desk guarding access to the stairs could summon more henchmen with a blast on the silver whistle that she wore on a chain around her neck.

"Good day to you, madam." He bowed, low and courteous. "I seek an audience with Lady Escarene."

The matron at the desk sniffed. "You can see her at the sale like everyone else."

"Excuse me, but I have other business with her," Zettis said politely.

The matron's gaze sharpened. "Are you known to her?"

"No," he said steadily, "but I wish to ask what she might know of any Lantir living in the Hemlock Commune."

The matron drummed well-manicured fingernails on the table, looking thoughtful. Just when Zettis was expecting her to send him on his way, she rang the silver handbell that stood beside her inkwell. A maid appeared from a rear door and waited patiently while the matron wrote a brief note on a card taken from a marble box.

She handed the card to the girl and nodded at Zettis. "Take a seat."

"By all means." He was happy to wait on one of the chairs against the wall. That gave Deshiri more time to learn whatever she could at the inn's kitchen door. As it turned out, the eager maid returned promptly and handed the card to her mistress. The matron read whatever reply was written on it, sniffed and tore the message in two.

"You may go up." She dropped the pieces of card into the wastepaper basket by her desk.

Zettis followed the demure maid up to the second floor where Lady Escarene had a spacious corner sitting room at the rear of the inn. An interior door presumably led to a bedchamber. The sitting room was comfortably furnished for business as well as pleasure, though the chairs and tables had been pushed inelegantly close together. That was to accommodate the row of leather-covered and metal-reinforced chests that were lined up against the wall. Judging by the scuffs and dents, those had seen a lot of travel. They looked solid enough to protect their contents regardless.

The lady herself sat at a desk dealing with a quantity of correspondence. She was neither overly plain nor strikingly pretty. She wore a simple black gown, and a necklace and earrings of some sort of shiny grey stone. Silver combs held her long black hair up in a complicated twist. Zettis was hard put to guess her age. He could see no sign of grey on her head and her face was unlined. On the other hand, she was clearly well past her girlhood. He settled for 'in her prime'.

She laid down her pen and looked over at him. Her pale grey eyes were unexpectedly penetrating.

Zettis bowed low. "My lady."

"Captain." There was a sardonic edge to her voice. "You seem very interested in my possessions for a man supposedly here to ask about his strayed compatriots."

He decided a straight riposte was safer than making any attempt to parry. "A man may have more than one interest."

"True enough." She smiled, though there was still a challenging glint in her eye. "Then let us deal with one thing at a time. There are seven Lantir families in the Hemlock Commune."

Zettis took his wood and wax note tablet out of his jerkin's outer pocket. "Do you know their clan names? Can you say how many there are from each clan? How many generations?"

Lady Escarene had already picked up her pen as she drew a sheet of paper towards her. "I will write down all that I recall of them."

Zettis waited patiently once again. Meantime, he made a mental note. Every sentence that she spoke convinced him that the lady was indeed born and bred in the Varra Hills Kingdom as she claimed. So that was one of Doctor Catt's questions answered.

His throat tightened. Her lilting accents reminded him of his childhood, when travellers and traders came and went across the Middle Kingdoms, bringing news and wares in peace and friendship. Before the Kinslayer and his hordes brought destruction, death and worse to the innocent.

She set her pen aside and blew lightly on the page to dry the ink. "Do you honestly believe that you will be able to return home? Only the foolish expect to see a frost-blighted branch bear any fruit." Her words were uncompromising, though her voice was warmly sympathetic.

Zettis sniffed and coughed to clear his throat. "We will never know unless we try. The more of our kin we can gather to work together, the better our chances."

"The more coin you can earn, the better equipped you will be for the return."

She looked at him speculatively, and for a moment Zettis wondered if there was any way she could know that he was working for Catt and Fisher. He couldn't see how, but if the lady had magic artefacts to hand? Tavern tales were full of supposed wonders to be found – for the right price.

Despite himself, his gaze strayed to the line of trunks. The lady laughed.

"You are here to see what I might have for sale, aren't you? You're interested in whatever might be of use in your people's quest?"

"That had crossed my mind, as well as seeking news of the Lantir in the communes," Zettis admitted. After all, it was true. "My company has had a profitable year, wielding our swords in other people's quarrels. There may be better uses for our gold than gathering dust in a strong room."

"Just as there are better uses for the gold and silver that I can raise by selling these precious artefacts that my family have gathered." She smiled briefly and sadly as she glanced over at the trunks. "An ever-sharp knife is no use if there's no meat or bread for it to cut so that hungry children may eat. A book of alchemical lore offers no meaningful shelter in a rainstorm."

She drew a deep breath and sat up straight, squaring her shoulders. "What sort of things are you seeking?"

Zettis spread helpless hands. "What sort of things do you have for sale?"

The lady sat motionless and looked at him for a long moment with those penetrating grey eyes. He tried not to fidget. She pursed her lips and then nodded, as if she were conversing with someone unseen. She opened a drawer in the desk and took out a sheet of paper with neat printing already on it.

"I am not selling anything in advance of the auction," she warned. "Every buyer will be treated equally. My people need all the funds that this sale can raise. Each bidder may be accompanied by a clerk, but no one with weapons or an armed retinue will be allowed to enter. Anyone buying items too large or too numerous to take away with them will be escorted home by Oerni."

"Of course." Zettis nodded. Even Yorughan walked warily around the massive traders. The Oerni themselves were peaceable folk. That was easy enough, since no one wanted to risk angering them, and not merely to avoid being flattened by a fist the size of his head. Offend one Oerni and word would spread through all their enclaves, making a malefactor's life very difficult indeed.

The lady held out both sheets of paper, printed and immaculately handwritten. He walked forward to take them.

"May I ask one further favour?" He folded the lists and stowed them in his jerkin's inner breast pocket. "When you return to the Hemlock Commune, would you take letters from me to the Lantir there? So these families may learn of our plans and the best ways to contact us if they wish to join us, or other communities of our people?"

She smiled. "I can do that, and gladly."

Zettis bowed low once again. "Many thanks."

"I look forward to seeing you at the sale tomorrow."

That was clearly a polite dismissal. The lady was already reaching for the next letter she wished to read.

"Thank you for your time, and for your consideration." Zettis bowed his farewell and left without further ceremony.

He went downstairs with a spring in his step. His first two tasks had been accomplished swiftly and easily. Of course, that was always a warning to stay alert. Complacency killed as effectively as a cut throat.

A woman in sunny yellow skirts and a well-fitted, well-filled maroon bodice over a white blouse was sitting on a chair in the entrance hall. She glanced up as he appeared at the top of the stairs. There was nothing remarkable about someone doing that, but her gaze lingered on Zettis as if she sought to fix his face in her memory.

As he came down the stairs, the matron at the desk was summoned into the salon by a querulous voice. "Mistress Lafide, a moment of your time, if you please?"

As soon as the doorman's back was turned as he looked to see who was calling, the woman in yellow darted forward to scoop the torn cards from the wastepaper basket. The doorman caught the flash of movement in the corner of his eye, but she had fled through the front door before his bellow of outrage rattled the candles in their sconces on the walls.

Zettis walked through the hallway and paused on the threshold at the top of the steps. He swiftly surveyed the street, looking for Deshiri. He saw the woman in yellow skirts loitering in a doorway opposite. She was looking back at him. As their eyes met, she smiled, flirtatious. She was fine featured and smooth skinned with a knowing look in her eye that made her even more attractive to a man of the world.

He considered his options. Heading that way was his most direct route back to the Dogged Drummer. There was no sign of Deshiri, but he'd bet good gold that the Grennishwoman would be close enough to see any encounter, if the woman in yellow accosted him. He walked down the steps and made his way along the street without undue haste.

As he drew near, the woman stepped out of the doorway. "Good day to you, Captain."

"Good day." He nodded politely, though he didn't curb his stride.

She fell into step beside him, white lace on her petticoats frothing under her hems. They were much the same height. Zettis was wiry and lithe rather than tall and muscular, while the woman was a little taller than most. They were much of an age as well. Old enough to have learned from the mistakes of their callow years, and young enough to make the most of the knowledge they had gained.

"We do admire your people, you know," she remarked, as though continuing a conversation. "So many recoil from the hard work of regrouping and rebuilding now that the Kinslayer is dead. They prefer to mope and wail and wait for someone else to magically restore all they have lost."

"We?" Zettis queried.

She replied readily. "I study with one of Cinquetann's foremost scholars. Doctor Ulpian. You may have heard of him."

"Indeed." Though people studiously avoided offering an opinion about him. That made Zettis wary.

The woman laughed, determined to be amiable. "You are a man of few words."

Zettis decided not to answer that. The woman didn't seem concerned.

"As you might imagine, the good doctor is most interested in what this self-proclaimed lady might be selling." Scepticism shaded her words.

"And in those who might be interested in buying from her,

whether or not she wishes to share her business affairs." Zettis decided it was time to test this stranger who had still not shared her own name. She had stolen those torn cards from the wastebasket right in front of him. She had to know he had seen her do that. He wondered idly where she had stowed the cards beneath her full skirts.

She laughed again. "I admit our methods may seem unorthodox, but the good doctor is concerned that the innocent may be cheated. Tell me," she invited, "what are you particularly interested in buying?"

She slipped her arm through his and drew him close. He felt the generous swell of her breast against his biceps, as he was forced to walk more slowly.

"I sought news of Lantir families taking refuge in the communes," he said steadily.

"I'm sure you did," she agreed, "but you sought more besides." That wasn't a question.

"What is that to you?" he asked, curious rather than challenging her.

"Doctor Ulpian is concerned that prices at an auction may be driven up by rival bidding, beyond an item's true value and beyond what people can afford. These are desperate times, and desperate people can be goaded into folly they will later regret."

"And so?"

"Doctor Ulpian is willing to act as assessor and also as proxy. He will offer his expert opinion on items of interest, as to their authenticity and value. He will bid up to a fair price on a piece and no further. It may well not be necessary to offer an agreed maximum price. The fewer buyers who attend the sale, the less fevered the bidding will be."

"The less money there will be for the Hemlock Commune," Zettis observed.

"The lady decided to take that chance when she opted to

hold an auction rather than sell to Cinquetann's established traders." For the first time, there was an edge to the woman's voice.

Zettis shrugged. "That is no concern of mine."

"No?" The woman forced him to a halt. "Then what are you doing for Doctor Catt? We know he called on you today."

"That is no concern of yours." Zettis pulled himself loose from her hold.

As he took a pace backwards, a passer-by collided with him. As the stranger stumbled and swore, he pushed Zettis into the woman. She rebuffed the captain with a swift shove.

"My apologies." She forced a smile. "Very well. Let us discuss your concerns. You wish to fund your people's return to their villages and farms in Lannet. Whatever Catt and Fisher are offering you, for whatever they have asked you to do, Doctor Ulpian will outbid them."

He looked her in the eye. "I have no interest in getting in the middle of their rivalry."

She met his gaze. "Then don't. Tell us what they want, and then tell them you have changed your mind. Doctor Ulpian will pay handsomely for that alone. Surely securing a profit without risk is in your people's best interests?"

"Alas." Zettis smiled without humour. "Don't you know that once Lantir are bought, we stay bought."

The woman wasn't smiling back. "Then you will earn Doctor Ulpian's enmity and that error will prove costly."

Zettis couldn't deny that prospect gave him a qualm, but he didn't show it. "That is unfortunate, but it is none of our doing. We will share this conversation with all and sundry, if the good doctor subjects us to some undeserved punishment. He will hardly profit from that."

With so many people unwilling to comment on Doctor Ulpian's character, Zettis guessed that he guarded his reputation zealously. That was all very well, but that meant there would be a lot of pent-up grievances in this town. Any crack in the dam would be followed by a flood.

The woman sneered, looking most unattractive. "I had heard you were a master tactician. You are as foolish as every other Lantir dreaming of a return to your ravaged lands. No wonder the Kinslayer found you people such easy pickings."

She turned away and strode off with a flounce of her yellow skirts. Zettis watched her go. When he lost sight of her in the busy street, he went on his way.

Deshiri appeared at his side as he turned into the lane leading to the Dogged Drummer. She offered him his wood and wax tablet.

"Thanks. Did she take the time to read it?" Not that it mattered if she had. A reminder to settle the company's bill with a local pastry maker was hardly vital intelligence.

"No, and you may rest assured that she'll have no idea where or how she lost it." The little Grennish smiled happily, though that had the unfortunate effect of showing her double row of pointed snaggleteeth.

Fasro had once told her to smile at some temporary captives to reassure them. He'd told the prisoners that meant she was choosing which one of them to eat. The captives had believed the sergeant. He was waiting for them both when they went into the room that Zettis had claimed as the company's office.

"There's a spy on the staff here," the captain said without preamble. "Selling gossip to Doctor Ulpian, most likely by way of—" He looked at Deshiri.

"Marincol," the Grennish supplied. "His fixer and lover, though she'll lie back and spread her legs for others if that's what a job takes."

Fasro grinned at Zettis. The captain grinned back. He knew what the sergeant was thinking, and yes, the thought had crossed his mind. It had been a long time since he'd last lost himself in a woman's tight embrace.

"Just find out who the spy is." He dismissed Fasro with a gesture. He didn't need to tell the sergeant not to alert the informer. It was always useful to have a conduit for misinformation.

Fasro left, closing the door behind him. Zettis took his usual seat at the scarred table and reached inside his jerkin. No pickpocket had ever succeeded in lifting anything he kept safe in there. He added the handwritten sheet to the papers inside his leather portfolio and handed the printed list to Deshiri.

She climbed onto the chair opposite. As she read, he poured wine for them both. He sipped slowly as he waited. Finally she looked up.

"What do you think Catt and Fisher want?" Zettis slid her cup across the table. "What could we use?"

"Flegen's Stenograph," she said instantly. "That's what we need. Those old men are welcome to whatever other trinkets they fancy."

Zettis' eyes widened. "That's there?"

Deshiri was amused. "You didn't read the list?"

"I didn't want to look too eager," he protested. Then he grinned. "That would be something to get hold of, wouldn't it?"

Deshiri raised a warning finger. "That's what everyone who reads this list will think. The bidding will be fierce."

Zettis finished his wine. "Catt said he would call at midnight, but now we know these walls have ears. Shall we go to the shop straightaway?"

"I see nothing to be gained by delay," the little Grennish agreed.

# THREE

CATT WAS PACING back and forth across the shop. He didn't dare go and enquire about Fisher's progress in the back room. The last time he had asked how things were going, Fishy had threatened to shove the silver ear-trumpet where it was most emphatically not designed to go. Though it had to be said, wondering what might actually happen if he did that had distracted Catt for at least a quarter of an hour. He was even wondering if there might be any way to experiment on some unsuspecting but well-compensated volunteer, when the bell over the door jangled.

Catt stared at the unexpected arrivals, appalled. "You have an odd definition of discretion."

The Lantir captain was unmoved. "You were seen in the Dogged Drummer and somebody there sells gossip. Doctor Ulpian's fixer knew I was visiting the lady on your behalf. She accosted me as I left."

"What did she want?" Catt demanded. "Marincol, I mean."

"To buy me." The captain's smile came and went in an instant. "She wasn't best pleased to learn I wasn't on the market."

Catt knew Marincol wasn't going to leave it at that, but he was content to let the captain think so, for the moment at least. "Well? What can you tell me about the lady?"

"She is from the Varra Hills, and her accent is from the region that includes Varra Hecklen." The captain had no doubt about that.

"This is what she has for sale." The diminutive Grennish proffered a printed list.

"Did you see the goods?" Catt demanded as he took it.

"No." Unconcerned, the captain looked at his Grennish companion.

Its fang-filled smile unnerved Catt despite himself. "I got close enough to her rooms to feel the resonance of powerful magic. If there are any fakes on this list, I will know them when they are presented individually for bids at the sale."

"Good to know." Catt wondered in passing what task this particular Grennish had been fashioned for. It was unusual to see one whose body shape and face was so close to human. He dismissed that as irrelevant, for the moment at least. He studied the printed list.

"There are some curios here we could be interested in acquiring. Ulpian may know that you are acting for us, but he will keep that to himself so you can still be of use." He made sure to keep his tone casual. "I will need to confer with Doctor Fisher. Call back here midmorning tomorrow. We will tell you what to bid for and what prices we are willing to go up to."

The captain didn't move. "We wish to discuss amending the terms of our agreement."

Catt looked up, woefully disappointed. "That is hardly the Lantir way."

"Revising an agreement is not breaking one's word," the Grennish said quickly.

Catt ignored the creature. He stared at the captain. "Well?"

"We have a use for Flegen's Stenograph," the Lantir soldier said steadily.

Catt was surprised into a laugh. "You seriously think you can afford to buy it? I know your company has a fine reputation, but I was not aware that you had found one of the Kinslayer's lost hoards."

"No, but everything we hear tells us that you have such wealth. We merely seek the loan of it, once it is in your possession."

Catt had to admire the man's audacity. "For what purpose, may I be so bold as to enquire?"

"To erase the dread runes at Dorhambri."

Catt was lost for words. He couldn't recall the last time that had happened. Had it ever happened? He managed the briefest of questions.

"Why?"

"There is still a fortune to be made working those mines. Seams of the finest iron ore remain untouched, which will yield both magical metal and inert. Everyone knows it. Bold gangs head down the shafts to see what riches they might win, now that Jocien Silvermort has been overthrown. But sooner rather than later, they succumb to the dread magic that still prevails. They are overwhelmed with the despair that kept the Kinslayer's slaves from revolting. Without his overseers' whips and brutality to drive them to work, they cannot focus on their tasks. They linger, listless, until they wander away, or until some carelessness or accident kills them."

Catt noted that the Lantir captain could be stirred to a lengthy speech when his passions were roused. "But if you erase the dread runes, the mines will be open to all comers."

"But we will be there first," the captain said confidently. "More than that, a good number of our kinsfolk toiled in those shafts when we were enslaved by the Kinslayer. We are familiar with the seams and adits. We know the tricks of processing the ore. We have contacts across the Middle Kingdoms and beyond who will be interested in buying high-grade metal."

Catt couldn't resist pressing the captain a little harder.

"What will you say to any descendants of the duke who used to own that land, if they seek to reclaim their inheritance?"

"The Kinslayer was well named," the captain said grimly, "in this regard at least. He eradicated that family root and branch, to the last and most distant offshoot. We have made certain of that. We are not thieves."

Catt acknowledged that with a nod. "But your people who laboured in those mines were treated with unspeakable cruelty. How can you possibly expect those who suffered such torments to go down into those depths again?"

"Many have already volunteered. They see it as a way to put such experiences behind them. They are focused on the gold they will earn for the good of all Lantir, to buy what we need to restore our homes when we return to Lannet."

"Well." Catt shook his head, his expression somewhere between admiration and disbelief. "I will give your proposal some thought." He stepped closer, lowering his voice and with a conspiratorial glance at the closed back door to the rear room. "I must warn you though, Doctor Fisher will take a lot of persuading. He won't like this in the least."

The captain was unmoved. "We will call here tomorrow for your answer and your instructions."

Catt nodded. "Very well. In the meantime, I'll wish you a pleasant and peaceful day." He beamed as he watched them leave the shop.

His smile faded as he turned towards the rear door. Fisher was coming through it. "I take it you heard that?"

"I did." Fisher laid the gleaming silver ear-trumpet on the glass counter. "We should be able to hear conversations including people we know now. Of course, we still have to establish its range."

"Later." Catt waved that aside as he handed Fisher the printed paper. "What are we going to do about this?"

Fisher studied the list. He raised a hand and a pencil flew

across the shop. He plucked it out of the air and ticked a few items. "These are the choicest picks. Of course, we'll have to disguise our interest with bids on lesser artefacts to mislead Ulpian and his lightskirt."

"What about Flegen's Stenograph?" Catt glanced at a high shelf where a row of leather-bound tomes sat shrouded in shadow and cobwebs. "We could really use that."

"Tell me something I don't know," Fisher said without heat. "That will go for a whole lot of gold. An emperor's ransom, if we're not careful. That will leave us seriously short of funds in the short term. How do we recoup at least some of that outlay?"

Catt smiled. "The Lantir want to borrow it. I suggest we hire it to them instead, for a deposit and full payment in due course."

"That would tell us if it's genuine, before we risk using it ourselves." Fisher looked thoughtfully at the shadowed shelf. "Though that also risks us losing it. Goodness knows what's lurking in those depths by now."

"Let's assume that it is the real thing, for the moment, and that this company are as good as everyone says, so they're well able to keep it safe," Catt countered. "If the Lantir can take control of the Dorhambri mines, and I wouldn't bet against them, they will soon earn themselves several emperors' ransoms. You saw they have a Grennish with them. One who can sense magical metals unless I am very much mistaken."

"And you so very rarely are," Fisher said gravely.

Catt's smile broadened with satisfaction. "Then it's reasonable to suppose these Lantir will secure a firm hold on the trade in magical iron. Sooner rather than later, most likely, as their one-time compatriots flock to help them. If you and I have been instrumental in helping them achieve this cherished aim, there's every chance of us securing a share in the wealth that results."

"While we take our time using the stenograph to unlock a

few profitable puzzles here." Now Fisher looked at the age-darkened books with barely veiled anticipation. "All told, I believe this proposed course of action has considerable merit."

"Besides, we can always keep an eye on them, and step in to retrieve the Stenograph if needs be." Catt rubbed his hands together before shoving his sleeves up his forearms. "Now we just need a plan to shove a spoke in Ulpian's wheel tomorrow."

Fisher turned to contemplate the array of figurines on the shelf behind the counter. He rubbed a long-fingered hand thoughtfully over his stubbled chin.

# FOUR

THE FIRST STROKE of the noon bell rang across the Oerni enclave. Zettis looked around the market place in front of the Exchange Hall. The trampled earth had been cobbled with river pebbles to reduce the mud underfoot and Oerni craftsmen and traders had erected stalls that were taking on an air of permanence. Trade was brisk as Cheriveni from Cinquetann and beyond mingled with humans and other races making a stop on their journeys up and down the river. He even saw a handful of Yorughan, clearly minding their manners. It would be a fair while before this enclave packed up and moved on, if he was any judge. As long as business was this good, the Oerni would stay put.

Deshiri plucked at his sleeve. "Come inside. We don't want to be locked out."

Zettis glanced over his shoulder at the two Oerni guarding the door. They looked in no hurry to him, chatting idly as the second bell sounded. "There's still no sign of him? Or of her?"

He had been looking for the woman, Marincol. He had studied every passing female, however dressed and whatever the colour of her hair. Making a few further enquiries yesterday, they had learned Doctor Ulpian's fixer had a talent for disguise. Even so, Zettis was pretty sure she hadn't passed him on her way into the hall.

Deshiri was keeping watch for Doctor Ulpian. She and Fasro had learned where the learned scholar was dining last night. They had paid a servitor to point him out to them, and made careful note of his appearance. A man who enjoyed his meals, Fasro had told Zettis, though with the height to carry off his excess weight. Dark and sleek of hair, with a precisely trimmed beard and manicured hands. The cost of his doublet would feed three generations of a large family for a month. His reputation said he would evict that same family without a second thought if they were a day late with their rent.

"He's not—" The little Grennish broke off and hissed with vicious exasperation. "Here he comes."

As the noon bell struck its third chime, Doctor Ulpian was hard to miss. His elegant hat with its jaunty feather was pushed back on his head to make sure that everyone could see his face. Add to that, he wore a long poppy-red cloak over a rich wine-coloured doublet and breeches, and his top boots were polished to a mirror shine. To make quite certain that everyone noticed him, he rode a glossy bay stallion across the cobbles at a leisurely walk. It was the first horse Zettis had seen in the market. Everyone else had more sense than to bring a beast here amid the bustling throng. Doctor Ulpian, however, evidently knew what he was doing. He sat in the saddle with the poise of an expert horseman, and rode with his reins loose in one gloved hand as he waved to acquaintances in the crowd. Those visitors who had no idea who he was stopped and stared, nudging each other, pointing and whispering. Those locals who recognised him, even if they were beneath his notice, either studiously avoided catching his eye, or played safe with a demure curtsey or a polite bow.

A horse neighed, but it wasn't Ulpian's stallion. Zettis looked around to see who else was riding to the sale. He saw a chestnut being led through the crowd instead. Where by the Guardians had that come from? He'd only just looked in that direction, and had only seen people on foot. Zettis couldn't quite make out who had hold of the rein attached to the beast's halter. They wore an oddly indeterminate-coloured cloak as they were walking away.

That gave him a clear view of the chestnut mare's rear end. There was no mistaking she was a mare as she held her tail high and swished it too and fro. Zettis looked back as Ulpian's stallion snorted. The bay's nostrils flared as his crested neck arched. Zettis realised the mare must be in season. The stallion's interest in mounting her was increasingly apparent beneath his belly.

Ulpian realised it too. He gathered his reins in both hands, Too late. The stallion had the bit between his teeth. As Ulpian tried to curb him with whip and boots, the horse stamped his front hooves impatiently. The bay's rump swung around as he gathered his hind legs under his haunches, eager to pursue the mare. Startled bystanders scurried aside. Unease spread through the crowd like ripples from a stone dropped into a pond. Somewhere, a child wailed.

Shouts rose, rebuking Ulpian. The stallion's ears flattened against its skull. Its whinny was a belligerent challenge now, though Zettis couldn't see where the chestnut mare had gone. The bay stallion reared up, his forelegs raking the air. A woman screamed. The horse landed on all fours again, but immediately kicked out with both hooves behind him. To Ulpian's credit, the man kept his seat and his stirrups, as he wrestled for control over the frothing animal.

People were hurrying away, shoving and jostling. There was a crash somewhere on the far side of the marketplace. Yells and abuse followed. Heads turned to see what calamity had provoked the altercation. Even Ulpian looked around. That moment of inattention cost him dearly. The stallion sprang forward, determined to slake his desire for the mare. Ulpian was carried away, unable to restrain the lustful horse. Those too slow to get out of their path were barged aside. Feet were crushed under the stallion's steel-shod hooves. Cries of pain cut through the shrieks of alarm. A rumble of outrage was building beneath the cacophony. The trade-lords who governed this enclave were soon going to be deluged with complaints.

"Come on!" For a small creature, Deshiri had a vice-like grip. She dragged Zettis back towards the Exchange Hall threshold.

He didn't resist as he realised he had lost track of counting the noon chimes. The bell's note was still lingering overhead though, and the massive, mottle-faced Oerni guarding the entrance let the two of them pass inside without comment.

To call this a hall was to flatter the building and the Oerni. It was built of wood rather than stone, and as Zettis looked around, he realised the wooden panels that made up the walls and roof were designed to be taken apart, transported and re-erected. There were no windows, merely an open clerestory with canvas blinds that could be lowered to keep out any rain. The floor was thick woven reed matting over a layer of oiled canvas that could be glimpsed by the doors.

Zettis saw those doors were being closed behind them. "It looks like Doctor Ulpian's plan was to make a grand entrance when everyone else had already arrived. So much for that."

"The woman's not in here either." Deshiri satisfied herself with a cursory look around before returning her attention to the printed list. The sheet of paper was now liberally annotated with Doctor Catt's looping script and Doctor Fisher's cramped scrawl.

Zettis wondered if chance or something else had foiled whatever plans Catt and Fisher's rivals had made to be here, and doubtless to direct the course of the sale in their own favour. He dismissed such speculation in favour of assessing the situation here and now. To his relief, no one was paying the least attention to him and Deshiri. Each pair of bidders was standing as far from the others as possible, with heads close together as they whispered to avoid being overheard. Some were human, a substantial number were not, and mixed couples like him and Deshiri were common enough. There were enough bidders present to promise a lively sale, but not so many that there was any fear of things getting out of hand. Not that such folly was likely with six hefty Oerni standing beside the trunks from Lady Escarene's rooms.

Zettis looked around again. "She's not here either. The Varran noblewoman, I mean."

"Would you want to watch your inheritance going under the hammer? Everything you salvaged as you fled from the Kinslayer?"

Deshiri fell silent as a tall Oerni with an attractively pied face strode to the lectern. An expectant hush filled the hall as one of her assistants opened the first trunk. A clerk sat at a desk, opened a ledger, and dipped his pen into his inkwell.

The auctioneer clapped brisk hands together. "Good day to you all. Let us begin. Lot Number One is Aralun's Shovel."

The sale began. Zettis and Deshiri split the bidding between them, just in case that might put their rival bidders off their stroke. They didn't bid turn by turn obviously, but in an order decided by the random roll of a dice as they had shared a midmorning plate of pastries.

Bidding was brisk on some items and not at all on others. Zettis couldn't see any particular pattern, and it didn't seem that what was paid related in any way to a piece's intrinsic value. A silver brooch set with opals went for a paltry sum. A nondescript clay cup went for a price that left him breathlessly relieved it was not on their list.

Some of the things that Catt or Fisher had desired were clearly fiercely sought after. Twice, Zettis was forced to drop out, as the price others were willing to pay soared past the maximum sum he had been authorised to spend. Other pieces went for less than half their estimated worth. For the most part though, they secured the items the old men had marked out. Most important, as far as he was concerned, Deshiri's was the winning bid for Flegen's Stenograph. While the price was far more than the company could have possibly afforded, it was some way short of Doctor Fisher's estimate.

As the sale concluded, Zettis felt reasonably sure the sum raised would go a long way towards restoring the flood-ravaged Hemlock Commune. He hoped that would console Lady Escarene. He wondered if there was some way to be sure that her people appreciated her sacrifice.

The Oerni opened the doors to let the disappointed and disgruntled leave. Zettis and Deshiri joined the line of contented purchasers at the auctioneer's clerk's desk. Zettis took the letter of credit Doctor Fisher had given them out of his inner breast pocket. Deshiri and the clerk agreed the total sum owed, and the clerk carefully inked it in the ledger and on the letter. Zettis and Deshiri each signed his ledger and the letter to witness the transaction. The clerk endorsed both with the trade-lords' seal.

Zettis breathed a whole lot more easily as he took the letter back and tucked it away. Not carrying that around any longer while it was incomplete for any thief to steal and use for their own gain was a great relief. The only thing that outstripped that feeling was his satisfaction at securing the stenograph. He held up a hand as he saw one of the Oerni about to stow it in the large, bucket-shaped basket that already held their other purchases, well padded with rags. There was a good supply of packing materials and baskets of all sizes. There always was in any Oerni enclave. It was said their children learned to weave cane and grass around the same time they learned to walk and talk.

"I'll take that." He held out his open palm.

The stenograph was an ebony rod as long as his hand and the diameter of his little finger. Silver caps at each end were extended with tendrils curling along the wood. What looked like some sort of runes were inlaid along its length in a spiral pattern. Zettis had no idea what the shimmering substance they were made of might be. He also had no idea what sorcery could imbue a device like this with such unearthly powers, but the fact that so many bidders had sought to buy the thing convinced him this was the genuine article.

He put it in his inner pocket as well as the annotated letter, and picked up the basket. Feeling the weight of it, he decided not to trust the handles on either side. Ignoring the Oerni's affronted glare, he wrapped his arms around the burden and hugged it to his chest. He'd risk insulting these traders before he'd take the chance of anything they had bought with Catt and Fisher's gold getting dropped and broken if the wickerwork gave way.

Walking at his side, Deshiri looked up as they left the hall. She chuckled. "That should slow you down to a sensible pace for a change."

Zettis was about to answer when he saw movement a short distance away across the marketplace. Marincol came striding towards them. She was splattered with mud and her blue dress was as dishevelled as her hair. He wondered what had happened to delay her, though he didn't bother to ask. He was more concerned with watching the five extremely muscular henchmen who were following close behind her. People passing by slowed and stopped to see how this drama would play out. Zettis wondered that himself.

"Where's Doctor Ulpian?" Marincol snapped at him.

"Negotiating the fine he must pay to the trade-lords, I shouldn't wonder," Deshiri remarked. "He lost control of his horse and that caused no end of trouble."

Marincol ignored the Grennish, still glowering at the Lantir. "What did you do?"

"Us?" Zettis would have shrugged, but he was too encumbered by the heavy basket. "Nothing."

Marincol glared. "Let's see what you've got in there."

She gestured to two of her henchmen. Zettis took a swift step backwards. Deshiri slipped in front of him. She had a long, three-edged knife in her hand. She carried all sorts of things under that loose smock.

The henchman on her right curled his lip in disdain. The one on her left looked more wary. Perhaps he had worked out that this shorter opponent's stabbing height was on a level with his groin.

Zettis looked over the Grennishwoman's head. "These things are bought and paid for. You have no right to examine them. Let us pass."

Marincol spat on the ground. "You think we're afraid of Catt and Fisher?"

"I think I gave them my word. I won't let you make me an oath breaker." He resisted the urge to look over his shoulder for the Oerni market guards who had been watching the hall door. He wanted to keep Marincol looking at him.

Deshiri laughed. "If you're not afraid of Catt and Fisher, my girl, you've got more hair than wits."

Marincol bared her teeth in a snarl. "I could wring your neck with my own hands, you misshapen little runt."

Deshiri carved a figure of eight in the air with the tip of her murderous knife. "By all means, come on and try it."

Provoked, Marincol took a stride forward. Her henchmen grinned, avid to see what happened next. They certainly looked confident in their mistress's ability to fight the little Grennish hand to hand, with or without a weapon.

Marincol wasn't going to get the chance. Zettis' obstinacy and Deshiri's taunts had given Fasro and his hand-picked team the time they needed to slip quietly through the gathering crowd. They stepped up behind the woman and her henchmen as smoothly as if they had rehearsed this dance. Each henchman's smile faded into uncertainty as they felt a heavy hand on one shoulder and the point of a dagger in their back.

Fasro took care of Marincol. He wrapped both of his arms around her, pinning her elbows to her sides. To her credit, she responded immediately, bending her knees and trying to force her arms outwards to slip free. Alas for her, he had his hands firmly locked together beneath her voluptuous bosom. She couldn't force his hold up past that barrier.

She wasn't about to give up. She sidestepped, shifting her hips. She thrust her foot backwards, trying to sweep it around and hook a boot behind Fasro's leg. He was ready for that, moving nimbly out of her way. Now she was unbalanced, and that gave him his chance to lift her clean off her feet. People often looked at Fasro and underestimated his strength.

Marincol screamed, more with fury than fear. If she had any hope of rescue, Zettis reckoned that died as derisive laugher rippled through the watching crowd, from those confident they could stay safely anonymous.

"Excuse us." The burly Oerni who had been guarding the Exchange Hall doors strode past him and Deshiri. A handful of others followed them.

Zettis was relieved to see that Marincol and her henchmen weren't about to try fighting back. They stood, sullen and silent, as the Lantir stepped back to allow the Oerni to take them into custody. Each offender had his hands bound tight to his sides with rope looped tight around his hips. What Zettis had taken for belts turned out to be the means of restraint that the Oerni carried.

The market guards marched their captives away at a steady pace. None of the Oerni jerked the ropes that they held, or tried any other malicious trick, but Zettis was pretty sure that if one of those henchman lost his footing, he'd be dragged along the ground and the Oerni wouldn't miss a step.

Fasro set Marincol back down on her feet as the Oerni who had spoken to Zettis approached. The guard raised a hand holding his rope with a slipknot already looped at the end.

Marincol offered him her hands, wrists pressed together. Her face was expressionless. The Oerni looped his rope over her clenched fists and pulled it tight before leading her away. She spared Zettis one last glance of burning fury.

"You've made an enemy there," Deshiri observed. The Grennish didn't sound overly concerned.

"You'll watch my back, won't you, Fas?" Zettis handed over the heavy basket.

The sergeant just grinned. Then he felt the weight of their purchases and frowned. He snapped his fingers and two of the company's most recently pledged recruits hurried up with a handcart that rattled over the cobbles. Fasro always came prepared.

Zettis looked at the detachment from the company now assembled around him and nodded. "Good work. Now, let's get Catt and Fisher's treasures delivered, and get back to the Dogged Drummer to pack up. I want to be on the road at first light tomorrow."

# FIVE

ZETTIS PRACTISED HIS gaming face as soon as he woke every morning on their journey to the Dorhambri. The company needed to see that their captain remained resolute, even when they came under the influence of the dread runes. Especially then. He left it to Fasro and the others who had been handpicked to come with them, to tell of the devastation they had found on their scouting trip here. That made for sombre tales around the cook fires as the company made camp a short while before dusk fell on each day of their journey.

Where there had once been a mining town where life was hard but fair, the Kinslayer had ordered a grim fortress raised to house his minions. Brutalised slaves had toiled and died to build windowless barrack blocks to hold still more in helpless, hopeless servitude. More than that, the Kinslayer had incised complex sigils into the very stones of the walls to assail everyone who ventured into this once prosperous vale high in the hills. The dread runes filled the air with crushing despair more deadly than the foul black smoke from the foundry fires that had burned day and night to smelt the steel that armed and armoured his hordes.

The vile magic drained the slaves and prisoners who worked in the mines of all hope and spirit. That ensured they would never rebel. More than that, many paid little heed to their own safety or that of others. What was the point, when they would labour here until they died a wretched death? Some even hastened their own miserable end, by stepping into the path of a rumbling wagon heaped with ore. Others threw themselves into the black mouths of the mineshafts to plummet to their deaths. That was most common among the Aethani, whose wing-limbs had been mangled on the Kinslayer's orders, to rob them of their power of flight. Did they relish the last fleeting sensation of falling through the fetid air before they died in an instant of unspeakable, shattered agony?

The guards did nothing to stop them. Why bother? There would always be more slaves. There would always be more opportunities to drown out their own terrors with the screams and weeping of those they lashed to work harder. As long as the guards could show they were doing everything they could to keep the voracious furnaces fed, they wouldn't be crushed by the Kinslayer's wrath, would they? There was no way to know for sure, of course, but they could ward off their fear of those who ruled over them with merciless brutality for those beneath them. Then, with what passed for luck in this hellhole, maybe someone else would be chosen for drawn-out and bloody execution, when an example was made to boost productivity.

Zettis realised they must be approaching the outer limits of that foul magic when such grim recollections filled his thoughts. He raised a hand to halt the company as their path through the hills crested a ridge. They had taken this circuitous route to reach a vantage point over the town, in order to see what might await them.

"No smoke," Deshiri observed.

"Really? I hadn't noticed," Zettis retorted, sarcastic. He immediately realised the magic was curdling his tongue. "Sorry. I shouldn't have said that."

Deshiri glanced over her shoulder at the rest of the company and raised her voice. "Now you see what the dread runes can do, even at this distance, even to the strongest willed."

Zettis tried to hide his embarrassment as he looked back at the array of apprehensive faces. He cleared his throat. "Watch yourselves, and watch each other. We must guard against any urge to retaliate, if one of us is goaded into offering some insult. If I can be caught unawares by this magic, so can any of you."

Deshiri was already studying the buildings beneath them. "It looks very quiet down there."

"Too quiet." Zettis scowled, mistrustful. Was that the magic or years of experience talking? He couldn't be sure.

"Perhaps." The little Grennish still showed no sign of being touched by the vile runes. "But Jocien Silvermort is dead, remember. He would have been a hard act to follow by anyone seeking to rule this valley."

"The murderers and thieves he had working these seams may well still be lurking around here. They were, last time we came. It's not as if they have anywhere else to go." Despite himself, Zettis laughed bitterly. "You have to hand it to that bastard Silvermort. He persuaded the local lords and councils to hand over their criminals to serve as his free labour and then he sold them the ore and iron that their own people's blood and sweat had produced. They might just as well have paid him twice."

"Much good it did him in the long run. His little fiefdom fell as soon as he was killed." Deshiri was unperturbed. "There's no sign that anyone else has managed to make a go of working these mines."

Zettis had to admit she was right. There were no fires that he could see. Their first visit had shown the great foundry chimneys no longer spewed their soot, but this time there wasn't even a faint thread of woodsmoke to betray a meagre cook fire surrounded by the vagabonds who had fought like cornered rats.

There was no sign of life anywhere. No figures out in the open, human or other. No one slinking from one ruined building to the next. No glimpse of movement in a window frame fringed with shards of glass like broken teeth. No one lurking behind the shattered remnants of a kicked-in door. There wasn't even a solitary bird flying in the sky.

All the same, he recalled the awful stories they had heard, as they had travelled from place to place in search of their scattered compatriots. An Oerni consortium had sent some venturers here, to assess how the mines might be brought back into use for the greater good, and yes, to earn themselves a reasonable profit. Only half of them had returned. No two told the same story of the fate of the rest, and the trade-lord responsible had hanged himself barely ten days later. At least one Yorughan expedition had come here, declaring they would seize the valley for themselves. No one had been prepared to gainsay them, but nothing had been heard of them since.

Even so, the lure of Dorhambri iron and the fortunes that were surely to be made was simply too strong to fade away. A handful of other expeditions had been put together across the Middle Kingdoms. One had fallen apart when a crazed Aethani had cut her leader's throat in the middle of a crowded tavern. She had gone to the gallows screaming that the graves of her people here should never be profaned. Another proposition had turned out to be nothing more than a confidence trickster's scheme to fleece greedy investors. At least two boldly confident syndicates had actually travelled here, so the stories went. Those men and women had returned before the season had changed. They had come back threadbare, footsore, starving and refusing to discuss what they had found or what they had suffered. A frightening number swiftly drank themselves to death.

Then Deshiri had found Zettis and between them, they had come up with this plan. The plan that had survived the Lantirs' first encounter with this vale's dread runes when they came here to reconnoitre. A plan that they had finally found the means to enact, even if that had meant leaving the strongbox holding the company's entire fortune in trust with Catt and Fisher.

That was what Zettis kept telling himself, over and over again. As long as he did that, he could keep the memories of that first visit here at bay. No story however dire could match the reality of encountering the dread runes' power as they had advanced by the most direct route up the valley. Every time he had seen a dead body, and corpses had lain everywhere, Zettis had heard the screams of his own slaughtered family. His mind's eye had shown him the countless ways his mother and brothers, his sisters and father might have been slain by the Kinslayer's minions, how their bodies could have been violated before or after they died in screaming agony.

Not that he would ever know, because he hadn't even been there when Lannet was obliterated. He had only been thinking of himself, travelling in pursuit of selfish pleasures and paltry coin. He should have died alongside those he had abandoned, but if he killed himself now he would have to face those beloved ghosts. They would shun him and he would deserve it. He wasn't fit to rejoin the living or the dead. The best he could do would be to hide his shame in the deepest, darkest hole he could find. If he shed enough blood and sweat as he toiled, perhaps that would wash away his guilt before he died.

Zettis had managed to fight his way free of that insidious suggestion, but others had succumbed to whatever torments the dread runes had stirred up in the silt of their darkest imaginings. When they stopped to make camp, Moumol had ripped his own guts open with his own sword before anyone could stop him. When they realised Rimaris hadn't come back from gathering firewood, they had gone looking and found her hanging from the noose of her belt. Zettis had seen Vikri advancing on the dangling body with a knife. He had thought the young sergeant was going to cut her down to see if she could be saved. Instead Vikri had cut his own throat with a single, unhesitating slash to fall dead at his lover's feet. No one had slept after that.

He didn't deserve to ever sleep again. If he did succumb to exhaustion, who would blame any of those he had led into such suffering if someone smothered him with a pillow? How could anyone respect a captain who had failed his people so completely? Zettis clenched his fists so hard that his own fingernails gouged deep welts in his palms. The pain brought him back to himself and he realised he was feeling the brush of the runes' foul magic more and more strongly. He drew a deep, resolute breath and told himself he had survived these horrors once. He could survive them again, and more than that, he would see this evil eradicated so that no one else ever need suffer such torment. There could be no turning back now.

"Fasro, you keep the company up here for the moment. Set sentries and keep watch ahead and behind. Deshiri and I will take a small detachment down first, to assess the situation. Let's be ready for anything."

He looked over and saw the sergeant understood what he was saying, as well as everything that he wasn't. Fasro had felt the insidious touch of the runes threading despair through his thoughts on their earlier venture into this valley. He had told Zettis horrors the captain would never repeat, as they drank themselves into oblivion after escaping with the remnants of their reconnaissance expedition. Still, every coin has two sides. That meant the sergeant would know who would be best able to resist the evil magic, and who to keep furthest away from this vantage point over the valley.

Zettis pointed, choosing soldiers swiftly before any doubts in his own judgement could creep in. "Listis, Sardana, Hutten, Tinanthe, you come with me and Deshiri."

He led the way down the slope. As he scanned the desolate scene ahead, he rested his hand on his sword hilt. He resisted the growing urge to draw the blade from its scabbard. If he did that, then so would the others. The closer they came to the fortress, the greater their sense of peril and fear would be. If one of them succumbed and lashed out without thinking, there was only so much damage that a fist could do. Panic edged with razor-sharp steel would be something else entirely.

They reached the first traces of the havoc that years of mining had wrought here. The hillside was scarred with old pits where the easy iron had been dug out first, close to the surface. Many of the holes had been filled in with spoil from latter diggings, Zettis guessed, as well as with sundry garbage. There was a faint scent of old midden in the air.

Then he heard Hutten whimper behind him. The faint rattle of leather and buckle as the old soldier drew his sword made Zettis shiver. So much for choosing a man who'd never shown any sign of an active imagination, despite the horrors he had seen in the war.

"What is it?" Zettis fought to keep his voice level.

"There." Emotion choked off Hutten's reply.

Zettis turned and saw the burly greybeard pointing with his sword. There were two – no, three – figures huddled in a pit. The most that could be said was the trio were most likely human rather than anything else. One was larger, two were smaller. They had been digging, if the disturbed earth and torn turf was some guide. Whoever they had been, their nearest and dearest wouldn't know their faces now. Wind and sun had dried skin to rags of leather over stained bone. Their eyes were empty hollows, which at least proved there was some wild life here. Other scavengers had gnawed at withered fingers and feet protruding from their torn and faded cloaks. Apprehension hollowed his stomach. If there were wolves in these hills, they now had a taste for human flesh.

Zettis was unable to stop himself thinking about what could have happened here. These three must have been trying to hide. A mother and her children? The largest figure was smaller than an adult man, he could see that. Hiding from whatever dreadful fate pursued them. Murder, rape or worse? They had been desperate enough to try digging deeper into this hollow with their bare hands. He clenched his fists against phantom sensations of torn fingernails and lacerated fingers.

Though they had not been found. That had not saved them. They had perished here, pressed close together. They had wrapped their cloaks tight in a futile effort to ward off the night's cold. Had they frozen to death regardless, too afraid of whatever awaited them below to seek warmth and shelter? Had they endured the agonies of death by thirst over three long, wretched days? Had they starved here, after fruitlessly digging for whatever roots and worms might remain in this barren wasteland? Or had they simply lain down and died from sheer terror?

His throat closed with anguish at the thought of their final moments. What must it have been like for the eldest, whether parent or sibling, to die bereft of any hope for a future? Now no one would even remember their names to mourn.

"Ow!" Very real and physical pain shot up his leg as Deshiri kicked him in the shin. The Grennish might be slightly built, but she wore steel-toed boots like the rest of the company. Zettis grimaced.

"Thank you."

"You're welcome."

Deshiri sounded calm, but she was holding her three-edged knife so tightly that Zettis could see the sallow bones of her knuckles through her dark skin. He decided against asking her to put the jagged blade away.

The others were standing still, waiting for him to proceed. They looked pale and uneasy. Hutten was frozen in place. His face was twisted with horror and grief. Zettis walked over, though he stayed beyond reach of the man's sword.

"Soldier!" he barked. "What are you doing? Look at me when I'm talking to you!"

With a visible effort, Hutten dragged his gaze away from the pathetic corpses. As he focused on Zettis, the shadow haunting his eyes faded somewhat.

"The dead cannot hurt us," Zettis said sternly. "Don't let yourself linger to look at corpses. They are beyond any help. Keep watch for movement because that's what signals danger. Remember that danger is not just for ourselves, but for all those depending on us. I don't only mean our brothers and sisters in arms on the ridge."

As he gestured back up the slope, he looked to see if the other three were paying attention. Satisfied they were listening, he went on.

"We are here for the sake of all Lantir. If we can secure the wealth from these mines, then we can rebuild what has been stolen from us. We can lay a firm foundation for our children's future."

Hutten squared his broad shoulders. "As you say, my captain."

They went on. Deshiri took the lead. They reached the rutted and rubbish-strewn streets that cut between the barrack blocks. The hairs on the back of Zettis' neck rose. It was harder to keep watch in all directions now, hemmed in by the buildings. He couldn't shake the sensation of being watched. It didn't help that the slightest breeze rolling down from the heights was channelled and strengthened by these narrow alleys. Movement constantly snagged his eye, as rags or debris were caught by the wind. He had to look and look again to be certain there was no threat. That meant seeing the bones of the dead and feeling the pull of the dread.

"Where are we going?" Sardana's demand echoed the cry of the child she had been, dragged away from her home and friends as the Lantir fled death and worse at the hands of the Kinslayer's armies.

"To the fortress," Deshiri hissed. "The real magic is scored into the stones there. These marks only serve to amplify it."

She waved a misshapen hand at the closest rune carved above a door lintel. Zettis barely stopped himself looking at it.

Listis wasn't so quick to realise the danger. He stared at the carving then growled with wordless disgust. "Why are we following this abomination, Captain? How do we know it won't betray us? The Grennish always scavenged amid the destruction the Kinslayer wrought!"

Deshiri spun around, her knife at the ready. "We had no choice beyond yield or die, the same as everyone else."

Zettis struggled to understand her slithering words. She blinked and he shuddered, revolted by the sight of a pale third eyelid sweeping across her slit-pupiled iris. He screwed his own eyes tight shut against a surge of nausea. An instant later, he found the force of the evil magic fade.

"Close your eyes, all of you! Now! That's an order!"

He wanted to look to be certain that they obeyed him. He wanted to see if any threat was sneaking up, while they stood like dumb animals waiting for the poleaxe. He forced himself to stay there, blind by choice, chin on his chest, even as his ears strained for any sound of purposeful, stealthy movement in the ruined town.

Deshiri spoke first. Now her voice sounded perfectly normal, just as it always had. "I should have realised. There must be some respite from the dread runes, or the slaves here and the rest would die faster than they could be replaced. Darkness and sleep must offer just enough relief for people to endure the day to come."

That was in keeping with the Kinslayer's character, Zettis thought grimly. Why kill a prisoner just the once, however brutally, when you could keep someone lingering on the edge of endless misery?

"So we have to walk around here with our eyes shut?"

Zettis was inexpressibly relieved to hear the faintest trace of humour in Tinanthe's voice.

"I think we should be all right if we keep our eyes down and just watch where we're putting our feet," Deshiri said judiciously. "As long as we get to the fortress as quickly as possible," she added fervently.

That prompted a murmur of heartfelt agreement. Zettis cautiously opened his eyes and raised his head just enough to see everyone's feet. "Stay close together."

He fell into step behind Deshiri. The little Grennish picked up the pace. Zettis concentrated on watching her heels, counting her steps. He could hear the others marching behind him. The regular rhythm of their boots on the cobbles echoed back from the buildings.

His stomach hollowed. If there was anyone left in this benighted town, they were sure to hear the Lantir presence now. He fought the desire to stop, to look around, to make ready to fight. He resolutely ignored the fear that was shrivelling his balls. All he had to do was concentrate on watching Deshiri as she walked ahead of him.

He couldn't have said how far they had gone before stepping into a shadow caught him by surprise. An unnatural chill cut right through to his bones. Zettis looked up to see the wall of the fortress looming above them. Terror that the stones were about to fall and crush them all paralysed him. He would have cried out, but his mouth was too dry.

"Quick!' Deshiri demanded. "The stenograph!"

Zettis fumbled for his pocket. Despair numbed his fingers. What were they doing here? It was surely pointless? How could this gaudy trinket possibly undo such mighty magic?

The little Grennish snatched it from his hand. "Tinanthe! Lift me up!"

The rangy woman dropped to one knee and offered Deshiri both her hands. Deshiri took hold and used Tinanthe's knee as a step to spring onto her shoulders and turn around, as lithe as any market-place tumbler. The Grennish stretched out her arms to keep her balance as Tinanthe got carefully to her feet, with her hands now holding Deshiri's ankles.

"Close to the wall. A little to your left. Don't look upwards, any of you," Deshiri warned.

She and Tinanthe were both facing the same way so it was easy enough for the tall Lantir woman to follow Deshiri's directions.

Zettis desperately wanted to watch what they were doing. He settled for looking at Hutten, Sardana and Listis.

Sardana's attempt at a smile was ghastly. Her face was gaunt with strain. "So how does this thing work, Captain?"

He forced himself to concentrate on answering her question. "Complex magic like this, well, it's a complicated business. To create such a widespread effect, a sorcerer would have to inscribe hundreds of runes and sigils. They would have to recite pages and pages of incantations. If anyone was able to interrupt the process, they would have to begin again. So lots of wizards and scholars searched for ways to shortcut the process. Several of them had some success and we've been searching for those devices ever since Deshiri told us about them."

The Grennish had offered up her knowledge as the price of her admission to the company, and as proof that she was equally as committed as they were to undoing the abominations wrought in the Kinslayer's name.

Zettis went on. "Flegen of Sidero created the stenograph. The spell-caster can use it to trace over the pages of sigils and chants that would make up a matrix of spells. Once that's been done, it can be used to write a single rune that will be imbued with all that magic."

"So..." Listis struggled for understanding. "Now it holds some spell that will override the dread?"

"No, it will simply erase the rune and that will dissipate the magic. Flegen was wise enough not to create something so powerful that couldn't be just as swiftly undone."

Zettis broke off as he took an involuntary breath. He felt as though he had been carrying some great burden without even realising it. Now that weight had been unexpectedly lifted. The deadening chill that surrounded them eased. He looked up and felt the sun's warmth on his face. Even the sky seemed a brighter blue, reminding him of bellflowers.

Up above their heads, Deshiri laughed. "Feeling better?"

"Captain?" Desperate hope lit Hutten's eyes. "Does that mean—"

"Ware!" Listis' shout interrupted them.

Zettis drew his sword, quick as thought, as he spun around. A shadow moved in a darkened doorway across the street. A Yorughan staggered into the daylight.

"That's the biggest Yogg I've ever seen," breathed Sardana.

"Tallest, maybe. He's missed a few meals." Listis was cautious nevertheless.

Zettis saw what he meant. The Yorughan would stand half a head taller than most of his kind, but he was reduced to skin and bone beneath the dented helm and rusted armour that he still wore. That didn't stop him stalking towards them, clutching a halberd clotted with old blood in both of his clawed hands. His tusked mouth gaped with dreadful hunger, blackened tongue lolling. He would kill them and eat them all if he got the chance. There could be no doubt of that.

"What's going on?" Tinanthe demanded. She was still facing the fortress wall.

"Five paces to your right, if you please." Twisting at the waist, Deshiri could turn just enough to see what was going on, but she refused to be distracted from her task.

Zettis couldn't decide whether to be flattered by her faith in him or angry that the Grennish wasn't about to help. Before he could make up his mind, the Yorughan charged. Half-starved or not, his hoarse bellow struck Zettis like a physical blow. Hutten and Listis immediately fanned out to either flank. That left Sardana at Zettis' side to defend the Grennish as she worked to obliterate the next rune. Their swords were ready. The Yogg swept his halberd around in a wide arc to ward them off. Hutten scrambled back to avoid the blackened blade. As the Yogg turned towards him, Listis hesitated when he should have been looking for any chance to attack from the rear, to cut a hamstring or thrust through some gap where that armour hung loose.

Then Zettis felt the second rune dissipate. His sword was instantly lighter in his hand and his fighting instincts were keener. He took half a pace forward, and Sardana immediately fell back to stay between the Yogg and Tinanthe. He could see her wits were as sharp as ever now the magic that had dulled their minds was fading. As soon as the Yogg attacked him, Zettis knew she would seize her best angle of attack. Hutten and Listis were ready to back her up, with renewed alertness bright in their eyes.

They waited, poised. That was one of the first things Fasro taught recruits. Let the enemy commit first in a fight. Keep your own options open for as long as you could. Zettis felt a surge of pride in his people, and growing confidence that they would succeed in their task. Once they had reclaimed these mines, they could embark on the next stage of their quest.

The Yogg seemingly abandoned any thought of sucking the marrow from Hutten's bones, and focused on Zettis with murderous, bloodshot eyes. He drove the spike of the halberd forward with a thrust that would have skewered the captain like a chicken on a spit if it had connected.

Zettis sidestepped just enough to avoid the spike. In the same movement, he advanced. Now he was within the polearm's arc. Listis stepped forward, to distract the Yogg, or to hack down the halberd's shaft if he raised it. Zettis couldn't tell, and it didn't matter. All his attention was focused on driving the point of his sword up and into the Yorughan's throat, where the gorget that should have protected that vulnerability sagged on the wasted muscles of his neck.

The gleaming steel slid through skin and cartilage. The Yogg's halberd fell to the ground. Zettis felt his sword point grate against bone and pulled it free as the Yogg collapsed to his knees. Listis stepped forward to deliver a killing blow.

"No. Wait." Zettis raised a hand as the Yogg sagged forward.

Now the Yorughan was leaning on his hands, but he was struggling to look upwards all the same. Blood flowed from the wound in his neck, thick, dark and sluggish as treacle. Zettis realised he was trying to speak, but he could not make out the words. He struggled to understand Yoggs at the best of times as their tusks mangled the common speech. He had no chance here. The Yogg's mouth was dry as dust and the slash to his windpipe stole away his dying breath.

The Yorughan crashed to the floor. He used the last of his strength to roll over to lie on his back. Then the light in his eyes was gone.

Deshiri landed lightly in the dust beside Zettis. She knelt and laid a hand on the dead Yogg's forehead, with a few quiet words in the dead creature's own tongue.

"What did he say?" Zettis asked.

"Sky. The sky." The Grennish looked up. "He wanted to die looking at the sky."

"He wanted to kill us and feast on our flesh," Sardana said roughly.

"No, I don't think he did." Zettis gazed at the dead warrior. "He lowered his guard for an instant, just enough to give me an opening."

"He wanted to die." Deshiri's wide eyes brimmed with tears. "Erasing that first rune must have lifted his despair just enough for him to get up and seek his fate instead of lying in the darkness till death came."

"Captain?" Listis asked with desperate appeal. "Can we get out of here now?"

"I think so." Zettis looked for Deshiri's agreement.

She nodded. "We certainly know that the stenograph works."

Hutten raised a hand. "Then could it—?"

"It could do. It should do, but that must wait." Zettis let them see the depth of his regret. "It belongs to Catt and Fisher and our agreement is limited to using it here. As soon as we have cleared the dread runes, and taken possession of this valley for our exiled people, we are honour-bound to return it to Cinquetann."

"Once you buy a Lantir, we stay bought," Tinanthe said with a wry twist of her mouth. She wasn't rebuking anyone. She simply voiced the regret they shared.

Zettis looked around the valley. "When we have won some wealth from the mines here, there may be another deal to be done."

"Maybe..." Deshiri began, only to fall silent.

"What?" Zettis demanded.

The Grennish shook her head and refused to be drawn.

# SIX

CATT PACED BACK and forth across the shop. Fisher stood behind the glass counter, polishing the figurines on the shelves.

"If you're still doing that when he arrives, he'll know we were expecting him," Fisher observed. "Would you like to be the one to explain how we know so much about what he's been up to? Without making the good captain think we didn't trust him?"

"No." Catt bit off the word. He went over to sit at his desk and scowled. "Though I wouldn't mind hearing his excuses for taking so confounded long to return."

"Good luck with that." Fisher smiled over his shoulder before he gave a bronze statuette of a wide-rumped horse one last flick of his rag. "Never apologise, never explain. Isn't that the Lantir way?"

Catt wasn't listening. He had a far more serious concern. "What if Ulpian hears that they're back in town? Or Marincol?"

"They wouldn't be so foolish as to try to rob them. Not after the spectacle Marincol made of herself after the auction. Not now they know we have an interest in the stenograph." Fisher spoke softly, but his hooded eyes were hard. He tossed the rag into the air, and it vanished in a burst of flame so intense that not even ash was left hanging there.

Catt drummed thoughtful fingers on the desktop. "Are you

sure you can't think of any other reason why the Lantir would want to borrow it again?"

He knew they wanted to, but he had no idea why. He had used the Forinthi ear-trumpet to listen in on the captain's conversations with the Grennish whenever he'd had some spare time each day, but he had heard nothing to explain that mystery. At least, he had done until the captain's remarks had grown so curt and uninformative that there seemed no point in carrying on. Catt had become positively demoralised. So demoralised in fact, that he had wondered if there was some chance that the dread runes' despondency was somehow leaking through the trumpet. He hadn't tried to use it at all after that.

Fisher had called him a fool for obsessing over the captain's reasons for wanting the stenograph. There was no reason for the mercenaries to discuss something they both clearly already knew, for the benefit of some passing eavesdropper, near or far. Fisher was right, of course, but that didn't make any difference. Not knowing chafed Catt like an ill-fitting shirt. The only secrets he liked were the ones he kept close and which nobody else knew about. Well, no one but Fisher.

The door opened and the little bell rang its cheerful jingle. Catt made sure his smile was just as sunny.

"Good day to you both. Welcome, welcome." He slid off his stool and walked towards the Lantir and the little Grennish. "Just the two of you have come to Cinquetann today?"

Captain Zettis nodded. "As far as Doctor Ulpian is concerned, anyway."

The little Grennish smiled, smugly secretive.

Catt wasn't interested in whatever scheme the Lantir mercenaries had contrived to foil Ulpian's vengeance. "I take it you have our property with you?"

"Of course." The captain reached into an inner pocket and drew out the stenograph. "I take it you have our strongbox still safely stowed?" He nodded towards the back room.

"It is, but I don't think you'll manage to carry it between the two of you." Fisher was amused.

Captain Zettis smiled. "I will call back with a handcart and a squad of guards."

"As you like." Catt reached for the stenograph. "Have you succeeded in securing the Dorhambri for your people?" he asked innocently.

The captain handed over the silver and ebony rod. "We have cleared the dread runes and established our presence in the valley. Now we wait to see if anyone disputes our right to claim the rewards for the risks we have run, above ground and below."

"We wish you every success," Catt said warmly as he ushered them towards the door. "We look forward to seeing you again – a little later on, if you please."

"Tomorrow," Fisher said as he came around the glass counter. "Call for your strongbox tomorrow."

The Lantir and the Greenish exchanged a glance. The captain shrugged and the ungainly little creature nodded. Neither looked concerned.

"We will be here first thing," Zettis said.

"That will be fine. Good day to you both. Have a very good day." Catt smiled as he escorted the pair over the threshold and closed the door quickly behind them.

As soon as he turned his back, the bolts on the door drove themselves home. The grime on the window panes darkened and thickened. No one would be able to see inside the shop now, even if they pressed their nose to the glass.

The shadows around the high shelf on the far wall were thinning and fading. Fisher was already reaching up to take down the first bulky tome. It was as tall as his forearm was long, nearly as wide and as thick as the breadth of his hand.

"So what are we starting with?" Catt twirled the stenograph end over end with deft fingers.

"How about Owain's *Philosophy of Sorcerous Command*?"

Fisher set the book down on the counter with a thud. The leather binding was so dark with age it was almost black. That made the runes seared into the front cover nigh on impossible to see, let alone read. The edges of the pages were yellowed and tattered. The leather tongue of a book mark stuck out at the bottom, with the woven end firmly sewn to the spine at the top.

Catt reached for the tab and tried to lift it. The pages stayed clamped together, as solid as a block of the wood that had been pulped to make them.

Fisher arched a brow. "What was the point of that?"

"Just making sure that nothing had changed." Catt was unperturbed.

Fisher laced his long fingers together and cracked his knuckles. "Go on then. Let's take a look inside."

"Get me some light." Catt held the stenograph like the pen it resembled and slid the band holding his lenses down over his eyes. Once the lenses had arranged themselves to their own satisfaction, he gently brushed the silver end of the stenograph across the grooves in the leather. The silver tendrils that extended along the ebony rod writhed. The inlaid sigils glowed iridescent as mother of pearl.

Fisher brought over a small oil lamp, lighting the wick with a snap of his fingers. He set it down on the counter and Catt began to trace the stenograph along the twisted lines of the runes.

"Not too fast," Fisher warned.

Catt ignored him, bending closer to his task. He had to concentrate. Glimpses of the spells that had been combined here flickered across his enhanced vision. The writing came and went too fast for him to read but the ghostly script was persistent enough to be distracting. As the stenograph moved, a trail of glittering smoke arose from the runes. It disappeared almost as quickly as it appeared.

Fisher sniffed. "Smells like hot tin. I wonder why," he mused.

Catt didn't answer, still focused on what he was doing. Finally, he reached the end of the last arcane symbol. He stood straight, shoved his lenses up out of the way, and laid the stenograph carefully down on the glass.

"Let's see what old Owain knew that some selfish bastard was so keen to keep secret." He smiled with gleeful anticipation as he reached for the bookmark again.

This time the pages parted. Catt eased the book open to reveal closely written text in crisp black ink, two columns to a page. The right-hand page began with a title in bigger, bolder script. The first capital letter T was beautifully illuminated in jewel-like colours and embossed with shiny gold leaf.

"Taikov's Spiderclimb," he breathed. "At last."

"Let me see that." Fisher laid another book down on the counter. "Get this one open – please," he added, belatedly.

"What's the hurry?" Catt protested.

All the same, he was curious. He looked to see what Fishy's next selection might be. This one wasn't as thick as the first book, though it was roughly as tall and as wide. The cover was fine red-scaled leather and the lettering seemed to flicker between orange and gold. The runes that sealed the contents were a black scar seared across the front, leaving the scales splintered and bulging.

Catt stroked the edge of the cover. "Zalila's *Thaumaturgy*," he said softly. "Of course."

He slid his lenses down and bent to his painstaking task a second time. The smoke that arose as he erased these particular runes was pungent with sulphur. Catt waved it away and coughed as he set the stenograph down. He took a moment to admire the evil beauty of the restored tome. The skilfully tanned hide gleamed, unsullied, tempting. Savouring the anticipation of reading the secrets within, Catt rubbed his hands together. He reached out to open the book.

"No!" Fisher roared. "No! Stop!"

Catt snatched his hand back before he realised the old fidget wasn't talking to him. "What's the matter?"

Fisher didn't answer. He was staring aghast at the great black book in front of him. Catt realised he had turned back to start reading Owain's secrets from the start. But Fisher was staring at an empty page.

"What is that?" Catt demanded, shocked. "It was a fake after all? Someone went to the trouble of sealing a counterfeit with Imbril's Admonition?"

Though he supposed that made obvious sense. The spell meant no one could open the book as soon as they had bought it, to find out they had been cheated. "Where is my best scrying glass?" he asked wrathfully. "I'll make Bodel rue the day she ever met us, just as soon as I track her down."

"Forget Bodel," rasped Fisher. "This is the real thing. At least it was. But look what's happening!"

He began turning the pages over and over, flipping them ever more quickly. He finally reached a page that had some writing on it.

"What—?" Catt pressed a horrified hand to his mouth. He could barely believe his eyes, and that was saying a lot after everything he had seen in the course of his long life.

The crisp black script was floating away from the page. Tiny globules of ink dissolved into nothingness as soon as they broke away from the paper. The capital L at the top of the next column was illuminated with an emerald green, twining vine. As Catt watched, the leaves dropped off their stalks to blow away and vanish. The sapphire blue of the background soaked away into the page, lost like water in sand. Without anything left to anchor it, the capital letter shivered. A moment later, it was lost as well.

"The stenograph has released all the magic in this book, not just the runes that sealed it," Fisher snarled. "That thing's not a blessing, it's a curse!"

"The thaumaturgy," Catt wailed. He reached for the dragon-hide book.

"Wait!' Fisher chewed a thumbnail as he stared at the red-bound tome. "Perhaps, if we don't open it..."

They both stared at the book. The golden letters shimmered, inviting, seductive.

"Perhaps, if I retrace the runes—" Catt snatched up the stenograph. "How do I...?"

He stared down at the ebony rod. The inlaid sigils pulsed with ominous light and the silver tendrils bristled around each end. They twisted swiftly around each other to make a many-pointed thorn. It would be impossible to touch anything with either cap now.

"Give that here." Fisher snatched it out of his hands.

Catt didn't object. He had no idea what to do. He followed Fisher around the counter. His partner was scowling at the racks of parchments. With an abruptness that made Catt jump, Fisher plucked two tightly wound scrolls from their niches. He set them on the counter and waved a hand over the first, muttering savagely under his breath. A stark black symbol appeared on the curved outer surface.

Fisher offered Catt the stenograph. "Erase that," he ordered.

"What have you got there?" Catt wasn't refusing, but he didn't take the ebony rod either. "What are we risking, Fishy?"

His partner waved an impatient hand. "A couple of copies of Haldu's *Maker*. Come on. We have no time to waste."

Catt grimaced. That particular spell was a very good seller and not cheap to make. Never mind that, he scolded himself. They could always make more. The books on that high, hidden shelf were irreplaceable, and they had already lost Owain the Grim's hoarded knowledge.

He ground his teeth with frustrated fury as he picked up the stenograph. He lowered his band of lenses once again, and blinked to set them shifting, so he could look through each one in turn as he examined the treacherous device. He saw nothing that offered any clue that might solve this new and unwelcome mystery.

He moved the stenograph towards the scroll that Fisher had just sealed. The silver spikes immediately unwound themselves, folding back down the ebony rod to leave the end caps undefended. The inlaid sigils stopped pulsating, though they glowed brighter than they had done before.

Catt carefully followed the lines of Fisher's seal with the stenograph. The dark pattern slid off the scroll to cloud the glass counter with silky dust. He set the perverse instrument down.

"Unroll it." Fisher was already spreading out the untouched scroll.

Catt did as he was asked. However fast he worked though, unfurling with one hand and re-rolling with the other, he could barely keep up as the words inscribed on the scroll vanished. He reached the end and looked up at Fisher with wordless dismay.

Fisher was staring down at the scroll before him, unblinking. Catt released the now uselessly blank one to do whatever it liked. He stepped close to Fisher's side and stared at the script on the untouched paper. This was his own writing, where the first scroll had been Fishy's work.

The stenograph's malign influence reached it a scant moment later. As he watched, Catt saw the words start to blur. The ink faded and turned to dust. It blew away slowly at first, though there was no breeze he could feel, obliterating the writing line by line. The destruction gathered pace, relentlessly wiping away his conscientious labour.

Fisher stepped back from the counter, letting the scroll reroll itself. Catt picked up the hapless cylinder and sadly watched the last smudges of fine dust trickle out of the end to vanish into some unknown void.

"Never mind that." Fisher took another scroll from the niche, and plucked a figurine from the shelf. "Come on," he said with fresh purpose, "and bring that damnable thing with you."

He walked around the counter to stand in the centre of the shop's floor. Catt cast a last, wistful look at Zalila's *Thaumaturgy*, but he followed all the same. Despite himself, he was intrigued.

"There have never been any whispers about the stenograph doing anything like this. Surely it would have been shouted from the roof tops?"

"And Flegen of Sidero would never have created something so spitefully destructive." Fisher spoke with absolute certainty. "Someone has gone to a great deal of trouble to repurpose this device."

"Who, and why?" Much as Catt wanted to know, he had an uneasy suspicion that he wasn't going to like the answers in the least.

Fisher handed him the scroll. He had already sealed with a crude spell. "Erase that, then run as soon as I drop this."

Catt didn't need telling twice. He had seen the figurine Fisher had chosen. "This had better be a short scroll."

"Akeman's Leak Bane," Fisher confirmed.

"Good choice." And thankfully, not an expensive spell to replace. Catt wielded the stenograph once more. This time he didn't bother looking to see what it did to the writing. He dropped the scroll to the floor at the same time as Fisher spat on the brass pig he was holding and let that fall as well.

The figurine transformed before it hit the floorboards. Now a full grown boar stood in the middle of the shop. He was a magnificent hairy beast with a bristling crest running down his grizzled spine and lethal up-thrust tusks. Nostrils wide and moist, his flexible snout was twitching as he looked around. Where were the luscious and receptive sows he was expecting, ready for his seed to swell their bellies with the promise of suckling pig and bacon?

Catt and Fisher were already back behind the counter. They were safe where the Prince of Porkers couldn't possibly see them, he told himself firmly.

Fisher cleared his throat. "There was just the one spell on that scroll, wasn't there?"

Catt was perversely amused to hear the faintest crack in Fisher's composure. He wasn't tempted to tease his oldest friend though, not in these circumstances. "That's right."

Fisher shook his head. "So it should be blank by now."

"I should say so." Catt nodded as he watched the boar.

The creature looked around again. Insofar as the boar could be said to have an expression, he looked puzzled. As he stamped, impatient, his sharp hooves scored the polished floorboards. He looked down at the floor and snuffled at what lay underfoot. His questing snout found the fallen scroll. The boar snatched it up with its fearsome yellow teeth. The wooden spindle splintered as the beast crunched. Rags of paper soiled with inky smears slid down the strings of drool that were hanging from his tusks.

Fisher sighed. "So the spell on that scroll is gone, but the Prince is unaffected."

"Whatever this sorcery is, it only eradicates written magic." Catt searched his memory for any mention of such foul mischief.

The boar heard them talking. He looked up and around. His little black eyes narrowed. Catt reminded himself that a pig's eyesight was none too keen at the best of times. Then he saw his snout testing the air. The pig's attention focused in their direction.

"Fishy," he said conversationally. "You know we said we really should add a muting spell to this mirror magic. Do we know anything that will stifle scent as well?"

"That is certainly worth considering." Fisher drew his arm back as the boar trotted purposefully towards them. He tossed the apple he was holding towards the creature. The shining red fruit rolled across the floor. Never mind the pig, even Catt could smell its sweet ripeness. His stomach rumbled with sudden hunger.

The boar found the treat in an instant. He gobbled it up, and vanished. The bronze figurine fell to the floor with a thud. Fisher walked over to pick it up. As he stalked back to replace it on the shelf, his scowl was thunderous.

Catt gestured, and a dustpan and broom floated out of a corner. They swept up the remnants of the pig-chewed scroll and returned to their niche. Muffled munching drifted through the silence.

"So who uses magic to eradicate magic?" Catt was utterly at a loss. Then something else occurred to him. "Do you suppose it *has* to eradicate the magic? I wonder if there's any way to make it suck the spells up instead. Then perhaps they could be used again. If we were talking about something as complex as dread runes..."

Fisher wasn't listening. He threw his head back and howled with rage. Catt was glad the great boar was no longer present. The poor beast would have soiled itself and Waldin's Broom would baulk at clearing that mess up.

Fisher slammed his hands down on the counter so hard that Catt feared the glass would break. "Luci!" he roared. "Pellucida! Show yourself!"

For an instant, a shadow shivered behind him. It was a monstrous, beast-headed figure, more than dog, more than wolf, shaggy-pelted and dagger-fanged. Fisher drew a resolute breath and the shadow faded. He still looked incandescently furious.

A handsome woman strolled through the window panes. She didn't break the wood and glass. The shopfront merely flowed around her and smoothed itself out again, like the surface of a pond as a breeze came and went. She was tall and shapely in the manner of women who spent their days constantly active rather than lounging around. She wore a well-fitted gown the colour of unbleached paper and her long hair fell to her waist, as straight and dark as a stream of ink.

"Good day to you, brother." She smiled serenely at Fisher before turning to Catt. "Doctor, it's a pleasure to meet you."

"I am honoured." Catt bowed courteously, then hesitated. He looked at Fisher. The people who knew his partner was in fact a hidden Guardian could be counted on the fingers of two hands, admittedly Grennish hands. As far as day to day life was concerned, Fisher expected no special treatment, not even from Catt. Especially not from Catt. When he was roused to his Guardian duties though, Fury could be as touchy as any other demigod.

Fisher growled, deep in his chest. There was honestly no other word for it. A shiver ran down Catt's spine. Then he spoke and to Catt's relief, his voice was level. The Guardian known as Fury had his anger under control. For now, at least.

"Doctor Catt, may I present my long-lost sister Pellucida, also known as the Diviner. She reserves the right to meddle wherever she sees fit. I should have recalled her style sooner."

Catt gaped, astonished. Then he realised he was doing that and shut his mouth with a snap. It didn't help. So many questions crowded his mouth that he was afraid he might choke. He swallowed hard.

Fisher – Fury – had no such problem. "So where have you been hiding out?"

His contempt was scathing, but the Diviner was unperturbed. "You say that and I say you're a mule mocking his neighbour the donkey's ears. There is unquestionably wisdom in withdrawing from a fight one cannot possibly win. Like you, I chose to live to fight another day."

"When have you ever bloodied your hands?" Fisher's contempt was scathing.

"I fight with other weapons," the Diviner said coldly.

Catt felt a chill. He had been caught up in rows between Guardians before and had no wish to repeat the experience. He steeled himself and raised a hand. "Excuse me?"

"Why? What have you done?" Pellucida smiled at him. That wasn't in the least reassuring.

Catt didn't rise to the bait. He held out the stenograph. "Might I ask? What can you tell us about this?"

Fisher interrupted. "Was this Varra Hills woman even real or was that you masquerading?"

"Lady Escarene is exactly who she claims to be," Pellucida said tartly. "A noble soul dedicated to her people's wellbeing, looking to establish their new home through honest labour and without magical shortcuts. I can see that her intent is pure, and that her people share her commitment."

Catt recalled one of the Diviner's powers was seeing the true nature of anyone's motives.

Fisher glared. "There is nothing wrong with using magic."

"You can say that as we stand here?" Pellucida challenged him. "In the midst of the unparalleled destruction wrought by the Kinslayer with the spells and devices he plundered?"

"Magic is a tool," Fisher insisted. "Knowledge is power."

"Tools and power alike can be far too readily abused. When an infant or a fool takes up a razor that is as likely to injure them as anyone else, regardless of innocence or malice. So it falls to those who care for those who know no better to remove the instruments of such harm. As the Guardian who can divine the most likely outcomes as events unfold, it falls to me to intervene at any crucial juncture." She looked at the two books on the counter and her lip curled. "I can easily foretell the evil consequences if the lore held within those is loosed on this wounded world. Now that will not happen."

Catt felt insulted, but he judged it would be unwise to say so.

Fisher had no such qualms. "You can guess, but you cannot be certain. You have no right to interfere with our affairs."

Pellucida raised finely shaped eyebrows. "You always think everything's about you, Fury. Does it ever occur to you that the world does not in fact revolve around your concerns?"

"Do you deny that you are responsible for that abomination? For the damage that it has done?"

Fisher swept the stenograph off the counter. The rod skidded across the floor and stopped at Pellucida's feet. She looked down.

"I did not make it, but I changed it. Flegen's motives were good, but I divined that uses would be made of its powers that he never envisaged." She glanced at Catt. "You are not the first to wonder if the device can be made to sequester magic rather than erase it. Believe me when I tell you any attempt to find out will assuredly end in disaster."

Catt wondered if the Guardian was saying she had foreseen catastrophe would follow such an endeavour, or warning him she would make it her business to ensure that it did, if he were so foolish as to ignore her warning. He decided not to ask.

Pellucida looked at Fisher and her smile was triumphant. "Once I had changed it to suit my purposes, I took the necessary steps to ensure it ended up where it would do most good."

Catt interrupted before Fisher could lose his temper completely. "For the Lantir?"

"Quite so." She looked at him, approving.

Fisher was far from placated. "So, we were just pieces moved around in your little game board?"

"We could have let Ulpian have what he wanted, and he could have suffered these losses." Catt felt aggrieved as he recalled the lengths they had gone to, in order to keep their rivals from attending the sale. "Instead we've made outright enemies of the good Doctor and Marincol for no profit to us at all."

"Not in the least." Pellucida's smile was enigmatic. "Ulpian wouldn't have loaned the stenograph to the Lantir in the first place. He would never have agreed to the request they will make of you when they return tomorrow."

Catt's curiosity overcame his resentment when he realised what that must mean. "You know what else they want it for, don't you?"

The Diviner nodded. "I do."

Catt waited. Eventually Fisher broke the silence with a huff of exasperation. "Tell us, or don't. Just stop wasting our time. You've had your fun, and rubbed our faces in it. You can leave as soon as you like. Sooner would suit me."

Catt clenched his fists, keeping them hidden in the folds of his robe. He really didn't want the Diviner to go, not before she shared this new secret. On the other hand, he wasn't about to risk fraying Fisher's threadbare patience any further.

Pellucida looked at Fisher for a long moment. Catt found her face impossible to read. Then she looked straight at him instead. She smiled. He was suddenly convinced that she knew exactly what he was thinking, and that she sympathised.

She scooped the stenograph up from the floor in a graceful, fluid movement. Walking across the shop, she laid it on the counter. "What do you know of the Silanti?"

The abrupt change of subject confused Catt. "They're one breed of the Kinslayer's minions? I've heard nothing of any note. They're still roaming the Unredeemed Lands. By all accounts, they're as vile and as ravenously destructive as any creatures he ever made."

But Fisher contradicted him. "They weren't made. They were corrupted."

To Catt's surprise, his voice was thoughtful, his irritation entirely gone.

Pellucida nodded. "They are an abomination created from one of the first peoples his hordes overwhelmed. The Yorughan didn't slaughter the Lantir they captured. They enslaved them, and the Kinslayer corrupted them to make his monsters. He bound a plethora of spells together to brand them with an intricate and excruciating curse."

Catt stared at the stenograph, horrified. "With that?"

"No," Pellucida said calmly, "though he used a similar device. He went on to use the same instrument to create the dread runes."

"The stenograph can erase those runes." Fisher looked at her. "That means it can restore the Silanti?"

She nodded. "So Captain Zettis and Deshiri the Grennish believe."

"What device did the Kinslayer use?" Fisher demanded. "To work such evil?"

"Are they right?" Catt wanted to know. "The captain and his Grennish? Can the Silanti be freed?"

"What are they to you?" Fisher's uncanny shadow flickered behind him again. "Why have you returned, when we had given you up for dead at the Kinslayer's hands? For the Lantir, of all insignificant, benighted people?"

Pellucida's smile was somewhere between wistful and rueful. "Who do you think they pray to, as they seek their scattered families and friends? In whom have they placed their trust, criss-crossing this land and defying countless dangers as they search for arcane lore to restore those who have suffered a fate worse than death? Who else should they call on, but the Guardian who can always, infallibly find that which is hidden or lost? The Diviner who can always see the best route for the journey ahead?"

Before Catt could ask her to elaborate, she vanished.

Fisher growled. "She always used to do that, and it was just as bloody infuriating then."

Catt didn't answer. He was recalling the woman he had seen stroll past the shop before Atrat the Arvennir had come in with news of that fateful auction. Had that been Pellucida? Would he ever find out?

"Come on." Fisher clapped him on the shoulder. "Stick that cursed thing on a shelf. It's no damn use to us. We can let the

Lantir captain have it tomorrow and we'll be done with this nonsense."

"We can sell it to the Lantir," Catt countered automatically.

"For what we paid at the auction?" Fisher shook his head. "You looked inside that strongbox of theirs, same as me. Don't deny it. They can't afford half of such a sum. No, we'll just have to charge our losses there to Pellucida's account. Believe me, I will find a way to collect." He sounded vengefully certain of that.

"Unless..." Catt's gaze strayed to the books still lying on the counter. The black tome was merely a battered collection of blank pages now, but the red dragonhide was as alluring as ever. "What do you suppose Doctor Ulpian would pay for a copy of Zalila's *Thaumaturgy*? Through a suitable third party."

"But the writing will erase itself as soon as he pays up and opens it. You heard Pellucida. That lore will never be loosed." All the same, Fisher's eyes gleamed. "Ulpian would be furious. Who do we owe that sort of misfortune, who won't immediately betray our involvement?"

"Or we seal it with a spell that the good doctor can undo – eventually. A spell which the seller could not possibly have cast, or indeed countermand." Catt felt a faint smile tug the corner of his mouth. "Then they cannot be blamed if Ulpian's clumsiness when he negates it causes some unexpected disaster."

"That is worth further thought," Fisher agreed.

Catt looked at the stenograph. "With Ulpian making good our losses, we could let the Lantir have that for a price they could afford. Not so modest as to arouse suspicion, but for a sum that wouldn't beggar them."

"How do we explain such generosity?" Fisher queried.

"For the same reason we let them take it to the Dorhambri." Catt's smile widened. "In return for the right to first call on any magical iron they mine, and at a favourable price. The Diviner just said we wouldn't lose out on this deal, didn't she? When I complained we would see no profit for our troubles."

"I'm not at all sure that's what she meant," Fisher said dubiously.

Catt's thoughts had already moved on. "Do you think that they can do it? The Lantir, I mean. Will they be able to save the Silanti from the curse that brands them?"

"They'll have to capture one alive to try it. That won't be easy." Fisher shook off that troubling prospect like a dog coming in from the rain. "But surely Luci wouldn't have gone to all this trouble, if she had foreseen they would fail?"

"You tell me," Catt said helplessly. "She's your sister."

He couldn't help thinking about the gulf that lay between a single victory and lasting success. Killing the Kinslayer had been a triumph, but this unhappy world was still full of people who hadn't seen any peace or prosperity coming their way because the wars were over.

Could the Diviner possibly change that, with such interventions, now that she'd returned? Catt allowed that the roll of a single pebble could start a mighty landslide, but could even a demigod truly foresee the path of every stone?

He decided not to test Fisher's patience by asking him. Time would surely tell.

# THE UNGUIS OF MAUG
### by K.T. Davies

## ONE

DOCTOR FISHER SQUEEZED the pom.

It wasn't entirely ripe; the smell was too sharp, the flesh unyielding, but its skin was the colour of a fiery sunset, bright and unblemished and in a day – two at most, it would be perfect. Of course, Catty wouldn't let it reach that state. He smiled at the thought of his associate's delight.

"If you touch it, you've bought it." The half-broken voice of a youth hooked Fisher's attention. He looked down. As was often the case it took him a moment to adjust his focus, to soften the spear of his gaze. The youth behind the stall adopted a bold stance and eyed him unwaveringly, too full of youthful insolence to know danger when he saw it. His clothes were typically grubby and patched hand-me-downs, but his copper-coloured locks were clean and combed, and his cheeks were rosy and full. The small improvements in the lives of the citizens of Cinquetann, if not exactly heart-warming, were satisfying. Gods knew it had taken long enough.

The lad folded his arms. "I said, if you touch it, you've bought it, Grandad."

At that moment, perhaps on hearing the sharpness of his tone, the costermonger in charge of the stall appeared from behind their cart and without breaking stride, cuffed the boy's ear.

"He doesn't mean to be rude, sir. He was just born as blunt as a river cobble."

The boy opened his mouth to protest, but on seeing the sharp edge in the woman's eye he settled into a fuming silence.

"No need to apologise, madam. How much for the pom?"

"A polly," the boy burst in earning another, light cuffing.

"It's four scits, sir," said the woman, no doubt gauging the size of his purse by the cut of his robe, which was excellent but well worn.

"It's Doctor, not sir." He paid her and nested the pom in his basket before re-joining the flow of people passing through the busy market. Catty would be pleased by the rare delight. Like Fisher, he would appreciate the significance of finding the fruit readily available in the market. After almost eleven years of struggle, of rebuilding and repairing and healing, real, boring everyday life was returning, and he loved it.

The world was opening up, unfurling like the petals of a flower, questing for the sun. *A flower? You're going soft in your old age.* The rebirth wasn't without strife; it was a long and painful labour restoring the mundane, even here in Cinquetann, nestled in Cherivell, the most central of the safe Middle Kingdoms. Years of war had left an ugly legacy. Beyond the bright stalls of food and drink, down a side street stacked with broken crates he spied a gang of youths. They were a rough-looking crew, one of many that roamed the docks and derelict districts. They were jostling each other, laughing hard and harshly as they goaded and cajoled a small human, made entirely of rags, filth, and wild hair, to drink from a leather jack. One of the group, an older youth with more hair on his chin than his head, waved a scit before the scrapling. Thus enticed, it raised the mug to its lips. The gang fell into a tenuous silence. It sniffed the contents and then, quick as a fish, hurled the mug to the cobbles and snatched the coin before running into the market shouting, "It's your piss, you drink it!" Some of the gang laughed but the eldest blanched with anger, kicked the mug, and punched the nearest fellow to him in the ear. The laughter died. Having reaffirmed his faith in human nature, Fisher lost interest in the gang and waded through the throng to his favourite pickle stall.

Although it was a peasant staple, their red gherkin chutney would go perfectly with the chops he'd bought for dinner; the acidic bite just enough to cut through the richness of the fat. His attention focused on the spicy acid tang of vinegar and peppercorns wafting towards him, he almost failed to notice the small, dirty thing weaving towards him like an angry bee until it was a stride away. The gang had spread out and were herding their quarry towards a sound beating if Fisher read the situation right. Their prey's head was down, so it didn't see that it was aimed at just the right height to poleaxe Fisher should it continue on its path unchecked. To save himself from both pain and embarrassment, the doctor thrust out his hand and stopped the little beast in its tracks. Upon hearing the oik exclaim, one of the gang, a girl with a pair of long braids whistled and arrowed in on Fisher's left flank. She leaned in, prepared to accidentally shoulder Fisher aside. On hearing her signal, the shave-pated leader shoved his way towards them from the right.

The scrapling squirmed in his grasp and fixed him with a defiant gaze, its small fists bunched at tight as budding apples. With the skill of a magician, Fisher thrust the child behind him beneath the cover of his flowing sleeves, swayed back a handspan, and extended his foot an inch beyond the hem of his robe. Gaze fixed on her prey, the girl tripped, and her momentum did the rest. Her accomplice was now in the awkward position of either catching her, or going after the scrapling. She hit the cobbles with a yelp. The bravo brushed past Fisher, but it was already too late. The little cockroach had scarpered. Frustrated, he turned on Fisher who was feigning ignorance.

"Don't mess with the Double Pockets, old man," he snarled before plunging into the haggling shoal to continue the hunt. Doctor Fisher stepped around the cursing woman and allowed himself a slight smile of satisfaction, for as Catty was fond of saying, '*One must take pleasure in the little things.*'

THE WALK HOME from the market was for the most part uneventful. The pink promise of the dawn, into which he had set out, had turned into a bright and blustery morning. The rugged horizon rising above the roofline shone like polished pewter beneath a pale sun. Somewhere amidst the distant mountains, a green flash lit the sky. Fisher slowed his pace and wondered what magic had caused the anomaly. It was many miles away, too far even for him to discern if the cause was malign or benevolent. The gut-cramping urgency that shopping and planning dinner had temporarily banished returned with a vengeance. There was still much to do. Out there, perhaps even here in the city, buried deep in some forgotten vault, lay the tools of the Kinslayer and gifts of the gods and their guardians. *Gifts. More like knives in a crib.* He spat in the dirt.

Another viridian flash scorched the horizon.

The murk of his mind having been stirred by dark thoughts, Fisher returned to the shop in a more sombre mood than when he had left. Grateful to be home, he took a moment to admire their neat little building. Through hard work and artifice soon after the war he and Catt had made sure their premises were well-maintained. Even when it had stood in the shadow of the burned-out shell of the Gracious One's Hospice, they had taken pride in their home and place of work.

Times were changing and their neighbours were more affluent. Indeed, the sign above their door which read, *Catt and Fisher, apothecaries, physicians, notaries of law, lawyers of note, dealers in the unusual* looked tatty compared to the newly painted sign above the bookmaker's next door. Not to mention, the weather mage two doors down had installed an ingenious eye-catching device above the bay of her window. By the cunning use of magic and mirrors, a miniature sky danced upon the parapet. Yes, Catt and Fisher would have to up their game if they did not want to appear as shabby as the drunk of an armourer three doors down whose sign was obscured by soot and grime.

Fisher put his hand to the door but paused when he caught sight of the hard-eyed leader of the Double Pockets in the glass. The doctor pretended to search for something in his basket while watching the four guttersnipes in the window. He kicked himself for allowing grim ruminations to distract him enough not to notice them following him from the market. The girl was with them, but it was the youngest member of the gang who once again caught his attention.

His cheek was swollen, his nose bloody, but the fierce defiance of the scrapling's gaze shone through the wild tangle of its hair as it met and held Fisher's gaze. The doctor recognised the steel in those eyes, the animal acuity, as sharp as that which he saw every time he looked in a mirror. Satisfied that they knew where he lived, the gang moved off. The scrapling was led away by the girl.

They were going to be a problem, but one for another day. Fisher opened the shop door and the bell shrilled on its spring. Before the echo had died, he was confronted by a sight that froze him in place. Sticking out from the side of the glass-fronted counter were a pair of feet. Catt's feet to be precise, silk-slippered toes pointing to the ceiling.

"Catty?" The name fell from his lips like a stone. The feet didn't twitch. "Catt!" He charged across the room. Catt sat up, clutched his chest, and looked most disgruntled.

"Are you trying to kill me, Fishy?"

Fisher put the basket on the cluttered counter. It was either that or throw it at Catt. "Me, kill you?"

"Yes, you, Doctor Fisher."

"Didn't you hear the bell?"

"Well, obviously not, or we wouldn't be having this conversation. Do keep up Fishy."

Fisher scowled. "I've more chance herding your namesakes than keeping up with you. What the hell were you doing down there?"

Catt climbed to his feet and knocked the creases out of his blue brocade overrobe. "I've noticed some stains on the ceiling." The little man beamed proudly as though announcing some great revelation.

"Please do go on, this is enthralling." At a loss, and yet relieved, Fisher folded his arms. It was either that or strangle his partner.

"I'm choosing to ignore your sarcastic tone because I am the better man." Catt tilted his chin so that he could look down his nose at Fisher. "However, when I saw the stains, I took them to be a common leak, after that dreadful downpour the other day. But upon inspection of the sitting room, I found nothing of the sort." He began to rummage through the bag of groceries. "I then noticed a slight luminescence and an odd, quicksilver quality to the marks. I therefore studied them for quite some minutes and, as evidenced by mine own eyes, saw the pattern of stains shift, bloom, and in some cases dissipate. Oh, a pom..." Catt plucked the fruit from the bag like a cormorant spearing a fish and would have scarfed it there and then but for a stern look from Fisher which he accompanied with a deep warning growl. Catt continued. "By that point, my poor old neck was as stiff as a broom, so in order to continue my observation of the phenomena, I lay down and then I suppose I must have dozed off." He brandished the pom. "But not before postulating a reasonable theory with regards to the fugacious blemishes."

"And that is?"

"Errant magical energy. Like candle smoke, it soaks into the boards. Why, one day, Fishy this whole building might get up and wander off. Now wouldn't that be something? What's for lunch, by the way. I'm starving?"

LUNCH CONSISTED OF a large bowl of icy silence, but by dinner time, after spending several hours apart, the atmosphere had thawed.

Catt had settled in the comfy armchair by the kitchen window. He was bathed in soft evening light by which he was reading a book, voraciously consuming the contents like a starving man at a banquet. "I've been thinking," he said without looking up, eyes locked to the page.

"Congratulations." Fisher was preparing dinner. It was an inane activity, but he found the simple chore of cutting, slicing, and peeling to be almost meditative.

"Thank you, Fishy. I was thinking that we should find a bigger place. Somewhere more impressive, as befits our rank and status."

"What's brought this on?"

"Glad you asked." Catt snapped the book shut and pulled a gilt-edged envelope from his robes. He tossed it on the table where it landed beside the carrot tops. It had been opened, an embossed invitation card peeked from under the broken seal.

Fisher raised his hands which were covered in chop juice. "Could you elucidate?"

Catt took another slurp of the Arvenni red he was throwing down his neck like it was cheap, tavern plonk. "We've been invited to dinner by Laurenta Castamere."

Fisher laid the chops in the pan and drizzled them with herb-infused oil. "Am I supposed to know who that... Oh. The weather mage?"

"Indeed. Our neighbour. Can you imagine? I mean, I guessed that she'd been doing well, given all the comings and goings and that outrageous some might say tasteless, signage, but a dinner party?"

"How dare she."

Oblivious or inured, Catt ignored the sarcasm. "Quite. Which has prompted me to consider that we also might 'up our game' as it were."

"I was thinking we should have the sign repainted."

"Or move into larger premises."

Fisher shook his head and wiped his hands on the towel before covering the chops in a colourful scatter of vegetables. "We can't."

"Of course we can. Unless you have squandered our money on wine, women, and song?"

Fisher gave him a hard look.

"I've even seen somewhere that might be suitable, and it's going for a song."

"I doubt that, the good burghers of Cinquetann do not place great value on the choral arts. Either way, it won't work, Catty."

Being possessed of a face entirely unsuited to seriousness Catty nevertheless did his best to frown. "Pray, why not?"

"A bigger building would require more maintenance. It would require staff." Fisher waited for comprehension to dawn. "*People,* Catty. People in our house, living in our home with us. Can you imagine?"

Catt's button-bright eyes widened. "Ah. I hadn't thought of that."

"You surprise me."

Catt put his now empty wine glass on the side table and let his gaze idly track to the window. "I don't think it's a good idea to have staff. Not with what we keep here, and then there are our more colourful visitors.

"Quite." Fisher relaxed again now that Catt had wisely poured cold water on his latest scheme. The city was growing again after years of laying fallow. New buildings, streets, and indeed entire districts were being raised in their place, but as far as he was concerned and he was *very* concerned about the matter, they would dwell in this modest abode until the arc of time cracked. Doctor Fisher did not like change.

"Fishy?" Catt tweaked the lace curtain.

He put the stock in the pot. "Yes, Catty?"

"There are some ne'er-do-wells loitering by the middens. They appear to be appraising our demesne avariciously."

Fisher put the pot on the stove and peeked through the curtain. It was the gang from earlier. "Ah, yes. I encountered them in the market. They style themselves 'the Double Pockets'."

"How very descriptive. It seems you've offended them."

"Clearly."

"Would you see them off? They're spoiling the view."

Fisher gestured to the kitchen table. "I am trying to cook."

"I would do it myself, but I'm wearing my slippers." He gestured to his feet.

"And you're lazy."

"That too."

Fisher snatched the Staff of Ways from the preserved, marsh-dragon-foot cane-holder and unlocked the kitchen door. Behind the row of shop premises were outhouses, workshops and stables that belonged to them and the neighbouring businesses. Beyond the outhouses were the middens. Rubbish and the contents of chamber pots were deposited there before being carted away once a month by the gong farmers. Fisher narrowed his eyes at the familiar faces of Shave-Pate and his cronies. Although they knew they'd been rumbled and were all casting surreptitious glances at Catt and Fisher's building, they made no attempt to flee when Fisher went outside.

"The outhouse is over there, old man," the leader called out, to the amusement of his grubby companions. "Hey, don't ignore me. I said, don't ignore me. You deaf?"

Fisher was faced with a dilemma. He could either ignore them, and hope they got bored, or he could make them regret stalking him. The latter option was most vexatious because it involved effort that he would much rather devote to cooking.

"Needs must when the rats are lurking in the middens," Catt called from the doorway.

"As no saying ever went," Fisher muttered as he trudged down the path and around the pond in which lurked some amphibians of dubious origins that they had discovered on one of their adventures. The gang held their ground. He continued past their testing shed from which emanated the faint smell of sulphur and sweet iron. The sign above the shed door read, "Keep out on pain of pain". It was an idiot test, and one he was inclined to let the gang take even though the smell of burning hair took hours to dissipate.

"You owe us old man," Shave-Pate called. "You beat up my little cousin. We demand recompense."

"Don't demand something you can't spell, and I did no such thing as you very well know." He leaned on the staff. Shave-Pate wiped his mouth on his filthy coat sleeve and glared insolently at Fisher, who wasn't sure if he was more amused than annoyed.

"I'll tell the guard. It's four against one."

"It is quality, not quantity that matters. As a lawyer I should know, but do go right ahead."

Flummoxed, the bravo's cheeks reddened, and he pulled out a rusted knife with a rag bound hilt. "Ten sollies or I swear I'll—"

Fisher raised his free hand. "Let me stop you there." He didn't shout, but the sepulchral severity of his tone commanded instant obedience. "You've picked the wrong mark. Go away or this will not go well for you." He struck the heel of his staff on the gravel path; sparks flew. The bruised child leapt from the midden. The others backed away and would have fled had the leader not stood his ground.

Fisher turned and made to head back down the path when, to his disappointment, if not surprise, he saw Shave-Pate reflected in the window, plucking a rotting cabbage from the midden to throw it at him. Before the improvised missile had flown ten feet, Fisher spun, aimed, and released a concentrated bolt of energy from the staff. The vegetable exploded, showering the belligerent gutterscum in burning fragments. Catt roared with laughter as he pointed at the gang stumbling away through a cloud of burning cabbage smoke. The child lingered longest and regarded Fisher with a defiant and curiously questioning gaze before following the others.

Fisher returned and closed the door. He put the staff back in the cane holder, relieved and a little disappointed that he hadn't had to teach them a more serious lesson.

"What will the neighbours think?" Catt teased.

"I would imagine that I've saved them from a spate of inept burglary attempts."

The shop doorbell rang. Catt's smile faltered. "Do you think that's the city guard?"

Fisher picked up his knife and with a deft stroke, sliced an onion in half. "They're never that quick, but why don't you go and find out?"

"You're already up..." Catt protested.

"I've got a pickle to prepare."

"But..." Fisher gave Catt a look that would brook no argument; the steel of his gaze as keen as the knife blade. "Fine." He climbed to his feet like a wounded soldier rallying for one last charge before flouncing from the kitchen.

# TWO

THE SOUND OF Fishy brutalising onions chased Catt from the kitchen. He threaded his way past the precarious stack of packing crates that were piled in the small hallway between the kitchen, the storeroom and the shop.

He paused before the silver looking-glass hanging by the crooked staircase that led up to their living quarters. They had found the mirror in a subterranean ruin where they had liberated it from the tentacles of something unmentionable. The mermaids etched in the frame always giggled and winked suggestively when he visited, all vying for his attention. He blew each one a kiss for he was not the kind of man to play favourites when it came to mermaids. They might be mere magical representations of their breed, but like the real thing, their teeth were sharp and their memories long.

These days when he looked in a mirror, there was always a moment of disorientation tinged with shock when he saw his father's face staring back at him. A resemblance that was growing stronger every year, it seemed. Thanks to a robust appetite, wrinkles were suggested rather than deeply etched, but they were there, a daily reminder that time was passing far too quickly for his liking. He flicked a few errant crumbs from his chest and rubbed at the redness where his eyeglasses had pinched his nose. Despite his thinning thatch of silvery gold hair, he was reassured that he was still a fine-looking fellow.

"Is anyone there?" an aged voice rasped. "Shop? Shop!"

Catt rolled his eyes at his mirror self and waved to the mermaids before sweeping through the bead-curtained doorway.

Judging by the sound of the quavering voice, he expected an older customer. He had not expected someone who looked like they had recently escaped from a crypt. Like a living statue, she was almost entirely grey with dusty skin, hair and clothes. She was garbed in what looked to be a wedding gown complete with a withered floral headband and tattered veil of cobweb silk which she threw back to reveal a profoundly shrivelled visage.

Her hooded eyes widened and beetle bright fixed upon him "Aha!" she exclaimed triumphantly. "You must be Doctor Catt."

Catt inclined his head. "I am, madam. And who do I have the pleasure of—" Before he had chance to finish, she began coughing so forcefully that he feared she would expire right there by the counter. Dust flew, and he was sure something flapped its tiny wings from within the nest of her elaborately coiffured powdered wig. He considered offering her a glass of water, but that would have meant he had to enter the billowing dust cloud that surrounded her. As she did not appear to be choking, he decided to wait for the situation to play itself out. After a few worrying moments more, she brought the attack under control.

"Blasted snuff." She wiped her nose on the frilly engageantes of her sleeve. "Now, where was I?"

"Honestly? I have no idea." Given her garb, a thought occurred. "Are you... have you been to a celebration?" Something – a mouse perhaps, blinked at him from within the round eye of a grey curl.

She huffed. "No. Quite the opposite, but there's only so long a person can sit and sulk without going mad, eh?" She chuckled.

For one dreadful moment Doctor Catt thought that she would start coughing again, but she refrained, and the laugh petered out without further catarrhal expulsions.

"Indeed, madam. Now, how may I help you? A tincture perhaps, to ease that cough?"

She eyed him testily. "What cough?"

He got as far as opening his mouth before she dipped down out of sight. Curious, and a little concerned, he peered over the counter to see that she was rummaging in a moth-eaten carpet bag. He caught a tantalising glimpse of sparkle and what looked to be a bag of mints before all manner of peculiar items were dumped onto the glass case. She stood back, put her hands on the broad panniers of her grey silk skirts. A small cricket hopped from under a tatty silk kerchief and bounded across the counter before making good its escape and leaping to the floor. He didn't know what to say. They remained there for some moments, silently eyeing each other over the pile of tat.

"Yes?" he enquired.

"It says on the sign that you deal in the unusual."

"It means objects, not people."

"What was that?"

"Nothing, dear lady, nothing. Let us take a look at these treasures, shall we?" He reached beneath the counter and took out his headband of magnifying lenses. Out of habit more than need, he breathed upon them and gave them a quick polish on his sleeve before setting them on his head. "What's this?" He picked up a small copper container. A flying dragon was etched into the pitted, verdigrised surface.

"Well, young man. It's obviously a cucurbit." She adjusted the fragile lace gloves she was wearing. "I thought you were supposed to be a doctor. It was used to turn base metal salts into silver."

He looked up. The view was not improved by viewing her

at ten times the magnification. "Do you have the alembic that goes with it?"

"No. It got broken some years ago during the fire."

He moved it aside. "I'm afraid it's no use without the alembic. And this..." he picked up a brass hourglass, "has a crack in it."

"What about the beads? They were blessed by the Lightbearer."

He picked up the beads. Each one was carved to resemble a tight fist. "For what purpose?" He flipped through a series of lenses. When viewed through the sixth and smallest of the seven lenses in the array, the amber beads glowed with a faint, magical light.

"To ensure chastity."

He dropped them and wiped his hand on his robe. "Not much call for such things these days." He took off the lenses. "I'm sorry, but there's nothing here for me."

Undaunted, she ducked down again and began rummaging in the carpet bag. Unable to curb his curiosity, Catt leaned over the counter. As her clawed hands raked through the assorted bits of tattery and draff, a small notebook book caught his eye, not least because it looked like it was bound in dragon skin.

"Madame, would you be so kind as to show me that?" he pointed at the notebook. She made to pick up a desiccated mouse corpse. "No, to the right of that er, rodent. Yes, that's it."

With many a creak and a click, she rose clutching the book which she slammed onto the counter like a prize catch.

"Bound in the skin of Vermarod himself." She tapped the book. "It belonged to a great scholar, much like yourself."

*And a liar, much like myself.* He knew Vermarod's skin when he saw it, and this wasn't it. "Is that blood on the cover?"

"Probably. Do you want it?"

Catt flicked through the handwritten journal. Although not intrinsically valuable, every page was crammed with captivating notes, sketches and diagrams. The hand was educated, if crabbed. The faint whiff of alchemical compounds clung to the pages that were scorched and stained with oxides and rare oils. He searched the usual places for a nameplate, or indeed any hint to the identity of the author but found nothing. Damn it, but he was intrigued. He rubbed his jaw and whistled thoughtfully. "I really shouldn't." The game was on. He put the book on the counter and took off the lenses.

"But you will, won't you?" She laughed wheezily.

"We are not a charity, Catty!" Fisher's voice boomed from the kitchen.

Catt put the lenses under the counter. "That's my business partner, and brusqueness aside, he has a point."

She swept the tat into the bag and picked up the book. "Very well. I'll go see that nice young lady down the street."

"Ah. Now, don't be so hasty." Catt leaned across the counter and lowered his voice. "I said he had a point, not that I wasn't… Well, that is to say, I do have a charitable nature."

"What?" she shouted as she cupped her ear and craned towards him.

"What?" shouted Fisher, evidently suspicious.

"Nothing!" Catt sang cheerily for Fisher's benefit. He returned his attention to the powdery eccentrix and bestowed upon her a smile pitched somewhere between warm and solicitous. "I'll give you a silver opal for the book." He patted her bony hand.

"I'll take a solly."

He almost choked. "Alas, dear lady there's a point at which an act of charity turns into culpability in one's own mugging. As a notary of law I know whereof I speak."

Huffing and muttering, she half turned.

"Two pollies."

She paused, her head snapped round shortly followed by the wig and its inhabitants. "Three."

"Done." He considered a moment after the word left his

mouth and hers broadened into a grin that he had been had. Feathers ruffled, he drew the coins from his almost empty 'muggers' pouch' pickpocket decoy and handed them over. Instead of thanking him and leaving him in peace, she again began rummaging in the bag. The delicious smells emanating from the kitchen made his stomach rumble. He gazed longingly at the beaded curtain and listened to the sound of the bread knife sawing through the fresh loaf that Fishy would soon slather with creamy butter. When he returned his gaze to the dowager, she was staring at him through a magnifying glass which was almost as big as her face. Momentarily disconcerted, he took an involuntary step back into the shelves, rocking a stuffed monk toad on its plinth. It regarded him with a baleful, glass-eyed stare. "Was there something else...?"

She produced a crumpled note and began to read with the aid of the glass. "Do you have any Yorughan Heart Taker tusk?"

"Powdered or whole?"

"Powdered."

He glanced to the door before retrieving the powder which was kept in a jar marked 'mustard powder' on the off-chance that Celestaine the Slayer dropped in with her Yorughan paramour. He made a paper cone and poured a measured scoop. "Anything else?" He gave the cone a twist and placed it on the counter content that she would not snatch it and run.

"A pint of Water of Doom."

"Alas, there's been a run on it, and I'm all out. That will be..." He so wanted to say 'three pollies'. But as it was common Yorughan tusk mixed with eggshell and chalk, he decided to be generous in his dishonesty. "Four scits." She handed over the coin and snatched up the powder. "Planning on a spot of cursing, are we?" he enquired politely.

"None of your beeswax, young man. Good day to you." She picked up her bag and strode purposefully from the shop, her ragged train adorned with snagged detritus. Like guests at a wedding, the captured leaves, twigs, and feathers clung to the lace. Bemused, Catt wondered what fool had excited the potty dowager's wrath.

LATER THAT EVENING thanks to Fisher's culinary wizardry, they retired with full bellies to their sitting room above the shop. Fisher chose to sit by the fire, all angular shadows delineated in fiery splashes of gold cast from the glowing coals. "Well?"

"Deep hole, full of water," Catt chuckled. "Speaking of which, I'm parched. Any chance of another glass of that Arvenni?"

"I would ask what your last slave died of, but I already know." Fisher stood up and swept his robe behind him pointedly and poured them both a glass of red. He moved with surprising grace and vigour for an old fellow, and despite an appetite that rivalled Catt's own, had somehow managed to maintain a lean physique. He was more aesthetic than athletic, but Catt was still envious of the trick.

"Did you find anything interesting, or did you waste our money?" His ever sceptical gaze fell on the book that Catt had devoured along with his dinner.

"The author was clearly in our line of business and, if they were being honest, they bagged a few very nice toys."

Fisher handed him a glass of wine. "Did they leave directions to where they keep them?"

"Alas, no. According to the notes, they sold up and apparently retired due to ill-health, after a disagreement with a Tzarkomen Soul Binder."

"Oh. Enjoy the wine. Given your reckless extravagances, it will be the last for a while."

Catt sensed that, not for the first time, his partner was about to deliver a lecture on the evils of profligacy. He raised his hand to distract him. "They did, however, leave directions to something that allegedly belonged to *him*."

Like sun after rain, Fisher's entire demeanour changed. He ceased to loom menacingly and took to looming interestedly. "Go on then, don't keep me in suspense."

"Something called the Unguis of Maug."

"Maug?" His eyes momentarily glazed as his gaze turned inwards. "Do I know that name?"

"Oh, let me read your mind and find out."

Fisher grew coldly distant. A frown cut deep across his brow. "There were so many…" Just like that Fisher was gone, off down some long and winding tunnel of memories to which Catt was frustratingly not privy. Even though he would swear before a magistrate that there was no one in the whole world he knew better, Fishy could become as remote as a mountain peak within the space of a breath.

"Fishy?" Catt enquired. The darkness that had momentarily seized his friend passed like a cloud across the moon. He looked at Catt like he'd just awoken from a deep and troubled sleep.

"No, it's gone. Never mind. Do you think there's anything to be gained hunting it?"

Catt drummed the notebook. "I'm not sure it's worth *our* valuable time, but we could send an agent to poke around. A little speculation with a view to accumulation?"

A slow smile spread across Fishy's grizzled face. "A modest exploration. Expenses upfront and bonus on completion, but only if they find something worth our while."

"Naturally. I'll put the feelers out, see who's in town and in need of earning some reasonably honest coin." Eager to get on, Catt drained his glass and headed for the door. As this was a speculative punt, he was not going to seek out anyone in particular, not least because if an agent knew they were in demand that always put the price up. He would head to the less reputable part of town and let it be known that he was offering work and that enquiries should be made in person on the morrow. Those who knew Catt and Fisher would either come or run a mile. It was always a toss of the coin which it would be, and most often dependent on how desperate the agent was.

Catt swapped his slippers for a pair of comfy, fur-lined boots. The sound of rain gently pattering on the roof prompted him to take his heavy cloak with the hood and the rather fetching blue satin lining. He was about to head out through the shop when he remembered it was night and he looked like easy prey. Tempting though it was to take the Staff of Ways he felt it was too much for a trip to the Pig and Skillet and opted instead for his trusty swordstick with the brass devil's head handle which when applied to a skull made a most satisfying crack.

Fishy appeared in the doorway. He was carrying a tray of dirty dishes. "Don't stay out all night but do stay out of trouble."

"Yes, mother," Catt smirked and pulled up his hood. "I'm going to drop into the Pig and Skillet and depending on who's about I might visit the Castle."

Fishy grunted. "I thought you were barred from there?"

"A misunderstanding, old boy, all dealt with now." He unlocked the front door and was about to step into the street when he noticed a dark bundle of rags on the doorstep. "What the blazes…?" He prodded the bundle. It moved. The sword hissed from the cane, foxfire lit along its length, illuminating the pile of rags. He didn't turn to see, but he felt Fisher's reassuring presence behind him. A moment later eyes blinked amid the rags. Fisher gently but firmly pushed him aside and grabbed whatever it was by the scruff and hauled it to its feet. It squirmed momentarily but then relaxed like a pup in the fierce grip of its mother, which was not a thought Catt had ever imagined he would associate with Fishy. "My, what big hands you have, Doctor Fisher."

Fisher scanned the street before dragging the wretch into the shop. Catt also took a look. Aside from the rain, the street was empty. He closed the door. Fisher released the ragbag. One of them growled deep in their throat. Catt wasn't sure which and neither did he care. He was more concerned that the little scrap was dripping on the floor.

"Where are the others?" Fisher demanded. "Speak up, boy."

The boy glared at Fisher. "I don't know. I ain't their keeper."

"What are you doing here?" Fisher folded his arms and narrowed his eyes.

"I want a job."

It looked like the unflappable Fisher had met his match. As amusing as it would have been to stay and watch the battle of wits, Catt eased himself around the scowling pair and slipped out of the shop.

As the night wore on, it became apparent that much like his namesake, Catt had decided to spend the night on the tiles. Fisher wasn't overly concerned. The port militia regularly patrolled the most dangerous parts of town, and despite his genial nature and scholarly appearance, his partner could handle himself. Nevertheless, he decided to ensconce himself in the sitting room until Catt returned. He banked the fire and doffed the candles, preferring to watch the shadows dance by firelight. As time passed, his senses opened to the thousand notes the house and the inhabitants of the darkness played upon the slumbering world. The creak of joists, the fluttering of birds roosting in the attic rafters, the wolf spider's light step as it prowled across the papers scattered under the desk.

The sound of a pebble hitting the kitchen window and boots crunching on gravel was intrusive but not unexpected. Though he lied well, the boy had obviously been set up as the inside man for the Double Pockets. Fisher closed his eyes and let his senses travel beyond the prescribed human limits.

"Open up, you little shit," someone hissed outside the kitchen door.

"No. I've changed my mind. Shove off," said the boy. From the sound of the scuffling and shuffling coming from outside, it sounded like there were three of them. Fisher was content that even should the boy fulfil his villainous obligations he could deal with the gang.

"Open the door, or I'll wring your bloody neck."

"How are you gonna do that from the outside, Ren?"

Fisher smiled. The boy made a good point. There followed more threats and some weak attempts at cajolement which were answered with resolute silence. With his hearing acutely focused, Fisher could clearly picture the comedy unfolding downstairs. Like a patron at the theatre, he sat back and enjoyed the farce which came to an abrupt end when someone tried to force the door. There was a flash, accompanied by a yell of pain which was swiftly followed by a lot of cursing. The neighbourhood woke up, dogs began, shutters were flung open, lanterns flared. A clap of thunder was followed by Laurenta Castamere shouting at the by now fleeing thieves.

Fisher waited for the fuss to subside before heading downstairs. When he wanted, he could move very quietly and so, when he peered into the kitchen, the boy was under the table and did not stir when Fisher checked that the door was still locked. The sound of the boy's breathing was deep and even untroubled by recent events. He had knowingly decided to betray his associates and was content with that decision. Fisher was quietly impressed. He headed to the stairs as the familiar strains of Catty singing "Last Port of the Chemina" drifted down the street. Why he had chosen to ruin the night with an Ilkand song was beyond Fisher, but he was certain that he didn't want to find out and tiptoed back upstairs. Half an hour and many curses later, he heard Catt finally get his key in the lock.

"Almost there, Catty, almost there."

# THREE

"DRINK IT." FISHER put the glass on the counter before Catt. The drink was fizzing and smelled like an egg that had been poached in sulphur. He shuddered and pushed it away. He'd managed to shave and wash and had even splashed himself with lilac water, but his skin was a fetching shade of dead fish grey, and his usually bright eyes were sunken and red-rimmed. "Just drink it." Fisher folded his arms.

Catt slumped against the counter and sniffed the glass. "Tincture of Balzantine?"

"With an egg yolk. It's the best non-magical cure for a hangover."

"Only if one believes the cure should be worse than the ailment."

"You mean 'self-inflicted harm'." Fisher put the pestle and mortar under the counter. Catt took a deep, preparatory breath as he summoned the courage to drink the tincture. To give him his due, he downed it without further complaint. "Did you find time while carousing to put the word out that we were looking for an agent?"

"I wasn't carousing." Catt affected a wounded expression. "As it was raining I thought I'd have supper at the Pig where I obviously ate something that didn't agree with me. Don't look like that, you know the quality of the food there can be variable. And yes, I put the word out." Catt shuddered. "Was the egg entirely necessary?"

"It disguises the taste of powdered tiger snail."

Catt gave him the sharp edge of his eye. "There are times I question our friendship and no, it doesn't." The sound of a pan clattering on the floor in the kitchen put an end to the conversation. Both men followed the ringing clash but only Catt was surprised to see a child wearing a cut-down pair of Fisher's breeches and an old shirt of his, if he was not mistaken. The boy was brandishing a dish mop and a copper pan like a gladiator about to enter the arena. He was however clean, and his wild hair had been washed and tied back from his freshly scrubbed face. All that remained of the midden-crawler was the fierce, challenging gaze.

"I say, Fishy. There appears to be a... youth in the kitchen."

"Yes. He is doing the washing up." Fisher brushed past Catt and took the pan from the boy and picked up a towel. "Be careful with this, I don't want it denting." He dried the pan and hung it on the rack before turning back to Catt who was still attempting to fathom what was going on through the painful after-effects of a thorough booze beating.

"Something wrong, Doctor Catt?" Fisher enquired, amused.

"I know there's a good explanation for this. I just can't imagine what it might be."

Fisher shrugged. "The pans needed scrubbing."

Catt glared.

"Oh. You mean *the boy*. He wishes to make amends for past misdemeanours and become an honest and useful citizen. As you had your heart set on moving up in the world, I thought I'd kill two irritating birds with one stone and train our own staff." He gestured to the boy with the towel. "Opportunity presented itself."

"Does opportunity have a name?"

Fisher was momentarily perplexed. It hadn't occurred to him

that the child might have a name, or that such a thing might be of import. He poked the boy with his questioning gaze.

"Ashina Tagan Illig," the boy recited like a well-drilled soldier.

"That's too much name for a pup," said Fisher. "We'll call you Ash. When you have done the dishes, mop the floor."

Catt put his hands on his hips "Do we have quarters for the boy?"

Fisher shrugged. Catt turned to the boy.

"And just where are you going to sleep?" He pointed to a nest of blankets under the table. "I suppose it's a step up from what you're used to."

Ash didn't venture an answer, but his lips thinned to a hard line and his brow knitted into a frown that was eerily familiar to Fisher. "Just don't break anything," said Catt.

"I'LL NEED TEN sollies now." Neska drawled as she leaned back in the chair and put her hands behind her head. "For expenses."

After interviewing seven other potential agents, all of whom had all failed to impress, Catt had drifted into a state of bored semi-consciousness. The mention of ten sollies roused him like a slap in the face. "We want you to have a snoop around, not raise an army." He looked to Fisher just to confirm that he was not being unreasonable. Fishy maintained a dignified silence but arched his brow.

The Lantiri mercenary gave Catt a slow smile. "Mistress Castamere paid me twelve suns not a month ago to harvest some fire hyacinths. Ten in advance, just to dig up some bulbs."

"Where were they – Nydarrow?" Catt dipped his quill in the ink then paused. Neska was the last name on his list. *Damn and blast Laurenta bloody Castamere*. At this rate he'd have to go himself and that simply wouldn't do. "I'm not paying ten suns 'expenses' just so you can sit in a tavern for a couple of days and then come back and tell us you haven't found anything."

She drew a sharp breath; her hand flew to her chest as though she'd been struck. "I'm hurt, Doctor Catt. You know I'm reliable, or else why offer me the job?"

"Because as well as reliable, your services used to be reasonably priced," said Fisher. The smile on Neska's face vanished. She stood up, straightened her faded, first Lannet Dragoon's uniform jacket and swung the rapier on her hip behind her. "I would say I've never been so insulted, but then I recalled the last time I worked for you." She pointedly turned her gaze away from Doctor Fisher and focused her attention on Catt who did not want to get in the middle of an argument just before supper.

"Six up front," said Catt. He felt rather than saw Fisher's withering gaze upon him and quickly added. "But that's an advance and expenses."

She smirked and threw on her cloak. "I'll be in town for another night. You know where to find me if you change your minds. Gentlemen." She inclined her head before striding to the door which swung open before she reached it. Silhouetted by the burning sunset bleeding on the roofline, a huge, armoured form filled the doorway. Neska took a step back. Her hand slipped to the hilt of her rapier, ready to draw. Catt didn't blame her; he recognised the bulky form.

"As I live and breathe, Bailey Dannoch," said Catt, trying and failing to hide his disappointment. "Come in man, come in." He beckoned him inside not out of politeness, he just didn't want the neighbours to see the wretched fellow at their door.

It was impossible to distinguish where beard began, and hair ended; both were shaggy and greasy, and more grey than blond these days. His drooping moustache was stained red from cheap wine and matched the broken veins in his booze-swollen nose. His armour, once richly enamelled in the blue and gold colours of the Ilkand Temple, was patched, missing pieces, and rusted. What repairs had been affected were crude. The hauberk, once bright quilted canvas, was now leathery, dark with years of accumulated dirt. His boots were odd and, like his clothes and armour, more patch than original. The steel loop on his belt where his hammer had once hung was empty. In short, he was a man whose future was all behind him.

"I've come about the job." He stank like a dead bear but spoke softly. His gaze shifted awkwardly between Catt and Fisher. The old arrogance was gone, washed away by gallons of cheap wine and years of bitter regret.

"Drink?" offered Fisher.

If he didn't know him better Catt would have thought it cruel, whereas it was merely a lack of thought on his partner's behalf.

Dannoch seemed to take it in good spirit and gave a lopsided smile. "Often, as you know. But not now, thank you. Doctor Catt said there was a job?"

"I did? I mean, I did..." He searched his memory, but Catt could not find the slightest recollection of speaking to the ex-Templar. "Although, having said that I don't recall bumping into you at the Pig."

"It was outside the Castle. You were... It was late."

"Ah, yes of course." *Damn, I was cupshot last night.*

"If you will excuse me?" Neska looked at Dannoch like he was something that had been dredged from the river and waited until he stepped away from the door. On her way out she turned to Catt. "Like I say, you know my price and where to find me." She smiled, no doubt heartened at the thought of the coin that would soon be winging her way given the competition. And damn her, she was probably right. On a good day, Catt might have employed Dannoch, but the disgraced ex-Templar hadn't had one of those for years. It was sad bordering on pathetic to see the relic from another time loitering awkwardly by the door. Silence fell like a blanket.

"Seems you've already found an agent." Dannoch turned to leave.

"Never one for listening were you, Dannoch?" Fisher sighed. "Did he manage to tell you anything about the job?" His gaze flicked to Catt.

The Templar went to rest his hand upon the head of a hammer that had once hung from a brass loop on his belt. A frown creased his brow when his fingers closed on air. "Another dread weapon of the Kinslayer may or may not be somewhere up near Berrinford." He wiped his mouth with the back of his hand. "I'll do it for half of whatever she wanted."

He should have felt pity for the broken shell of a man, but Catt remembered the war and Dannoch's insufferable arrogance when crowds had cheered him and his company until they were hoarse. "Two suns?"

Dannoch's head went up at that. "She only wanted four?" He might have been a drunk, but he wasn't entirely stupid.

Fishy lowered the herb creel and took a bunch of thyme from the rack. While hidden from the warrior's view, he shot Catt a questioning glance. Catt replied with an affirmative wink. It wasn't like they wanted him to be anything other than a bloodhound. "We'll give you an extra solly if you take our apprentice, show him the ropes," Fisher added. "It'll be like having a squire again." Sending the boy was an unexpected rider, but Catt went along with it.

"I work alone."

"Then you don't work for us." Fisher sniffed the bunch of thyme. "It is that simple. Make up your mind, it's getting late."

The warrior straightened, squared up, and adopted a defiant expression. To his credit, he held the pose for a good three breaths before conceding. "Damn it."

"I take it we have an accord?" Catt wasn't confident that they hadn't just lost three gold suns, but if the unwanted house guest got lost with them it would be worth it.

He looked at Fishy, who he expected to smile conspiratorially. He didn't, he looked through him with the cold, dead-eyed gaze he reserved for strangers and those occasional moments of maudlin introspection to which he was given. "Come back tomorrow, first light."

The big man lingered.

"What is it?"

"I need to pick up a few supplies."

Fisher sighed and dug four scits from his grubby 'mugger's pouch', the one he used in public to avoid the attention of filchers and others of their ilk. He slapped the coins on the counter.

Trying to hide his limp, Dannoch came over and palmed them. He was taller than Catt, more of a height with Fisher, although twice as wide. Having said that, although his armour was snug around the middle, it hung in places where muscles had once challenged the straps and tested buckles. With a polite nod to both of them, he turned to leave.

Fisher called after him. "First light, Dannoch. Don't let me down." The warrior nodded without turning and prowled into the gathering darkness.

When he was sure he was out of earshot, Catt rounded on his partner. "Care to tell me what in the name of the Watcher is going on?"

Fisher blinked and breezed past him. "What do you mean, what's going on? We have a little job to do, and a big man to do it."

Catt followed him upstairs to the sitting room. On his way through he noticed that the kitchen floor tiles were gleaming and that the smell of lavender soap perfumed the air. The boy was squatting under the table gnawing on the ham bone Fishy had given him as a reward for his diligence.

"What's going on, Fishy?"

"Again, I don't know what you mean." He threw himself on the couch. Dust billowed.

Catt knelt by the fire he'd set earlier and sparked life into the lint and kindling with one of the long-stemmed matches they kept in a flowerpot next to the hearth. "Are you punishing me?"

"Don't talk nonsense, Catty." Fisher huffed. "I work with the clay given me by circumstance. In this case, an ill-advised purchase followed by a drunken invitation to a handful of greedy rogues and a dangerous drunk." He stretched, bones cracked. "That's better."

"You... I didn't invite a waif to live with us."

"You want to move up in the world. You want a grand house for which we will require servants. If you can't deal with a kitchen boy, I doubt you'll have a chance standing up to any housekeeper worth her salt."

"The kitchen boy is chewing on a bone like a starving dog, or hadn't you noticed?"

Fisher chuckled. Fire leapt amid the kindling and firelight rooted in the bright metal objects in the room; the brass astrolabe hanging above their acre of desk, the crystal vase filled with glitter-eyed Tzarkomen corpse pins, gilt scroll frames, silver ink wells.

"It's good for his teeth. And I told you, it is circumstance. Sometimes you have to play with the cards you've been dealt. Have faith, Catty."

Doctor Catt patted his robes. "I think I lost it in the frozen north, you remember, when the gods died. I don't need faith, I need assurances."

"In that case, I assure you, everything will be well."

Catt used the sagging armchair by the fire as support as he climbed to his feet. "I don't suppose you could assure me that our hound will sniff out something that will provide a down payment on a delightful townhouse on River View?"

# FOUR

"IT'S FAR TOO big."

Catt took a step back, flicked the tassel of his nightcap over his shoulder and appraised his handiwork. "He'll grow into it."

The boy peered at them from over the folds of a waxed cloak that hid all from the nose down. Catt had attacked it with scissors, but it was still far too big. For his part, Ash endured the ill-tempered fittings stoically, even on the numerous occasions Catt mistook him for a pincushion. Fisher made a mental note to visit the market and purchase a suit of clothes that would actually fit upon his return from the scouting mission. For the time being, he would at least be dry, which was more important than sartorial elegance. It would be terrible form if their first servant caught a chill and died of a fever – not unlikely since it had rained for the best part of the night. The sky was grey, pitted here and there with the slightest suggestion that it had ever been blue and full of light and warmth. It was poor weather in which to hunt: tracks were washed away as soon as they were made, and scents drowned in the deluge. Luckily for Dannoch, he was hunting an artefact, not a herd of deer.

"I'll do it myself then." Catt swept past him.

"Do what?"

"Get the door," he called over his shoulder.

"The bell rang," said the boy as he shed the cloak which

folded at his feet like a sloughed skin. "He asked if you'd see who it was."

Fisher grunted. "I must have drifted off." It was happening too much of late; something would happen that would set his mind to tunnelling into old memories that he hoped he'd forgotten. Catt returned, followed by Dannoch. Muttering under his breath, his partner began to pack away the contents of the sewing box that were strewn across the kitchen table. Alongside the sewing box was a small knapsack of what they deemed to be essential items for the boy's first 'job'. It occurred to Fisher that on a whim he'd decided to send a child and a drunk to find a weapon of the Kinslayer that probably didn't exist. He hid the chuckle under a throat-clearing cough. He'd never expected to go mad in old age, but then, who does?

Dannoch lurked in the doorway, awkward and restless. He had nevertheless made an effort to appear ready for work. He had a blanket roll tied across his shoulders. Someone, most likely himself judging by the lack of skill, had hacked a good six inches off his beard and his hair had been loosely braided. He still smelled like a dead bear, but Fisher appreciated that he had made some effort not to look like one.

"Doctor Fisher," he acknowledged in tone and manner that was half apology half challenge. It was as though he had not entirely reconciled himself to being on the wane. His pride made him vulnerable, kept him in that dreadful state of 'hope'.

"You know, the more I think about this, the more I am convinced this is a less than sensible arrangement." Catt closed the double lid of the sewing box and drew a silver locket on a chain from his dressing-gown pocket. A lone ruby winked on the lid. He rubbed the etched case with his thumb, paused a moment, then thrust it back in his pocket.

"Nonsense," Fisher exclaimed. "They're going to wander around the countryside, not wage war against the Ice Worms of Galdinnion."

"And what of our reputation?" Catt demanded.

Ah. There it was. "I think you overestimate our importance. Now hand that over to Ash."

His partner frowned and drew the locket from his pocket once again. "Wouldn't it be better to give it to Dannoch?" Catt glanced at the big man leaning against the doorframe.

Fisher saw a flicker of concern cross Dannoch's face. "No. Give it to Ash. The boy needs to learn how such things work."

"If you insist." He crouched before the youngster. "This is the Bijouterie of Whispers." He flicked the ruby from the lid. "I keep this. If you find the Unguis, open it like so." Catt thumbed the well-worn lid on the locket. It opened with a metallic pop. "And whisper where you are."

"What if I don't know where I am?"

"Find out before you use it."

"What if I can't?"

Catt looked to Fisher for help.

He couldn't offer any, but he was enjoying watching Catt struggle. He handed the book that he'd wrapped in a piece of oiled cloth to Dannoch. "Don't lose it."

"I'll do my best... sir."

"I'm here!" the boy shouted into the locket, causing the ruby to leap from Catt's hand like a glittering frog.

Quick as a snake, he snatched it from the floor. "I'm not deaf! Just whisper, and we will come," he said to the boy who was examining the locket, turning it this way and that. Finally, he sniffed it before looping the chain over his head.

"You were serious about me taking him with me then?" Dannoch did not look pleased at the prospect, but he did look sober, which was something. He was still wearing his armour and still weaponless, but he had at least brought a shovel. "I've no skill with children."

Catt again fixed Fisher with a look that said, 'I told you this was a bad idea.'

Fisher ignored it. "He's not a weapon you have to master. Just feed him and keep him safe. I recall you had some skill at that once."

"You're paying me to find this Unguis, not care for a child."

"I can take care of myself." The boy picked up his knapsack. He looked resolute, determined, and very bloody small. Like a startled fish darting for the shadows, a flicker of doubt shot through Fisher. He crushed it like a bug. The boy was old enough to run with a gang, so he was old enough to learn a trade. "You might as well go out the back way, cut across the Tein Street Bridge." He handed Dannoch a letter. "Show this to the watch if they stop you."

Dannoch took the letter and gave a wry smile. "Must be nice having connections." He sized up his travelling companion and shook his head.

*Penitents cannot be choosers, warrior*, thought Fisher as he and Catt watched the ill-matched pair trudge to the end of the street, the boy running to keep up.

"Well, Fishy. I hope you know what you're doing," Catt said, his gaze fixed on the rooftop horizon, his pale eyes filled with scudding clouds.

"And I hope that book isn't just expensive arse-wipe."

As SOON AS they rounded the corner, the boy stopped. "We need to talk," he said.

Dannoch kept walking until it became clear his companion wasn't following. "Can we walk and talk? Only I want to get out of the city before the road gets busy."

"You're going through with it?" He sounded as much disappointed as surprised.

Dannoch reassessed his companion. He was a sharp-eyed little thing. Skinny, pale, spotty, as befitted a street-bred gutter-rat, but he was also possessed of a calm, self-assurance. "Yes.

*We're* going through with it. This town... this country, is too small to cross the good doctors. You may smile but don't be fooled by their doddering old codger act. They've hearts of flint and a vengeful nature – both of them."

"I just wanted to be sure you weren't going to do one and leave me somewhere."

"Oh, did you by... How old are you?"

"Nine."

"Nine?"

"I'm small for my age."

Such a little thing should be home with his family, not robbing tombs for greedy old men with decrepit old drunks.

"Well?" Dannoch looked down. The boy was tugging on his cloak. "Are you all right?" the lad asked.

"Aye. I was just thinking."

The boy squinted up at Dannoch. "So do we have an accord, or what?"

"I give you my word that I won't 'do one' and abandon you." It had been a long time since he'd heard himself say that and mean it. He felt foolish. The embarrassment, the sting of ingrained cynicism, burned like acid in his throat. He swallowed the bile, and resolved to make less of a fool of himself as they made their way through the dawn-lit city.

The river was on their left and would stay there as it curved north-west like an old silver scar. They were headed due north. He hoped to reach Berrinford by mid-afternoon if the weather held. He looked up; the clouds were heavy and grey, and even though they burned within from what scant sun's rays they had captured, iron plumes braced the sky from edge to edge. "It looks like rain."

The boy also looked up, his small hand gripped the pack straps like they were made of gold, his scabby knuckles as white as hens' eggs. His feet kicked the hem of his cut-down cloak with a rhythmic *thap, thap, thap* as he walked. Although he didn't dawdle, Dannoch soon began to outpace him and had to stop more than once and wait for him to catch up. He reassessed the situation and decided that they would do well to reach Berrinford by nightfall.

"You ever been to Berrinford, boy?"

"It's Ash. My name. It's Ash, or Ashina Tagan Illig. I'm not just 'boy.'"

"You're an insolent pup."

"Called Ash, and no, I've not been to Berrinford. I lived on the river and then when ma died, in the city."

The marks of civilisation that defined 'the city' soon fell away as they pushed beyond the margins of what was currently inhabited. The districts of Cinquetann furthest from the river had by and large been rendered down. The first felling had been through war, the second years of neglect. Now scavengers and entrepreneurs were moving in, robbing out seasoned timber and dressed stone, as well as what treasures lay buried where they had been abandoned by their owners. What mortals didn't want had been swiftly reclaimed by nature.

The boy, *Ash*, was watchful but not fearful. Dannoch wondered how far his courage would stretch from the relative safety of the city. Even here in the warm heart of the Middle Kingdoms, the roads weren't patrolled often and drew rogues like a corpse drew flies. *And you saw fit to bring, not a hammer or an axe, but a shovel.* He laughed in his head and as was often the case, mocked himself for mocking himself; like a drunk gazing into a fairground mirror seeing his own stupid face reflected to eternity.

Today the joke amused him less because his long quest for oblivion had not included a child. The boy was an unwanted complication, a consideration he did not wish to take into account.

\* \* \*

THEY CONTINUED IN blessed silence for a good fifteen or so miles by which time evening was pressing the light from the day and filling the void with stars. Dannoch's knees ached. This was the furthest he'd walked in months and he was feeling it. Up ahead some hundred feet or so, the road forked.

"Which way?" the boy asked.

"We take the smaller road on the right. The main one on the left goes north."

"To Ilkand?"

The name of his home still held venom when he heard it, but it had weakened over the years. "Aye, eventually."

Somewhere near Berrinford a pall of smoke rose and stacked its grey billows through the dying light, spinning ghostly threads towards the darkness. He thought it an odd place for a caravan to pull over when the town was so close. Wary as well as weary, he pressed on.

As they got closer to Berrinford, Dannoch could smell burning meat. Half a mile later, the smell was stronger and accompanied by the sound of voices.

"Do you think it's bandits?" the boy asked, again more calmly than Dannoch would expect from someone his age.

"Not even the worst highway robbers would light a bonfire if they were planning to ambush travellers."

A little further along, the road widened into a clearing in which the pyre they had smelled was burning. Sitting around the clearing blaze were half a dozen blood-soaked hunters. They didn't look like Cheriveni. They were all garbed in brown and green leathers, and at least three were wearing Varran ancestor beads around their wrists, necks, and waists. Three dead star-crown stags lay in a pile waiting to be skinned. Another five of the majestic creatures had already been skinned and decapitated. Rather than salting the meat, the bodies had been consigned to the flames.

"It seems a waste," said Dannoch half to himself, half to the boy.

One of the hunters who was cleaning blood from a barbed spear acknowledged him with a curt nod. "Bad meat," she said.

"Poison?" Dannoch asked.

"Bad spirits," said the hunter, her gaze tracking to the forest. The woodland was dense and overrun with thick coils of razor-thorned reaper vine and the ghostly umbels of fell bane that choked everything smaller than a tree. Before the war, foresters would have cleared the undergrowth and kept trails open. Varran hunters made their own trails. Driven from their mountain homelands by the Kinslayer, the Varra had become nomads, surviving by dint of their formidable hunting, and tracking skills. Independent and proud, they were friendly enough, even to vagabond knights, but a pall hung over this group and they seemed to be in a hurry to pack up and leave.

"I'd head to the town if I were you. Our ancestors won't be able to protect you come nightfall."

"These bad spirits, have you seen them?"

She nodded. "Come." She took him to the pile of star crowns. Up close, he could see that they were all suffering from some kind of mange. Their features were distorted, and their teeth too long, and too many for their mouths. One even had sharp bone spurs growing from its shoulders. "Their hides are no good. We killed them as a kindness. Do you smell that?" He couldn't smell anything except the greasy stink of burning meat. He shook his head. "It's wrong. No animal should smell like they do, dead or alive."

He glanced over his shoulder to see another of the hunters hanging a string of beads around Ash's neck.

"For your son," said the hunter when he saw Dannoch looking. "For luck."

"He's not my son."

"We're business partners," said Ash.

"Business partners?" the woman seemed both surprised and

378

amused and said something in Varran that caused the others to laugh.

Dannoch felt the colour rise in his cheeks. *Seems I do have some pride left after all. Fancy that.* "Well, we'd best be on our way. Come on, *partner.*"

"Be safe, and be swift, Templar," said the woman. "And do not tarry."

When they were out of earshot, Ash turned to Dannoch. "Why did she call you 'Templar'?"

Old wounds began to ache. "No idea. Now come on, it's getting late."

# FIVE

"Settlements most often grow in places where Nature bestowed its bounty," said the warrior, his deep voice rolling through the threatening darkness of the forest, startling Ash, and scaring a pair of crows to flight. "Some areas are blessed with rich soil, some a fair climate, others a clear lake with an abundance of fish. Before the war, Berrinford was an open-pit mining town."

The buildings were log-built, greened with age and squat as toads. A pair of short-legged, skinny dogs barked at them before chasing rats under the walkway that ran alongside the rutted main road. A couple of bored-looking militia stared down at them from a gateway that bestrode the road. A watch bell silhouetted against the light of a feeble brazier flame swung gently between the men.

"Did the Kinslayer come here?" Ash asked.

"His army swept through Cherivell, but no, it did not come here. Hard to believe, isn't it?"

The boy nodded. "It's a dump."

"Welcome to Berrinford."

"Where are we going?"

Dannoch slowed to a halt. "It's too late to do any exploring now. Let me see, there's a tavern and a coaching inn. I usually go to the tavern. It's a bit rough, but the booze is cheap." He rubbed his jaw looked at Ash like he was a puzzle waiting to be solved. "We'll go to the inn. As I recall it's on the west side of town."

The few stores and houses were shuttered tight, but soon enough he got a whiff of beery, smoky air. The soft babble of conversation floated towards them, accompanied by the sound of bleating lunnox and slamming doors.

The closer they got to the inn, the quicker Dannoch's pace. Ash almost had to run to keep up, but rather that than be left behind. He shuddered at the memory of the malformed beasts, pain and sickness locked in their dead eyes. Not for the first time that day, he wondered if he'd made a mistake leaving the Double Pockets. As gangs went, they were terrible, but at least they'd stayed in the city that he knew.

*Trust your gut, Ash.* That's what his ma had always said. Well, the moment he laid eyes on Doctor Fisher he'd listened to his gut tell him that his prospects would improve if he got in with the old gaunt. It didn't tell him that Fisher would send him out of town with a walking midden in rusty armour.

He hastened after Dannoch, imagining the prickle of eyes upon his back, of claws reaching from the darkness. He risked a glance over his shoulder, daring the monsters to strike by acknowledging their presence. His heart stuttered. There was someone lurking in a doorway, but it was a man not a monster, his face shining pale in the moonlight.

The inn was busy, bright, and warm; the lantern light and pipe smoke made his eyes water, the smell of stew made his stomach rumble. All eyes turned to the door when he and Dannoch entered. Some drew their packs closer, wrapped their hands around mugs protectively, as though he might try to snatch them away. The big man drew a breath, straightened up, and strode through the milling crowd to the bar. Ash followed as close as a shadow. A group of giant Oerni standing at the bar made Dannoch look small, but there was something about him, something dangerous, that even they shuffled aside when he approached.

A woman was serving behind the bar. Her cheeks were red, her hair prisoned in a big white bonnet save for a few errant strands that framed her face. Hanging from the rafters above her were a row of pewter tankards and swags of fell bane blossoms, their sweet smell lost in the booze-drenched air. A few emotions crossed her face when she saw Dannoch. The first Ash recognised all too well. It was suspicion mixed with disgust; the kind of look those with gave those without. In his experience, it was most often followed by a sharp admonition, an accusation and then finished with a threat should he not get lost quick enough. She frowned, puzzled a moment, and then Dannoch dropped some coins on the counter. She smiled.

"Good evening to you. A jug of your house wine and a room, for two nights, if it please you." He spoke haltingly, like he was reciting a half-remembered story rather than making a simple request.

She swept up the coins up. "Will you be wanting dinner?" She looked pointedly at Ash and gave him a smile laced with pity.

Dannoch glanced over his shoulder. The look of confusion on his face turned to one of embarrassment. "Aye, mistress."

"Yannis!" An older boy with a mop of dirty blond hair and tombstone teeth side-stepped through the crowd. "Table for two, in the corner by the fire." the innkeeper commanded.

The boy nodded. "If you'll follow me... sir." He turned before Dannoch saw him smirk. Ash saw it though and took an instant dislike to the potboy who flourished a washcloth and wiped up some spilled beer before inviting them to sit. Although it was a novelty not to be called 'vagabond' and be chased from the inn, Ash made sure not to grin as he took a seat like a legitimate customer. The potboy danced back and was swallowed by the crowd of travellers.

Dannoch pulled the shovel from the strap of his pack and rested it against the table. The pack he dumped on the floor before sticking his right leg out straight. His stool groaned under the testing weight and the table rocked when he rested his rust enshrined arms on the scarred wood. Ash had seen plenty of old soldiers begging on the streets of Cinquetann. Mostly they were harmless, but sometimes through drink or madness, their mood would curdle, and they would turn like wild dogs and grow strange and frightening. Sometimes, they would cry and mumble in drunken tongues, weep and lament lost friends, lost battles, and lost limbs. The man sitting before him was well on his way to joining that regiment of the forgotten and forlorn. When his knee finally gave out, and he couldn't work enough to keep himself in cheap wine, he'd sell that rusting armour and take up the beggars' cup, and that would be an end of him. Ash had seen it happen many times. *I will never be a beggar* he silently swore.

As Dannoch wasn't one for talking, Ash set his ears to picking over the bones of others' conversations. Most were passing through, discussing the road, the bad food, the worse drink. The group of Oerni traders stooped beneath the low roof beams were talking excitedly about pelts they'd bought. Ash toyed with the beads the hunter had given him, his thoughts turned by their conversation back to the wrong animals and the coppery stink of burning blood.

Dannoch hunched over the table, dug his fingers into his thick beard to scratch his chin, all the while casting sly, needful glances towards the bar. Eventually, the potboy burst from the throng, carrying a tray of food and drink. The warrior straightened, his gaze fixed on the wine bottle. Ash could have taken a shit on the table for all Dannoch would have noticed, which suited Ash well enough because he was intent on the food and ate until his stomach was uncomfortably full. Lulled by the gentle babble of conversation, warm, and with a hard, round belly Ash began to drowse.

"Something wrong?" Dannoch's growl intruded into the cushioned bliss of his dozing. He jerked awake. The warrior wasn't talking to him. He followed the direction of his heavy-lidded gaze to three travellers sitting in the opposite niche by the fire, rain dripping from steaming cloaks hanging off their chairs told him they had recently arrived. A Ystachi with blue scales and amber eyes smiled and leaned across the table. Her companions sat back. One was a woman with a half-shaved, tattooed head. She was wearing a mail coat and armour. In contrast, the third member of the group was a skinny fellow wearing a mud-splattered, homespun robe. He looked like a travelling scholar or a priest save that his boots were made of fine leather, etched, and inlaid with silver. Ash couldn't place where they were from, but it certainly wasn't Berrinford.

"Your armour. It looks…" She paused, canted her head as though trying to dislodge the right word from wherever it was hiding. "You don't belong here." Her friends sniggered. The tattooed woman put her feet up on a stool, showed them the soles of her muddy boots. Ash didn't know much about good manners, but he knew that was a sign of contempt.

Dannoch sighed quietly and took a drink from his mug of wine. "No. We're just passing through."

"On your way to Ilkand?" she enquired, her voice softly sibilant.

"None of your business," growled Dannoch. His warning tone muted nearby conversation and drew patrons' attention to the parties sitting in the inglenook. Ash took the remaining bread roll and stuffed it his knapsack, ready to make a quick exit should this go badly.

"There's no need to take that tone, my man." The skinny fellow plucked a loose thread from his robe. "We were just curious to see such a relic, is all. I mean your armour, of course. It is antique, is it not?"

"Fuck off." His weary tone coupled with the deadness of his

gaze reminded Ash of the guard dogs kept in the grounds of wealthy houses, the kind that would cause the Double Pockets to pass and pick somewhere less dangerous to rob.

Before the Ystachi or the skinny fellow could add more fuel to their pyre, the tattooed woman intervened. "Leave it, you two," she said. The Ystachi shrugged and turned her lambent gaze to the fire.

The skinny fellow rolled his eyes. "I meant no offence. It was just a little—"

The sound of the door almost being torn from its hinges cut him off. An Oerni woman crashed through the door, scattering patrons as she fell into a table that collapsed under the weight. "We're being attacked. A monster!" Her voice rose shrilly above the sound of breaking mugs and splintering wood. The others of her clan ran to her aid and by dint of their prodigious size cleared a space around them as they helped her to her feet. In panic and confusion, people started shouting, dogs barked excitedly, while outside, lunnox were screaming.

Some instinct saw his companion leap from his seat and charge outside, shovel in hand. Compelled by the force of Dannoch's sudden exit, Ash followed.

"There. The beast is there."

A terrified stable hand jabbed towards the paddock behind the inn where something was tearing a lunnox apart. Dannoch ran towards it as torches flared and lit the grisly scene. Something that looked part wolf, part bear was feasting on one of the dying lunnox. The rest of the pack animals were cowering in a corner, horned heads lowered, they kicked the fence and each other while crying out in terror.

Although his legs were trembling with fear and excitement, Ash fought his way through the crowd from the inn, pushing his way forward while trying to keep Dannoch in sight. When he got closer, he could see two more dead lunnox laying in the paddock. They were on their backs, limbs splayed as though in supplication to the night sky, their black and white fur stained scarlet, their spilled innards steaming beside their mangled bodies. Someone opened the gate, and the remaining lunnox thundered from the pen and ran towards the inn. The crowd scattered. Ash pressed himself against the fence. What he hadn't seen straightaway was the body of an Oerni laying trampled in the muddy paddock. His head was tilted back, and his eyes were open, staring from behind a mask of blood.

"On me!" His sore knee forgotten, Dannoch leapt the fence.

The beast looked up from its meal and snarled, revealing uneven rows of bone-splitting fangs. Axe in hand the tattooed warrior yelled a battle cry, and bounded after Dannoch followed by two Oerni.

"Hey, you, get away! Go on. Get out, get out!" It was the innkeeper. She was standing on a stack of hay bales shouting and waving her arms. The creature lowered its ragged crown of antlers. Dannoch swerved at the last minute, ducked, and swung up into the beast's maw. The handle of the shovel shattered, the beast's head snapped back.

Dannoch barrelled into its flank. Antlers screamed against steel and scored gouges in the rusted metal. The beast was the size of a large deer, but he threw it across the paddock. Ash didn't know much about monsters, but it seemed to move with unnatural agility and whipped around in the air before landing on its feet. Monster it might be, but it did not have eyes in the back of its head, so it did not see the tattooed warrior run up behind it and bring her axe down on one of its hind legs.

It tried to take a step and stumbled, giving Dannoch time to grab a broken fence post. In horror and awe, Ash watched him sway aside as the beast lunged, its bloody maw snapping at his face. He ducked and drove the jagged post into its chest. The tattooed warrior swung again breaking its other back leg. It collapsed with Dannoch beneath it.

No one moved, no one spoke, the sound of his heart beating

resounded. The spell was soon broken when the crowd descended on the paddock like crows, some just to get a look at the beast, others to congratulate the axe-wielder who was hoisted onto her comrades' shoulders. The Oerni gathered around their fallen comrade. While they wept, some latecomers began to hack at the beast with a collection of improvised weapons. Ash didn't know if they were trying to make sure it was dead, or to take a grim souvenir. Either way, it did not go down well with Dannoch.

"Enough. Damn it. Enough!" he shouted from under the beast. "It's dead already. Now get it the fuck off me."

# SIX

"WELL?" FISHER DEMANDED impatiently.

Catt popped the ruby from the centre of the monocle and rubbed his eyes. "I fear I have a headache coming on." Fisher thrust a crystal goblet of brandy into Catt's waiting hand. He threw it back and grimaced. "That's better."

"Did you see anything?" Fisher asked.

"Yes, yes. I'll spare you the gory details – and they are gory, trust me. But suffice it to say, I think they might be onto something."

"I'm a big boy. Don't spare me. Tell me."

"They arrived in Berrinford, which is unsurprisingly still a dump. There appears to be some unnatural creatures roaming around. Anyway, one of the aforementioned *things* attacked an unfortunate Oerni and ate some lunnox. I didn't get a clear look, but it had something of the vilewolf about it." He shivered. "Anyway, our hero hit it with a shovel and another warrior type slew it."

"A vilewolf? Are you sure?"

"No, not really. I've been looking through the eyes of an untrained child. Scrying clear images is difficult at the best of times."

"I am aware, yes."

"I think it had antlers."

"Vilewolves do not have antlers."

"Yes, thank you, I know. It was more the way it acted. It was feral, insanely savage. Like I said, I couldn't see it clearly; there was a heavy fog clouding my view. If they survive the adventure, remind me to teach the boy how to attune." The last log of the night crashed into a crust of grizzling embers. It was getting late. Catt sighed and dramatically fell back in his chair. "I feel quite dizzy."

"I wish you'd told me that before I gave you the good brandy." As ever, he was milking his part, but Fisher had to admit that scrying through the Bijouterie could be difficult. He poured himself a snifter of the twenty-year-old Arashun and swirled the honey-coloured brandy around the glass, releasing the light, delicate bouquet.

Catt massaged his temples. "Please, accept my heartfelt apologies."

"We might have made a mistake sending them instead of going ourselves."

Catt leaned back in his seat and sought inspiration in the ceiling before answering. "I don't understand your concern. Your man dealt with the situation adequately enough. So long as there aren't any more, all he has to do is poke around the countryside."

He knew he should ignore the barb, but something in Catt's tone irked him. "My man? I thought we both hired him."

Catt shrugged. "You offered him the extra solly."

"To pay for the boy's food and lodgings. You have an unreasonable dislike for Dannoch. He is not the worst of those who've worked for us by far, and you know it."

Catt huffed. "He was a braggart and an egotist and got his company killed playing the hero. I think my dislike is perfectly reasonable."

"Did you see him? Guilt has consumed him. He's trying to change."

"He's trying to drown himself in cheap wine so that he doesn't have to admit what he did."

Catt would never understand men like Dannoch, and Fisher could never explain it to him, at least not without destroying their friendship.

"I don't want to argue with you, Fishy. I'm just tired."

"Then perhaps you should go to bed."

"Very well. I shall. Try not to brood too loudly." He stood up, flicked the silver tassel of his nightcap over his shoulder, and buttoned his dressing gown under his soft, peach-fuzzed chin. "Goodnight, Doctor Fisher."

"Sleep well, Doctor Catt," said Fisher, and he meant it knowing that he would not be able to do the same.

THE ROOM HAD one full-sized bed and a truckle bed that had already been pulled out and pushed over by the fire. A bowl and jug of fresh water stood on a painted washstand. There was even a ball of clove-studded lavender soap. It wasn't as grand as Doctor Fisher and Catt's kitchen, but it was the finest establishment Ash had ever had cause to visit legitimately.

"Shall I light the fire?" he asked and hoped Dannoch would say yes.

"If you like." The warrior sounded tired. He went over to the window and watched those still loitering by the paddock.

"What was that thing?" Ash asked, even though part of him did not want to know that such things had names.

It took Dannoch a while to answer. Eventually, he closed the shutters, and with a voice full of pity said, "Something broken."

Ash lit the fire with flint and tinder, and felt relief when the sparks caught in the wool, and tiny snakes of flame wove through the faggots. "Do you think there are any more of them out there?"

"I doubt it. You don't get many creatures like that. Not any more." Dannoch sat on the bed. Blood dripped from a gash on his wrist which wasn't covered by the worn vambrace. He saw Ash looking and wiped it on his filthy cloak. "Don't worry. You're safe."

He didn't feel safe. But he didn't say it. Neither did he mention the blood running down Dannoch's hand, or that he was swaying drunk, covered in mud, and stank worse than the dead lunnox. He didn't say Dannoch scared him. The warrior lay on the bed without taking off his armour and stared up at the rafters taking occasional swigs from the bottle of wine.

Ash rubbed his sore feet and took off the cutdown cloak. He lay down, closed his eyes, and listened to the crackle of faggots and the slosh of Dannoch's wine. More distantly, he could hear the wind combing through the forest's edge, the sobbing Oerni, and the chatter in the bar, bleeding through the floorboards. As sleep enfolded him, it felt like he was floating through the sounds, weaving in and out of the fretful weft of the shattered night.

THE BOY FELL asleep as soon as he put his head down. Dannoch got up and pushed the truckle bed away from the hearth. The last thing he wanted to deal with now was a fire. His right arm was throbbing where the creature had raked him with its teeth. He'd been lucky; it had been trying to chew his face off. Old memories stirred, lost voices sang in the wind that was rattling the shutters.

For want of something to do, he took Catt's notebook from his pack. The doctor had marked relevant passages relating to locations to search. He'd also added his own notes, in bold, underlined, and pointed out with arrows just in case Dannoch missed them. Aside of oblique references to the 'Unguis of Maug' the notebook was filled with fanciful nonsense that ten years ago he would have called heresy before burning the book.

But then ten years ago, he had believed absolutely in the power of the gods and his own divine calling. So much had changed since then; for him, and the world.

He tossed the notebook aside and picked up the bottle of red he'd been given by the innkeeper. It was empty, and he was still too sober, but the common room was packed and given the excitement of the night, wouldn't empty any time soon. They had cheered him when he'd returned, and some had bought him drinks, but he'd had his fill of stupid questions for the night. He closed his eyes, and when he opened them again the velvet night had turned into a grey dawn.

He sat up. Everything ached. The pain in his creaking knee was warm, but the gash on his wrist was now a pink rope of scar. In a week it would be silver. He crept to the window and unlatched the shutters. The sky was hidden behind thick cloud, and the buildings floated in a heavy, milk mist that shrouded the ground. Crows swooped onto the paddock fence posts. Pinions stretched their wings like fingers as they summoned their kin to the feast with raucous calls. Dannoch stoked the embers in the hearth and coaxed life back into the fire before he left. Avoiding the common room, he slipped outside through the stables.

The Oerni were camped behind the inn, close to the paddock. Their huge wagons were drawn up in a circle. Ringed by tall, cloaked figures that huddled like monoliths a woolly twist of smoke rose from their campfire. Having long since forgotten words of comfort, he kept his head down as he headed to the paddock. The Oerni had been moved, but the dead lunnox lay where they had fallen and were already being investigated by carrion. The beast was also where it had died, but not even flies troubled its carcass.

Whatever it was, it had been a sick animal. Its ribs were clearly visible under matted fur, its vicious teeth protruded at random angles and cut into lips and gums that were scarred by pustulent scabs that could never heal. It must have been in agony. Even in death, its eyes seemed to burn with fever. He crouched and picked up its foreleg to get a better look at its claws. The stench was like a punch in the face, but he'd smelled worse.

"What the hell do you think you're doing?" A deep voice rumbled through the ground. He turned and was not surprised to see one of the Oerni lumbering towards him. His mottled face was pale with ashes.

"I'm taking a look at this thing."

"Leave it alone! It's diseased... Oh, it's you. Forgive my brusqueness, but scavengers have been hanging around. They wanted this, can you believe it?" The giant shook his shaved head. "Marroc not cold and these... *ghouls* come looking for trophies. No respect." Tears threatened, but then he caught sight of something, and his face darkened. "Look. Do you see?" He chinned in the direction of a group of humans, lurking in the edgeland between forest and town. Their clothes were ragged, their hair wild. They were watching them with hungry eyes.

"Like you say; they're scavengers," said Dannoch as old memories of battlefield horrors surfaced.

"You're wasting your time!" the Oerni's voice boomed. "We're going to burn it. Do you hear me?" The whole town must have heard him. The scavengers drifted away.

"Pay them no heed. Something like this draws all kinds like..." He was going to say *like a corpse draws flies*, but given the circumstances he refrained. "...like the greedy bastards they are. Some hunters had a pyre going on the way into town. I'll help you take it there and burn it if you'd like?"

The Oerni stood head and shoulders above him, but despite the mourning ashes, he was a gentle-looking fellow with a merchant's soft hands and comfortably rounded body. He nodded, clearly relieved. "Aye. We did some business with them. We bought pelts to sell in Cinquetann. But I cannot ask any more of you, Templar, you've already done enough."

"I'm not a Templar. And it's no bother."

"But you wear the armour of a Hegumen."

"Someone gave it to me." It wasn't entirely a lie. His Archimandrite had presented him with the breastplate when he was inducted into the order.

"Well… thank you. The Wayfarers say that those who show kindness on the road are a blessing from the gods."

*The gods are gone.* "I've got to fetch something from the inn. Hitch a wagon and we'll drag it." He cast a glance to where the scavengers had been, saw movement in the mist, sensed eyes upon him. "And have one of your people keep watch until I get back."

The Oerni nodded. "Thank you…?"

Given that the Oerni had recognised the Hegumen armour, the possibility existed that he might have heard of him, but he was young, hopefully too young to remember the name of a disgraced Templar. "Bailey." He offered his hand.

The Oerni smiled and wrapped his prodigious hand around Dannoch's. "Aerin."

"Sorry for your loss, Aerin. I'll be back soon."

"Do you see those spurs?" Dannoch pointed to the barbs on the beast's forelegs. Ash nodded, a look of deep concentration on his face. "What do these things tell you?"

"I don't know."

Dannoch cinched the knot tight around the monster's legs. Wiped his hands on his cloak. "Have a guess."

"I don't know. I've never seen anything like it. I don't…" Ash bit his lip, and stared harder at the beast that was starting to decompose far quicker than it should have done. "It wasn't born like this?" He scratched his head to give himself time to order his thoughts. "I mean, it wouldn't have lived if it had been born with those teeth and all those spikes and its feet are wrong. They look like one foot pushed its way through another." He shook his head. "It just isn't right."

Dannoch smiled and experienced a rare moment of genuine pleasure. "Aye, something changed it." *Or someone.* "That's good observation. Now get in the back of the wagon. Shout if anything falls off it." The boy swallowed hard but nodded and scrambled into the back of the wagon. Dannoch checked that the rope was secure to the tailgate before joining Aerin upfront.

"Thank you again," said the Oerni. "We're just merchants; this is beyond anything me or my brothers have ever experienced."

"He was your brother?"

"No. Marroc was our mother's sister's son. I don't know how I'm going to tell them. Until last night it had been the best trip. We'd sold in Ilkand, and replenished stock on the way back to Cinquetann." His voice caught in his throat. "It's like a nightmare from which I cannot wake."

"I understand." What he didn't tell him that it was a nightmare that would never go away. It would lodge like a splinter in his mind and from time to time would make itself known. Awake or asleep, it didn't matter. The memory of it would leap unbidden into his mind as sharp as the moment it had happened.

Aerin released the brake and clucked the pair of lunnox into movement. The goat-like animals were still skittish from almost being eaten, but with a combination of gentle coaxing and a firm hand, he got them trotting along at a fair clip. Some townsfolk stopped to watch, and when they reached the guard post, one of the militia waved them to stop. Dannoch sat on his disgruntlement and waited, tensely silent while she inspected the creature and poked her head over the back of the cart before coming to speak to them.

"What are you doing?" she asked.

Dannoch waited for Aerin to speak because his tongue was primed for rebuking stupidity and he didn't want to fight today.

The Oerni inclined his head to the woman. Some colour had returned to his cheeks, but his large grey eyes still swam with tears for his fallen kin. "We're going to burn this thing away from the town."

She frowned. Dannoch got the feeling that no matter what he'd said she would have pulled the same face. "I don't know..."

"It killed my cousin."

"Aye. And I'm sorry for your loss," she said without meeting his gaze. "But we need to inform the local magistrate. They will decide what's to be done with it."

The giant began to fume. Although they were not inclined to violence, it was a brave or stupid person who riled an Oerni.

"Now you listen..." he began, his knuckles paling on the reins.

"Don't you take that tone with me sir..." The militia woman flushed.

"What tone...?" He loomed over her.

"That tone!" She took a step back. By now, a sizable crowd had gathered ensuring that the militia woman could not back down without losing face.

If Dannoch let this continue it would end badly. "Enough!" He surged to his feet, prayed that the lunnox didn't start and throw him on his arse. "By the power vested in me by Archimandrite Lerriven of the Order of the Redeemers of Ilkand, I say unto you: no unclean beast shall be buried in the ground, or left to foul the air." He drew breath, tried to summon some of the righteous fire that used to burn within him. "The beast must be burned! And woe betide any who stand between wrath and the Righteous. Evil must be purged in fire!" The last he said directly, accusingly, at the militiawoman. She leaned away from the fury of his onslaught, eyes wide lips drawn as thin as a flatworm.

It had been a while since he'd spoken similar words. They sounded hollow now, devoid of the passion he'd once felt, but he must have done a good job because some of the crowd cheered. "Drive on." The Oerni cracked the reins. Dannoch sat down as the wagon lurched forward, leaving the militia woman speechless.

"I knew you were a Templar," the Oerni side-mouthed, his eyes locked on the open road ahead.

"All that I said?" He glanced over his shoulder where the echo of his speech still held the militiawoman in place.

"Aye?"

"Lunnoxshit."

The hunters had gone, leaving nothing save the burned black eye of the pyre inches deep in bone ash that was as grey as the sky. Aerin pulled the wagon over.

"Ash, go gather some kindling, big pieces mind." As with everything, the boy thought about it before climbing off the cart. He wouldn't make a good Templar – they obeyed first and thought after, but Catt and Fisher might well have found a useful apprentice.

The Oerni stepped off the cart. A strong gust of wind whipped through the clearing carrying scents that caused the lunnox to bleat and stamp.

Like the animals, Dannoch suddenly became aware that they were being watched. He jumped from the cart, ruing again his vow never to carry weapons. He scanned the treeline, saw Ash drifting towards them, eyes down scanning the ground. His heart began to run at a pace. "That'll do, boy, bring them over," he called managing to keep apprehension from his voice.

Ash hooked another branch with his foot before sliding around twisting arches of reaper vine. The feeling that they were being watched intensified. Dannoch pretended not to notice as he willed the boy to walk quicker. Blood pounded in his ears, his palms began to sweat. A plume of ravens took to the sky, carved black crescents in the wind. He smelled blood sweet as iron, bound with the smell of fell bane blossom. Something dangerous was close, ready to pounce.

He wanted to scream at the boy to run.

"We have company," said the Oerni. He didn't sound as concerned as he should. Dannoch followed the track of his gaze and saw a group of the townsfolk led by the militia woman marching down the road. Some were carrying jars of oil, others logs. As suddenly as it had arrived, whatever had been lurking was gone. The militiawoman marched over while the others hung back. "We've come to help, Hegumen." Braced for a rebuke, she fixed her gaze on the middle of his chest. There was a time he would have catechised her, but that time had long since passed.

With all the extra hands, the pyre rose quickly. Someone handed Dannoch a torch, and then they all stepped back. He could see that they wanted him to say something meaningful, something profound. Caught up in the moment, he gave it serious thought, but that would be a lie too far. "Thank you all," he said and thrust the torch into the wood. Flames roared, lit borrowed life in the beast's dead eyes.

# SEVEN

WHEN THEY RETURNED from the burning, the crowd drifted away, and the Oerni returned to his camp. Dannoch had intended to go straight to the room and plan a search pattern for the morrow. Suddenly aware of a terrible thirst, he instead found himself forging a path through the crowd to the bar.

"When are we going to look for the thing for the doctors?" the boy asked as though the events of the previous day were no longer of consequence.

"Tomorrow. That is, I'm going. You will wait here."

"Why?"

"I'll cover more ground without you." The boy tilted his head and gave him the side-eye. Dannoch relented. "And there's something else out there."

"Like that thing we burned?"

*Worse.* "Perhaps."

"I thought I was here to learn the ropes."

"You won't learn much by being eviscerated."

The innkeeper saw him shouldering his way through the crowd and waved. "Over here. I saved you a seat." She pointed to the end of the bar where a corner had been closed off by chairs piled on a table. "Yannis!"

The potboy deposited a tray of mugs on the bar before arranging the chairs around the table in the corner. He looked pleased to see Dannoch, which made him uncomfortable. He had grown accustomed to being looked upon with a mix of disgust and pity. He let the boy take the corner seat.

Dannoch leaned on the bar and surveyed the faces in the crowd. He'd hoped to see the axe wielder and perhaps buy her a drink, but she and her comrades were nowhere to be seen. A group of mercenaries just passing through. A group of friends. He missed the camaraderie even though he didn't deserve it.

"A scit for your thoughts." The innkeeper slid a horn mug of wine across the bar. It had a silver rim. She smiled. "On the house, and before you say anything, it's not charity. Someone's paid your bill in advance." She wiped her face with the back of her hand and caught the swag of fell bane blossom hanging over the bar. There was a sudden burst of perfume and a drizzle of pollen and tiny petals.

He raised the mug before tipping it to his lips and forced himself to take a sip. It was good and wasted on him as he had long since ceased to care how wine tasted.

"So, why so glum?" she pressed as she poured a mug of warm ale and served another customer. "You look like you lost a solly and found a scit."

He shrugged, uncomfortable under her scrutiny, suddenly aware that he was filthy. "It's just how my face falls."

She laughed, exchanged the mug for coin, scooped empties from the bar and threw them in a tub before turning her attention back to him. "I don't believe you. I mean, I can't be sure, as I can't see much of it under all that fur."

It suddenly struck him that she might be flirting with him and that he liked it. "I assure you, ma'am, my face is more pleasing with the 'fur' than without it."

"Aye, well that's as may be, although I do like a man with a beard, and call me Sarna..." She held out her hand. The warmth of the wine began to spread from the pit of his stomach. The smell of the fell bane sweetened the air. "You know, this place hasn't seen so much life since the thorn fever swept through. You're good luck…?"

"Bailey." He shook her hand. The contact was almost shocking. It had been such a long time since he'd touched another person a thrill ran through him. Despite the heat of the room, her hand was pleasantly cool. "Thorn fever?"

She looked away, loosed the pain in her gaze at the floor. "Folk say we escaped the Kinslayer, but we didn't, not really. A sickness came at the end of the war. Just a scratch or a graze was all it needed to get in. So many died. That's why the mines closed. And those that recovered were…" She sighed her weary sorrow. "It took a toll."

"I'm sorry." The door swung open and ushered in a cool breeze. He turned, grateful for the distraction.

"Ho, Bailey," Aerin called and hunched apologetically as he made his way to where Dannoch and the boy were ensconced. He looked better than when they had parted after burning the beast. He had changed his robes, and instead of ashes, his shaved head was covered in ochre powder. "I came to say goodbye."

"Tonight?"

The big man raised his hand to try to get the attention of the innkeeper, but she was elbow deep in a barrel of dirty mugs. "Aye, we need to get Marroc back home to Cinquetann."

"Ah, yes, of course."

"We must find a Wayfarer before the fourth night after…" He sighed. "I hear myself speak and still cannot believe what has happened."

"I understand. When someone dies and the world doesn't stop even for a second to acknowledge that fact." He gestured to the bar. "It doesn't seem real."

The Oerni's shoulders sagged. "Aye. That's it. When my grandsire passed, bells rang. We shut stalls for five full days. We wore mourning blue. We prayed. Offerings were made, and the Wayfarers sang. The world took note. Here it's like nothing happened." Incredulous, he shook his head.

*That's because it doesn't matter to anyone except you and your kin.*

"I'm sorry, I've soured your mood," said Aerin.

Dannoch looked up. "What? No, you haven't." The big man winced. "I mean, I feel for your loss, obviously. I'm sorry, I hope your family's pain heals soon." He downed the wine.

"It was good to meet you, Bailey." Aerin smiled. "I hope you don't mind; I settled your account."

"Not at all."

The Oerni placed his dinnerplate hand on Dannoch's shoulder. "You know, I had always been led to believe that the warriors of Temple Ilkand were…"

"Arrogant? Violent? Proud?" Dannoch smiled to show that he was teasing.

The Oerni flushed. "Proud is perhaps the word I was looking for. But you're not like that."

He gestured to himself. "Clearly." They laughed. It seemed a relief to the young merchant to expand those big lungs and give vent, momentarily unimpeded by sorrow. "Would you do me another favour?"

"Of course. What is it?"

"Deliver a message to some… friends in Cinquetann."

"HE SAID *FRIENDS*?" Catt was astounded. "Un-ironically?" He finished grinding the Orris root and poured it over a bag of dried iris petals. They were in the kitchen the curtains drawn against the flaming sunset.

Fisher dropped the ruby monocle into his palm and blinked away the fishbowl vision imparted by the magic of the Bijouterie. "I believe he dissembled for appearance sake."

"Hard to tell unless you look a person in the eye." He made

finger prongs and pointed at himself. "That's where the truth lies. Or most often where the lies lie. And with regards to our hirsute friend, if he is to work for us again, you must insist that he visits a bathhouse and a barber – or perhaps a gardener would be more appropriate."

Fisher grunted. "He's taken a vow. He doesn't bathe because he hasn't taken that damn armour off in ten years."

"What an idiot. Why you give him the time of day is beyond me. He was an arrogant fool when he was at the Temple, and now he's a stinking drunk – literally." He snorted. "So much for us not being a charity."

"I knew his mother," said Fisher quietly.

Catt peered at Fisher who was avoiding his gaze. "Indeed?" He coughed.

Fisher looked up. "Don't look at me like that. It was a long time ago." His gaze was fixed on a place and time far from here and now. "She was a good woman and deserved better than she received."

Catt ached to find out more, but his friend's face darkened, precluding further enquiry. Not for the first time, a gulf opened between them, encapsulated in the pained expression on Fishy's silly, grumpy face. "Oh, enough of this. What was the message he wishes to convey to us?"

"I don't know. He wrote it down."

"How very inconvenient. And surprising. I didn't know he could write."

"We should go to Berrinford, tonight."

"You sound serious..." He peered hard at Fisher. "Oh, my. You are serious. Oh, no, Fishy." He shook his head, paused a moment then shook it again. "No, no, no. It's too late to go galivanting. I've got a pot of hot chocolate on the stove, and I don't think our agent will appreciate our interference. Not when he's doing so well." He tried to sound like he meant it, but the last bit of garnish went a touch too far.

"I don't like it, Catt. There's something bad there. I can smell it."

Catt opened his mouth.

"Don't you dare."

"I was just going to agree with you. Of course there's *something bad* there. There is something bad everywhere, my dear Doctor Fisher. But do any of the miserable, parochial little dramas of Berrinford and its roaming beasties have anything to do with the Unguis of Maug?"

"Yes. I think so."

"Oh." Catt was stumped, which was not a feeling he enjoyed. He pulled the drawstring on the bag of dried flowers and shook it for wont of occupation while he tried to find a way to wheedle out of going. "Well if that's the case then it's been going on for a long time. What say we save the Berrinfordians on the morrow, after a good night's sleep?"

"I was thinking more of saving Dannoch and the child, now."

"Pish. Dannoch killed the monster with naught but a shovel and the boy grew up in the shitheaps of Cinquetann. I'm sure they'll survive a night in a country inn."

Fisher dropped the monocle in his pocket. Contrary to what Catt had expected, he looked relieved as though he had settled some private matter to which Catt wasn't privy. "Very well. Tomorrow it is then."

Ash didn't think much to being an adventurer after spending half the day watching the monster burn and listening to straw-chewing theories as to what it was and where it came from. Bored and cold, he'd watched the crowd drift away, leaving Dannoch the Oerni and the militiawoman to ensure nothing remained of the beast. They had then trudged back to town. His mood had been as glum as the weather until his gaze lit on the inn. The common room was shoulder to shoulder, packed with locals, travellers, some dogs, and at least one pig. The rafters were lost in a blue haze of smoke. It was wonderfully, almost painfully hot, and smelled of beer, smoke, and roasting meat.

Despite telling him they were going to their room as soon as they got back, after saying goodbye to the militia woman and the sad Oerni, Dannoch ploughed a well-worn path to the bar. Ash followed eyes down so he could avoid the milling feet crushing his toes. Probably because he'd slain the beast, the innkeeper smiled when she saw Dannoch and they were shown to a corner near the bar that it seemed she had saved for them.

Ash felt like king of the walk as he slid into the nook and what must have been the best seat in the room, between the bar and the chimney stack. He didn't think anything could be better until the innkeeper who introduced herself to Dannoch as 'Sarna' gave him a slice of pom pie. Pom pie tasted like something from a dream. It was sweet, tangy, and creamy. Ash had smelled it before, had seen it tantalisingly close, but he'd never actually eaten any. He thanked his good luck that for some reason he couldn't fathom, Sarna liked Dannoch.

It wasn't that *he* didn't like his companion, but he did smell, drink too much and when he wasn't shouting, he mumbled and hid his gaze like someone might steal it. Yet, whenever she looked at him, the innkeeper smiled like she knew a secret. It was a puzzle he had no wish to solve, but he was grateful for it because the pie was the best thing he had ever eaten.

When the Oerni came over, Sarna moved away. Ash noticed her jaw tighten as she gave the Oerni the hard edge of her eye. No doubt she was annoyed that he was interrupting her and Dannoch. Ash settled his head on his arms, lulled by the babble of conversation.

"Wake up, boy. Ash wake up." Dannoch was shaking him. "Go to your bed, lad."

Hardly awake, he complied without complaint, leaving the warrior to flirt with the innkeeper.

He hadn't realised he was so tired, but by the time he reached the top of the stairs, he was almost on his hands and knees. The corridor was empty; the door to their room was swinging gently. He pushed it open and staggered to the truckle bed and was asleep before he hit the mattress.

Dreams came quickly, strange, and sad. He dreamed his mother was kneeling beside him. Her hair was hanging loose around her shoulders, and her pale eyes were fever bright. He blinked. It wasn't his mother. "Who are you?" He was too tired to be afraid of the stranger looking down at him and smiling.

"Hush, little rabbit." She stroked his face. Her hands were hot and bloody. Leaf mould and twigs clung to her ragged shift; her bare arms were scarred with a brocade of deep scratches, some were old and silvered, others new and bleeding. "Close your eyes," she said, as she picked him up and held him against her. He could hear her frantic heart, smell loamy soil, and the scent of fell bane. She carried him to the window where a cool breeze caressed his face; kissed him goodnight. He felt like he was falling, like he was drowning in sleep.

# EIGHT

DANNOCH WATCHED THE procession of Oerni wagons until the light of their lanterns was nothing but a glow-worm in the distance. Before going back to the, by now, quiet inn, he paused by the water trough. He wasn't entirely drunk, but now he was in the fresh air, he could feel the numbing effect of the wine that had crept up on him, taking the edge off his senses.

He plunged his head in the water; the cold stung. Thus sharpened, he shook his head, wrung the water from his beard, and tried to run his hands through his hair. For the first time in many years, he lamented the lack of a comb.

It was late, and the bar had closed. The locals had staggered to their homes, and the guests had retired to their rooms. Dogs slept in the hearth, and the dying fire bathed the common room in a soft, honey glow.

"Your friends have gone then?" Sarna was wiping down the bar. She was still wearing her apron, but she'd taken off her bonnet, and her hair hung down her back in a long dark braid. She was not the most beautiful woman he had ever seen, but she was comely. "Why are you smiling?"

"I didn't know that I was."

"That'll be the Arvenni red that I plied you with. Don't look so shocked, as the Oerni was paying I thought I'd treat you."

"That was very generous... of Aerin."

"Ack. I've never met a poor Oerni. Can I get you another? You still have a tab."

He should have said no because he had work to do in the morning, not that Catt and Fisher had paid him to do much work, but he wanted to be back in Cinquetann by nightfall... *And then what*? He was hit by the sudden realisation that there was nothing to go back for. "Aye, why not?"

She wiped her hands on her apron and took the bottle from under the bar. "I was hoping you'd say that. Do you mind if I join you?"

"Not at all."

She poured two mugs and raised a toast. "To a bright future."

He tapped her mug with his and took a polite swig.

"You don't share my optimism?" She took a deep drink.

He tried not to look at her breasts and failed, although he was quietly pleased to discover that he wasn't dead yet. "I have no thoughts on the matter. I wish the world well, hope it heals."

"But you don't feel yourself part of it?"

"This is quite the discussion for—"

"A country inn?" Her brow raised like a knife blade.

"No, I mean, it is unexpected, but no." *Fool.* "I mean, it's late. Forgive me. I've never been much of a conversationalist."

"You spoke most eloquently earlier, Hegumen."

"Any fool can learn a speech, trust me." He drained the mug, put it on the counter and tried to leave before he made an even bigger fool of himself, but she refilled it.

"But not everyone can be kind and brave. The girl with the axe enjoyed the fight, but she didn't give a damn about the Oerni or what happened to the hybrida."

"The what?"

"The animal you killed. They come out of the forest sometimes. We call them hybrida because we don't know what else to call them." She shuddered. "Anyway. You showed kindness and bravery. They're rare qualities not often found together."

All he wanted to say was that she smelled good and that he liked the way her eyes were neither green nor blue. But that was the wine trying to loosen his tongue. "Thank you for the wine, Sarna. And the conversation." He drained the mug and made for the stairs before she could stop him with wine or kind words.

"Goodnight, Hegumen Dannoch." He was many things, a liar amongst them, but tonight it did not sit well with him – much like the wine that was already making his head pound. He climbed the stairs looking forward to a few hours' blessed oblivion. He crept along the corridor as much as a big man in armour can creep and opened the door to the room as quietly as he was able.

The absence of life struck him immediately. In a glance, he took in too many telling signs of mischief. Only the ghost outline of the boy was imprinted on the mattress by the dead fire. The window shutter swung gently, and claw marks scarred the windowsill. That there wasn't any blood or other signs of a struggle was of little comfort. He checked under his bed, found nothing but dust. He went to the window and peered into the night. Panic engulfed him. The boy was gone. The pale scratches on the window ledge taunted him. Not just gone, taken.

He did not leap from the window, because he didn't want to destroy what tracks there might be. He instead snatched the boy's blanket to keep his scent in mind and ran. Sarna was still in the common room and looked up as he bounded down the stairs.

"What is it? What's wrong?" she asked as he made for the door.

"Something's taken the boy." The heart-hammered words almost choked him.

"Are you sure? He might be in the privy…"

He scanned the quaggy ground and tried to unpick the planished tapestry of tracks and sift the scents of all that had passed through. Alas, they all blended into a distempered wash, diluted by the petrichor of rainfall. A deep pair of heel marks stood out from the patination of drunken, dog-danced steps. He followed the tracks, peripherally aware that the watchtower was in darkness and that Sarna was following him. The prints were small, mostly human save for the clawed toenail gouges. They led through the paddock and into the shrouding menace of the trees.

Reaper-vine thorns scratched his armour and fired sparks into the indigo gloom. The footprints ran along the pale rib of an animal trail that was illuminated by a faint scatter of starlight. He quickened his pace, sure he could feel the heat of his quarry clinging to the trees.

"Dannoch wait!" It was Sarna.

"Go back," he shouted. She kept coming, her lantern a bright pendulum in the darkness.

"No, I'll come with you," she called. "This place is dangerous, full of old mine pits, and you don't have a lantern."

"I don't need one." He could see well enough in the dark.

He plunged deeper into the dark heart of the forest. Something growled, low, and rumbling. He pulled up instantly transported to the past, to a time when he had heard, not the roar, but the mere breath of Vermarod the dragon. Then as now the dreadful sound shook the very roots of the earth and promised an end to everything… He shook his head and cursed himself for a fool as it came again, and he heard it more clearly. It wasn't a dragon. It was just cave breath; the low growl of an underground wind breathing into the forest shaped by cave mouth and tunnel. He wiped sweat from his eyes and followed the path. The tracks were indistinct, but the smell of the boy was stronger. He ran on, past the derelict shells of buildings bound in the spiny tendrils of reaper vine and draped in the faint luminescence of fell bane flowers.

FISHER WAS PROWLING. Catt could hear him pointedly wringing accusatory creaks from the floorboards as he paced heavy-footed; back and forth, back and forth across the sitting room floor. And had it not been directly beneath his bedchamber he wouldn't have minded. But as the old frame house was but a box of joist and timber, the walls flexed, and the rafters sang like old violins beneath Fishy's discontented stride.

"Bloody, bleeding heavens!" He tore off his eye mask and threw back the quilt. He didn't bother fumbling with the candle, but found his slippers by feel and plodded downstairs to find Fisher standing by the window, his hands knotted behind his back, long fingers pale as bone in the darkness. "Why don't you have another look, just to put your mind at ease?"

"I don't know what you mean. My mind is perfectly at ease." He unlaced his fingers and his right hand drifted to a pocket in which Catt guessed his partner had dropped the Bijouterie.

His pride was as ridiculous as it was endearing. "Indulge me, then would you and have a peep. I can't sleep for worrying." *That you'll wear a hole in the carpet.* He sat down.

Without further prompting, Fisher slipped the monocle from his pocket and pressed the ruby into the glass before throwing himself into the armchair and setting the monocle against his eye. He tensed. Catty wasn't worried… to begin with, but then Fisher began to breathe heavily, like he was running for his life. Catt snatched the monocle away by its silver chain and was forced to take a step back as Fisher surged to his feet, his gaze still locked on whatever the boy was seeing.

"Fishy?" Catt inquired, suddenly fearful. With his back to the window, the heavy brushstrokes of shadow made Fisher look almost feral. "Fishy? Are you all right?"

He blinked and dragged his gaze to the present, away from whatever dark vision had seized him. "Yes, but our agents are not. We need to go. *Now.*"

Catt desperately wanted to argue that they didn't, because all he wanted to do was go back to bed, but in this, he trusted Fisher. "Give me a minute to throw some clothes on."

\*   \*   \*

STRIPPED OF CLOUD, the moon and stars contrived to throw a silver light over the clearing, casting every rock and stone in shades of pewter and old bone. The footprints led to the far side of the clearing where shadows pooled in the rock rimmed eye of a sinkhole. A sound like a beast growling bored through the substance of the ground, shivering the trees and an underground wind roared from the hole carrying the stench of deep places, death, and foul magic. Dannoch's hackles rose, sweat ran cold down his back. Dark forms detached themselves from the shadows, yellow eyes shone.

He could see seven pairs of shining eyes, and from the way they were moving – creeping slowly through the arching boughs of reaper vine – he could see that whatever they were, they were trying to surround him, leaving him nowhere to go but the clearing. He didn't know what they were, but he was confident he could make a run for it and break through before they closed in. "Stay close," he whispered over his shoulder. "And be ready to run."

"I'm not going anywhere, Hegumen…" The guttural tone of her voice chilled the blood in his veins.

He smiled at his stupidity. "You called me Dannoch. How did you know my name?"

"I know lots of things." She smiled.

He walked into the starlit eye of the clearing. The wind sighed from the hole gathered in the darkness. He turned and wasn't surprised to see the innkeeper's eyes shining with the same unnatural light as the rest of the pack slinking around the clearing. He heard groans turn to growls as bones snapped, tortured flesh split, and bodies changed.

Sarna kicked off her shoes.

"Do you like the shoes? They're new." A woman emerged from the night-cast glamour behind Sarna. He knew her. She was one of the scavengers. "You've not been formally introduced. This is my sister, Urnna. Urnna, this is Bailey." The woman snarled and bared jagged, blackened fangs. "Urnna got the thorn fever, but she was one of the blessed."

"Where's Ash?"

Sarna put her arms around her sister's shoulder. "All in good time."

"This is the best time there's going to be, trust me. Where is the boy?"

She shook her head. "Don't be like that."

"Where's Ash?" he asked, the words cold, hard lumps in his mouth.

Sarna smiled and unlaced her bodice. "It was you I wanted. Maug spoke to me in a dream and said you would come and run with us." She smiled. "The moment I laid eyes on you, I knew who you were, and that you were the one."

"I won't ask again, Sarna. Where is the boy?"

"Your armour is your fortress, isn't it, Hegumen?" She let her gown slip from her shoulders. Her sister gave a low, rumbling growl and collapsed, bones popping and snapping, skin flowing like wax over distended limbs.

"Dear gods." The curse came unbidden.

Sarna smiled with a mouth that was too wide for her face and gazed upon him with animal eyes. "Ah, yes. Gods. About those. Care to test your faith? Or will you just surrender willingly to Maug?"

"I swear if you've hurt him..." The numbness that had cloaked his heart like ice began to calve as anger woke within him.

She laughed hard and sharp on the cusp of a snarl. "Hurt? He is an honoured sacrifice. The little whelp will achieve more by his death than anything he could have done in life. Don't worry, I drugged his pie. He won't feel a thing when Maug takes him."

Dragged from the subterranean depths, the wind roared from the cave. "*Мauuuuug*," it seemed to say. The beasts howled and a shudder ran down his spine. The howls recalled to him a time when he had stood against unknown evils with his brothers and sisters; righteousness their weapon, unquestioning faith their shield. Now they were all dead, and the gods were gone, and he was alone.

"Join us, Dannoch. Join our family."

He drew a shuddering breath, fought through the painful recollection of his comrades' faces. "I had a family…"

"Had. And now you have nothing. You are alone, without a pack, in a world that doesn't want you. You are yesterday's hero." Agitated, she cast aside the thorn and paced just beyond the bright arc of the clearing. Dark blood dripped from her claws.

"Aye, true. The world has turned, the sun is shining on another dog's arse. What's your point?"

Her luminous eyes seemed larger. "You can't hide what you are from me. I see you. I see what you are trying to imprison in a suit of steel."

"They say a little knowledge is a dangerous thing." It was a concession. The beast in her sensed the beast in him, but there was more to it than that. So much more.

"I see the wildness. I see your guilt, your pain."

She was good, but for the most part guessing. "I refer you to my previous comment." They shared a moment of accord, both smiled too wide.

"You don't have to be alone any more. You don't have to hide what you are. We can be your family, your pack. We live to run, to hunt, and with your help, we will make the world a better place; fit for the strong, safe for the weak."

He shook his head. "You spoiled it right at the end." They always did. No matter if they were prowling in a forest, or preaching from a pulpit, there was always someone who wanted to remake the world in their image, according to their values, their way of thinking. Why couldn't they just let people be? And by people, he meant him.

She spread her arms. "Be Maug's warrior. Join us. With or without you, our pack will flourish and grow." The hulking shapes drew closer, growling and snapping.

"At least you didn't say, 'join us or die'."

"I was saving it. Now take off your armour, Hegumen. Show me what you're made of."

"You don't know what you're asking for."

"I'm asking you to join us. I sense your potential. Grasp the vine, let Maug unleash that which lies within." Her words were distorted by the pale fangs that were pushing through her bleeding gums.

"I don't need Maug, whatever the fuck that is." He could run, might even escape but the boy would die, and these... whatever they were, would infect more with their madness. It wasn't his business, but the boy was.

He fumbled with the buckles of his armour. After ten years, they were stiff. He gave them a hard tug and the breastplate crashed to the ground. The backplate had moulded itself to him over the years and he had to drag it from his back. The warding spell worked into the steel faded. The beast that had slumbered within woke. Sweat beaded his brow. He felt sick. "I can't believe you chose this."

"I didn't, not at first. All I wanted was my sister back. This" – she gestured to herself, to the hulking watchers pinning him with their predator stares – "was an unexpected benefit of finding the source of the thorn fever. I say fever. It was a test. And I passed." She dropped to all fours.

Dannoch ripped the buckle from his pauldrons. His blood began to burn, his limbs ached. He had forgotten what it felt like, how much it hurt and how much he liked it. "You shouldn't have taken the boy. All I wanted was the boy." *Hope. All I wanted was hope.*

"Yes!" Sarna's sister exclaimed. "Join us, Hero of Kyne's Bridge. Curse the Ilkand Temple, and join the Children of Maug."

"'Children of Maug'? Fuck. Couldn't you come up with something better than that?" His teeth were too long. He bit his lip, tasted sweet iron. It tasted good. "No matter. I'm done with cults whatever they're called."

Sarna growled deep in her throat. "Are… you… sure?"

"Quite sure." He spat blood.

"At least you're honest. Stupid, but honest. You… you could have lied… tried to. Oh. Here we go…" All the while she'd been speaking she'd been fighting to slow the change but he knew from his own experience that you could only hold it for so long. Her birthing scream turned to a howl of triumph as her skin split and sloughed to reveal a dark, scaled body. She was not a vilewolf, but most certainly some kind of benighted kin.

The beast she had become regarded him with storm-lit eyes.

Dannoch slashed at the straps of his leg harness. The buckles were rusted and no match for his claws. "When I was a child, my mother told me that the gods had favoured me. I believed her. I thought I was invincible." He tore at the prisoning armour, eager to be free now that he had accepted his fate. "I was a champion of Temple Ilkand. Strong, arrogant, powerful." The monsters closed in. "My brothers and sisters followed me, and I led them to their deaths. Me, the hero of Kyne's Bridge. Sole survivor! I survived the ambush because I killed everyone, friend and foe alike. I fought for my survival, like an animal. That day I realised I wasn't favoured." He saw them all again, torn apart; dead by his hand. "Do you think I would turn my back on fucking gods that cursed me so that I could bend the knee to yours?"

He fell to his knees as the agonizing spasms of the change stole his breath. The man he was dissolved in the fury of the transformation. He was erased and remade. Perceptions shifted, senses that had slept roared to painful life. The world became sharper, brighter, louder. It was annihilation; death and rebirth in a breath. The scaled thing howled, and bounded towards him. The beast he had become answered in kind and rose to meet it.

# NINE

THERE COMES A time in every parent's life where they must look upon their child as an adult; a creature acting under its own volition. They must trust them and respect them or else the relationship will be flawed. So it was that Doctor Fisher, the Guardian Fury, ex-messenger of the gods, had made a vow as constricting in its way as Dannoch's prison of armour. He would not only trust his friend Doctor Catt, he would respect him as an equal. He wasn't entirely in agreement with himself on the matter and had therefore nudged Catt into an agreement with regards to Dannoch, but that part of him that wished to better understand the mortal condition felt that progress had been made.

Catt and Fisher appeared outside of an inn. Fisher brandished the Staff of Ways. Catt leaned upon the Staff of Faultless Striding which had brought them here. They'd expected trouble and found... a quiet, deserted street. Their magical arrival marked by none.

"Where are they?" Catt demanded.

"No idea. What did you focus on?"

"The Bijouterie of course. I don't understand." Catt picked up his robe. "Urgh, I'm wearing the wrong footwear for mud."

Fisher plucked the monocle from his pocket, put it to his eye, and scanned the darkness. A faint glow emanated from the water trough. He strode over and plucked the locket and its broken chain from the bottom of the trough.

"Do you think he dropped it?" Catt asked.

Fisher shook his head. "The hasp has been snapped."

"I'll set up a seeker spell. Now, let me see what I've brought with me." Catt unslung his pack. "Aha! I have the Alembic of Trantos. Give me a moment." He drew the elaborate brass stand from the Endless Satchel. Fisher saw a flash of movement out of the corner of his eye. Quicker than one might expect an old man to move, he crossed the ground between the water trough and the inn door. He kicked it open and grabbed the spy by the scruff of the neck.

The boy squirmed in his grip. "Please, sir, I haven't done anything. It wasn't me."

Fisher spun him to face them. "What haven't you done, boy?" Even in the darkness, he could see the colour drain from the boy's face. Fisher shook him just enough to show him that trying to break free was a bad idea. "Speak, boy."

"I can't. Sarna will kill me. Please, let me go. I didn't do anything." He looked, sounded, and smelled genuinely terrified. *Good*.

"There's a man and a boy staying here. The man is particularly grubby, wears old armour, has a lot of hair. The boy is quite small for his age."

"I didn't do it. I swear. It's Sarna."

"What is?" This did not bode well.

"She'll kill me."

"Slap him around a bit, Doctor Fisher," Catt called over his shoulder as he put the finishing touches to the Alembic. "Rough him up until he spills, as they say in the vernacular."

"Please don't rough me up, sir." The youth didn't know Catt was bluffing and shielded his head.

"I'm not a sir, I'm a doctor."

"Please don't rough me up, Doctor. It's Sarna. She ain't right."

"Go on, slap him." Catt encouraged. "Matches, matches. I know I put some in here."

Fisher raised his hand. The boy cowered. "All right. She's done for travellers. Her and them scavs. They used to just drug folk and rob them but then... after the fever. They changed."

"What do you mean?" Fisher shook him.

"They got meaner and they... they go into the forest and..." He almost choked on a sob. "They really *change*."

A ragged chorus of howls shredded the comfortable familiarity of night noise. "Stay here." Fisher released the youth and bounded past Catt. There was blood in their call. The song of a pack closing for the kill.

"But:... what about the Alembic?" Catt wailed. Fisher ran across a muddy, blood-scented paddock and through the neglected edgeland of the town; the firebreak between wild and civilised. He ran towards the fight, towards the inevitable. '*This will not end well,*' she'd said.

'*It never does,*' he'd answered. And then, for a brief moment in time, they had forgotten who they were.

"Fishy?" Catt cried breathlessly. "Don't worry, I'm coming... Where are you?"

IT WAS DARK, and Ash was in his ma's arms. She was singing a nonsense lullaby, her breathing was laboured, her arms cold like the night she'd died. He realised then that it wasn't his ma singing, it was the wind whistling through a cave. He wasn't wrapped in her arms, he was lying on a floor and it was wet and hard.

He dragged his eyes open. He lay in a pool of silver-grey moonlight. He tried to move, but he was so tired, his limbs were leaden. His heavy eyelids closed, and he felt himself slipping back into the delicious oblivion of sleep.

Something stung his ankle. He twitched, kicked out, and

opened his eyes. A pale centipede was squirming near his foot. No, it wasn't a centipede. Was it a snake? No, snakes didn't move like that. And then he saw it for what it was. It was a tendril of reaper vine, but it was deathly pale, like something that had never seen the light, and it was twitching blindly towards him. He groped around, his hand closed on a rock that was colder than death.

Ash brought it down on the vine, smashed it into the gravelled floor, ground it to a sickly smudge. The wind growled; something above howled. He withdrew from the light, as far into the darkness as he dared. After a few minutes of listening to his breathing and blinking away the terrifying mirages conjured by shadows, his eyesight adjusted. But what he saw was no less monstrous. He was in a tunnel, not much different to the sewers and cellars he'd scavenged and slept in back in Cinquetann. The wind whistled through fractured gaps in the rubble that choked the tunnel like a frozen waterfall of pale stone. At the far end, a rough-hewn column of stone supported the roof.

It was what lay slumped against the stone that froze his heart. Bigger than a Yorughan, its elongated, armoured head had fallen forward into its chest. Shreds of fur clung to its long muzzle. Its skin had shrivelled, accentuating the snarl that had accompanied its death and revealing fangs that were longer than his fingers. Its body resembled that of a human, albeit a giant one covered in fur. It was garbed in rusted armour, which was as fantastical as it was vicious, adorned as it was with cruel, iron barbs that looked like thorns. Swirling patterns were etched into the metal and inlaid with black enamel. Most striking and horribly reassuring, the slender shaft of what looked like a glass spear was sticking out of its chest. Entwined with the creature's body, poking through bones, and twisting around armour were the pale, fleshy stems of reaper vines.

He traced the path of the offshoots that spidered across the ground. They were wrapped around desiccated corpses, the thorns buried in their ravaged flesh. He'd seen, and even robbed unfortunates who had died in the alleyways of Cinquetann, but he had never seen any like this. There were dozens, a couple of Oerni, something he didn't recognise, men women, children like him. The mother vine had burrowed through the giant wolf-headed beast before punching through the roof of the cave. He scanned the floor, alert for any more tendrils that might be questing for his blood.

Someone crashed through the undergrowth. He opened his mouth to shout for help when whatever it was snarled.

"Where's Ash?" Dannoch's voice rang clear and loud.

"All in good time." It sounded like the innkeeper. He didn't understand. She'd been so kind, she'd given him the lovely pom pie. He suddenly felt very cold but also very calm, much like the time he'd got stuck in a chimney when the Double Pockets had been on the rob. He'd got stuck in a bend, eye to eye with a dead rat that had been smoked to death. He couldn't move, couldn't go up or down. If he called for help, the householder might dig him out, or they might do what they'd done to the rat. Either way, he would be in for a roasting. So instead of panicking and shouting, he'd controlled his breathing and eventually, calmly, he'd managed to wriggle his way out of the damned chimney.

He would have to do the same thing now or face a worse fate than being thrown in the town gaol. He slowed his breathing. The sound of metal hitting the ground echoed in the hole. Shadows cut across the starlight window, and rivulets of dirt poured down. A chorus of howls shook the trees, and savage things snapped and snarled no further than twenty feet above him. Where the hell was Dannoch? *Stay calm*. He was a steady hand, not given to weeping and wailing, but even he trembled when the eye of light darkened. A massive, shaggy beast with the head of a wolf backed towards the hole, its fur shining silver in the starlight.

Ash backed towards the wall, tried to keep his distance from the nearest bodies and any vines. Something yelped above him. The sound died suddenly. A thing of scales and claws that gleamed like thorns, leapt on the beast with the wolf's head. It wrapped its bone-barbed arms and legs around the wolfish thing and tried to bite its neck through its thick mane of fur. The wolf beast howled, and grabbed its attacker monster by the throat. Ash stumbled on some rubble, the beast's head snapped round, and its fierce green gaze fell upon him and although nothing of the human was obviously recognisable, something in the fire of its eyes told him it was Dannoch. Ash shrank back and pressed himself against the wall. He was steady when the gang went on the rob, and had survived plenty of scrapes without blubbering or pissing his pants, but the sight of the monsters was a sore test of his mettle.

The wolf creature, *Dannoch*, tore the thing off his neck. Blood darkened his fur. He shook it vigorously from side to side. There was a loud, crunching sound. It went limp, and he hurled it away from him. Another dark shape moving too fast for Ash to see clearly rushed him from the side. His claws flashed. There was a horrible wet, tearing sound and the hot stink of the slaughterhouse thickened the air. It fell, and as far as he knew, it did not rise. Another of the long-limbed, black-furred beasts pounced on him. He caught it in his huge, shaggy paws but the creature's weight and speed drove him back. Ash watched in horror as he overbalanced and fell, dragging his attacker into the pit with him.

They fought as they fell and landed hard. Bones broke, blood sprayed the walls. Their howls were deafening and almost drowned out the wind that was howling through the cave. Ash pressed his hands to his ears and, rather than be crushed by them as they tried to tear each other apart, he ran toward the skeleton, which at this beggar's banquet seemed to be the safest place. The creature attacking Dannoch was smaller, but it was ferocious. It fastened its fangs on his shoulder, and blood flowed. Howling, he wrenched it off him and hurled it against the wall. Rocks tumbled, dirt cascaded from the roof. Dannoch was bleeding profusely.

Without the slightest rumble of warning thunder, a jagged bolt of lightning split the sky. Ash stumbled and tripped over an armoured, skeletal foot. When he managed to blink the flash away, he saw the thick mother root of the reaper vine. It had grown where the blood of the beast had stained the ground, and it was pulsing like the blood running through his veins, as were the dozens of tendrils that had spread across the cave in a living web. Horrified, he quickly scrambled to his feet, mindful to avoid the hooked thorns.

The smaller beast recovered quickly, crouched, and pounced on Dannoch. He stumbled as it scored deep wounds that stained his fur. He was weakening. Ash didn't want to watch him die, but neither could he tear his gaze away from the dreadful battle. Another flash turned the night to day. Something yowled. The choking smell of burning fur filled the air. Unable to see anything but stars, Ash put out his hand and found the cool, glass shaft of the spear.

# TEN

POWERFUL AND SINUOUS, he could feel the drumbeat of its footsteps through the ground before it leapt. Claws flashed. Fisher aimed, and the Staff of Ways spoke. Eldritch briars of thorned white fire ensnared the beast and hurled it into a tree. Bones broke. It howled and tried to bite the flames that had taken root in its fur.

Fisher aimed again and put it out of his misery as he continued to run towards the sound of fighting. Catt was some way behind, cursing as he battled through the undergrowth in entirely the wrong outfit for running through thickets of thorns.

"Watch your step, Catty," he called over his shoulder.

"You make it sound like a threat," he replied, his pale face bobbing through the trees like a little moon. "And don't worry, I am watching my step."

A mangled corpse lay on the ground in a clearing. Beside it was a pile of rusted armour and shredded clothes. *Finally.* The sounds of a savage fight resounded from a sinkhole, the howls bound in a swift wind that carried the stench of blood and death and dark magic. Fisher prodded the body with his staff. Like the one he had dealt with, it seemed to be something between human, dog, and wolf; it also smelled like it had been dead for a month. He peered into the pit, saw Dannoch locked in furious combat with one of the beasts. They were not vilewolves, but they were uncomfortably close.

Fisher raised the staff, ready to finish the fight below when an explosion in the forest rocked him on his heels and lit the clearing. He turned to see a ball of fire roll through the canopy. Something wreathed in flames ran into the darkness.

"Catt!" he yelled.

"I'm fine, thank you, Fishy."

Fisher turned back to the hole where the two beasts were too closely entwined to put a blade between them. "Damn it. Get out of the way, Bailey!"

The shout momentarily distracted Dannoch. The vile beast latched on to his throat. If Fisher used the staff, he would undoubtedly slay the beast. But it wasn't a subtle weapon and would most likely kill Dannoch as well as his attacker. In the time it took him to consider his actions, the matter was taken from his hands. Something small and pale rushed from the shadows of the cave and speared Dannoch's attacker in his back. The beast howled and tried to turn, to rip the gleaming spear from its body. It was Ash. With everything that was going on, he'd quite forgotten about the boy. He watched as, with uncommon bravery, the boy drove the spear deeper.

The beast arched, clawed at its back.

"That was a damn good thrust for such a scrap of a thing," said Catt.

Fisher had been so intent on what was happening that he hadn't noticed his partner approach. Catt was singed, smelled of sulphur, and his robe was smoking like a recently snuffed candlewick. Back in the hole, Dannoch fixed his feral gaze on the boy and snarled.

"Bailey!" Fisher shouted in a tone of voice that few mortals could ignore.

The man in the beast heard him. He staggered to his feet and grabbed the spear shaft with both hands and hoisted the beast above him. Its ribs shattered as the spear tip burst from its chest. Dannoch fell back with the dead creature on top of him. Catt almost fell into the cave as he leaned over to get a better look, but Fisher pulled him back. "What the hell happened to you?" he asked.

"Something that looked like a dog wearing a cat mistook me for its dinner. I had to improvise." He grinned as he patted at his smouldering sleeve. "I see Dannoch has forsworn his vow not to change into the beast. I'm sure people only make them so they can break them. Perverse, if you ask me."

"I'm sure the next time the Ilkand Temple synod is in session you will be the first learned theologian they call upon for advice."

"I could at least present legal precedents."

"Could you present me with a ladder?"

"I'll have a look in the satchel... which I dropped somewhere over there." He peered into the burning trees. "Oh dear."

As THOUGH OUTSIDE of itself, beyond pain and emotion, the beast that had been Dannoch watched as Sarna clamped her jaw around his neck. He had always known it would end like this, and the part of him that was still Bailey was reconciled to that. Until he saw the boy. His mouth was moving, he was shouting something...

Then there was a moment of silence. The world began to dim and then silver fire blazed.

He was sure he heard his name. Noise rushed in; howls, screams, growling wind rushing through the cave. He opened his eyes, saw Sarna with a shining splinter of light spearing from her back so bright that it hurt his eyes. He gathered what strength he had and lunged for the blade of light.

It burned his hands. Before his inhuman strength failed him, he hoisted the monster into the air. Blood gushed down his arms as he fell back under the dead weight.

Dissolution. Dragged beneath the wave of change, for a time he was neither one thing nor the other. A spark of consciousness floated somewhere on the edge of self-awareness as the beast was broken and washed away. Dannoch returned to himself and a world that was less bright in every way. His limbs were leaden, his sense blunt, and his arse was wet because he was lying in a puddle. To add to his discomfort, Doctor Catt was standing over him, looking at him like he was something he might put in a pickling jar.

"Ah. You're back with us. Do put this on, there's a good chap." Catt thrust a rough homespun robe towards him. He took it, not least because this was the first time in years he had been naked, and there was a bitter wind blowing through the cave. He looked around, saw a ladder stood at the far end of what looked like a collapsed tunnel cut into pale stone. Doctor Fisher was finishing applying a poultice to the boy's ankle. A collection of lanterns had been arrayed around the huge, armoured skeleton of a vilewolf that was overgrown with recently burned reaper vines.

The heat of battle had fled, leaving him drained and stiff and ashamed that when he had been tested, he had failed. Misery engulfed him.

Catt narrowed his eyes. "Cheer up, Hegumen. You did it. You smote great evil and found the Unguis with hardly a scratch upon you. I might have done things slightly less... violently, but a win is a win. What's the matter? You look like you lost a solly and found a scit."

"Someone else said that to me recently." He looked to where Sarna's body had been dragged, at the gaping hole in her human chest, and her lightless eyes staring into eternity. He struggled into the robe, his skin was burning like he'd been flayed. In a week, the thick, pink scars would be little more than traces of faint silver, but right now they hurt like hell. "What's he doing?" He chinned towards Fisher.

"He's examining the vilewolf that met its demise in this cave and from what a cursory examination suggests, seeded doom in Berrinford and its environs."

"I don't understand." Not only that, he also didn't care. He'd seen more than enough of the monsters during the war. He wasn't awed by the sight of a few old bones. It was his own sins that troubled him. "Who did I kill?"

"My, but aren't you jolly." Catt gave a weary sigh. "As far as I can tell you did for two of the beasties." His gaze flicked to Sarna. "Although I think you have to share that one with my apprentice." He beamed like a proud grandfather. "Fisher and I dealt with the rest. No need to thank us."

"I just want to know if I hurt anyone who didn't deserve it."

"Hard to say, isn't it? Who is the arbiter of such things? Ah. That isn't what you meant, is it?"

"Not, really, no." He put his head in his hands.

"Don't worry, Templar, I think your conscience is clear, *on this one*."

"Were there...? Didn't I see other bodies down here?"

"You did, but they weren't yours, so to speak. We've taken them up. We'll let the locals know when we're done."

"Catty, come here," Fisher called over his shoulder as he poked at the corpse with a silver stylus. "You have to see this. Ash, hold the lantern steady."

The boy yawned, his arm sagged, and the lantern swung. "I'm really tired."

"We all are. But we have to work quickly before the local 'authorities' get wind of what's going on and come riding in to save the day *and* steal the spoils of our labour." He raised an eyebrow and fixed the boy with his best sincerely insincere stare. "We don't want that, now do we?" The boy shook his head and raised the lantern.

Even though he felt as weak as water, Dannoch had to smile. There was something reassuring about the doctors' cold-blooded avarice. It was an anchor to the mundane and allowed him to ignore the beast that prowled restlessly in the depth of his being, just waiting for the chance to be free again. He watched Catt tiptoe across the bloody floor, holding his thorn-snagged and singed robe out of the filth like he was about to dance a minuet. All Dannoch wanted to do was sleep for a year, and could have quite happily curled up on the rubble.

"You too, Bailey. Come and look at this," said Fisher in a tone of voice that was more telling than asking. Tempting though it was to tell him to go fuck himself, Dannoch climbed to his feet. Everything had seized up, and his knee creaked like a rusty hinge. He buttoned the robe which came to his knees and hobbled over.

"Now, you will note that even though the armour was girded with some very impressive warding spells," – Fisher pointed to the flowing script etched into the skeleton's armour – "the spear went through it like the proverbial knife through butter."

Dannoch's gaze tracked to Sarna. "How did the vine cause her to change?"

"What? No idea." Fisher grunted dismissively and continued to probe the hole in the breastplate. "It is unbelievably clean, it really is."

Catt cleared his throat. "As it happens, I have a theory. Based on my extensive arcane knowledge." He beamed. "And, I must say, peerless powers of observation."

Dannoch folded his arms as much to stop his teeth from chattering as to show his impatience. The wind blowing through the cave was bitter and he was freezing. "Care to explain, Doctor?"

"I shall indeed elucidate!" He flourished a rigidly pointed finger like a wand. "I believe that, mortally wounded, the beast staggered into what was a tunnel. Probably from that direction given the angle of descent." He pointed to the uphill end of the tunnel. "It bled out and died where we see it now; an unknown victory for the forces of good in the war of the Kinslayer." He smiled at the boy. "A few years before you were born, I should think. Fancy that, eh?"

Dannoch cleared his throat.

"Ah yes, where was I? Over time, the tunnel collapsed at both ends, and that should have been an end to it. Alas, some things don't want to stay buried." Fisher grunted at that and wandered around the back of the column where he began to rummage through Catt's slightly singed satchel.

Catt continued. "The reaper vine like many of the genus *Rubus vulpes* thrives on a drop of claret. Alas, this blood was laced with dark magic. Anything scratched by the thorns of this particular plant either sickened and died or became what we had the misfortune to encounter."

"So, this is Maug?" Dannoch gestured to the skeleton.

Fisher returned carrying a long, leather-bound case. "No. Of course not." Frowning at Dannoch like he'd just said something particularly stupid, he put the case on the ground, opened it, and retrieved the spear from its bed of padded velvet. "If you look closely you can see the Argathian script." He pointed to fine symbols etched onto the glass blade.

Dannoch had exceptional eyesight, but he struggled to make out the fine marks that seemed to have been drawn in light. "What does it say?"

Fisher sighed again, wearily disappointed. "It says it is the Unguis. I therefore find it unlikely that the vilewolf is Maug. The Kinslayer's vilewolves – created to mock the Guardian Fury, his most ardent foe – did not kill themselves, unless expressly commanded by their master." He turned the spear in the light of the lantern and threw rainbows across the wall. Like glacial ice, it was a thing of dreadful beauty. "And as we all know that prick didn't come to Berrinford."

"But I heard it," said Ash. "I heard the wind say 'Maug'." The boy's gaze turned to the rubble, and to the fractured voids through which the cave wind breathed.

Catt and Fisher shared a calculating look. Fisher looked at the boy, raised an eyebrow. Catt squared his hands and sized up one of the gaps in the rubble before nodding conspiratorially.

"Now wait a minute," said Dannoch guessing what they were thinking and wanting none of it. "We have to report this to the authorities. Sarna's—"

"Not going anywhere. And don't fret. Everyone who needs notifying will be notified. We are lawyers, you know." Fisher's intense gaze fell on the boy. "Ash has proved himself to be a most capable agent."

"And he is quite small for his age." Catt closed one eye, spread his hands, and estimated the size of one of the bigger holes in the rubble and then compared it to the boy. "Ash, how would you like to earn a nice, shiny solly?"

He eyed-up the hole then smiled at Catt. "Make it two."

Fisher grinned wolfishly. "That's my boy."

# ACKNOWLEDGEMENTS

THE EDITOR WOULD like to thank the following people for their invaluable contributions to the existence of this book.

First of all the writers, for their hard work in creating great stories, mostly in a world not of their own making: Adrian, Freda, Juliet and KT, you all did a wonderful job.

Michael Rowley did the 'having an idea to make this book' and 'getting this project together in the first place' work and the overseeing of the whole scheme from Rebellion's end – so major thanks to him and those other powers at Rebellion who agreed, because without that this book wouldn't even be here. He also took a punt on hiring me as an editor, which wasn't an inconsiderable risk given I've previously only shown up as a writer. A big personal thank you from me for the opportunity.

In the day-to-day work he was aided and abetted by Kate Coe, co-ordinating the workers, organizing the money, sourcing the contracts and scheduling all the many business-end things that must be done in order to publish a book.

Sam Gretton designed and typeset the interior and cover. Thanks to him it looks appealing to read and smartly turned out.

Tomasz Jedruszek made the dashing cover painting, according to some very vague notes about adventure and tomb-raidering type activities, issued before even word one was written

– I love that it reminds me of the adventure books of my youth!

Paul Simpson did the copy editing and highlighted all the mistakes, possible conflicts and gaffes that we'd made during our journey with the Doctors.

After we fixed them Donna Scott did the final proofreading for the last errors. Any mistakes remaining are down to me, therefore, as everyone else has done their best.

# ABOUT THE AUTHORS

ADRIAN TCHAIKOVSKY IS the author of the acclaimed ten-book Shadows of the Apt series, the Echoes of the Fall series, and other novels, novellas and short stories including *Children of Time* (which won the Arthur C. Clarke award in 2016), and its sequel, *Children of Ruin* (which won the British Science Fiction Award in 2020). He lives in Leeds in the UK and his hobbies include entomology, and board and role-playing games.

FREDA WARRINGTON LOVES rural Leicestershire, where she lives and makes things up. Throughout school, art college and a career in graphic design, writing was a constant. Her first novel, *A Blackbird in Silver,* was published in 1986. Twenty-two more books followed, ranging from epic quests to contemporary/supernatural fantasy. Her novels include *Dracula the Undead* and *Elfland*, both of which won Best Novel Awards. Most recent is *Nights of Blood Wine* (Telos), a collection of dark short stories.

Freda continues creating new magical worlds, in between mentoring/editing assignments. For full info, visit her author website FredaWarrington.com, Facebook, or Twitter @FredaWarrington.

JULIET E MCKENNA is a British fantasy author living in the Cotswolds, UK. Loving history, myth and other worlds since she first learned to read, she has written fifteen epic fantasy novels so far. Her debut, *The Thief's Gamble*, began The Tales of Einarinn in 1999, followed by The Aldabreshin Compass sequence, The Chronicles of the Lescari Revolution, and The Hadrumal Crisis trilogy. In association with Wizard's Tower Press, she's re-issued her early backlist as well as publishing original short story collections and contemporary fantasy novels rooted in British folklore. The series so far is *The Green Man's Heir*, *The Green Man's Foe* and *The Green Man's Silence*. She writes diverse shorter fiction, enjoying forays into dark fantasy, steampunk and SF. Recent short stories include contributions to the anthologies *Alternate Peace*, *Soot and Steel*, and *The Scent of Tears* (Tales of the Apt). Visit julietemckenna.com or follow @JulietEMcKenna on Twitter.

KT DAVIES WAS born and raised in Yorkshire, and has a degree in literature. A nerdy gamer, KT also plays with swords, sometimes on horseback. Author of the bestselling fantasy series The Chronicles of Breed, you can find KT on Facebook @KTScribbles.

JUSTINA ROBSON IS the UK author of thirteen science fiction and fantasy novels and many short stories. In addition to her original works, including a novel set in the Catt and Fisher universe – *Salvation's Fire* – she has also written The Covenant of Primus, the 'bible' of *The Transformers*. She has tutored for the Arvon Foundation and been an awards judge for the Arthur C Clarke Award. She sometimes works as a freelance developmental editor. Visit www.justinarobson.co.uk or follow @JustinaRobson on Twitter.

# AFTER THE WAR

A DECADE AGO THE TERRIBLE DEMIGOD, THE KINSLAYER, RETURNED FROM HIS LONG EXILE IN DARKNESS, LEADING AN ARMY OF MONSTERS AND LAYING WASTE EVERYTHING IN HIS PATH.

BUT WHAT HAPPENS WHEN THE FIGHTING'S DONE?

*AFTER THE WAR* IS A STORY OF CONSEQUENCES.

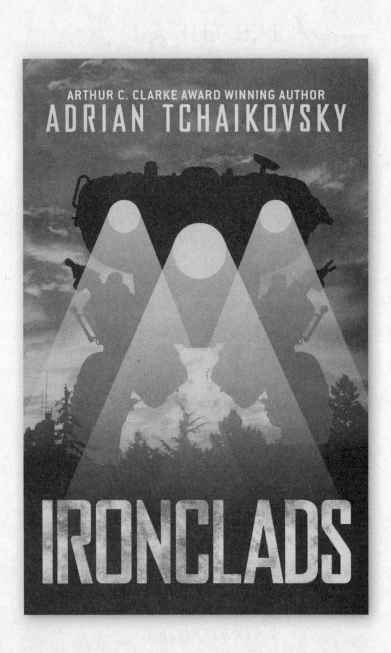

ARTHUR C. CLARKE AWARD WINNING AUTHOR
# ADRIAN TCHAIKOVSKY

# WALKING TO ALDEBARAN

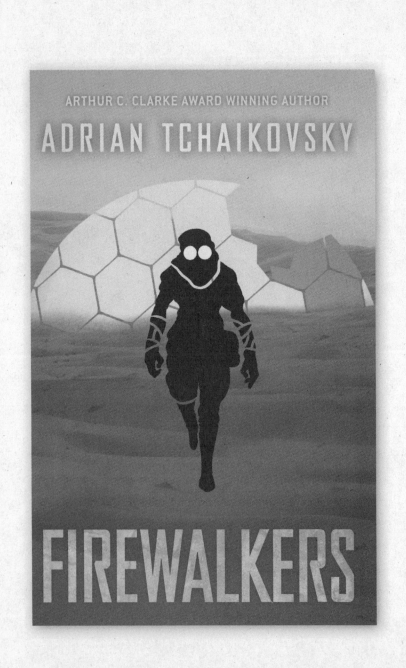

# ADRIAN TCHAIKOVSKY

# FIREWALKERS

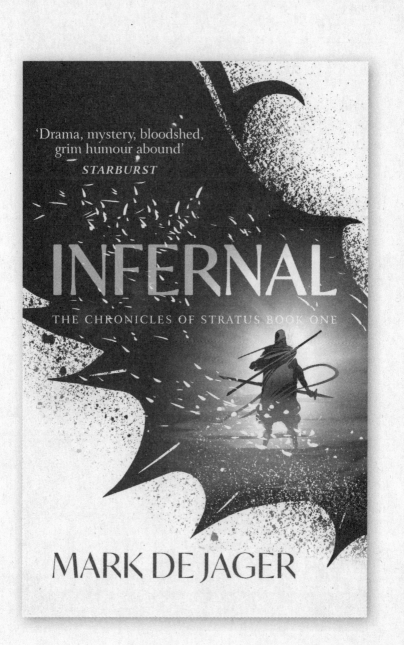

'Drama, mystery, bloodshed,
grim humour abound'
*STARBURST*

# INFERNAL

### THE CHRONICLES OF STRATUS BOOK ONE

# MARK DE JAGER

# FIND US ONLINE!

## www.rebellionpublishing.com

/rebellionpub      /rebellionpublishing  /rebellionpublishing

## SIGN UP TO OUR NEWSLETTER!

rebellionpublishing.com/newsletter

## YOUR REVIEWS MATTER!

Enjoy this book? Got something to say?

Leave a review on Amazon, GoodReads or with your
favourite bookseller and let the world know!